## Praise for *Virtually Perfect*

"In *Virtually Perfect*, newcomer Paige Roberts serves up a
fresh take on reinvention and acceptance. Light and
satisfying, *Virtually Perfect* is the perfect weekend read!"
—Amy Sue Nathan, author of *Left to Chance*

"Roberts's spot-on debut novel delves into the virtually
perfect façade of an internally imperfect family. The author also
eloquently splashes in a dash of humor. . . . Readers who enjoy
novels with cooking themes will laugh and commiserate with
Lizzie as she sweats her way through a summer of gourmet
requests, grandiose demands, and secrets she learns about
almost too late."
—*Library Journal*

"Entertaining and incisive . . . Lizzie's intelligence and
moral compass grounds the story. . . . Her self-awareness
makes her an inspiring heroine. Readers are treated to ample
helpings of snappy dialogue and vivid characters."
—*Publishers Weekly*

**Also by Paige Roberts**

*Virtually Perfect*

*The*
# LAST HOUSE ON SYCAMORE STREET

## PAIGE ROBERTS

KENSINGTON BOOKS
www.kensingtonbooks.com

KENSINGTON BOOKS are published by

Kensington Publishing Corp.
119 West 40th Street
New York, NY 10018

All Kensington titles, imprints, and distributed lines are available at special quantity discounts for bulk purchases for sales promotion, premiums, fundraising, and educational or institutional use.

Special book excerpts or customized printings can also be created to fit specific needs. For details, write or phone the office of the Kensington Sales Manager: Kensington Publishing Corp., 119 West 40th Street, New York, NY 10018. Attn. Sales Department. Phone: 1-800-221-2647.

Kensington and the K logo Reg. U.S. Pat. & TM Off.

ISBN-13: 978-1-4967-1011-6
ISBN-10: 1-4967-1011-8
First Kensington Trade Paperback Printing: October 2018

eISBN-13: 978-1-4967-1012-3
eISBN-10: 1-4967-1012-6
First Kensington Electronic Edition: October 2018

10 9 8 7 6 5 4 3 2 1

Printed in the United States of America

For Alex and Charlie

# Chapter 1

The moment Amy stepped out of the realtor's car, she knew she'd been had. Not that she was surprised. She and Rob had been looking at houses for, what was it now? Three months? By now, she'd gotten used to disappointment. But this one had looked so promising online. Granite counters! Stainless-steel appliances! A cute backyard with azalea bushes and a vegetable garden! In her heart, she'd hoped this would be "the one." Finally they could stop making weekend trips to Philadelphia from Washington, DC, and move on with their lives.

But this wasn't "the one." She could already tell. She'd never been the kind of person who believed in that kind of kismet. Whenever people asked how she and Rob met, the follow-up question, at least from a certain type of person, was always, "And did you just *know* the second you met him?" The truth was, it took her months to realize Rob might be the kind of person—if not *the* person—she wanted to marry. She was never sure if that was because love at first sight didn't exist in general, or just not for her, but she didn't tend to make snap judgments one way or the other.

And yet somehow she knew they wouldn't buy this house. Even from the outside, it looked nothing like the listing she'd seen online. What had, in photographs, looked like a cute, stone Cape Cod, now looked more like a tired house in need of a facelift. How had she not noticed the paint flaking off the shutters in the photos? And the roof . . . was that moss?

"A beauty!" crowed Cynthia, their realtor.

Amy and Rob locked eyes. They were on the same page.

Cynthia must have caught their look because she fiddled with the rhinestone broach on her bright yellow blazer and added, "Of course, it needs a loving touch, but then doesn't every house?"

She rushed ahead to open the front door.

"I guess everything looks better when you're also the listing agent," Rob whispered in Amy's ear.

She laced her arm through his and leaned her head on his shoulder. "I really wanted to love this one."

"You still might."

She glanced up at him. "Wishful thinking."

"Come on. Let's take a look."

They held hands as they walked up the driveway, and Amy surveyed the neighborhood. She liked it. A lot, actually. The houses were close together, but in a friendly, "meet your neighbors" kind of way. She could already see at least five houses with swing sets and immediately pictured kids running from one yard to the next, their squeals filling the air on a warm summer day. Oh, what she would give for Noah to be one of those kids. Even if they moved here, he would probably still want to sit inside and play math games and wouldn't want to—

No. Amy put the brakes on her runaway train of thought. *He's never had a yard*, she reminded herself. If he did, he'd probably want to play in it. That's why they were moving here, wasn't it? Well, that and to be closer to Rob's family. But they both knew they'd never be able to afford a decent-size house with any property in DC, and they'd decided that was a lifestyle Noah would need if he was going to come out of his shell. They just needed to find a nice house in a friendly neighborhood that wasn't too expensive and didn't require many renovations.

"So basically a unicorn," her friend Jess had said.

Amy laughed off the comment at the time, but she was beginning to think Jess was right. Why was finding a house so hard?

She'd always thought she had good taste, but after seeing so many houses she considered hideous, she was starting to wonder if maybe she was wrong. Maybe it was a known fact among her friends and family that she dressed horribly, bought terrible furniture, and was otherwise aesthetically blind. She peered down at her brown leather boots. Were they maybe a little too rugged? And the skinny jeans—they were still "in," weren't they? She'd thought so when she'd bought them, but now she wasn't sure. Nothing was making sense, least of all Cynthia's comments about the house.

"I think you'll see it has an understated elegance," she said as she led them through the front door.

The first thing Amy noticed was the smell. Cigarettes. Having grown up with a smoker, Amy knew the thick, musty smell of to-bacco would linger long after the current owner left. Her mom had quit years ago, and yet every time Amy visited her back in Rhode Island, the house still bore the same stale, almost sweet smell her Parliaments had left behind. The smoke had latched on to every-thing it could—the curtains, the carpet, the walls. Amy knew this house would be no different. At the very least, they'd have to prime and repaint everything, rip out the carpets, and buy new window treatments. If that was all, Amy wouldn't mind, but she had seen enough houses by this point to suspect that wouldn't be the end of the problems.

"The dining room." Cynthia gestured to the left and let Amy and Rob go in first. "Perfect for entertaining."

Amy walked around the dining room table, and as she did, she felt as if she were walking downhill. "Is it me, or . . . is the floor slanted?" she asked.

"Slanted?" Cynthia sounded baffled by Amy's question, but in a way that made her seem disingenuous rather than truly confused. Any idiot could tell that the floor wasn't level.

"Yeah, see?" Rob reached into his pocket and pulled out a bouncy ball he had confiscated from Noah earlier that morning. He placed the ball on the floor and it began rolling toward the wall.

"Ah. Well. It *is* an older home, and homes settle. But it isn't a problem. Your son might even enjoy it!"

Amy didn't consider this a selling point. She had visions of Thanksgiving dinner sliding off the table, the centerpiece tumbling into the gravy and cranberry sauce.

"Let's move on to the kitchen," Cynthia said, wisely bursting Amy's thought bubble.

As they entered the kitchen, Cynthia began talking very loud and very fast, but Amy barely caught any of what Cynthia was saying because she was distracted by an inescapable funk. This one was different than the cigarette smoke. It smelled of damp, as if a pipe had been leaking under the sink, or mold had been growing beneath the dishwasher. Instinctively, Amy made her way to the sink and opened the cupboard beneath it. She bent over to identify the source of the smell, when she heard a rustling in the trash can. Before she knew what was happening, a small mouse leapt out of the can, scurried down the side, and disappeared through a small hole near the drainpipe.

"Aaaahhh!"

"What is it?" Cynthia asked.

"A mouse—under the sink."

"Are you sure? Maybe it was a—"

"I'm sure."

"Well, obviously if it *was* a mouse, that's something the owner would take care of before settlement."

Amy had to admire Cynthia's ability to dismiss or pretty up any potential problem. Part of her wondered how Cynthia would address the decaying roof, but she realized it didn't matter because she and Rob officially would not be buying this house.

"Shall we move on to the family room?" Cynthia continued.

Amy looked at Rob. He tugged at his earlobe, their agreed-upon signal that the house was a no go. "I don't think so," Amy said.

"Would you prefer to see the powder room first?"

"No, I mean we don't need to see any more of the house. We aren't interested."

"Oh. But in your e-mail you said—"

"I know. I really did think this could be the one. I love the neighborhood. Just not this house."

Cynthia stroked her chin. She had strong features and weathered skin but maintained a sophisticated look with cropped silver hair and bright red lipstick. "But you do love the neighborhood," she said.

"Definitely. The swing sets, the vibe—I could see us living here. Just not . . . *here*."

"Well, if you like the neighborhood . . ." She narrowed her eyes and scrunched up her lips, apparently in deep thought. "I probably shouldn't even mention this, but there is a property a block or so away. It isn't officially on the market yet, but it will be in a few days."

Amy's and Rob's eyes met. "What's it like?" Rob asked.

"Four bedrooms, two and half baths. Brick colonial. The kitchen was redone a few years ago. It's a beautiful house. A young couple like you. A young child, too, I believe. I'm not exactly sure what the story is, but they contacted another person at our firm and seemed anxious to move quickly. I think the photographer was there earlier this morning."

"But it's not on the market," Amy clarified.

"Not yet. But if I . . . Hang on." Cynthia pulled out her phone and began scrolling through her contacts. She put the phone to her ear and waited while it rang. "Connie? Hi, it's Cynthia. I'm calling about that house in Glenside Park, the last one on Sycamore. I know they haven't listed it yet, but I have some buyers who might be interested. Do you think they'd mind if we . . . you're sure? Because we're at the place on Juniper now, so we could be there in a minute or so. Could you? That would be great. I can hold."

Cynthia raised her eyebrows excitedly with the phone pressed to her ear. Amy couldn't help but be excited, too, even if she knew better than to get her hopes up about any house, particularly one for which she'd never seen so much as a photograph. But she was so tired of combing through listings and living in limbo that she found it comforting to think that their dream house could be right around the corner.

"Yes?" Cynthia directed her attention back to her phone call. "Oh, wonderful. Wonderful! We will be there in just a minute. Thanks for your help—the next coffee is on me!"

Cynthia hung up and clapped her hands together. "Today, my friends, is your lucky day."

Cynthia slowed the car as they approached a brick house with black shutters and a glossy black door.

"Is this it?" Amy asked, looking out the window.

"Yes, 120 Sycamore. What do you think?"

Amy sized up the property. From the outside, it was just the sort of house she'd imagined them buying when they initially decided to decamp to the Philadelphia suburbs: an old but well-maintained brick colonial that was brimming with character and warmth. There was a brick walkway extending from the front door to the street, surrounded by shrubs and flowers, and the front of the house was flanked by bright azalea bushes, in shocking shades of pink and purple. She didn't want to get too excited before seeing the inside, but she couldn't stop smiling.

"I like it," she said, trying not to come on too strong for Cynthia. She looked at Rob, who nodded in approval.

They got out of the car and made their way to the front door. It suddenly occurred to Amy that they were about to barge in on a woman with a young child, having given her about two minutes' notice. If someone did that to Amy, she would panic, and the house would most likely look like a war zone.

"Are you sure it's okay for us to stop by like this? I feel bad not giving the owner much notice. If it were me—"

"It's fine," Cynthia said. "Like I said, the photographer was here this morning, so everything is clean and organized."

Amy glanced at Rob. "How long do you think it would take for Noah to tear the house apart? Three minutes? Five?"

"Somewhere in that ballpark."

"Well, then, you'll understand if it isn't pristine," Cynthia said. "I'm sure it isn't a problem. If they're anxious to sell, they aren't going to turn away a qualified buyer."

She hurried ahead of them, rang the doorbell, and thumped the shiny brass knocker. Amy and Rob came up behind her just as a slim woman with long dark hair opened the door.

"You must be Cynthia," the woman said. She extended her arm. "Grace Durant."

Cynthia shook her hand. "Thank you so much for letting us in on such short notice. This is Amy and Rob Kravitz. I think your house might be just what they're looking for."

"Wouldn't that be nice?" She smiled at Amy. "Come in. Have a look around. I was just putting in a load of laundry, but I promise I'll stay out of your hair."

"Please—we're the ones in your hair," Amy said as she walked through the front door. *And what nice hair it is,* she thought, as she compared Grace's glossy chocolate locks to her own limp auburn ones. "We really appreciate you letting us in like this. We have a four-year-old. We know what it's like."

"Thankfully mine is at preschool," she said.

"Well, we're grateful anyway."

"Don't mention it."

Grace closed the door behind them. Amy pretended to size up the foyer, but really she found herself eying Grace. Already, she could tell Grace had probably always been popular in school, the kind of person everyone wanted to be friends with but also envied. Amy had never been that person, nor had she managed to befriend anyone who was, at least not until college. Aside from the fact that Grace was gorgeous—exotic, even, with upturned narrow eyes, olive skin, and glittery hazel eyes—she had a relaxed, Bohemian vibe and exuded confidence and style. She wore the sorts of clothes whose origins Amy couldn't immediately ascertain. Amy was hardly a clotheshorse, but she could generally tell if someone had bought her shirt at a place like J. Crew or Gap or another mainstream store. But Grace's clothes—her linen pants, her dip-dyed tank, her brown leather sandals—looked expensive and rare, and Amy was certain she'd never encountered anyone wearing their likeness.

"I love your sandals," Amy said before she could stop herself.

"Thanks." Grace looked down and studied her foot. "My parents took us to Greece last summer, and I bought them super cheap."

Sandals from Greece. She was even more worldly than Amy had assumed.

"Anyway, let's have a look around, shall we?" Cynthia suggested.

Grace disappeared down the hallway, and Amy and Rob began looking around the first floor. Grace's distinctive style extended to the décor. All of the furnishings were tasteful yet unique—a living room chair that hung from the ceiling like a swing, fabric patterns and materials that were at once lush and relaxed, a coffee table made of an antique wooden trolley. Amy knew she was buying the house and not the things in it, but Grace made the house look so effortlessly chic. And with a four-year-old! Amy's vision of her family in this house suddenly became more fashionable as well, as if the house itself would confer her with impeccable taste. Maybe then she'd know for sure whether her skinny jeans were a fashion faux pas.

They wandered through the house, into the bright and airy renovated kitchen and upstairs to the cozy bedrooms. Amy stopped in the doorway to the bedroom that obviously belonged to Grace's son. The letters E-T-H-A-N hung above his bed, surrounded by bright and sporty decals—soccer balls, basketballs, footballs. A tent shaped like a rocket ship sat in the corner, surrounded by toy rockets and cars and a light-up globe. Amy looked up and noticed glow-in-the-dark stars and planets affixed to his ceiling. Her heart swelled.

*Noah would LOVE this*, she thought. Again she knew the space paraphernalia wouldn't come with the house, but Noah had been obsessed with the planets since he was three, which made visualizing him in this room a no-brainer. She noticed framed photos of Ethan with other kids (Friends? Cousins?), and a part of her clung to the idea that if they lived here, Noah would make friends that he could pose with in photos, too. Maybe he would have the social childhood he hadn't so far and that she never did.

"What do you think?"

Rob had snuck up behind her and rested his hand on her shoulder.

"I like it," she said. "It feels . . ."

"Like home?"

She turned around to face him. "Yeah, or at least as if it could."

"I know."

Amy peered over his shoulder. Neither Cynthia nor Grace was in site. "It's kind of awkward with the owner here, isn't it?"

"A little. She seems nice, though. Cool taste. Did you see the painting hanging in the family room?"

"The abstract sunset?"

"Yeah, pretty rad."

Amy sniggered. "Rad? Since when do you call anything rad?"

"I don't know. Since now? See, this house is making me hipper already."

"I'm not sure I'd go that far. . . ."

Rob nudged her in the side. "So what do you think? Do you want to make an offer?"

Amy looked back into Ethan's room. It felt so . . . right. She hadn't had this feeling in the three months they'd been looking at houses. "I do. Do you?"

"Yeah, let's talk to Cynthia."

Rob headed downstairs, and Amy trailed behind but stopped when she reached a closed door she hadn't noticed before. "I'm guessing this is a linen closet?"

She looked for Rob, but he was already downstairs trying to find Cynthia. Amy attempted to open the door, but it fit snugly against the frame and wouldn't budge. She pulled harder, but the door remained shut, until—*pop!*—it swung open, catching her by surprise. A pile of sheets that had been stacked on the top shelf tumbled to the floor with a loud thump, followed by the crash of an orange prescription pill bottle hitting the hardwood floor. Amy was still scrambling to pick everything up when she heard a voice coming up the stairs.

"Sorry about the closet—it's a mess," Grace said.

Amy turned around. "It's not—I was just—"

Her cheeks flushed as she stammered through a response. She felt as if she'd been snooping, which she supposed technically she had been, but then wasn't that what looking at any house was, in effect? Still, she couldn't shake the feeling that Grace had caught her doing something wrong.

She clumsily attempted to refold the sheets and slide them back on the shelf, then picked up the pill bottle and handed it to Grace. "Sorry, I'm not really sure where this went."

Grace took the bottle and quickly glanced at it. Amy thought she noticed Grace's expression harden, if only for a moment.

Amy flashed an embarrassed smile. "I was just looking for—"

"Ah, there you are!" Cynthia appeared right on cue. "Rob says you'd like to talk?"

Amy looked back at Grace, whose gaze had returned to the pills. "I'd like to see the backyard first," Amy said. She didn't want to discuss the potential for an offer in front of Grace, but mostly she wanted to get away from the linen closet. Something about it had laced the air with tension, and Amy wanted to diffuse the situation as quickly as possible.

"Of course," Cynthia said. "I think you'll absolutely adore it— let's have a look."

Amy followed Cynthia down the stairs, and as they walked down the hallway and toward the back door, Amy pretended she didn't hear Grace slam the linen closet door shut, a little louder than she thought was necessary.

# Chapter 2

"The Durants want to discuss a settlement date."

Cynthia's voice boomed through Amy's phone, which she held between her ear and her shoulder as she scooped a helping of macaroni and cheese into Noah's bowl. They'd been back in DC for less than a day, and yet Amy felt as if she had lived a year in that amount of time. She and Rob had made an offer on 120 Sycamore the evening after they saw it, and by the next morning, the Durants had accepted. The house was going to cost them more than they'd wanted to spend, but they had crunched the numbers, and they could afford it.

"It's perfect for you," Cynthia had said when she was trying to convince them. "And perfect doesn't come around every day."

Amy gestured at Noah to put away his activity book. "Rob and I need to discuss our timeline."

"They'd like to settle as quickly as possible," Cynthia said. "It's mid-May now, so what about Memorial Day?"

"I was thinking more like July."

Cynthia took a deep breath. "I'll ask. But between you and me, I don't think that will fly. I'm not sure what the story is, but Connie tells me they want to close within the next few weeks."

"We haven't even done our inspections, and our bank still needs to send out an appraiser."

"Yes, but those things take days, not weeks."

"Unless we find out the house is infested with termites."

"Well, obviously, but I don't think you'll run into any problems there."

"Mommy?"

Amy gestured at Noah to eat his macaroni. "Let's hope not."

"Mommy, what are termites?"

Amy covered the receiver. "Bugs."

"What kind of bugs?"

"They eat wood."

"Why?"

"Because that's what they like."

"So what do you want me to tell them?" Cynthia asked. "July first?"

"Can I get back to you? I need to talk to Rob."

"Our new house has bugs that eat wood?"

Amy shook her head and covered the receiver again. "No. At least we hope not. Eat your dinner."

"If they eat wood, then what if they eat my bed?"

"They're not going to eat your bed."

"It's wood."

"I know, but—"

"And you said they like to eat wood."

"Yes, but—"

Noah began to tear up. "I don't want them to eat my bed! I don't want this house!"

"They aren't going to eat your bed! Eat your dinner!" Amy realized she was yelling.

"Is this a bad time?" Cynthia asked.

"No, it's fine."

In truth, it wasn't a great time, but these days, it was no worse than any other. If it wasn't dinnertime it would be time to pick Noah up from the preschool he attended three days a week, or she'd be working on a freelance project, or she'd be lugging four too-heavy bags of groceries into the elevator to their apartment. One of the first houses Cynthia had shown them had a hammock hanging between two old oak trees. Amy tried to envision herself lounging in it while reading a book, but she couldn't because even in a fantasy she had trouble imagining that kind of downtime. It would come, or so people told her, but some days she had trouble believing them. How on Earth had her mother done it with two? And on her own, working a full-time job? As she got older, Amy began to understand why her mom had been gruff and unsentimental. Who had time for sentimentality when you barely had enough time to shower?

"So you'll talk to Rob and let me know," Cynthia said.

"Yes," Amy said. "Tonight."

"Good. I'll wait to hear from you."

Amy hung up and looked at Noah, who sat sullenly in front of his bowl of macaroni. Amy tried to conceal her irritation. She loved her son more than she thought it was possible to love anything, but he had a tendency to get weepy over the most trivial things, and tonight she wasn't in the mood.

"Noah, sweetie, what's wrong?"

His lip began to quiver. "You yelled at me."

"Because you interrupted me when I was on the phone. We've talked about that."

"But you said the house might have *bugs*."

"No, I was just trying to negotiate with our realtor."

"What's negotiate?"

Amy took a deep breath. She loved Noah's innate curiosity, but on nights like tonight she wished he'd show no interest in language or semantics and just eat his mac and cheese. "When you talk back and forth with somebody until you come to an agreement."

"Like when I ask for another story and you say no, but I ask again and then you say okay?"

Amy smiled in spite of herself. "Yes, kind of like that."

He poked at a piece of macaroni. "Will our new house have the same stories?"

"Sweetie, of course." Amy sat down next to him and rubbed his shoulder. "Everything is coming with us—everything in this whole apartment."

"Even my markers?"

"Even your markers."

"And my pillow?"

"That too." She pulled him in for a hug. "And you know who else is coming?"

"Daddy?"

"Well, of course Daddy is coming. But, did you know . . . the *tickle monster* is coming, too?"

She wiggled her fingers under his armpits as Noah giggled wildly. He had the most wonderful laugh—a full belly laugh that seemed to fill the room with joy. It was like a drug. No matter how many times she heard him laugh, the effect never dulled.

Amy stopped tickling him and kissed him on the head. "Now eat your dinner."

"But first let me tell you something."

"No, first eat your dinner."

"But, Mommy, I'm trying to *negotiate*."

Amy laughed and rolled her eyes. In moments like this, she never knew whether to be proud of him for mastering a concept, or exasperated because her precocious son was utterly exhausting. "Let's leave the negotiating to the adults for now, okay?"

"But, Mommy."

"Noah?"

"Okay, fine." He shoveled a forkful of mac and cheese in his mouth. "I just want to say—"

"Don't talk with your mouth full."

He swallowed. "I just want to say I'm excited for our new house. But a little bit scared, too."

Amy wrapped her arms around him and squeezed him tight. "I know, sweetie. But it's going to be great. I promise."

"Really?"

"Really."

"Okay." He wiggled from her arms and scooped up another helping of his dinner. Amy watched as he proceeded to scarf down the rest of the meal, his worries over the new house seemingly gone. She always marveled at the way kids could generally move on from an emotional state so quickly. One second they were worried or angry or sad or elated, and the next they would flip to another emotion, like taking off one T-shirt and putting on another. She wished she had that ability, especially now, because the truth was, for all of the assurances she gave Noah about their move, she was a little scared, too.

# Chapter 3

The Kravitzes and Durants came to a compromise: They would settle the second week of June. When the day came, they sat across from each other at a long conference table as a woman from the title company shuffled and copied papers they all needed to sign.

"All right," she said. "First, here is the settlement sheet for you to look over."

Everyone smiled politely at each other. It was all a little awkward. After today, they'd probably never see the Durants again, yet for the next hour or so, Amy and Rob would be sitting directly across from Grace and her husband, Julian, forced into an unnatural intimacy.

"So you guys are moving from DC?" Julian asked. Like Grace, he was very attractive, with model good looks. His dark brown hair was held in place by just the right amount of product, giving it a handsome sheen without looking greasy. He had chiseled cheekbones and a slight cleft in his chin, and his teeth were bright white, perfectly straight, and completely symmetrical.

Amy and Rob nodded in unison. "I grew up around here," Rob said.

"No way. So did Grace. Where did you live?"

"Jenkintown," Rob said.

"Me too!" Grace chimed in. "Until I was ten. Wait, where in Jenkintown?"

"Jenkintown Manor."

"Oh, okay. I grew up in the borough. Then my family got a place about two miles away in Meadowbrook. I can't believe we never ran into each other! Where did you go to school?"

"Abington."

"I think I knew a few people there. Adam Simpson? Leah Goldberg?"

Rob shrugged. "Don't think so. But it's been a while."

"I went to Germantown Friends, so my friends were sort of all over. But you look my age . . . thirty-five?"

"Close. Thirty-six."

She smiled. "Too funny. Such a coincidence."

Amy craned her neck to check on Noah, who was playing on the floor in the corner of the conference room. She'd brought some of his favorite activity books and puzzles, which he played with happily. The Durants had also brought their son, Ethan, who was also four and played on his iPad a few feet from Noah.

"Now if you'll just sign at the bottom." Cynthia placed another set of papers in front of Amy and Rob. She and Connie had been chatting across the table in hushed tones ever since settlement began. Amy hadn't caught much of what they were talking about, but she knew it had nothing to do with housing. At one point she thought she heard them discussing the billing system at a local salon.

Amy signed and passed the paper to Rob. She heard some giggling from the corner of the room and, a moment later, one of Noah's joyful belly laughs.

"What are you two up to over there?" Grace grinned as she peered over her shoulder.

Amy's and Rob's eyes met. Was Noah really . . . laughing? With another kid his age?

"Nothing, Mommy," Ethan replied, stifling another giggle.

Amy raised herself from her seat and looked toward the boys. Her heart swelled. The two boys were lying next to each other on their stomachs, watching something on Ethan's iPad. Noah's mop of strawberry-blond hair nearly covered his big blue eyes—he desperately needed a haircut—but even still, Amy could see them dancing. He let out another belly laugh.

"What are you watching?" Amy asked.

"*Minions*," Noah said. He snorted as some sort of explosion detonated on the screen.

Grace caught Amy's eye. She looked skeptical. "You don't have *Minions* on your iPad," she called back.

"It's on YouTube," Ethan said, rolling his eyes dramatically.

"Ah. Of course." Grace shook her head as Amy settled back in her chair. "I swear," she said in a lowered voice, "these kids are going to be running circles around all of us in, like, two years."

Rob chuckled. "Two years? I already feel behind."

So did Amy—not least of all because all of these four-year-olds seemed to have a device she hadn't yet bought for herself. All of Noah's preschool friends in Washington had their own iPads, and Noah had begged for one for ages, but Amy couldn't bring herself to buy one for him yet. It seemed like so much money to spend on a present for a four-year-old. The problem was, Noah had all but appropriated Rob's device, loading it up with so many math and spelling games that Rob had no storage left. Rob's phone was due for an upgrade, and as part of that they'd offered him an iPad mini for only (only!) $99, so Amy knew it was only a matter of time before Noah joined the ranks of the spoiled.

"So are you guys staying in the area?" Rob asked.

Grace caught Julian's eye, then looked away. "Not too far. Only ten or fifteen minutes away."

"Will you keep Ethan in the same preschool?" Amy asked.

"Oh, definitely. He would lose his mind if we moved him. He *loves* his school."

"Where does he go, if you don't mind my asking? We're looking for someplace to send Noah."

"Beth Israel. It's Jewish, but you don't have to be Jewish to go there."

"Rob is Jewish, so that could actually be a good fit," Amy said. "Are they still enrolling for the fall?"

"Oh, sure. I mean, I know people who've registered the week before. It's super low-key. The director is—well, she is just the best. Like a super-energetic and organized grandmother who also plays guitar. Like I said, Ethan adores it. I can't imagine sending him anywhere else."

Amy smiled at Rob. Tedium aside, the closing was getting Amy very excited about settling into 120 Sycamore. Already she felt more relaxed about life. She knew it wouldn't be all giggles and guitar songs, but that was the vibe she was picking up from Grace and Julian. She barely knew them, but somehow she wanted to be like them—effortlessly cool and unquestionably attractive, the kind of people who instantly make friends with anyone and everyone. She'd always been attracted to those sorts of people, perhaps because she'd always wished she could be one of them.

"And here is the last paper."

Cynthia placed the last document in front of Amy and Rob, and they signed and returned it to the title company. There was more shuffling of papers and chitchat, and finally, the woman from the title company clapped her hands together. "Looks like we're good. Congratulations on your new home."

Amy and Rob smiled as Grace passed the keys across the table. "Enjoy," she said. She was smiling, but her eyes also looked wet. Amy thought it sounded as if there were a lump in her throat. "Let us know if you need any recommendations on plumbers or electricians or anything like that. We have a great tree guy, too, if you ever need it."

"Thanks," Amy said. She and Rob stood up and shook hands with the Durants across the table. "Noah?"

She heard Noah titter in the corner before Ethan whispered, "Your mommy wants you."

Noah gathered up his books and shuffled over to where Amy and Rob were standing. "Are you done?"

"We are. Do you have all of your books?"

He nodded. His mood had become less ebullient than a few minutes ago, but Amy figured he was probably just tired. He'd perk up when he saw the new house. At least she hoped so.

She pulled her purse over her shoulder, when she felt something tugging at the hem of her shirt. She turned around and saw Ethan standing behind her, his wavy russet hair sticking out in all directions.

"Can Noah come play sometime?" he asked.

"Ethan," Grace said, her head cocked. "What have I told you about—"

"No, no, it's fine," Amy cut in. She didn't mean to undermine Grace's parenting, but she didn't want Ethan getting in trouble for uttering words Amy longed to hear. A cute, normal kid with cool parents wanted to play with her son—*her* son, the introvert most kids at his former preschool overlooked because he was content playing word games by himself. Okay, so they would now be living in this kid's old house, but never mind. A friend was a friend, and Noah didn't have many, and certainly none in Philadelphia.

"Of course Noah can play," Amy said.

"Yippee!" Ethan shouted and jumped up and down. Then Noah started jumping up and down, too.

"Yippee!" he said, mimicking Ethan, and the two of them proceeded to hop around the room together, hooting and hollering and acting like silly four-year-olds.

Grace slipped Amy a piece of paper. "Here's my cell and e-mail. Let's set something up once you've moved in and caught your breath."

Amy held the piece of paper in one hand while she squeezed Rob's hand with the other. Life in Glenside Park was going to be even better than they thought.

Amy quickly realized that while life in Glenside Park might eventually be idyllic and lovely, any semblance of that life would have to wait until they finished unpacking, and at the rate they were going, that might be December. There were just so many boxes. How and when had they acquired so much stuff? She knew exactly how many boxes she had packed—and had a spreadsheet identifying each one by number and contents—and yet somehow there seemed to be more in Glenside Park than there had been in Washington. Had the boxes mated on the truck?

The other problem was that although they had much more

space, all of it was new. Had she been unpacking things into their apartment, Amy would know exactly where to put everything. The cutlery would go in the drawer to the right of the kitchen sink. The vacuum would go in the coat closet. The wedding china would go into boxes beneath their bed. But now there were multiple possible locations for every item. Unpacking wasn't merely a matter of taking something out of a box and putting it somewhere else. It involved making decisions, and Amy had never been particularly good at that. She found the entire process excruciating and exhausting.

Two weeks after settlement, she was still organizing her bedroom. As she arranged some framed photos on top of her dresser, Noah thumped up the stairs and stood in front of her with his hands on his hips.

"When are we going to play with Ethan?"

"I told you, sweetie. Once we've settled into the house."

"But we've been here for a thousand *years*," he groaned.

Amy couldn't deny that, indeed, it felt that way. But she also knew that for all of Noah's intellectual strengths, time was still a vague concept for him, and so in his mind, he probably thought it had actually been one thousand years.

"It's only been two weeks," she said.

"But I want to play now."

At the moment, the last thing Amy wanted to do was arrange a playdate. What she really wanted was a warm bath and a glass of wine. But she couldn't remember the last time Noah had begged to play with another child. Wasn't this part of the reason they'd moved? To make a better life for their son? And anyway, if she waited until she'd fully unpacked and settled in, it might be Christmas. She couldn't make Noah wait that long.

Amy sighed as she broke down an empty box. "How about this: I'll call Ethan's mommy after I take these boxes outside, and we'll see what she says."

Noah clapped his hands together. "Tell her I want to watch *Minions* again on YouTube!"

"Sweetie, Ethan might not want to watch *Minions*. He might want to play outside or go to the park or . . . I don't know, something else." She narrowed her eyes. She'd suddenly become suspicious. "Do you actually want to play with Ethan, or do you just want to use his iPad?"

He gave her a look so brimming with irritation that for a moment Amy thought she'd time-traveled to the future and was conversing with a sixteen-year-old. "I want to play with *Ethan*," he said, clearly indignant.

"Even if he doesn't bring his iPad?"

Noah rolled his eyes. "YES!"

"Okay, okay." Amy searched for the piece of paper Grace had given her at settlement. She'd put it in her purse, but then she thought she moved it to the room they were setting up as a home office. Clearly she had not, however, because it wasn't there. She made her way downstairs as Noah trailed behind.

"Mommyyyyyyy," he whined.

"Noah, relax. I just need to find the—Ah! Here it is." She pulled the scrap of paper off the counter, next to a stack of papers and lists. She dialed Grace's number.

"What does she say? Can Ethan play?"

Amy shushed him. "She hasn't picked up yet."

Amy hated Noah's tendency to interrupt her when she was on the phone. She supposed from his perspective, he couldn't hear anything on the other end—whether the person was speaking or the phone was merely ringing—so technically he wasn't interrupting or talking over anyone. All he heard was complete silence. Still, it drove Amy crazy.

"Has she picked up—"

"Hi, Grace?" Amy held up a finger and gave Noah a stern look. "It's Amy Kravitz. We're great, thanks. I mean, we're still buried under boxes, but we're starting to see some light. No, no—nothing with the house. The house is great. I was actually calling because Noah has been asking about Ethan, and I was hoping we could get the two of them together."

"You'd come, too, right?" Noah began to look worried. Amy waved him away.

"It's funny you should say that," Grace said. "Ethan has been talking about Noah, too. I figured you were up to your eyeballs with house stuff, so I didn't want to bother you. But I know Ethan would love a playdate. What does your week look like?"

"What day is it today? Tuesday?" Amy was embarrassed to admit she truly wasn't sure. Without the structure of an office job, every day since the move had pretty much seemed the same: wake up, unpack, unpack some more, sleep, repeat.

"Yes, the . . ." She paused. "Twenty-first."

"To be honest, we don't have much on the schedule at the moment, other than unpacking. We can be free whenever."

"Ethan is at camp three days a week, but he's home on Fridays. Maybe we could meet up at a playground this Friday? There's a really cute one a few minutes from you—Montgomery Park. You can walk. We used to do that all the time."

"That would be great. What time are you thinking?"

"I don't know . . . maybe eleven? The kids could play a while, and then we could have a picnic."

"Perfect. I'll see you Friday at eleven then."

"Yay, yay, yay!" Noah jumped up and down and pumped his fist in the air.

"Oh, and I should mention—Ethan has a tree nut allergy. He's fine with peanuts and almonds, actually, but he can't have anything with traces of walnuts, cashews, pistachios, or pecans. We have an EpiPen, but considering the drama and cost of using one, I'd rather not have to."

"Got it. No nuts."

"Why no nuts?" Noah asked.

Amy shushed him. "See you Friday—looking forward to it."

She put her phone on the counter, and Noah crept toward her, his brow furrowed. "Why no nuts?" he asked again.

"Ethan is allergic."

"Like Daddy is to shrimp?"

"Yes, like that."

Noah's eyes widened. "Then we *definitely* can't have anything with nuts."

Six months ago, Rob had accidentally eaten a Thai dish with shrimp paste in it, and Noah had watched in horror as Rob's face had puffed up like a balloon, his eyes had swollen shut, and his upper and lower lips had inflated like two cocktail sausages. Rob had immediately grabbed his EpiPen and stabbed it into his thigh, only adding to Noah's terror. He'd had nightmares for weeks after that, and only in the last month or so had stopped asking Rob before every meal, "Is this going to make you explode and die?"

"Don't worry," Amy said. "We won't bring anything with nuts. I promise."

"Good," Noah said. "Because Ethan is going to be my bestest friend, and I don't want him to die."

Amy chose to ignore Noah's fixation on death and instead focused on the positive: Noah saw a friend in Ethan, and for that, Amy was eternally grateful.

When Friday arrived, Amy decided she couldn't have ordered better weather: seventy-nine degrees and sunny, with an occasional light breeze. It was perfect, and Amy hoped the favorable elements were an omen for what would be a perfect playdate.

She finished packing up their cooler bag, which she'd managed to dig out of a box in their new garage. The house looked better than it had even two days ago, but they still had numerous boxes to unpack. At least the bedrooms and kitchen were finished. They'd hung Noah's pictures, posters, and glow-in-the-dark planets, so as far as he was concerned, there was nothing left to do.

Amy zipped the bag shut. "Noah, come on, we're going to be late!"

Noah came bounding down the stairs and rushed into the kitchen. "There's no nuts in there, right?"

"Nope, I triple-checked everything."

"You should check one more time."

"Noah . . ."

"What's one more than triple?"

"Quadruple."

"I don't think I can say that."

"Kwa-droo-pull."

"Kwa . . . droo . . . pull." Noah beamed. "I did it! Kradoople!"

Amy smiled. Part of her loved that he still mispronounced things. She knew she should encourage him to pronounce everything correctly, but given how advanced his vocabulary was, she let the occasional metathesis slide. He was only four. Sometimes she enjoyed the reminder.

"So can I kradoople-check it?"

Amy sighed. "I guess if you want to be late . . ."

Noah frowned. He hated being late. Amy knew threatening tardiness was one way to avert a pointless food inspection. "Okay, fine," he said. "Let's just go."

They headed out the front door and held hands as they walked along the sidewalk to the park. Amy breathed in the grassy, summer air as she admired the hulking oak and maple trees lining their street. She'd always dreamed of living on a street like this, from her earliest days in Woonsocket. She'd grown up on a nice street, one that even had sidewalks, but it had lacked the Norman Rockwell quaintness of Glenside Park. There was plenty about Rhode Island that she missed—her family, coffee milk, clam cakes, chowder—but she could never envision herself setting down roots there. This, this was the sort of place she'd imagined for her family.

The walk took less than ten minutes, and as Amy and Noah approached the wood-chipped play area, she saw Ethan flying down one of the slides.

"Ethan!" Noah let go of Amy's hand and charged toward the slide. Amy stopped momentarily and watched with widened eyes. She'd never seen Noah so excited to see another child. Ethan certainly seemed like a nice boy, but was he really so much nicer than the kids at Bright Futures Academy, his DC preschool? Maybe Noah liked that Ethan didn't know anything about him. He could start fresh. Amy knew what that was like (hadn't her entire college experience been a social reboot?), but she also knew the appeal of a blank slate didn't usually apply to four-year-olds. Then again, Noah was advanced in so many ways. Perhaps he was more socially aware than she'd given him credit for.

"You made it."

Amy snapped out of her trance as Grace approached, her head covered by a floppy straw hat. She wore a breezy gray-and-white sundress and another pair of stylish leather sandals. *She even looks chic on playdates*, Amy thought.

"The walk isn't too bad, right?" Grace nodded toward the parking lot. "Ethan couldn't understand why we had to drive. He doesn't quite get the concept of distance yet."

"Neither does Noah. He told me the drive from DC was at least five thousand miles."

Grace laughed. "I've done that drive. It can definitely feel that way."

"So where should I drop our stuff?"

"I saved us a spot over here." Grace nodded for Amy to follow her and led her to a picnic table beneath a maple tree, just beyond the monkey bars. Amy heard a squeal and turned to see Ethan chasing Noah up a ladder.

"Careful!" Grace shouted. "Ethan?"

"I'm a monster!" he shouted back. "ROAR!"

"Does Noah like you being a monster?"

"Yes!" the boys screamed in unison. Amy studied Noah's face. He seemed thoroughly delighted.

"It's my turn next!" he said as he raced down a bumpy slide. Ethan took off behind him.

Grace shook her head and took a seat at the picnic table. Amy laid down her cooler bag and sat across from her.

"So are you guys finally settling in?"

"I think so. It's starting to feel more like our home, as opposed to . . ." Amy trailed off.

"Our home?"

"No. Well, I mean, yes."

Amy's cheeks flushed. She knew it might be a little awkward socializing with the former owner of the house she'd just bought, so she'd made mental notes not to dwell on 120 Sycamore or any of the changes she and Rob planned to make. But already she felt as if she'd screwed up.

"Sorry," Amy said. "I didn't mean to—"

"It's fine," Grace said, smiling. She had a way of making Amy feel at ease. "I went through the same thing when we bought the house five years ago. Only at that time the seller was this cranky old man who was totally horrible to us, so I felt like I needed to have a shaman purge the house of evil spirits." She pulled on the brim of her hat. "Hopefully you don't feel the same way about us. . . ."

"Not at all! You and Julian made everything so easy. Oh, but that reminds me." She reached into her purse and pulled out two envelopes. "These came for you."

She handed them to Grace, who glanced at them briefly before sticking them into her purse. "Sorry. Julian was in charge of forwarding our mail. You can see how that worked out."

"Don't worry about it. I've already had an Amazon package delivered to our old apartment because I forgot to change my address on Amazon. I'll just pass along anything that comes for you."

"Thanks. And if it's junk, feel free to trash it."

The boys came barreling toward the picnic table and stopped right in front of them, both of them panting. "Mommy, I'm staaaaaarving," Ethan said.

"Well, you're in luck because I'm staaaaaarving, too, and I have lunch right in here."

She opened up her cooler bag, and Amy followed suit. Amy laid out the carrots and hummus she had packed, along with some cream cheese and jelly sandwiches, a bunch of grapes, and some strawberry yogurts. She glanced at Grace's offering, which included a large bowl filled with what appeared to be a lentil and butternut squash salad, a container of falafel, some sort of vegetable tart, berries, and oatmeal raisin cookies.

"Wow—did you make all of that?" Amy asked. She thought her lunch was pretty bourgeois, but Grace took it to another level.

"Just the salad and the cookies."

"I'm still impressed."

"Don't be. It's basically last night's leftovers combined with stuff I bought at Whole Foods. Frankly the only reason I made the cookies is because it's hard to find a bakery that makes ones without possible nut contamination."

"None of this stuff has nuts," Noah chimed in, waving his hand over the food Amy brought. "My mommy kadroople-checked."

Grace raised her eyebrows and gave Amy an impressed look. "Quadruple, eh? That's a big word."

"It means four times," Noah said.

"I see."

"Anyway," Amy said, trying to move the focus away from her son's precociousness. "Our stuff is, indeed, nut free, so you are welcome to any of it."

"Same," Grace said. "We have more than we could possibly eat."

Somehow Amy doubted Grace would have any interest in cream cheese sandwiches when she could be eating a delicious salad and vegetable tart, but she was glad she'd made the offer, if only so that she could feel justified in trying some of Grace's food. She couldn't stop thinking about how delicious all of it looked.

In the end, Ethan and Noah ate the sandwiches and most of what she had packed, and she and Grace ate the majority of her spread, though the kids happily wolfed down the berries and cookies.

"So how do you like camp, Ethan?" Amy asked.

"Good," he said.

"What kinds of things do you do there?"

He shrugged. "Games and swimming and stuff."

"That sounds great. Better than what we've been doing." She looked at Grace. "A little too much TV and Y-o-u-T-u-b-e . . ."

"I have not been watching too much YouTube!" Noah protested. "I don't even have an iPad!"

Grace's eyes flitted from Amy back to Noah. "Wow, you're a good speller, huh?"

Amy shrugged timidly. She never wanted to seem as if she were bragging about Noah's intelligence. Back in DC, whenever Noah would read something in front of another parent or demonstrate his early grasp of mathematical concepts, at least one parent would latch on to her with frightening interest: "What method are you using?" "Is he enrolled in a program?" "Have you had him tested?" Amy would shrink back and explain truthfully that Noah had pretty much done all of it on his own, which never seemed to satisfy the other parents. It's as if they thought she was holding back some secret that, if shared, would be the key that would unlock their child's future success. She didn't want to get caught up in some helicopter parent rat race.

But more than that, Amy didn't want to say or do something that would encourage other people to label her kid a "nerd." He was, but in the best possible way, and she didn't want his intelligence to hold him back socially, like it had for her in her childhood. She was never nearly as smart as Noah was, but then it was always harder for smart girls, especially when she was a kid. Sometimes she wondered if she hadn't been quite so precocious and openly geeky in elementary school, maybe her social life in high school would have been a little better (or frankly would have existed at all). She'd started afresh in college and had blossomed as a social creature, but that seemed like an awfully long time to wait. She knew all the exclusion and heartache she experienced as a teenager had made her the person she was today (a lesson in resilience, character building, and so forth), but a part of her wanted to save Noah having to go through all of that if he didn't have to. He didn't need to feel isolated—or worse, get bullied—to become an enlightened human.

"If you're looking for something for Noah to do, I bet he could still enroll. Ethan only started this week."

"You think?"

"Sure. I could talk to the owner, Donna. She is the sweetest. It's like a ten-minute drive from you, so it would be convenient, too."

"How much does it cost? Is it expensive?"

The hat hid some of Grace's face, but Amy swore she saw her cheeks turn pink. "Not too bad, I don't think. . . . You can check the rates online. Green Hills Day Camp."

"Cool, I'll do that, thanks." She felt a tug on her shirt.

"Mommy, can I go play now?"

She examined Noah's lunch. Nothing was left. "Of course."

He jumped down and scampered off with Ethan.

"It's like he's a different kid," she said.

"Why, what was he like in DC?"

"Introverted. A little quiet. But ever since we closed on the house, he's like Mr. Social. Some days I can't believe what I'm seeing."

"Maybe it's the house. It changes people." She paused for a beat. "It did us."

Amy smiled but noticed Grace wasn't really smiling back. She looked wistful and a little sad, and Amy wondered if the house had changed the Durants for the better or, as Grace's glum expression indicated, for the worse.

# Chapter 4

Amy enrolled Noah at Green Hills Day Camp, if only to give Noah something to do other than watch her unpack boxes all summer. They could only afford to send him three days a week, but since Ethan only went three days, that was just as well. The two had become nearly inseparable since the move, and Amy knew Noah would have little interest in Green Hills if Ethan wasn't there.

On at least one of the weekdays Noah wasn't at camp, they would meet up with Ethan and Grace for an outing of some sort—a museum, a park, a playground, an ice cream shop. They never met at each other's homes. Amy was self-conscious about inviting Grace into her old house, a house Amy had changed in small ways that Grace would surely notice (new wall colors in the bedrooms, updated hardware in the hall bath). Grace also hadn't offered to have them to her new place, though Amy got the distinct impression in their conversations that wherever the Durants were living wasn't a permanent situation.

On the days Noah was at camp, Amy continued to set up the house, but she was also able to devote more time to work, or at least some semblance of it. She had left her job as an education analyst at a nonprofit about a year after Noah was born so that she could freelance, the idea being that she could spend more time with Noah and also pay less in childcare while still bringing in a bit of money for the family. She would write and edit grant proposals, help with promotional materials, and analyze pending legislation. None of it was super exciting, but it had given her the balance she was looking for at the time. That said, drumming up freelance work wasn't easy, even in DC when her clients were often a quick Metro ride away. Now, in the suburbs of Philadelphia, she was finding it even harder.

By the time Noah had been going to camp for two weeks, Amy decided to buckle down and get going on editing a proposal for yet another education nonprofit. She also planned to send out friendly reminder e-mails to a few clients to attract new work. For a time, it was true that she'd been too busy with the move to devote any time to these things, but by now, she knew she was using unpacking as an excuse. It was time to get serious.

She had just opened the Word document on her computer when her cell phone rang. It was her mom.

"How's the house coming along?"

Amy had only spoken to her mom once since they'd moved, which was more than a month ago now.

"Pretty good. I've finally gotten to the point where I can think about something other than boxes, so that's a promising step."

"I think I have a box or two in the basement that I still haven't unpacked from our move thirty years ago."

"I feel pretty comfortable saying you don't need anything in those boxes if you haven't opened them in thirty years."

"You never know. Could be something useful in there."

"You say that as if you have no way of knowing."

"How am I supposed to remember? It's been three decades."

"You're not supposed to remember. You're supposed to open them. Then you'll know. Mystery solved."

Her mom groaned. She always acted as if Amy was lording her superior stature over her. Yes, Amy had gone to college, which her mother, Ellen, had never done, and yes, at her peak Amy had earned more than her mother could ever have hoped. But Amy never felt superior. If anything, she felt grateful for the opportunities she'd had and humbled by the sacrifices she knew her mom had made. Ellen never seemed to see it that way, though. On some level, she always seemed a little resentful that Amy had done things she'd always wanted to.

"Anyway," Ellen said, "I'm calling because . . . you know how last time we talked I said I was supposed to get a raise in July? Well, I guess they changed their minds, or I guess not changed their minds, but decided on a lot less than I'd hoped, which frankly, if you ask me, is bullshit because I've been their receptionist for a zillion years, but anyway—"

"How much do you need?"

Her mother paused. "Just two thousand."

"*Just* two thousand? Mom . . ."

"I'm still digging out from Timmy's rehab costs, and you know—"

"I thought we'd settled that."

"Well, we'd settled his first time, but I'm still a little in the hole from the second."

"He went back?"

She cleared her throat. "In May. He didn't want me to say anything—you know how your brother is. But he relapsed, and he couldn't afford another go, so I helped him."

Amy took a deep breath. She didn't blame her mom for helping her son—as a mother now, Amy couldn't imagine ever turning her back on Noah—but the truth was, they weren't really talking about the "first" and "second" times Tim had gone into rehab. They were talking about the first and second times *this year*. Tim had been in and out of rehab for what felt to Amy like his entire adult life, but what had probably been more like the past ten years or so. It had started with prescription pills and had progressed to heroin, and Amy lived with a constant, low-level fear that someday her mother's call would be to tell Amy that Tim had overdosed and was dead.

"I'll talk to Rob," Amy said.

"Oh, thank you. Thank you so much. You know I wouldn't ask if I didn't really need it. Tell Rob that Timmy is serious about getting clean."

"He always says that."

"And you always act like he doesn't mean it. It's a disease. Don't you understand that? He wants to get clean. He just can't silence whatever demons make him do that stuff in the first place."

"I know. I do. It's just . . . we've been through this so many times. Sometimes I wonder if he'll ever . . . if it's even possible . . ."

"It's possible. This was a new place. It's supposed to work wonders. You don't know what it's like up here. You're living in your little yuppie bubble. But up here, these drugs . . . they're just everywhere. They're ripping families and towns apart."

"I know. I'm sorry."

"You don't know. Not really. I'm sure you've read about it in one of your magazines or newspapers. But we're living it every single day."

Amy rested her forehead on her palm. She knew her mom was right. Amy's knowledge of the opioid crisis didn't extend much beyond her own family and the stories she read in various news outlets, from *The New York Times* to *The Philadelphia Inquirer*. But she did have that knowledge. She had watched her brother go from a sporty, fun-loving teenager to an aimless junky, and she had already invested a large amount of her own time and money to help him. She may not be living the crisis 24/7, but it had touched her personally more than it had anyone else she knew.

"Okay, I'll let you know what Rob says."

"Thank you. I really think this could be the last time."

Amy hoped her mother was right, but she wasn't holding her breath.

"Where's my favorite guy?"

"Here, here, here!"

Noah came bounding down the stairs and greeted Rob, who stood in the foyer. Rob crouched down as Noah leapt at him and threw his arms around Rob's neck. Amy smiled. Their bond made her heart swell.

"How was camp today?"

"Pretty good."

"Only *pretty* good? What did you guys do?"

Noah shrugged. "I don't know. Games and stuff."

"Did you play with Ethan?"

Noah rolled his eyes. Amy couldn't believe how much he acted like a teenager lately. "Of *course* I played with Ethan."

"Then that's more than pretty good, right?"

"I guess. But then Carter and Henry wanted to play with him, too, so he played with them at the end."

"Didn't you want to play with them, too?"

He shrugged. "No, I just wanted to play with Ethan."

Amy's and Rob's eyes met. They'd talked about how happy they were that Noah had finally made a good friend but also how they worried he'd become a little obsessed with Ethan as his *only* friend.

"Sometimes it's good to play with other kids, too," Rob said.

"I don't want to play with other kids."

"Why not? I bet Carter and Henry are pretty cool."

"Carter doesn't even know what Minions are," Noah said, as if this proved Carter was completely socially unacceptable.

"Maybe you could show him."

He looked at the ground. He always got sulky when he felt Amy and Rob were trying to pressure him socially. Amy backed off because she knew she would have reacted in the same way.

"Anyway," Amy said, "why don't you let Daddy get changed, and we can talk more about camp over dinner."

"I don't want to talk about camp."

"Then we can talk about whatever you want," Rob said. "But not until I've gotten out of this monkey suit."

Noah giggled and looked up. "*Monkey* suit?"

"It's what they call a man's dress suit sometimes. What, you don't think I look like a monkey?" Rob began scratching under his armpits and making loud monkey sounds. "Ooh ooh ooh, ah ah ah!"

Noah threw his head back and laughed. "You're silly, Daddy."

"But adorable," Amy said, and leaned in and kissed Rob on the lips. Even after eight years of marriage, she still felt a rush of attraction every time she looked at him: those big green eyes, that dirty-blond hair, those strong shoulders and defined waist. He was the cutest. And he was such a good dad to Noah. He could always lighten the mood, even after a long day at work. His days had been longer and more intense since they moved, but that almost never soured his mood, at least toward his son.

"Ewwww, yuck," Noah said as their kiss lingered. He burrowed between them.

Rob pulled away and smiled at Amy. "Good day?"

"Not bad," she said. "I talked to my mom."

Rob raised an eyebrow. "All okay?"

"We can discuss later."

He glanced down quickly at Noah and back up at Amy. *"Ton frère?"*

Amy nodded. They didn't like to go into detail about Tim's problems in front of Noah. They used to, albeit in very vague terms, but about six months ago he started asking questions that made it clear he understood more than they'd thought. Now they either waited until Noah was in bed or spoke elliptically, often invoking a foreign language.

Rob rubbed Amy's arm. "We'll talk. Oh, but before I go up, these things came in the mail for Julian. When are you next seeing Grace and Ethan?" He handed her three letters.

"Yeah, Mommy, when?"

"Friday." She glanced at the letters. They'd received mail for the Durants nearly every day since they moved—some of it standard junk, but some of it serious and official, from the likes of tax agencies and banks. She'd pretended not to notice how much official (and seemingly urgent) mail they received every time she handed it over to Grace, but it was becoming increasingly difficult. One of these letters said "FINAL NOTICE" in bright red letters. She'd have to be blind not to see it.

"Has she said anything?" Rob asked, lowering his voice as he pointed at the red lettering.

Amy shook her head. Grace had seemed a little awkward the last few times Amy had handed over the mail, more in her demeanor than anything she'd explicitly said. But Amy told herself the discomfort could stem from embarrassment over not having properly forwarded their mail. Amy knew that if Julian had done it through the Postal Service like he has supposed to, much of this mail would have ended up at their new address and not at 120 Sycamore. Certain things would have fallen through the cracks, sure, but not this much. They were obviously living somewhere, though Amy still wasn't sure exactly where. Why hadn't they simply forwarded their mail there? It seemed odd.

"See if you can find out any details on Friday," he said.

"It's none of our business," Amy said.

"It will be when some debt collector comes knocking at our door, demanding payment."

Amy rolled her eyes. "Let's not get carried away."

"I'm just saying. You don't have to ask anything specific. Just see what you can find out."

"Okay, Mr. Nosey Neighbor," she said, nudging him in the side, but the truth was, she wanted to know what was going on just as much as he did.

Amy circled around the library parking lot three times before getting out her phone to text Grace.

"Mommy, what are you doing? Let's *go*!"

"Noah, stop it," she snapped back. She knew her reaction might make Noah cry, but she didn't care. She'd had a rough morning—an e-mail had arrived from one of her regular clients saying they wouldn't need her help this quarter—and now she couldn't find a parking spot. The lot was about half the size it should be for such a big library, and being unfamiliar with the area, she wasn't sure where else to go.

"Are we here?" he whined.

She shot off a text to Grace and put down her phone. "Yes, but I've never been here before, and I don't know where to park."

"There's no spaces?"

"Not that I can see. But Grace says the story time is supposed to be really fun and lots of kids come, so I'm sure there are other spots somewhere."

Her phone trilled with a reply from Grace.

Ugh, sorry, parking is a bitch here. I usually park across the street. Fifty cents for an hour.

Amy sighed and pulled out of the parking lot and into a metered spot across the street. It was a blazing ninety-three degrees that day, which meant even the short walk from their car to the entrance felt like walking through fire, but they were greeted by a welcome blast of air-conditioning when they passed through the automatic doors into the library. Grace was waiting by the circulation desk with Ethan.

"Ethan!" Noah shouted.

Amy shushed him. "Remember, this is a library. You can't yell."

"I wasn't yelling," he said in a loud whisper. He let go of Amy's hand and ran toward Ethan.

"Hi, guys," Grace said as they approached. She had such a warm smile. She always made Amy feel at ease, even now, when Amy could feel Julian's mail burning a hole through her tote bag.

"Sorry about the parking," Grace said. "I forgot to mention that."

"Don't worry about it. We found a spot across the street."

"But we almost *melted* on the walk," Noah chimed in.

"So did we!" said Ethan.

"Oooh—pretend you melted into the carpet," Noah said, "and then you needed me to spray you with ice, and then when I did you turned back into Ethan."

Ethan smiled and started doing pretty much exactly what Noah suggested. Amy looked at Grace, who shrugged.

"Oh, to be four . . ." she said.

Amy watched as Noah pretended to blast Ethan with ice, then glanced up at the clock. It was nearly 10:30. "So where is the story time?"

"Right through there." She looked at her watch. "Ethan, sweetie, story time is about to start."

"I'm covered in ice!" He groaned as he rolled around on the floor. Amy looked around and saw a few older patrons in the adult section frowning at them. Were Noah and Ethan making a scene? Probably. Sometimes Amy forgot what it was like not to have kids. Her baseline had become so much more chaotic than it had been before having a child.

"Noah," she said in a tense whisper. "We're going to be late to story time."

Noah immediately stopped his ice blasting. He hated being late. "Sorry. I didn't know."

"It's okay. You can play that game again later. Outside."

"Then maybe he really *will* melt!"

They followed Grace through the archway into the children's section, whose walls were decorated with famous characters from children's books—the Cat in the Hat, Clifford, the Wild Things, Babar. The room was airy and bright, and at the back there was a colorful alphabet carpet with beanbag chairs and brightly painted step stools. It reminded Amy a little of one of the classrooms from Noah's old preschool.

A bunch of other children and their caregivers were already sitting in a circle, and Amy and Grace squeezed in with their boys, sitting next to the librarian.

"Welcome, everyone! Who's ready to have some fun today?"

The children clapped excitedly. Noah looked up at Amy and smiled timidly.

"So, in keeping with the weather we're having, today's theme is . . . the sun! Who here knows about the sun?"

Several kids raised their hands. Amy noticed that Noah didn't, despite the fact that he had recently talked to her about solar flares.

"What can you tell me about it?" the librarian asked.

"It's hot!"

"It's yellow!"

"It helps plants grow!"

"It's almost ten thousand degrees!"

Everyone turned and stared at Noah.

"I . . . well, I think it probably is almost that hot," the librarian said.

"Not probably. It *is*," Noah said. "More like ninety-nine hundred."

Amy could feel her cheeks getting hot. She hoped the librarian wouldn't push it. She knew how Noah was, and she didn't want a scene, at least not this kind. She could deal with four-year-old silliness, like blasting a friend with an ice blaster, but she didn't want a tantrum over scientific accuracy.

"Okay," the librarian said, moving swiftly along. She turned back to the group. "And how big do we think the sun is? Is it . . . the size of a beach ball?"

Noah sighed wearily and looked up at the ceiling, but Amy nudged him and gave him a stern look. "Be nice," she whispered in his ear.

"No!" the other children screamed. "Bigger!"

"As big as . . . the Earth!"

There was a mix of yeses and nos.

"Nope, it's not the same size as the Earth," the librarian said.

"It's the size of a million Earths!" Noah shouted. Again the group turned to look at him.

The librarian smiled politely. "Sounds like someone knows a lot about the sun!"

"And space," Noah said.

"Well, then you're in for a treat because we have some super-exciting stories to read about our favorite ball of fire."

"It's actually a star."

"Yes, well . . . Yes, that's right. So let's read about it!"

She held up the first book and began reading. Amy sighed in relief as Noah looked on, elbows on knees, and listened to the story. She was glad she wasn't one of those mothers who treated her bright child like a performing monkey and reveled in his precociousness, but she wished she could be a little more relaxed about it all. So her kid was smart. So what? That was a good thing—a great thing. She knew that. But she also knew that no one liked a know-it-all. She was something of an expert on that subject. She'd been a know-it-all herself in elementary school, and it wasn't until she stopped getting invited to sleepovers and birthday parties that she realized maybe she should have toned it down. Noah was only four, so he still had plenty of time to tame his smart-aleck tendencies, but she couldn't help but worry his intelligence would eat away at his social life.

The librarian moved from story to story, asking the children questions in between, though Amy noticed she avoided any more specific queries about the sun or other celestial bodies. Noah seemed to be enjoying himself, which Amy knew was the entire point of the outing, but she was a little disappointed that the nature of the story time meant she and Grace couldn't really chat. Occasionally one of them would whisper something to the other ("How's Rob liking the job?" "Did you see the latest tweet from the president?"), but there wasn't really an opportunity to have a conversation. They'd had several playdates at this point, but Amy wanted to get to know Grace better, and it was hard to do that when you were being shushed by a librarian.

Aside from wanting to develop a friendship with Grace, she also wanted to learn more about her life. She'd given Rob a hard time about being nosy, but she had to admit, she, too, was curious about the Durants' living situation. Amy had gotten the distinct impression from Cynthia—and the Durants themselves—that there was some urgency to their moving. Amy assumed this was due to a contingency on the new house they were purchasing, but in all of their time together, Grace had never mentioned anything about her moving and unpacking travails, even when Amy had talked about hers. Maybe Grace was just very private, but it struck Amy as odd. Moving was such a chaotic and all-consuming experience. If you had a friend going through the same thing, wouldn't you want to commiserate?

The librarian finished the last story and clapped her hands together. "Now, who's ready to make their very own sun?"

The children squealed excitedly as she passed out tissue paper, glue, construction paper, and crayons. They began chatting merrily with one another, the room permeated by giggles and high-pitched babble. Amy and Grace hung back as Noah and Ethan started in on their projects.

"So Noah's a sharp one, huh?"

Amy smiled and shrugged. "I take no credit, I take no responsibility."

Grace laughed. "Aw, come on. You guys are smarties. Where'd you say you went to college?"

"Georgetown. Rob went to Yale."

"See? Smart parents, smart kid."

"Ethan seems bright, too."

"Meh. We'll see. He's smart enough, that's for sure. But let's just say he doesn't have Noah's genius."

"Yesterday he threw toilet paper with poop on it in the trash can, so let's hold off on the 'genius' diagnosis for a while."

Grace laughed out loud. "That's called being four and a boy. I'm telling you: that Y chromosome is a little fucked up."

She threw her hand over her mouth as another mother gave her the evil eye. Amy bit her lip but couldn't stop smiling. She reached into her bag and pulled out Julian's letters. "Speaking of Y chromosomes . . . these came for Julian."

Grace's eyes landed on the bright red lettering. Her cheeks turned a little pink. "Oh. Thanks. Sorry you keep having to deal with that."

Amy cleared her throat as Grace took the mail. "Julian still hasn't changed your address . . . ?"

Grace sighed. "No, long story. He said we don't have to because he's manually changed the address for anything that matters. He says the only stuff coming to the old place is junk we don't care about anyway." She paused awkwardly as Amy's eyes landed on the top envelope: FINAL NOTICE. It definitely didn't look like junk. "I'll talk to him," Grace said.

"It's not a problem—I don't mind collecting it for you. I just figured it would be easier to have it sent directly to your new address." Amy tucked her hair behind her ear, trying to seem casual. "Where is your new place, by the way? I keep meaning to ask."

Grace looked away and stuffed the mail into her tote bag. "It's . . . well, like I said, it's a long story." Something in her demeanor had changed. She seemed very uncomfortable.

"Sorry. I shouldn't have—I didn't mean to pry."

"No, it's fine." She looked up and met Amy's eyes. "We're sort of in transition at the moment. We're staying with my parents."

"Oh. I didn't realize. I thought . . . never mind."

"We had an offer on another house, but the deal fell through," she said, before Amy could feel too awkward. "So now we actually think we might build something. In the meantime, my parents have a guesthouse on their property, so that's where we are for now."

"Sounds like everything sort of worked out then."

"I wouldn't go that far."

Amy flushed. It *did* sound like rather a lucky break that her parents had a guesthouse. If the same had happened to Amy and Rob, they'd either be stuck at his parents' house with their two Rhodesian ridgebacks or—a far less likely but more unpleasant option—crammed into her mother's tiny ranch in Woonsocket. Having an entire guesthouse to oneself, or one's family, seemed like a pretty sweet deal. No mortgage, no rent, someone else to do the gardening and pay the bills. . . . To Amy, it sounded kind of perfect.

"Anyway," Grace said, "it's only temporary. We're looking at a lot in Rydal this weekend, so we may have more news soon."

"Nice. You'll have to keep me posted. I'm happy to pass along your mail until you sort everything out. Unless you'd rather I just drop it at your parents'?"

"No," Grace said, a little too quickly. She collected herself. "You can just give it to me when we get the kids together. Julian has been changing our contact info site by site, so hopefully there won't be much more."

"Okay, no problem," Amy said. She didn't mind. It was the lowest of low lifts to pass along their mail when she would be seeing Grace and Ethan anyway. But the more she talked to Grace, the more she got the impression that something with the Durants definitely wasn't quite right, and though it was none of her business, she couldn't help but wonder what it was.

# Chapter 5

The Durants' mail continued to arrive. Contrary to what Grace had said, the amount wasn't lessening, and the senders were the usual suspects: state and local tax departments, utility companies, credit card companies. Amy continued to collect the letters and pass them on to Grace, pretending she didn't find it odd that aside from a few catalogs and promotional coupons, the bulk of the mail came from organizations demanding some sort of payment. How could Julian not mind that Amy and Rob saw all of these notices? It seemed so . . . personal. Maybe he had changed his address, and the organizations just needed time to process the information. Or maybe he'd rather Amy and Rob know about his financial problems than his in-laws—though if he was living with them, wouldn't they already know? Amy couldn't figure it out.

She also couldn't figure out how to make her professional life work in the outskirts of Philadelphia, and she was beginning to worry. The freelance work had always come in dribs and drabs, and historically, just when one line of work seemed to peter out, another would pop up and fill its place. But now everything seemed to be tapering off at once, and nothing new had materialized. Was it because she had spent so many weeks unpacking? She knew that might be part of it. The move had been a major distraction. And the change of city definitely put her at a disadvantage.

But truthfully, work had been a bit precarious even before they moved. Working freelance and part-time provided great flexibility—she could spend time with Noah and take him to and from preschool without a problem—but over time, it also made her feel out of touch. She wasn't going to conferences or workshops on the latest research in the education field. She was writing grant proposals and editing policy papers, and the truth was, a lot of people could do that. She felt herself drifting further and further from the circle of policy experts she'd known in DC, and she wasn't sure how to make herself relevant again. She didn't want the long hours and intensity of her pre-Noah career, but in a year he'd be starting kindergarten, and she wanted something more for herself—and their bank account. Rob's job paid well, but they both still had a few student loans to pay off, and they wanted to give Noah the option of private school someday, if he truly needed it. She knew she still had time to come up with a plan, but the worries niggled her beneath the surface, even when she tried to ignore them.

She had just sent off another batch of anxiety-induced freelance pitches when she looked at the clock on her laptop and gasped. It was 3:05. She should have picked Noah up five minutes ago.

She grabbed her purse and rushed out the door. The camp was only ten minutes away, so she would be there by 3:15—sooner if she drove quickly. Noah wouldn't be happy, but . . . Oh, who was she kidding? Noah would be borderline hysterical. As much as he hated being late himself, he especially hated it when other people were late, especially when it came to picking him up. She once got tied up on a call in DC and was fifteen minutes late picking up Noah from Bright Futures, and when she arrived his eyes were swollen and his face was streaked with tears. "You *forgot* me!" he shouted accusingly at her. It took a full hour to bring him back from the edge.

Amy flew down the driveway and down their street, but—as if the universe were trying to teach her a lesson—she encountered road construction or traffic at every turn. Traffic in the suburbs? What was this?

When she finally tore into the camp parking lot, it was 3:20. Noah would be furious.

She parked the car, jumped out, and ran for the pavilion. By the time she got there, she was out of breath.

"Ah, there you are," said Donna, the director.

"So sorry," Amy said, panting. "Traffic was terrible."

"This summer has been the worst. I've never seen so much road work in my life. Our tax dollars at work, I guess."

Amy scanned the pavilion. It was filled with kids hanging around, playing cards, weaving lanyard, and trading fidget spinners. "I hope Noah didn't freak out too much. . . ."

"Noah? Oh, he's fine. Right over there playing Go Fish with a friend."

Amy followed Donna's gaze and saw Noah sitting cross-legged on the ground, across from a boy who—to Amy's surprise—wasn't Ethan.

"Who's that?" Amy asked.

Donna craned her neck. "Jake. Sweet boy. Just started this week."

"And here I thought Noah only had eyes for Ethan." Amy laughed.

"Well, Ethan is his number one. But the three of them were playing nicely together today."

She looked on as he and Jake played cards, when he looked up and saw her.

"Mommy!"

He leapt up and ran toward her. She loved how excited he always was to see her. She dreaded the day—probably not too far off now—when he'd roll his eyes upon seeing her and harrumph his way past her to the car.

"I'm *so* sorry I'm late," Amy said, giving him a hug.

He shrugged. "It's okay. I got to play Go Fish with Jake. I beated him two times."

"We'll see you tomorrow, okay, Noah?" Donna said.

"Not tomorrow—Tuesday," Noah said. "I don't come Fridays."

"Sorry, of course." Donna shook her head. "Can't get anything past this guy, can you?"

"Not much . . ." Amy said, she hoped not too wearily.

She and Noah walked toward the car, holding hands as they walked along the crushed gravel path.

"So you had fun playing with Jake today, huh?"

"And Ethan," Noah added quickly.

"Well, of course Ethan."

"Is Ethan coming over tomorrow?"

"Not to our place. We're getting together, but I'm not a hundred percent sure where yet."

"Are you sixty-eight percent sure?"

Amy smiled. With Noah, everything was quantified, even if he didn't really have a concept of what sixty-eight percent was. "I'd say I'm like fifty percent sure. Either the park near us or another one near Chestnut Hill."

"Why can't Ethan come to our house to play?"

"It's not that he can't. It's just . . ." Amy chose her words carefully. "I don't want to make Ethan feel funny."

"Why would he feel funny at our house?"

"Well . . . because it used to be *his* house. But we bought it from his mommy and daddy, so now it's our house, and I don't want him to feel sad that he doesn't live there anymore."

"He could come live with me in my room if he wants."

Amy kissed Noah's hand. She loved his generosity. "He has to live with his mommy and daddy. But don't worry—soon he will barely remember he ever lived there, and then we can have him over anytime you want."

"Like next week?"

"I think he'll need a little more time than that."

"Then when?"

"I don't know. Soon. A few months."

Noah smiled. The answer satisfied him. The truth was, Amy knew the awkwardness of having the Durants over would persist for months, maybe even years. Ethan might forget he ever lived at 120 Sycamore, but Grace never would. She'd decorated the house with such care. It's where her baby was born! That wouldn't stop Amy from inviting them over. She would. She knew that. But for now, she hoped to delay that eventuality for as long as she possibly could.

\* \* \*

Just as Amy pulled into their driveway, her phone rang. It was her mom. They hadn't spoken since she'd called about money for Tim's rehab costs.

"Mom, hi—sorry, I still haven't had a chance to talk to Rob," Amy said as she parked the car. She got out and held the phone between her ear and shoulder as she helped Noah out of his car seat.

"Oh. Okay. I just figured . . . it's been more than a week."

"I know. Stuff has just been crazy with the house and his new job and everything."

In truth, she and Rob had discussed the issue, but he wanted more time to think about it. He'd been so generous with her family over the years, having helped with Tim's previous stints at rehab and a few of her mom's bills, but they'd just moved and had so many expenses at the moment that he wanted to sleep on it. Amy assumed he'd meant for a night, but it had been more than a week and he was still mulling it over. She didn't blame him. Two grand was a lot of money.

"Could you try to bring it up with him tonight? I'm kind of running out of time."

"I will. But try to understand—two thousand dollars . . . it's a lot."

"I know, but look at you two. You just bought a big house in a nice neighborhood. I'm sure you can manage it."

Amy hated this tendency in her mother—to ask for a favor and then make it seem like it would be selfish and cruel of Amy *not* to help. Whether it was helping Tim with a science project in middle school ("It's not like you have to think about it—you've already taken that class so you know what the teacher is looking for.") or shuttling Tim and his friends to and from parties in high school ("You don't have any plans anyway."), her mother didn't so much ask for favors as expect them. It's not that Amy minded helping. She loved to lend a hand and knew her mom was stretched thin. But as she'd gotten older, the requests had become more monetary—and more substantial—and she hated the guilt that came along with knowing someday, she truly might not be able to help.

"Things are just a little tight right now," Amy said as she ushered Noah into the house. She opened the lid to their wall-mounted mailbox and pulled out a bundle of mail from inside. The postman had come sometime while she was picking up Noah.

"Tight? Maybe you should come stay with me for a while. Then you'll know tight."

Amy sighed as she dumped the mail on the kitchen counter and began to sort through it. She'd regretted using that word as soon as it had slipped out, but there was no taking it back now. Her mom was right: What she and Rob considered a precarious financial position would be total comfort, if not opulence, for her family. But there was no comparing the two lifestyles. What was a suitable income and savings level for her mom—a single woman in Woonsocket—wasn't even close to what Rob and Amy needed for a family of three in a middle-class Mid-Atlantic suburb.

Amy opened their latest PECO bill and took a deep breath. She still hadn't gotten used to paying the electric bill for an entire house. They could manage it, but in light of the conversation about finances, she couldn't help but hold her breath.

"Hello?"

Amy let out the air in a gust. "Sorry. I was just checking . . . Never mind. I will talk to Rob tonight. Okay?"

"Thank you. Like I said, Timmy is doing really great. This program is much better."

"Glad to hear that. Is he happy with it?"

"He hasn't really wanted to talk about it. He's embarrassed."

"Why? It's not like you're judging him."

"It's hard for him to understand that when everyone else is."

"I'm not."

"Oh, really? His big sister with her successful husband and adorable son and wonderful life? How do you think that makes him feel? You think he likes being the fuckup?"

"I just meant—"

"This is hard, okay? Hard for both of us."

"I know. And I'm sorry."

"Mommy, who are you talking to?" Noah whined.

Amy covered the phone. "Mimi."

"I want to talk, I want to talk!" Noah jumped up and down.

"In a second."

"No, I want to talk now."

Amy rolled her eyes. "Mom? Noah wants to say hi."

"Then put him on! I can't say no to my only grandchild."

Amy handed Noah the phone and continued opening the mail. She marveled at Noah's ability to change her mother's mood. Ellen hadn't been a particularly warm and fuzzy mother to Amy, but to Noah, she was all joy, all the time. Amy supposed she'd be all joy, all the time, too, if she didn't have to deal with tantrums and discipline and mealtimes and endless laundry. But her mom had done plenty of that with Amy and Timmy. She'd put in her time. Now she got to enjoy the fun bits. Being a grandparent sounded excellent.

Amy tore through letter after letter—the usual bills, forwarded mail from Washington, credit card solicitations—when she opened a bank statement from Wells Fargo.

> *Dear Mr. Durant,*
>
> *We are writing to inform you that the assets in the Lloyd F. Sterling Trust for the Benefit of Ethan James Durant have fallen below the $50,000 set threshold as stipulated in the trust agreement. Please be advised that the trust holdings are currently valued at $500.*

Amy felt her stomach drop as she flipped over the envelope. It was addressed to Julian. She hadn't even noticed. She and Rob used Wells Fargo, too, and she'd assumed it was meant for them. Her eyes flashed back to the letter as its contents sunk in. Ethan had a trust fund, and someone had drained it. Julian? It had to be. If he was receiving the letter, he was obviously the trustee. But what had he done with the money? And did Grace know?

"Mimi says goodbye!" shouted Noah, startling Amy out of her trance.

"Tell her I'll talk to her tomorrow," Amy said, even though, at the moment, her mother's financial problems weren't the ones that concerned her.

\* \* \*

"What am I supposed to *do?*"

Amy fiddled with the stem of her wineglass as Rob finished chewing a mouthful of chicken. They'd decided to eat dinner after Noah went to bed, so that they could discuss things they didn't want him hearing. Amy had led with the letter from Wells Fargo instead of her mother's financial request.

"Honestly, I don't know," Rob said. "It isn't really our business."

"True. But Noah worships Ethan. This was supposed to be his money, and now Julian has stolen it."

"You don't know that."

"He is the trustee."

"So? Maybe Lloyd F. Sterling—whoever he is—gave Julian permission."

"I think Lloyd is Grace's dad. Her parents have a guesthouse."

"Guesthouses and trust funds. Wouldn't it be nice?" Rob sighed.

"It just seems fishy to me, after all of the other mail we've gotten for Julian. The Durants are obviously in some sort of financial trouble, and all of the threatening mail comes in his name."

"That doesn't mean anything. Mail comes for me all the time, but that doesn't stop you from opening it."

"True." She swirled her wineglass. "So you think Grace knows?"

"I have no idea."

"Maybe she's in on it. Maybe they're running some sort of scam together or something."

"Slow down, tiger," Rob said. "It could be totally innocent."

"You don't usually drain a trust fund when everything is hunky-dory."

"You're an expert on trusts now?"

Amy clenched her jaw. Why wasn't Rob backing her up on this? He took her side on almost everything—not merely to keep the peace but because they were of the same mind on most issues.

"No, but you aren't either. And you've been saying from the beginning that something smells off."

Rob took a deep breath. "I have. And I still think that. But I just . . ."

"You just what?"

"I worry about Noah. Ethan is his best friend—frankly the only real friend he's ever had. Haven't you seen the change in him since we moved here?"

"Of course I have."

"Right. So I'm hesitant to make wild accusations about his best friend's parents."

"I'm not making wild accusations."

"You're basically saying they've drained their kid's trust fund to finance a shady criminal enterprise."

"I never said that!"

Rob smiled. "Have I told you how sexy you are when you get indignant?"

She kicked him playfully under the table. "You're not getting sex tonight, so you can stop that right now."

"Because I won't agree with you about this?"

Amy rolled her eyes. "I actually have my period, so it was never going to happen. It just sounded good."

Rob laughed as he wiped the corners of his mouth. He leaned his elbows on the table and sighed. "Listen, you're probably right. There is almost definitely something shady going on with the Durants, or at the very least Julian. But at this point, I honestly don't see what we can do about it. Frankly, we shouldn't even know about the trust fund. You committed mail fraud by even opening it."

"But I thought it was for us! I didn't read the name on the envelope!"

"I'm not a lawyer. I don't know if that excuse would hold up." His eyes wandered to the letter, which Amy had laid on the table. "You should probably throw it out."

"Throw it out?"

He nodded. "Lloyd F. Sterling's lawyer will get a copy of this letter, too, so eventually, if he doesn't know already, he will. And, Grace . . . well, if she doesn't know, she'll probably eventually find out, too. It isn't your job to tell her."

"But we see each other all the time."

"So? It's not as if you're super close. You really only see her on playdates at this point. You're not best friends or anything."

"I know, but . . ."

Amy didn't finish the sentence, which was: *But I* want *us to become friends*. She wasn't exactly sure why. Actually, she was: She was lonely, and Grace was cool, beautiful, and worldly. Who wouldn't want to befriend someone like that? But Rob was right. They weren't best friends, at least not yet, and so she had no responsibility to pass along the information in the letter. She reached for it and took a deep breath as she read through it one last time. Then she crumpled it up, walked over to the recycling bin, and tossed it inside.

"Anyway," Rob said, "wasn't there something else you wanted to discuss? You said there were two things."

"Oh, right," Amy said, feeling her stomach sour. "We need to make a decision about my mother."

# Chapter 6

Amy spent all of Friday morning dreading the playdate with Grace and Ethan. She kept mentioning to Noah that her stomach hurt (which was true—her stomach always ached when she got nervous), hoping to lay the groundwork for an eventual cancellation. But when she saw how excited he was about seeing Wissahickon Valley Park's Forbidden Drive, she didn't have the heart to disappoint him.

"Are you packing lunch again?" he asked as she dabbed concealer beneath her eyes.

"No, Grace says there is a little café where we can buy lunch."

Noah looked skeptical. "What kind of café?"

"I don't know, a regular café. They sell sandwiches and salads and stuff like that."

"I don't like salad."

Grace sighed. "Then don't order one."

"But what if everything has nuts in it?"

"Everything won't have nuts in it."

"But what if it *does*?"

Amy clenched her jaw and turned, ready to shout at Noah until she saw the expression on his face. He was worried. He thought they were going to eat somewhere that would kill his friend.

"Ethan's mommy is the one who suggested the place, so I'm

sure it's fine. They've been there before, and he has been able to find something to eat."

Noah hesitated. "Okay."

"Just let me finish putting on a little makeup and then we can go."

Noah sidled up behind her and watched as she swept a little blush across her cheeks. "Why do you wear makeup?"

She shrugged. "To look pretty."

"But you already look pretty."

She looked back at him and smiled. "Thanks, sweetie."

She took out her mascara and swept it across her lashes. Did she really need it? She thought so, but then she always found herself questioning her looks before meeting up with Grace, who was so naturally beautiful she didn't seem to require makeup of any kind. She wasn't comparing herself to Grace . . . okay, so maybe she was. But it was hard not to. Grace had such effortless style that Amy couldn't help but feel dowdy next to her. Some days she felt as if she were in high school again, trying to keep up with the popular girls, except this time one of the popular girls actually wanted to hang out with her.

She threw on a coat of lip gloss, threw her hair in a ponytail, and grabbed her sandals. "All right," she said. "Let's go."

They hopped in the car and wove their way through the suburbs until they reached the Forbidden Drive, a seven-mile crushed gravel trail along the Wissahickon Creek. Amy parked on the outskirts of the park and, holding Noah's hand, made her way across the street and through the barrier beyond, which cars were not allowed to travel. In the distance, she saw the Cedars House Café, a butter-yellow cottage nestled among the trees, set back from the gravel path. As they got closer, Amy saw Ethan running around one of the picnic benches situated outside.

"Ethan!"

Noah let go of Amy's hand and bolted toward the picnic table.

"Noah, slow down—"

But as the words came out of her mouth, he tripped on a rock and came crashing down. He let out a piercing wail.

"Shit," Amy muttered under her breath as she took off toward him. *Please say he hasn't lost a tooth.*

She lifted him up and brushed his hair off his forehead. "Oh, sweetie." His nose was bleeding—rather a lot—and his knees and hands were pretty scraped up, but he still seemed to have all of his teeth, and he didn't have any cuts on his face.

"I-I . . . n-n-need . . . s-s-some . . . iiiiice," he howled.

Amy kissed his forehead. "I'm sure the café has ice. Let's go."

She stood up just as Grace and Ethan came to join them.

"That looked like a nasty spill," Grace said.

"He's okay, aren't you, buddy?"

He sniffled and nodded as the blood trickled down his nose. Her heart broke for him a little. He'd shown so much enthusiasm for his friend. To them it probably looked like he got so excited that he was, quite literally, tripping over himself. They didn't seem to mind, but Noah was a lot like she was as a kid—sensitive, worried about being judged. Some of his tears were probably more to do with his embarrassment over tripping in front of a friend than from the injury itself. Amy remembered bashing her nose on the blacktop at recess one day when she was about ten, and although the resulting gash and swelling hurt, the stares from her classmates hurt a lot more.

"I told him the café would have ice," Amy said.

"Oh, definitely," said Grace. "Come on, let's patch you up. The café also has some pretty amazing cookies, which I hear can heal boo-boos like that." She snapped her fingers.

Noah looked up at Amy, unsure of her position of a cookie before lunch, but his uncertainty morphed into something resembling a smile as Amy nodded gently. She handed him a tissue and showed him how to hold his nose to stop the bleeding.

They went inside, and the cashier made up a small baggy of ice for Noah. She handed him a malted chocolate chip cookie. "On the house," she said.

"Oh, no, I insist," Amy said, holding out two dollars.

"Honestly, it's fine. Poor kid. Look at him."

Amy looked down at Noah. His nose had swollen, and his upper lip was caked in dried blood. Her son would always be gorgeous to her no matter what, but at the moment, even she had to admit he looked pretty bad.

He scarfed down the cookie, and in no time he started to seem like himself again.

"Shall we go for a little walk before we come back for lunch?" Grace suggested.

"Works for us," Amy said.

The group headed out, and before long the boys were chasing each other down the trail, weaving around puddles and piles of horse manure.

"Noah, be careful!" Amy shouted. "Please don't trip again."

He slowed down, only slightly, and gave her a puckish smile.

"It's not like he gave himself a bloody nose fifteen minutes ago or anything," she groaned, shaking her head.

"Typical boy behavior," Grace said. "Ethan is the same way."

It was the first time in a long time that anyone had referred to Noah as "typical." Amy found it refreshing.

"So how are things with you guys?" Grace asked.

"Pretty good. . . ." Amy said. Her stomach tingled. *I did get an interesting letter about Ethan's trust. . . .*

"Yeah? Doesn't sound that way. Everything okay with you and Rob?"

"Me and Rob?" Amy tried not to sound too taken aback by the question. It was so . . . personal. They talked kids and houses and schedules, but not marriage. It's not that Amy didn't want to talk about those things. Frankly she was eager for a friend with whom she could share personal and private details, and she really liked Grace. But their friendship was still in the early stages, so the question caught her by surprise.

"Sorry, I didn't mean—I just thought . . . moves can be stressful, and they can put a lot of pressure on relationships. And you said your work wasn't going that great due to the move, so I figured maybe . . ." She waved her hand. "Never mind. I didn't mean to pry."

"No, it's fine. Things with Rob and I are great. I mean, you know, there's the usual stuff with couples who have been married for nearly ten years, but nothing out of the ordinary."

"You guys have been married almost ten years?"

"Nine this September."

"Wow. Next year is a big one. Any fun plans in the works?"

"For next year? Uh, no. We haven't even figured out what we're doing this year."

"You should go to Vetri."

"This year?" From what Amy had heard, Vetri was one of the best restaurants in the country, but it was also more than $150 a head, and that didn't include wine.

"No, for your tenth. Though I guess if you can afford it for your ninth—"

"We can't."

Grace smiled. "It's amazing. Julian and I went in February for our fifth anniversary. Best meal of my life."

"We will have to check it out. Sounds perfect for a milestone anniversary." Amy found it a little odd that Grace and Julian were able to afford what was probably a $400 dinner when (from what Amy had seen) they couldn't pay some of their bills and, apparently, had all but liquidated their son's trust fund. But then she couldn't very well ask about any of that.

"By the way, totally off topic—did you happen to get any more of our mail?"

Amy's heart started beating a little faster. "I think there was a letter or two. . . ." She reached into her bag.

"Okay, great, because Julian said he actually stopped by your house yesterday to check, so that you wouldn't have to keep bringing the mail to our playdates, but you must have been out."

"Really? When did he come by?"

"I have no idea. Late afternoon maybe? Before dinner for sure."

Amy knew she had been home from 3:40, but he could have come while she was picking up Noah from camp. Then again, if what he was so anxious to pick up was the trust fund letter, couldn't he have just pulled it from the mailbox himself? Or was that mail fraud, too? Amy wasn't up to speed.

"I was super late picking up Noah from camp, so he must have come while I was racing like a maniac down the streets of Glenside Park."

Amy expected to get a laugh out of Grace, or at least an acknowledgment of her attempt at humor, but instead she seemed to be doing some sort of calculation in her head. "No, I think . . . well, anyway, the point is, you brought the mail, so it doesn't really matter."

Amy handed over the only two pieces of mail she had for the Durants this week: a newsletter from Ethan's preschool, and some sort of letter from Colgate University for Grace. Grace looked at the envelopes and rolled her eyes.

"I'm so sorry you're still having to deal with this. At least it's only two letters this week."

"It's fine," Amy said. "Really."

"Very kind of you to say that, but if it were me, I'd be a little sick of dealing with someone else's mail by now. If Julian had just— Ethan! You stop that right now! Slow down!"

Ethan veered precariously close to the edge of the gorge as he and Noah played some sort of chasing game. Grace ran ahead and grabbed Ethan by the arm and pulled him back.

"What have I told you? *Never* get that close to the edge. Do you understand? You want to plunge into the creek and die?"

Ethan shook his head solemnly. Noah's widened eyes landed on Amy's. They would be discussing death by falling off a cliff for at least two weeks.

"Now go back to playing safely—on the other side of the trail. Okay, boys?"

Both boys nodded their heads and scurried to the other side of the path.

Grace sighed. "You know what I need?"

"A stiff drink?"

She turned and looked at Amy. "Yes, actually. How would you feel about a girls' night out?"

"When?"

"I don't know. Sunday?"

"We're having dinner at Rob's parents', but Noah is usually at home in bed by eight or eight-thirty, so I could meet up after."

"Works for me. There's a new brewhouse in Jenkintown—really good, and if you're not into beer, they have good cocktails and wine, too."

"Sign me up."

"Perfect. It'll be great to have an adult conversation that isn't interrupted by these monsters. I mean, look at them. ETHAN! What did I tell you?" She sighed. "Is it Sunday yet?"

Sunday arrived before they knew it, and Amy and Rob spent the day weeding the garden while Noah ran through the sprinkler in his bathing suit. Amy hadn't weeded in . . . come to think of it, she wasn't sure she ever really *had* weeded. She remembered helping her mother occasionally in the summer, but Ellen actually enjoyed tending to her garden, so Amy's chores revolved mostly around the dishes (cleaning them), the floors (sweeping them), and the trash cans (emptying them). Once she moved to Washington, she lived in dorms and apartments, none of which had yards, front or back. She didn't have a lot of experience pulling up crabgrass and clover.

And there was a lot to pull. In all of the hubbub surrounding the move—unpacking, buying new furniture, signing Noah up for camp, trying to settle in professionally—Amy and Rob had sort of forgotten about the yard. Rob mowed the lawn every week (an activity that Amy found surprisingly sexy), but otherwise, the flowerbeds were largely ignored. Then one day last week, Amy noticed every last bed was overrun by hairy, green invaders, and she realized there was more to maintaining a garden than just looking at it and smiling.

By the time they finished, she and Rob were both smelly, sweaty messes, and Amy was pretty sure she'd pinched a nerve in her neck. She could already hear her mom mocking her ("Fancy-pants city girl can't handle a little gardening! Now you know what *real* work is like."). Amy wasn't sure why her mother's voice was so dismissive when she heard it in her own head. Ellen did often sneer at Amy's relative privilege, but Amy knew there was more to it than that. Her mother's voice somehow fused with her own conscience, the part of her that felt a little self-conscious about where she came from and guilty about leaving her family behind.

Rob volunteered to help Noah change while Amy showered, and once the three of them were clean and dressed, they piled in the car and headed to Rob's parents' house in Jenkintown Manor.

"Did Bubbe make me cake?" Noah asked as they stopped at a traffic light.

"I don't know, bud. Do you think you've been good enough for cake?" Rob gave Amy a playful look.

"YES!" Noah shouted. He sounded a little panicked. "I wasn't the one who tried to die by falling off a cliff."

Amy suppressed a groan. She'd been right: the topic had been discussed at length ever since their outing with Ethan and Grace.

"Well, if that's the case, then I bet Bubbe has made you cake. Or something as good as cake."

"Like cookies or pie or chocolate," Noah volunteered. "Or maybe ALL of those."

"Let's not get ahead of ourselves," Amy said, though she knew it was, indeed, a possibility that Rob's mother, Sherrie, had prepared every baked good imaginable. She loved to spoil Noah rotten, and food was her indulgence of choice. Most visits to her house ended with Noah so hyped up on sugar that he was literally running in circles, and they needed to carry him kicking and screaming to the car. Amy appreciated Sherrie's generosity but sometimes wished she'd tone it down.

Rob pulled up his parents' driveway, and Sherrie and Bruce were already standing out front, chatting with their neighbors. Like Glenside Park, the neighborhood Rob grew up in had sidewalks and tree-lined streets and the sort of friendly neighbors who regularly stopped by to say hello while they were walking their dog or taking an evening stroll.

"BUBBE!" Noah shouted as he bolted from the car once Amy had unfastened his car seat.

Sherrie beamed and clapped her hands together as Noah charged at her. "Look who it is!" She crouched down and gave Noah a big hug as he leapt into her arms. Amy's heart swelled. This was why they moved. If Noah couldn't have this relationship with her own mother, she wanted him to have it with Rob's.

"Did you make me cake?" Noah asked.

"Noah!"

Sherrie waved her off. "Of course I made you cake."

Noah jumped up and down. "Yay! See, I told you she'd make cake!"

"A strawberry shortcake," Sherrie added.

Noah squealed. "With whipped cream?"

"*Extra* whipped cream."

Amy thought Noah's head might spin right off his body. "I want a big piece. A gigantic piece. Like . . . like the size of Jupiter."

"I'm not sure the cake is *quite* big enough for that."

Noah frowned. "How about this much?" He gestured with his hands, showing a size of cake Amy and Rob definitely would not approve.

"That I think we can do," Sherrie said, winking.

She and Bruce said goodbye to their neighbors, and the group moved indoors to a screened-in porch on the side of the house. Sherrie had already put out snacks and drinks, and there was a nice breeze from a ceiling fan.

"So," Sherrie said, as they all took a seat around the table. "Good weekend?"

Rob shrugged. "Not particularly eventful, but we got some yard work done."

"Oh, well, that's good. I drove by the other day and noticed your beds could use a little TLC. It's a transition, moving from the city, isn't it?"

Amy knew Sherrie meant this in the nicest possible way, but she also knew that Sherrie was the type of mother (and mother-in-law) who would casually "drive by," just to check on their property. She was house proud when it came to her own home, and since Rob was the only child in the area (his only sister lived in Arizona), the interest in home maintenance now extended to their place as well.

"I ran through the sprinkler!" Noah exclaimed.

"You did? That must've felt good."

"It was very"—Noah searched for the right word—"refreshing," he finally said.

Sherrie gave Rob a knowing smile. "*Refreshing*," she repeated. "That's a very good word, Noah."

Noah looked pleased with himself. He loved impressing adults.

"What about you guys?" Rob asked as he dug into the crab dip. "Any weekend excitement?"

"We saw an excellent movie at the Hiway," Sherrie said. "About a foster care boy in New Zealand. Funny and touching—I highly recommend it."

"You want to watch Noah . . . ?" Rob joked, although Amy knew he wasn't really joking, and she wouldn't have been either. One of the main reasons they'd moved here was to be closer to Rob's family—for the relationship building, of course, but also for the childcare support. But so far, his parents had been busy every weekend, and they hadn't yet found any reliable sitters.

"Just say the word," Sherrie said. She gave Noah a smooch on the forehead. "I could never say no to this boy."

"Uh, Mom, I think you have. Several times actually."

She shrugged. "It's not my fault your father and I have a social life."

"I'm not blaming your social life."

"I think you are."

"Mom . . ."

"Why not try a weeknight?"

"Because lately by the time I get home, I'm exhausted. Sit me in a darkened room, and I'll fall asleep. No question."

"So take the movie part out of it. Just go to dinner." She nodded at Bruce. "We're free Tuesday, right?"

Bruce gave a droll look. "Like I'm the keeper of the social calendar. . . ."

"I just meant you don't have golf or anything."

"Oh, no, no—golf is Mondays."

"So? What do you say? Tuesday?"

Amy and Rob looked at each other and nodded. "Sure," Rob said. "It's a date."

"Great! It'll be you and us, kiddo," she said, tousling Noah's hair. "You know, you two really should go downtown. So many restaurants to explore. There's a new place in Passyunk Square that does . . . I don't know, farm to table small plates or something. But it's supposed to be very good. I think the chef was on *Top Chef*. Very popular."

"I'm guessing we won't be able to get a table with only two days' notice," Amy said.

"You never know," she said. "Anyway, it'll be good for the two of you to get out. You've been cooped up in the house too long at this point!"

"Amy is actually going out tonight," Rob said.

"Tonight?" Sherrie sounded surprised.

"With Noah's friend's mom," Amy said.

Sherrie raised her eyebrows. "You mean the woman who used to own your house?"

Rob groaned. "Geez, Mom."

"Well, she is, isn't she?"

"Yeah, but when you say it like that—"

"We've actually gotten pretty friendly," Amy said. "We certainly see enough of each other. We get the kids together at least once a week."

"Is it ever . . . you know, awkward?"

Amy's and Rob's eyes met—only briefly, but enough for Sherrie to catch a whiff of something off.

"Mmmmm," she said knowingly.

"There's nothing awkward about the house," Amy said quickly.

"Then what?"

"Nothing. It's nothing."

Sherrie pursed her lips. *It doesn't* sound *like nothing*, her expression said.

"Ethan doesn't come over to play," Noah said, and they all turned to look at him, as if they'd forgotten he was there. Amy knew they shouldn't have said anything in front of him. He heard and understood more than adults gave him credit for.

"He doesn't?" Sherrie said.

"Because Mommy doesn't want him to miss his old house too much."

"That's *very* thoughtful of her."

"Maybe in a year he can come," Noah said. He smiled, as if something had occurred to him. "Hey, maybe by then we won't get his mommy and daddy's letters anymore!"

Sherrie's eyebrows lifted to nearly the ceiling, but before she could ask any questions, Amy lifted Noah's empty glass from the table. "Looks like you need a refill, buddy," she said. "Bubbe, would you mind?"

*    *    *

Amy and Rob managed to escape his parents' house without another mention of the Durants. Bruce didn't seem particularly interested in any of it, but Sherrie always loved a juicy story and could smell one a mile away, like a hungry grizzly.

Amy didn't like thinking about their departure as an escape—she actually really liked Rob's parents, and she loved the way they treated Noah even more. Watching them together made her realize what she'd missed growing up. Her mom's parents had died before Amy was old enough to remember them, and her father's parents hadn't ever gotten along with her mother, so once he died, they didn't come around very much. Would her childhood have been markedly better if she'd had a Sherrie and Bruce? Probably. Rob grew up with his entire immediate family within a 20-minute drive, and to Amy the experience always sounded so cozy. Safe, really. That's what she wanted for Noah. A safe, cozy, supported childhood. It wasn't that she didn't want him to take risks. It was that she wanted him to feel as if he had a family network of support beneath him, like a safety net, so that he *could* take those risks. Already she could feel them weaving that net with Rob's parents, and she knew it would grow even sturdier as the years went on.

But of course the more they interwove their lives with her in-laws, the more Sherrie was going to catch wind of any minor issue that cropped up. Her relationship with Sherrie to this point had been great, but they'd also maintained that relationship from afar. Now, they would be in each other's business all the time. The Durants were the latest bit of drama in their lives, but who knew what would be next? What if they ran into money trouble and Amy couldn't land steady work? What if they got into a fight with their neighbors? What if there was an issue at Noah's school? Amy realized she was going to have to put up boundaries, but ones that wouldn't offend Sherrie and Bruce or put their relationship with Noah at risk.

By the time they got home, it was after 8:00 (they always stayed at Rob's parents' later than they should), so Amy quickly changed purses and left Rob to put Noah to bed.

"I won't be late," she said as she gave Rob a kiss.

"Stay out as late as you want. You deserve it."

"Part of me wishes *we* were going out."

"Two days," he said. "You and Grace will have fun tonight. It'll be nice to talk without the kids around for once."

"Hey!" Noah protested. Once again, they'd forgotten he was listening.

"Sometimes mommy needs time just with *her* friends," Rob said. "It's nothing against you and Ethan. She still loves you very much."

"Of course I do!" Amy squeezed Noah and kissed him on the head. "I'll see you at breakfast, okay?"

She hurried out the door, and a sense of liberation washed over her as she turned on the engine. She knew it was a little silly. She was just going for a quick drink. But the idea of not having to do bath or story time, or answer the seemingly endless number of questions Noah asks to get out of having to go to sleep . . . all she could hear was George Michael's "Freedom" ringing in her ears. She was so glad Grace had suggested this. It was exactly what Amy needed.

She found a parking spot in a lot across from the brew pub Grace had suggested and hurried across the road. The brew pub sat next to an old movie theater, one of those old-timey cinemas with neon lighted signs, promoting arthouse and indie flicks. Amy noticed they were promoting the movie Sherrie and Bruce had just seen. *Maybe next weekend*, Amy thought to herself.

A friendly, college-age woman greeted Amy as she came in the door.

"I'm meeting someone," Amy said as she searched the room. Her eyes landed on Grace, who sat at a table along an exposed brick wall. "There she is."

Amy made her way across the room, a hip, industrial space with concrete floors, exposed beams, and warm wood tables surrounded by metal chairs. Grace stood as Amy approached the table.

"You made it!" She reached in for a hug, which caught Amy a little by surprise. They'd spent a lot of time together, but it was always with the kids. Maybe tonight was the first step in developing their own friendship, separate from the boys.

"This place looks great," Amy said as she slid into her chair. She slung her purse over the back.

"I know, right? Look at you, Jenkintown. Almost hip."

Amy laughed. Rob had always described Jenkintown as an old-fashioned town that was always on the edge of being cool, but somehow never managed to spill over that edge. From what Amy had seen, the spill was finally happening. A bunch of new restaurants had opened in the area, and the town seemed to be having a bit of a renaissance. If this brew pub was any indication, things were heading in the right direction.

"So have you been here before?" Amy asked. "What's good?"

"I haven't been, but Julian has. He says the tacos and empanadas are a must. He also recommended the IPA, but I'm more of a stout girl myself."

*Of course she is*, Amy thought. Grace seemed to embody the laid-back, stylish, guy's girl everyone wanted to hang with in college, the kind of woman who could drink a beer and watch the football game while looking sexy and feminine and totally desirable. Amy had never been that woman, even in college, when she'd managed to turn her social life around. Even then, she was more of a cocktail and wine girl.

"They have cocktails, too, by the way," Grace said, as if reading Amy's mind. Amy wondered if she'd inadvertently made a face at the mention of IPAs and stouts.

"Hmmm, so many choices . . ." Amy said as she scanned the menu, even though she already knew she would order the cucumber gin cocktail.

The waiter came and took their order, and before they knew it the drinks and food started arriving. The conversation flowed easily, mostly relating to the kids but occasionally drifting to topics like must-try Philly restaurants and reality TV. Amy found Grace refreshingly approachable. Despite what she knew about the Durants' financial situation—so many unanswered questions, so many unsavory possibilities—Amy couldn't help but feel drawn to Grace. She was so easy to talk to. Amy was no longer the socially awkward girl she'd been in high school, but in new situations where she didn't know anyone, she could occasionally still be a little shy. But not with Grace. She had a calming effect.

"You guys have any trips planned this summer?" Grace asked as she took a sip of her second beer. Amy was still working on her cocktail.

"The move was pretty much it for trips this summer. We were talking about visiting my family in Rhode Island, but the timing isn't great."

"You're from Rhode Island?"

Amy nodded. "Woonsocket."

Like almost everyone Amy had met outside of Rhode Island, Grace looked mystified. "Is that near Newport?"

"Not even close. Newport is all the way across state."

"Oh, I didn't realize Rhode Island was that big."

"It isn't. When I say 'all the way across state,' I mean like an hour drive."

Grace laughed. "So basically from here to West Chester."

Amy didn't know the area well, but she knew West Chester was another Philadelphia suburb west of the city. "Yeah, all my Rhody friends talk about Newport like it's so far away. I guess culturally it is, at least from the part where I grew up."

"Is your whole family still there?"

"Yep. Well, what's left of them. My dad died when I was six, but my mom has lived there her whole life. My brother, too."

"I'm sorry about your dad."

Amy shrugged. "It's been almost thirty years. To be honest, I barely remember him. It was a freak accident—he was swimming super early one morning in Wallum Lake while we were on vacation, and he had a heart attack in the water and drowned."

Grace's jaw dropped. "Amy, I'm so sorry. That's . . . horrible."

"It was. Looking back on it, I have no idea how my mom carried on. I was six, my brother, Tim, was four. I mean, can you imagine?"

Grace shook her head. "Your mother must be an amazing person."

"She is I guess. I never really thought of her that way. She wasn't exactly a sentimental person, but then again, after something like that, with two kids to support, who'd have time for tears and hand-wringing?"

"I'd never make it. Doing all of this alone? I couldn't."

"Of course you could. You'd do it for Ethan."

"True." She took a deep breath and sighed. Amy felt guilty for having steered the conversation in such a negative direction.

"Anyway," Amy said, "regardless of what happened to my dad, my mom can be a little, shall we say, difficult, so aside from lacking the funds at the moment, visiting her always comes with headaches that none of us are in the mood for at the moment."

"I hear you. What about your brother? Are you guys close?"

"Not exactly. We used to be but . . ." Amy hesitated, but she'd nearly finished her cocktail, which was proving to be much stronger than she'd thought, and she felt her inhibitions melt away. "He's had some problems over the past few years," she said. "It's made staying close difficult."

"Oh. That's a shame."

"It is. It's both of our faults, but mostly his." Amy finished the last sip and laid the drink on the table. "He got into drugs. Pills first. Then heroin. He's been in and out of rehab for years."

"Wow. That's . . . oooh."

Amy knew Grace probably didn't know what to say, and she didn't blame her. Drugs was one of those dark, shameful topics that most people didn't want to talk about, and when the topics of addiction and rehab came up in conversation, the responses were usually lots of wide eyes, shaking heads, and strange filler words and interjections like, "Mmm," "Ohhh," "Yikes," and "Ugh."

"It's been tough. Noah barely knows him. He met Uncle Timmy once when he was one, but he doesn't remember it."

"Is he in rehab now? Or in recovery?"

"A little of both? Last I talked to my mom he'd tried a new program that was longer and more intensive, with a price tag to match. Getting off heroin doesn't come cheap."

"Yeah," Grace said, in a way that suggested she knew exactly what Amy was talking about. She finished her beer and flagged the waiter for another.

"Another cocktail for you?" the waiter asked.

Amy vacillated. "Eh, what the hell. You only live once, right?"

"That's the spirit," he said. "Back in a minute."

Amy almost immediately regretted ordering another drink—she was going to feel terrible tomorrow, she already knew it—but she was enjoying Grace's company and didn't want to bring the night to a premature close.

"Sorry," she said, once the waiter returned with their drinks. "I've turned this conversation into a real downer. First my dad, then my brother. Moving on!"

"No, no, I totally get it—trust me." She took a sip of beer. Her cheeks had turned a little pink. "In the interest of full disclosure, since we're sharing family secrets, there's something I should probably tell you."

Amy felt her stomach gurgle. She'd been waiting for Grace to spill the beans, but now that Grace seemed to be on the cusp of doing so, Amy wasn't sure she was ready to hear the truth.

"You don't have to—"

"Julian had a problem with drugs, too," Grace blurted out before Amy could stop her.

"Oh," said Amy. "I didn't—I had no idea."

That was actually true. Of all the things that occurred to Amy, drugs—the issue with which she had the most personal experience—hadn't entered her mind. Why not? Was it because the Durants seemed so together? Because they had a kid Noah's age? Because they were inarguably much more successful that her brother?

"He's clean now," Grace said. She gripped her beer tightly. "But it got bad for a while. He spent all of our savings on pills. Oxy mostly. That's why we needed to sell the house so fast. We needed the capital."

"So the new construction . . ."

"There is no new construction. We never had anything else lined up. The plan was to sell the house and move in with my parents while Julian put the pieces back together and got a fresh start."

"So your parents know?"

"Sort of. They don't know it was drugs. They think it was his business. He runs a nonprofit that promotes access to healthy food in poor urban communities. Nonprofits always have budget troubles, so we didn't go into details."

"Ah. Got it."

"I know we probably should have told them the truth," she said, her guilt gushing onto the table, "but my parents can be pretty judg-mental, especially about things like drugs. We figured it was better to keep it simple."

"And Ethan—"

"Oh God, Ethan has no idea. And for obvious reasons, we want to keep it that way."

"Of course."

Grace had cut Amy off before she could actually ask her ques-tion. She assumed Ethan didn't know, and regardless, she certainly wouldn't bring the matter up in front of him or Noah. What she'd really wanted to ask was about Ethan's trust fund, but she realized bringing that up would reveal that she'd opened their mail by acci-dent, which would open a can of worms she didn't want to deal with. Besides, given what Grace just told her, the liquidation of Ethan's trust was probably something both Julian and Grace knew about. If they had to sell the house, who knows what other finan-cial sacrifices they had to make?

"It's been really hard on both of us," Grace said. "But he's clean now, and he's throwing everything into getting his nonprofit back on track. He'd really neglected the business at the height of his problem."

"That's great. It's really encouraging to hear that he's getting his life back on track."

"Thanks. You know, I have to say, I feel so much better after talking to you about it. It's like this horrible, shameful secret no one knows about except me and Julian, and it's been eating me up inside."

"It isn't shameful," Amy said. "Addiction is a disease."

"I know. But the way most people talk about it . . . Anyway, it was good to get it off my chest, especially with someone who has personal experience in the area." She raised her glass. "How about a toast? To clean slates and new beginnings."

"I'll drink to that."

Amy clinked her glass against Grace's and bit her tongue to keep from saying that, in her personal experience, when it came to addiction, a new beginning didn't always mean the end.

# Chapter 7

Amy was exceedingly excited for date night. She and Rob hadn't been on a date since they'd moved, and even before that, it had been quite a while. They'd been to a few "going away" parties before they moved, but at those events they hadn't been able to talk in any sort of meaningful way. That was part of the reason they hadn't been to the movies in a long time either: If they were lucky enough to score a babysitter, Amy wanted to be able to have a conversation with her husband, not sit next to him in the dark for three hours.

"You okay out there?" Amy poked her head out of the bathroom as she tousled her wet hair with a towel. Noah was lying on her bed watching PBS.

"Uh-huh," he said, his eyes fixed on the screen.

"Good. I'll just be in here drying my hair. Let me know if you need anything."

Amy tried to spray and blow-dry her fine hair into some sort of style—if not a sexy one, then at least one that maintained some semblance of togetherness. She hadn't exactly let herself go lately, but a few days ago she had realized, with some horror, that she had worn her hair in a ponytail for the last thirty-four days. She was basically a few weeks away from showing up places in an oversize sweatshirt with no bra underneath. She needed to stem the tide.

She finished her hair and put on what felt like a ton of makeup, given her current barebones regimen of mascara, concealer, and blush. When she opened the bathroom door to grab her dress from the closet, Noah turned and raised his eyebrows.

"*Mommy*," he said. "You look *beautiful*."

"Thank you, sweetheart."

He furrowed his brow. "But . . . where is your pony?"

"My what?"

He pointed to his head. "Your pony. For your hair."

"My ponytail?"

"Yeah."

"That's just for when I'm busy. When I dress up, I like to wear it like this."

"Oh." He scrutinized her head a bit more. "But I like your pony. You should wear it like that."

"Not tonight. Tonight, I'm going for a different look."

Noah sighed and had turned back to the TV when the doorbell rang. Amy glanced at the clock.

"Shoot. That's probably Bubbe and Zayde."

"I can get it!"

Noah bolted from the bed before Amy could stop him and hurried down the stairs. Amy quickly grabbed a navy sundress from her closet and threw it over her head as she heard the door open.

"Mommy?"

"Tell Bubbe and Zayde I'll be down in two seconds!" Amy called down the stairs.

"It isn't Bubbe and Zayde. It's Ethan's daddy."

Amy froze halfway through putting on an earring. Julian? What was he doing here?

"Oh," she said. "Sorry—coming right down."

She slipped on her shoes and hustled down the stairs as she popped on the other earring. Julian stood on their front stoop—his old front stoop—looking sharp in a pair of tailored white shorts and a dark chambray shirt with the sleeves rolled up.

"Sorry to barge in on you," he said as Amy opened the door wider.

"It's fine, it's fine," she said, even though she wasn't entirely sure how she felt about this surprise visit. She tried not to look at him differently now, after what Grace had told her, but she couldn't help herself. What was worse, she knew better. Her brother hadn't always been a screwup. Before the pills and heroin, he'd been a funny, personable guy with a real talent for soccer. At his core, that was still who Tim was. But that was the problem with drugs. Once you'd gotten into trouble with them, people didn't think about you as you'd been before. Now you were a miscreant, a delinquent, a loser. Even when you tried to get clean—even when you *were* clean—your every move was tinged with a veneer of transgression. Maybe that's part of what made fleeing addiction so hard. If everyone sees you as a sinner already, at some point it must just be easier to give in to that assumption.

"What can I do for you?" Amy asked.

"I was in the area and just wondered if any more of our mail had arrived."

"I don't think so. Actually, I take that back. There was something small, like a reminder from your dentist. Hang on, let me grab it." Amy turned toward the kitchen, then spun back around. Should she invite him in? It seemed like the friendly thing to do. "You want to come in for a second? It's awfully hot out."

"Sure, thanks."

He came in and looked around the foyer and halls as they walked toward the kitchen. "Looks like you guys are pretty settled in."

"Looks can be deceiving," Amy joked.

"Really? From what I can see, you've done a great job. I like what you've done with the place."

"Thanks." Amy knew the house wasn't nearly as together and polished as it had been under their ownership, but she appreciated the compliment.

She rifled through the stack of mail on the counter until she found the postcard from Dr. Edward Chaswick, DDS.

"Here you go. A friendly dental reminder."

She'd meant to sound congenial, but now she wondered if that was a mistake. Her words implied she was looking at who was sending them mail, which she was, but she didn't want Julian knowing that. Admittedly, she would have to be blind to miss the bold red lettering on some of their mail, but pretending she did not see or care to see anything about their correspondence was part of the ruse.

"Thanks," Julian said. He waved the postcard in the air. "Better get those teeth cleaned."

"Mommy, I have to go potty," Noah called from the foyer.

"Okay," Amy said. She rolled her eyes as she heard the powder room door slam. "I don't know why he needs to make an announcement every time he uses the toilet."

"Ethan is the same way. He wastes at least ten precious seconds telling us that he has to go before he actually goes."

"Kids." She shook her head and escorted him to the front door. When she opened it, Sherrie and Bruce were on the other side.

"Sherrie! Hi!" Amy could tell that her face was flushed. Despite the fact that she was expecting them, they'd caught her by surprise.

"Hi," Sherrie said, a foil-covered platter in her hands. Her eyes landed on Julian.

"I'm Julian," he said, extending his hand. "I was just picking up some mail. I used to live here."

"Ah," Sherrie said. She pretended to sound satisfied with that answer, even if Amy knew she wasn't. Sherrie already thought it was odd that Amy and Grace hung out with the kids. She probably had a dozen questions as to why Julian was visiting his old house.

"They forgot to forward their mail, so we've been collecting it for them," Amy said. "I usually give it to Grace at our playdates, but I guess Julian was in the area so he stopped by."

Amy realized continuing to explain probably only made Sherrie more curious, but she couldn't help herself.

"You can start forwarding at any time, you know," Sherrie said. "I think you can even do it online now."

"You can," Julian said. "But by now I've changed our address with most of the important places anyway, so it's not really worth it. Plus we're living with my in-laws for the time being, so it's not our permanent address anyway."

"Mmm." Sherrie didn't sound as if she bought his story. Amy wasn't sure she did either.

"Anyway, he was just leaving," Amy said.

"Actually—sorry—would you mind if I used your bathroom? I'm meeting Grace and Ethan at some sort of picnic, and I'm not sure what the bathroom situation will be there."

"Of course. Only . . . Noah?"

"I'M POOPING!" Noah called back.

Amy took a deep breath. "That's what I thought. You'll have to use the one upstairs, if that's okay. It's at the top of the stairs—"

"To the right. Yeah, I remember."

Amy blushed. "Obviously. Sorry."

"I'll only be a second."

He hurried upstairs, and Amy let Sherrie and Bruce into the house. "Sorry about all of the chaos. He really caught us by surprise."

"So I see."

Amy felt her ears. Both earrings were in. Shoes were on. Dress was zipped. The only thing she needed was her purse, which was in the laundry room.

"Dinner is on its way," she said. "I ordered a pizza and some salad. And for dessert . . . well, I'm guessing you've got that covered." She nodded at the platter Sherrie had placed on the counter.

"Triple-chocolate brownies," she said.

"Oh, boy. Noah will go crazy. Better leave some for Rob, too." She craned her neck to see if Julian was in the foyer, but then she heard footsteps above her. He was still upstairs.

"As soon as I let Julian out, I'm going to run. But after dinner, Noah can play for a while, and then we usually start the bedtime routine around seven-thirty or eight. He's been begging to use our shower, so if you feel like giving him a treat, you can let him do that. Up to you. Oh, and we have a bunch of movies recorded on our DVR if you want to watch any of them, or you can order something on demand."

"Don't worry, we've got it covered," Sherrie said.

"I'M WIPING!" Noah shouted.

"Does he need help?" Sherrie asked tentatively.

"He's pretty much got it down," Amy said. She heard footsteps on the stairs. "That sounds like Julian. I'll let him out."

She hurried down the hall, reminding Noah to wash his hands as she passed the powder room. She and Julian reached the front door at the same time.

"Thanks for that," Julian said. "I really appreciate it."

"Not a problem. Have fun at your picnic. Tell Grace and Ethan I say hi."

"Will do."

He slipped out the front door and Amy watched him walk to his car. Something about their entire encounter had left a strange taste in her mouth, but at the moment, she couldn't pinpoint exactly what it was.

Traffic on Broad Street was terrible, so Amy was late to dinner. They couldn't get a reservation at the place Sherrie and Bruce had recommended, but they had managed to snag a table at Osteria, a popular Italian restaurant run by one of Philadelphia's preeminent chefs. The drive there had involved navigating through some of Philadelphia's less savory neighborhoods, but thankfully the restaurant had valet, so she didn't have to stress about finding a parking spot in an area of town she didn't know well.

She hurried through the front door into the restaurant, which bustled with activity—the clanking of pans, the chitter chatter of patrons bouncing off the rustically appointed interior. The hostess immediately led Amy to the small, wooden table where Rob was sitting, already scanning the menu.

"Sorry I'm late," Amy said as she leaned in for a kiss. She slung her purse over the back of her chair. "Broad Street is . . ."

"Something special?"

"That's one way to put it. I don't understand the timing of the traffic lights. It's as if they are designed to make the drive as long as humanly possible."

"I know. It's the worst."

The waiter arrived and went over the specials, then took their drink order and left them to peruse the menu. One dish looked better than the next: wood-grilled octopus, bucatini with lobster and roe butter, a pizza with baked egg and cotechino sausage. Amy didn't know where to begin. She wanted to order all of it.

"I can't believe we're finally out," she said as she studied the menu intently.

"Feels good," Rob said. "I've missed you."

Amy looked up. "I've missed you, too. It's weird, right? Like, we're living together. Neither of us has gone anywhere. And yet I feel as if we've been apart for months."

"It's the move. Everything has been so crazy. When are we supposed to talk? Over dinner, with Noah interrupting us every five seconds?"

"I know. A bunch of my friends eat with their husbands after the kids are in bed, but by that point, I'm basically useless. You'd be dining with a vegetable."

"A tasty one, though."

They grinned at each other, but their moment was interrupted by the waiter, who came with their drinks. They ordered some appetizers, a pasta, and a pizza to share and clinked glasses when the waiter disappeared.

"To a happy life in our new house," Rob said.

"And many more date nights."

"I'll drink to that. Cheers."

Amy took a sip of Prosecco and rested the glass on the table. "So Julian stopped by," she said.

"Julian? Why?"

"To pick up their mail. He said he was in the neighborhood."

"Where is his office?"

"I'm not sure. I've never asked. I don't think he was coming from work. Or maybe he was. I don't know. It was kind of awkward, to be honest. Your parents arrived just as he was getting ready to leave. I'm sure your mom has a million questions."

"She always does."

"Your parents' arrival wasn't the only thing that made it awkward. We've already established that the mail situation is weird in and of itself, but for him to stop by . . . I just saw Grace two days ago. Is he expecting something important that he doesn't want her to see?"

"You mean like a trust fund statement?"

Amy flushed. Of course that's what he was looking for. What would he do when it never arrived? Would he think they'd thrown it out by accident, or figure out that they'd opened it?

"All I had for him was a reminder from his dentist. I made the whole situation even more uncomfortable by commenting on what it was—'A friendly dental reminder!'" Amy shook her head. "If you'd been there, you would have been like, 'Stop talking right now.'"

Rob laughed. "Where was Noah while all of this was happening?"

"Pooping."

Rob nearly spat out his red wine. "Of course."

"I know. That was another weird moment, now that I think of it. Julian asked to use our bathroom before he left, but Noah was using the powder room, so he had to use the upstairs bathroom. I started directing him how to find it, but of course he knew how to find it because it used to be his house." Amy took a sip of her drink and shook her head. "Painful."

The waiter returned with a platter of roasted and grilled vegetables and a plate of grilled octopus. Amy and Rob dove in.

"So," Rob said as he cut into a roasted beet. "What are we going to do about your mom?"

She and Rob had discussed the matter at length the previous Thursday evening, after her mom had called, but they hadn't come to a resolution. Initially, Rob said they didn't have $2,000 to spare right now, so Amy had proposed meeting her mom halfway at $1,000. But Rob hadn't seemed entirely comfortable with that idea either, and by the time they'd talked about it for thirty minutes, Amy was so exhausted she didn't have the energy to discuss it any further and had, once again, kicked the can to a later date. To her relief, her mom hadn't followed up about it yet, but she knew she owed her mother an answer ASAP.

"I don't know," Amy said. "What *are* we going to do?"

Rob took a deep breath. "I've crunched some numbers, and we could do $1,000. I love you more than anything, and your family is part of you, so I'd like to help them. But I feel like your mom needs to understand that giving her this money means some sacrifices on our end. If we do this, we can't afford to send Noah five days a week to pre-K, for example. He's a smart kid. He'll be fine. But sometimes I feel like she thinks we're rolling it in, when really we are living on a budget like everyone else."

"She knows that."

"Does she? Because from what you said, she isn't so much asking if we'll help as she is expecting that we will."

"I've made it perfectly clear that we are not an ATM."

"Good. Thank you."

"And trust me, I am as uneasy as you are. We've been down this road so many times with Tim. I don't want to flush our money down the toilet. But my mom says this time is different."

"Isn't that what people always say? If Tim thought it were the same as all of the other times, why would he even bother?"

Amy wished she had a good answer, but she didn't. What terrified her most, what made it hard for her to sleep sometimes, was the thought that what would make this time different was that when he fell off the wagon, he'd end up dead instead of just using again. Because isn't that where so many of these stories ended? The accounts she'd read in the paper and in magazines made heroin seem like a one-way road to death. Tim had taken detours time and again, but somehow he always ended up back on the highway. Amy hoped he'd stay clean this time, but she knew there was always a chance he wouldn't. She had to keep hoping, though. She had to help Tim try.

"I'll call my mom tomorrow," she said. "I'm sure she'll be very grateful."

*Either that*, Amy thought, *or she will give me hell for not doing more.*

When they got home, Sherrie and Bruce were sitting in front of the TV, watching a home improvement show on HGTV. Bruce didn't actually seem to be watching. He was reading an issue of *Sports Illustrated* and occasionally peering above the rim of his reading glasses when Sherrie made a comment about the tile or curtain selection.

"We're back," Rob announced.

Bruce put down his magazine, and Sherrie muted the television.

"Good dinner?" she asked.

"Delicious," Rob and Amy said in unison.

"Did you get the polenta budino for dessert?"

"We shared it," Rob said.

"And? Was it the best thing you've ever eaten in your life?"

Amy wasn't sure she'd go that far, but it was definitely in the top ten desserts she'd ever had. It was a polenta pudding with hazelnut mousse on top, with caramelized hazelnuts sprinkled over the top. It hit all the right notes: creamy, crunchy, sweet, and nutty.

"Might have been," Rob said. "How was Noah?"

"An angel. He ate all of his dinner and dessert, and then we played Sums in Space. I didn't realize he could add and subtract so quickly on his own."

"I told you he's into numbers," Rob said.

"Well, yeah, but I didn't realize . . . Have you had him tested?"

"We will," Amy said. "When he starts kindergarten."

"That's more than a year away."

"I just don't see what purpose it serves right now," Rob said. "We know he's smart. It's not like we're going to start him in kindergarten early."

"You could . . ."

"Mom. Enough."

"Okay, okay . . ." She raised her hands defensively. Amy knew Rob had spoken to his parents many times about Noah's giftedness and had argued with them about whether to push him more, faster, harder.

"So I don't know if Amy mentioned," Sherrie said as she and Bruce collected their things, "but the former owner stopped by earlier."

"Julian. Yeah, she mentioned. He came by to pick up some mail."

"Kind of strange that he hasn't changed his address, isn't it?"

Rob and Amy exchanged a look. "It is," Rob said. "But I'm sure he has his reasons."

"Does he always stop by like that?"

"That was the first time," Amy said. "I usually give it to his wife, Grace, when the boys get together."

"Hmmm." Sherrie stroked her chin, as if she found all of it *quite* perplexing.

Rob's and Amy's eyes met again, and she could tell Rob was trying not to laugh. He found his mother's nosiness both exasperating and hilarious.

"Let me make sure the light by the driveway is on for you," Rob said as he ushered them down the hall.

"I left you some brownies," Sherrie said. "They're on the counter, next to the toaster."

"I can't wait to try them," Amy said, even though at the moment she was so stuffed from dinner that she actually couldn't think about eating without feeling a little sick. "I'm sure Noah was in heaven."

"He went crazy for them."

"The boy is a fiend for chocolate."

"And these were *triple* chocolate."

Rob leaned in and kissed Sherrie on the cheek. "Bye, Mom. Thanks again for sitting."

"Our pleasure. We had fun, didn't we, Bruce?"

"Always a laugh with that little guy."

"You're welcome to do it again anytime," Rob said.

"We'll talk." She motioned toward Bruce as she opened the door. "Come on, honey. Where are the keys?"

They waved goodbye, and Rob locked the door behind them. He looked at Amy and smiled. "No such thing as a free lunch, huh?"

"Listen, when it comes to sitters, that's as close to free as it's gonna get."

"Never mind her unquenchable thirst for gossip."

"I think she just likes the idea of something juicy."

"Juicy, eh?" He ran his fingers down her arms. "I'll give you juicy."

He scooped her up and carried her up the stairs and tossed her on the bed, like they were newlyweds or teenagers. She couldn't help giggling a little. They hadn't had impromptu sex in . . . well, she couldn't even remember, it had been that long. For years, sex had been timed and scheduled—both when they were trying to get pregnant with Noah and when they tried again for a second. They gave up on the idea of a sibling for Noah a few months ago (it had been nearly two years, and Amy was sick of trying), but it was hard to get out of the habit and mind-set that sex was a planned task with the specific desired outcome of pregnancy. Now that they weren't trying for a baby anymore, they could just enjoy each other. Amy hoped she could remember how.

The sex was fun and at times surprising, and afterward Amy turned to Rob and said, "We need to do that more often."

"You won't hear an argument from me."

"I just . . . Noah really uses up a lot of my bandwidth. And then we had the move, with all the packing and unpacking, and stress about work. By the end of the day, I'm zonked. I just want to stare at a wall, or sleep."

"I get it. Trust me. I just don't want us to eventually become, like, roommates."

Amy raised an eyebrow. "What we just did . . . is that what you did with your roommates? Because if so, I clearly got a raw deal in college."

He elbowed her in the side. "You know what I mean."

"Of course I do. I'll be better. Or at least I'll try."

"Me too."

He kissed her on the head and slipped out of bed toward the bathroom. Amy stretched out on the bed, too lazy and tired to go anywhere. She wished she were the type of person who could fall asleep right then and there, without washing her face or brushing her teeth, but she was far too uptight for that, even after all these years. So after a few minutes of enjoying the silkiness of the sheets against her bare skin, she got up and threw on a T-shirt. She was just about to follow Rob into the bathroom, when she heard whimpering coming from Noah's room.

She tiptoed toward his door, and just as she put her hand on the knob she heard him cry, "Mommy!"

Amy opened the door and crept toward his bed. "What is it, sweetie? Did you have a bad dream?"

"My head hurts," he said.

"Your head?" She reached down and rested her hand on his forehead. He felt a little warm. "Let me get the thermometer."

Amy scampered across the hall to his bathroom and grabbed the thermometer. *Please don't let him be sick*, she thought. He'd been fine when she left, and Sherrie said he'd been an angel all night. But she'd learned with kids, sickness could come out of nowhere and disappear nearly as fast.

She swiped the thermometer across his forehead: 99.9. A fever, but barely.

"You're okay, sweetie," she said. "Just a very low fever."

"I need medicine," he whined.

"I'll get you some Tylenol. One second."

She headed for her own bathroom, where she was storing all medications on the top shelf of their linen closet. At this point she trusted Noah not to get into anything he shouldn't—and all of the medicine bottles had childproof tops anyway—but out of an abundance of caution, she still stored all of the medicine out of sight and out of reach.

When she entered the bathroom, Rob had just finished brushing his teeth. "Did I hear Noah?" he asked.

"He has a fever," Amy said. Rob groaned. "I know—but it's very low. Only 99.9. I'll give him some Tylenol, and hopefully he'll be better by morning."

"Will you have to keep him home from camp?"

Amy hadn't even thought of that. She wasn't used to weeknight date nights and forgot it was Tuesday. "Depends how he is in the morning. We'll see. Hopefully not."

She opened the door to the linen closet and reached for one of the baskets on the top shelf. Amy had divided the drugs between two white plastic baskets (stomach/GI drugs in one basket, Tylenol and other pain-relief drugs in the other), neatly arranging all of the bottles and pill packets in organized rows. But as she laid the basket on the counter, she noticed everything was all jumbled up. Bottles were tipped on their side, Noah's stuff was scattered with theirs, and her fastidious system had been scuppered.

"Seriously?" Amy groaned. "Did you not notice I'd gone through a lot of trouble organizing this?"

"What are you talking about?"

"The medicine. I had it perfectly arranged in rows, and now it's a mess."

He looked over her shoulder. "I haven't touched any of that. Maybe everything toppled over when you took the basket off the shelf."

"Did you hear anything toppling?"

"No, but that doesn't mean it didn't happen."

"Rob . . ."

"Honest to God—I didn't even know that's where you were keeping the meds."

"Then who messed everything up? Noah?"

Rob rolled his eyes. "You're sure you didn't knock it over some time when you were getting something else out of the closet."

"Definitely not."

"Then I don't know what to tell you. Maybe you aren't as neat as you think." She whacked him with a hand towel. "Ouch."

"Oh, please, that didn't hurt."

"It did a little. And you are very neat. But I don't know what to say. Maybe my parents needed something when they were here. Want me to text them?"

"No, that's okay. You're right—that's probably it. Your dad has been complaining about his knees a lot lately. He probably took some Aleve."

"See? Mystery solved. No one else has been in our bathroom anyway."

But as Amy retrieved the children's Tylenol, she realized that wasn't entirely true. Someone else could have been in their bathroom recently: Julian.

# Chapter 8

*Had Julian been sifting through their medicine basket?*

Amy couldn't shake the thought. She tried to convince herself it was Bruce or Sherrie. Bruce *had* complained a lot recently about his knee. And she distinctly remembered Julian reminding her that he knew where the upstairs *hall* bathroom was. There was no reason for him to use the master bathroom. Unless he was looking for painkillers.

*Was he looking for painkillers?*

He wouldn't have found any. Rob and Amy were very boring in that respect. They only had the basics: Tylenol, Advil, Aleve. The few times they'd been prescribed something stronger like Percocet (Amy after her C-section, Rob after an ankle operation), they'd thrown the pills out after a few days. Narcotic drugs nauseated both of them something terrible, and neither of them saw the appeal. After living through her brother's downward spiral, Amy saw their aversion as something of a blessing. She also felt a little guilty. If Tim had felt as awful as she and Rob did on prescription painkillers, his life would have gone a lot differently.

But Julian wasn't her brother. He was the smart, successful founder of a respectable nonprofit, and he had an intelligent and attractive wife and an adorable, fun-loving son. Maybe Tim could have been that person or that would possibly still be that person someday, but he wasn't that person now, and when he'd started down this path at eighteen, he was naïve enough to think he didn't have anything to lose. Julian had everything to lose—his family, his job, his reputation. Grace said he was clean now, that he was throwing all of his energy back into his nonprofit. If that were the case it wouldn't make sense for him to be snooping through their closets and drawers. Unless—

*No.* Amy told herself to stop letting her imagination get the best of her. She had no proof that Julian had done anything wrong, and he was the father of her kid's best friend. She owed him the benefit of the doubt.

Whatever meager amount of sleep she was able to get was cut even shorter when early the next morning, she heard Noah whimpering in his room again. She stumbled in, only half awake, and took his temperature: 100.1. He definitely wouldn't be going to camp today.

She gave him a little more Tylenol and encouraged him to go back to sleep, in the hopes that she could carve out another hour of sleep for herself, but Noah wasn't having it.

"I want to watch *Ready Jet Go!* downstairs," he said.

"You need to rest, sweetie."

"I can rest in front of the TV."

"It's only six o'clock. Maybe close your eyes for a little bit longer, and then you watch a show. Or a movie—whatever you want."

"What movies do we have?"

"*Finding Nemo, Finding Dory, Toy Story*—the usual. And I think Daddy might have recorded *Despicable Me* the other day."

Noah's sleepy eyes widened. She never should have mentioned *Despicable Me.* Now he definitely wouldn't go back to sleep.

"I want to watch *Aspicable Me,*" he said, crawling out of bed.

"How about in a few—"

"Mommyyyyyyy," he whined.

Amy heaved a sigh. "Fine. Let's go."

She and Noah trudged down the stairs, and she queued up *Despicable Me.* Noah curled up on the couch with his blanket, a blue-and-white crocheted one that her mother had made for him. Amy could hear Rob thumping around above her, getting ready for work. He usually made the coffee, but since she was up and in desperate need of caffeine, she started the pot going and poured Noah a glass of apple juice.

"You should drink something," she said, holding out the cup as she nudged him to sit up. He shook his head. "Noah, you have to—it's important when you're sick."

He propped himself up a little and took an infinitesimal sip. "It's cold," he said as he handed the cup back to Amy.

"Juice usually is."

"It's too cold."

Amy tried not to lose her patience, but she was exhausted. "Want me to warm it up in the microwave?"

"Yeah. I mean no. I'm not thirsty."

"You have to drink."

"I don't want to."

Amy closed her eyes and took a long, deep breath. For all of Noah's intellectual strengths, he was still four, and negotiating with him was as enjoyable as stabbing herself repeatedly in the leg.

"Let me warm it up for you," she said, in as calm a voice as she could muster, which at the moment was somewhere between annoyance and exasperation.

She stuck the cup in the microwave just as Rob came downstairs.

"Hey, the gang's all here!" he said. Amy usually appreciated Rob's optimism and cheerfulness in the morning, but today she was jealous that he could muster any enthusiasm at all.

Rob came over and gave Amy a kiss on the head. "How are you?"

"Tired."

He peered from the kitchen into the family room. "Take a nap while he naps."

"He isn't napping. He's watching *Despicable Me*."

"He'll fall asleep at some point."

"By which time I will need to do some work. I'm almost finished with that grant proposal and planned to finish it today."

Rob shrugged. "There's always coffee."

"Helpful."

"I'm just saying. Hey, by the way, I've been meaning to ask: What are we doing about school for Noah in the fall? I looked at the calendar and realized it's almost August."

"I've been meaning to call the place Julian and Grace send Ethan, but I haven't yet. Grace says the director is very chill, so it shouldn't be a problem. I can try to call today."

"Keeping that connection with the Durants alive, huh?"

"What am I supposed to do? Noah is obsessed with Ethan. Wherever we send him, it'll be a new school in a new city. Why not make it someplace he already has a friend?"

"I'm not arguing. It's probably the best move for Noah. I just feel like . . . I don't know. We've established that they seem a little shady. Do we really want to keep our families so closely intertwined?"

Amy hadn't told Rob about Julian's history of addiction, and now she wasn't sure she wanted to. Aside from the fact that Grace had told her about Julian's problems in confidence, she worried if she disclosed Julian's history, Rob would be even less likely to want Noah and Ethan to socialize. She knew she probably wasn't giving Rob enough credit. After all, recovering from drug addiction was infinitely better than *selling* drugs or doing something shady like laundering money or credit card fraud. Rob had watched Tim struggle for the entirety of their relationship. Surely he would have sympathy for the Durants' situation.

But something in Amy's gut told her that although Rob would sympathize with the Durants, he also wouldn't want to knit their lives too tightly together. He'd been great with her brother—patient, generous, kind—but she suspected that was partly because Tim was an extension of her. Julian Durant was just some guy who owned the house they now lived in. Amy knew Rob was as happy as she was that Noah had finally found a friend—a best friend—but Rob was also very protective of his only son. He wouldn't want Noah to get sucked into another family's drama. Amy didn't want that either, but she didn't want to break Noah's heart. She also liked Grace and didn't want Rob to start dictating whom she could befriend.

"I'm not saying we have to start vacationing together," said

Amy, as she poured herself a cup of coffee. "It's preschool. They'll play together during the day, maybe have a few playdates on the weekends, and then they'll go off to kindergarten and will probably barely see each other again."

"Unless they end up at the same school."

Amy sighed. "In which case, who cares if they spend the next year together in pre-K?"

"I don't. Sorry. I didn't mean to start something."

"Well, you did. Congratulations."

Amy knew she was being bitchy, but she was so tired that she couldn't help herself. In her mind, Rob had already said Noah and Ethan couldn't be friends, and neither could she and Grace. He hadn't, of course, but that's where Amy saw the conversation heading, at least in her sleep-deprived head.

Rob came over and squeezed Amy's hand. "Hey. Can we start over, please?"

Amy squeezed back. "Yes, sorry for snapping. I'm just wiped, and now my day is pretty much shot."

"It isn't necessarily shot. You can—"

"*Mommyyyyyy. . . .*"

Rob frowned. "Okay, so it's probably shot. But I'll see if I can leave early to free up a few hours for you this afternoon."

"Really?"

"I have to talk to my boss, but I'll try."

"Thank you."

"*Mommyyyyyy, where ARE you? . . . I want my JUICE. . . .*"

Rob poured his coffee into a travel mug and kissed Amy on the cheek. "Gotta run. Good luck."

Amy watched him head out the door, thinking what she really needed was a break.

Later that afternoon, Amy got a text from Grace:

Ethan said Noah wasn't at camp today. Everything ok?

Amy was sitting in front of her computer, working on the grant proposal she'd hoped to finish that day. Rob had, indeed, been able to leave work early, so he was currently playing Scrabble Junior in the family room with Noah, who seemed to have improved in the last few hours.

**Noah had a slight temp this AM, so we kept him home. He'll be there tomorrow, though!**

She added the exclamation point to express certainty and enthusiasm, when really she knew there was a slight chance Noah could take a turn later that evening. But she was trying to think positive. Tomorrow would be a great day! She would be productive!

**Oh good—was worried! Ethan missed his buddy. :)**

Amy smiled. Someone thought of her son as a buddy. That made her happier than she ever could have imagined.

Noah's bubbly giggles filled the hallway, and Amy smiled. She shot Grace another quick text:

**Btw, I'm planning to call Beth Israel today. Totally dropped the ball on that. You think they still have openings?**

Moments later, Amy's phone rang. It was Grace.

"I figured it was easier just to call you instead of texting back and forth a million times," she said as soon as Amy picked up.

"I know, what are we, millennials?"

Grace laughed. "Anyway, yes, I'm sure there are still spots at Beth Israel. If I were you, I'd give a call and arrange to go over in person to make sure you like it."

"If you guys recommend it, I'm sure it's great."

"It is—it really is—but that said, Ethan isn't Noah. Noah is clearly a genius. You may want to check it out to be sure it's up to your standards."

"We have no standards. Or I guess our standards are, 'Is this a welcoming place where he will make friends?'"

"In that case, I think you'll love it. But still. I'd check it out if I were you."

"Will do. How was your picnic last night, by the way?"

"What picnic?"

"The one last night. With you, Julian, and Ethan."

"Who said anything about a picnic?"

"Julian did."

Grace hesitated. "When?"

"Last night. When he came to pick up the mail."

There was a long pause on the other end. Amy suddenly felt as if she'd outed Julian, even though she still didn't know whether he'd done anything wrong. Or rather, she now knew he'd done *something* wrong, which was that he hadn't told his wife he'd stopped by 120 Sycamore.

"I didn't realize he'd been by," Grace said.

"He was only here for, like, three minutes," Amy said quickly. She'd meant to assuage Grace's fears, when in fact she realized it probably sounded as if she were covering up the fact that Julian had stayed longer.

"What time?"

"I don't know . . . sixish?"

Grace let out a sigh. "Ohhhh, okay. I see what happened. We'd talked about doing a picnic this Friday, but he mixed up the days. He called me from his car last night when he was on his way, and I was, like, 'No, stupid, the picnic is Friday.' I swear, it's amazing to me that the guy runs a nonprofit. He can't even keep his days straight."

Amy relaxed. Julian hadn't lied about the picnic. What a relief.

"Rob is like that, too," Amy offered. "I go over our schedule a million times, and then he'll come to me and ask, 'We're not doing anything Sunday, right?' when I've told him at least six times that I promised Noah we'd go to the zoo or something. It's infuriating."

"Tell me about it."

Amy sat back in her chair. "Sorry—I didn't mean to create any problems by mentioning he'd stopped by."

"Not at all. He told me he was planning to, but he made it sound like he'd do it later in the week. As we've established, he isn't so good with keeping to a schedule."

"There wasn't much mail. It seems to be trickling off. Whatever he's done to change your address is working."

"I wouldn't go that far," Grace said. "*Working* would imply the mail was actually coming to us at my parents' house."

"It isn't?"

"I guess technically it is, but we'll get, like, two pieces of mail one day and then nothing for four. We used to get a fat bundle every day."

"Most of it was probably junk, though, right? Because we still get plenty of that for you."

"This is what I mean about the system not working. We're burdening you with our junk, as well as the occasional extremely important document."

This was the first reference Grace had made to the threatening notices Amy had passed along week after week.

"It's not a big deal. We recycle all the junk anyway."

"I will apologize for the hundredth time anyway. I'm annoyed with Julian all over again every time I think of it."

"How's he doing?" Amy asked gently. "With . . . you know. Everything."

"Good. Really good. He has one of his meetings tonight. The people have been a really good support network for him. We told my parents he plays poker with friends on Wednesdays, just to keep the whole thing quiet, so of course now they think he has a gambling problem. Guess we didn't really think our cover story through."

Amy thought it was sad that the Durants needed a cover story, but she understood. The Sterlings were Grace's parents, not his, and they probably didn't know anything about addiction, other than what they'd seen on TV or read in books or newspapers. They'd obviously been generous with Julian, and they'd never look at him the same way again if they knew. Still, Amy thought they deserved to know a recovering addict was living under their roof. How would they react if they discovered the truth? No one liked being lied to.

"I'm glad he's doing well," Amy said. "If you ever need help, or just someone to talk to, you know where to find me. I'm not an expert, but I've been through enough with my brother to know more than your average bear."

"Thanks. That means a lot."

Part of Amy wanted to mention the disorganized medicine basket, but she didn't want to stir up trouble. She didn't know Julian was the one who'd rifled through the drugs, and anyway, even if it *had* been him, he wouldn't have found anything because there was nothing to find. Telling Grace would have no benefit other than easing Amy's own conscience, over a scenario she had entirely concocted in her own head. So instead she let the matter slide and wrapped up their conversation, hoping the issue didn't come back later to bite her in the behind.

To Amy's relief, Noah *was* better the next day. She dropped him at camp and set off for a day of editing. She was nearly finished the project she'd been working on and had set up a call with a new nonprofit for the afternoon. The group focused on college prep for kids from disadvantaged backgrounds, and it needed someone to help draft and edit materials for their big fall conference in Washington. Amy had corresponded with the director of operations a few times, and she felt fairly confident their conversation would lead to work for her. She didn't know how much it would pay (from experience, her guess was probably not much), but it was something.

Amy settled in at a cute café she'd found about fifteen minutes from home. Despite its location in the suburbs, it had a distinctly urban feel—brushed concrete floors, ceilings with exposed ducts, a juice bar behind which sat wire baskets filled with fresh pineapples, bananas, carrots, and apples. The pastry case heaved with crackly topped muffins and thickly frosted layer cakes, and Amy knew working from here more than a few times a month would be risky for her waistline. As it was, she'd already ordered a frothy caffè latte and a softball-size blackberry-apple muffin.

As she got to work on the proposal, she saw, out of the corner of her eye, someone approaching her table. She tried to focus on her work. The pastry case was enough of a distraction—she didn't want to look up every time another customer passed by. But soon it became impossible for her not to look up because the figure—whoever it was—stopped right in front of her.

Amy tore her eyes from her computer screen. A woman in multicolor neon Lycra pants and a hot pink Lycra top stood beside the table. Her honey-hued hair sat in a bun atop her head, and she smiled as Amy's eyes landed on hers.

"Hi," she said. "I don't mean to bother you. You just looked familiar, and I realized . . . are you Noah's mom?"

"I am. How did you . . . have we met?"

"No, no—I just recognized you from . . . sorry. Let me start over." She took a deep breath and extended her hand. "I'm Emily. Jake's mom. From camp? I've seen you drop off and pick up your son a few times, and I know Noah and Jake play together sometimes at camp."

"Oh, right, Jake—of course." The truth was, Amy didn't recognize Emily at all, which was odd because Emily seemed like the kind of woman you would notice. To begin with, she was wearing neon from head to toe. Amy realized the attire was specific to this particular day and time, but she strongly suspected this wasn't the only neon outfit Emily owned. Emily appeared to be in great shape—elegant but defined biceps, no mom-paunch to speak off—and so it followed that she probably exercised a lot. And if she exercised a lot, she probably wore neon because all of the activewear these days seemed to be "statement" activewear. Also, Emily was tan and pretty and tall. How could Amy have missed her?

But a bigger question in Amy's mind was, *How did she notice ME?* Amy had been so consumed with the move and settling in that most days she showed up to Noah's camp wearing an unremarkable shorts-and-T-shirt ensemble, with her hair pulled back in a ponytail and no makeup on. Had she let herself go so much that Emily noticed her because she was such a hot mess? Or had she maybe caught Amy in a bad moment one morning, when she was yelling at Noah to *just get out of the car for crying out loud?* Amy's mind raced through several unpleasant scenarios.

"Anyway, I just wanted to introduce myself," Emily went on. "Jake always talks about how Noah knows how to spell 'all the words' and wants to know why he can't spell 'all the words.' Sounds like Noah is a little smarty-pants." She smiled.

"Noah definitely doesn't know how to spell *all* the words," Amy said, though she knew to another four-year-old, it probably seemed as if he did.

"More than Jake, I'm guessing. He can barely spell his own name."

"Kids learn at different paces. They're only four."

"Oh, I'm not worried. Please. My eldest is seven and didn't even speak until he was, like, two, and now he won't shut up. They all get there eventually. I mean, hello—have you ever met an adult who never learned to talk or walk or spell?" She paused. "I take back the spelling bit. I've read the comments section of too many articles. Crap. Jake is going to be one of those people, isn't he? Damn it."

Amy smiled. She liked Emily. She managed to be both high energy and low-key, and although Amy didn't like making snap judgments about people, she felt fairly comfortable giving Emily a thumbs-up. She knew part of her quick approval was due to her desire to befriend someone other than Grace. Not that there was anything wrong with Grace. She liked Grace—a lot. But Grace was the only friend she'd made since they'd moved, and she was hoping to have more than a single friend.

"I'm sure he'll be fine," Amy said.

"Let's hope so. That's what an education is for, right?"

"Exactly."

"So do you know where you're sending Noah in the fall?"

"Funny you should ask. I was going to stop by Beth Israel today to check it out, as soon as I finish up my work and this muffin."

Amy nodded toward her plate, but when she glanced down she noticed the muffin was gone. All that remained were a few moist crumbs, which clung to the paper wrapper. She'd finished it? When? Had she been eating it the whole time they'd been talking? Amy suddenly had visions of herself shoveling hunks of muffin into her mouth like a wild animal, while Emily, horrified, pretended not to notice. Had she enjoyed it? She thought so. She remembered the first few mouthfuls, before Emily came over. Those were good. But the rest . . . She honestly couldn't remember.

"That's where Jake goes!" Emily cried, interrupting Amy's panicked and somewhat mortified interior monologue. "Oh my God, it's the best. You will love it. It's like one big family. The kids are all so happy."

"That's what I've heard," Amy said. "It sounds super."

"So exciting! Jake will be thrilled."

"Really?" Amy tried not to sound surprised, but for Noah to have not one but two friends . . . it made her wonder. Had they done something wrong in Washington? Maybe Noah's lack of friends hadn't been his fault at all. Maybe she and Rob had screwed something up, and now that they were in a new place with new people, Noah had a chance to start again. She knew she sometimes projected when it came to Noah, but maybe she'd gone too far. Maybe he was more social and well-adjusted than she'd ever been.

"Oh, yeah. Jake, Noah, and Ethan have been like the Three Musketeers all summer."

"I didn't realize. Noah isn't great when it comes to sharing details about his day."

"Well, I wouldn't exactly call Jake a detailed and reliable narrator. But I usually manage to get a few things out of him. I'm talking bare bones, but Ethan and Noah's names always come up, so I figure they spend a lot of time together." Her eyes flitted to Amy's laptop. "Anyway! I should let you go and finish your work. I just wanted to pop over to introduce myself."

"I'm so glad you did. We should get the boys together sometime."

"That would be fabulous. What's your number?" She got out her phone and plugged in Amy's number as Amy recited it to her. "Perfect. I will definitely be in touch. In the meantime, good luck with your work. And enjoy your muffin . . . or whatever's left of it!"

Amy forced a smile, wondering if the real person who would have trouble making friends in this town would be her, and not her son.

# Chapter 9

"So wait, you don't remember eating the muffin?"

"No! It's like one minute it was there, and then I looked down and—poof!—it was gone."

Rob snorted on the other end of the phone. "Could it have fallen on the floor?"

"The wrapper was still there. And a few crumbs."

"That definitely suggests consumption. Hmmm."

Amy hugged her phone between her ear and shoulder and checked the mailbox. There was one letter for Julian, but the rest was for them.

"I do remember taking a few bites while I worked on that grant proposal," Amy said, "but that's it."

"Was it good?"

"I think so? I remember really liking those first few bites, but the rest . . . I mean, what if I was just pounding chunks of muffin into my face while this woman was talking to me?"

Rob laughed. "You probably finished it before she even came over. Why do you care so much anyway?"

"Because I basically blacked out while eating and probably made an ass of myself in front of a potential new friend!"

"You didn't black out. You remember the conversation you had, right? And the work you were doing? You were probably so invested in both that you weren't thinking about something as trivial as a muffin."

"You know how I feel about muffins."

"Whatever. You didn't make an ass of yourself, if that's what you're worried about."

"How do you know? You weren't there."

"Because I know you, and you're smart and sweet and delightful, and anyone with a brain picks up on that the second they meet you."

"I feel like I've heard you give Noah this pep talk before."

Rob sighed. "I need to get back to work. You're fine. Everything is fine. Oh, but did you end up talking to that nonprofit?"

"I did. They definitely have work for me."

"That's great!"

"Sort of. The pay blows."

"How bad?"

"A thousand bucks. For what will probably be a month's work."

"That's not . . . terrible. Remember how Carly said she was only making like fifty dollars an article?"

"Just because the pay isn't 'journalism terrible' doesn't mean it isn't bad. I could probably make more than that working at Starbucks."

"Probably," Rob conceded.

Amy groaned. "A college degree, and I'm making what amounts to less than minimum wage."

"You've been a little busy."

"Doing what?"

"Uh, being a mom? Moving cities? Do I need to break this down for you?"

Amy sighed. "No. But how long is the 'mom excuse' going to fly?"

"It isn't an excuse. You made a choice to step back from work to focus on our kid. End of story."

"I know, but . . . I guess when I made that decision, I didn't realize I'd feel so professionally . . . anemic. Like, I'm so glad I've been there for Noah, and I wouldn't trade that for anything—*anything*—but at the same time, I feel as if I've lost a part of myself. Who I used to be."

"Don't you think that would have happened anyway? I've

changed. I mean, if you were the exact same person before and after you had a kid . . . I kind of think maybe you wouldn't be a particularly good parent."

"Agreed. But what I'm talking about . . . Noah will be in kindergarten next year. He's growing up. Soon he won't need me so much. And I just worry that I won't have anything to fill the space he leaves behind."

"Listen. You're doing the best you can. It's not as if you've been doing nothing the past four years. You had a job. You've been freelancing. You have something to show for yourself—maybe not as much as you would have if you'd kept working full time, or if Noah hadn't come along, but something. And I have no doubt in my mind that you'll be able to build that something back into a full-time gig when the time is right. Okay?"

Amy let out a gust of air. She hoped he was right. He sounded so authoritative and . . . *certain*. She did love that about him. Her husband was not a man who dabbled in what-ifs. *You make decisions based on the information in front of you*, he always said, *and if the situation changes, you adjust.* It sounded so simple when he said it, but Amy was a planner and a worrier, and some days she couldn't see how it would all work out.

"Okay," Amy said. "Sorry for sucking up a chunk of your day."

"Please. This is nothing compared to earlier when my mom called."

Amy snickered. "What was it this time?"

"Oh, you know, the usual. The neighbor's dog keeps shitting on their lawn. Dad got a fender bender in the Giant parking lot. His knees are driving him crazy. Et cetera."

"Doesn't she realize you're at the office?"

"Realize? Yes. Care? No. Oh, but she did mention something interesting."

"Interesting?"

"Well, maybe I shouldn't go that far, but anyway. She was going on and on about Dad and his knees, and she said something about it being so bad that the night they babysat, he ended up rooting through our bathroom in search of Aleve or Advil."

Amy's eyebrows shot up. "Really?"

"Yeah, so he was the one who undid your 'system,' or whatever you call it."

"That's great!"

"Uh . . . I thought you were pissed about it being messed up."

"No, I mean . . . it's not great that he messed with my system, just that I now know he's the one who did."

"As opposed to . . . me?"

Amy remembered that she still hadn't told Rob about Julian and his issues, and now that it was clear Julian hadn't done anything wrong, she hardly saw the point in bringing it up, at least in this context.

"Or me, I guess. The whole scenario had me feeling like I'd gone a little crazy."

"You organize your medicine by type and letter, and have no memory of eating an entire muffin. I . . . think the boat has sailed on crazy."

Amy clicked her tongue. "Yeah, well, you're stuck with me, so there." She glanced at the clock. "Crap. Gotta run. Time to pick up Noah."

"Give him a kiss for me. I'll be home for dinner. Want me to pick up anything on the way?"

"Other than a new brain?"

"Preferably something we can eat."

"Maybe Chinese. We haven't had that in a while."

"Done. And hey, if you're lucky"—Amy could hear him smiling through the phone—"maybe I'll even pick up another muffin."

"I hate you," she said, and they both laughed.

As Amy made her way from her car to the camp pavilion, she ran into Grace and Ethan walking to their car.

"Glad to see Noah made it back today," Grace said.

"Not as glad as I am."

Grace glanced at Ethan, who was momentarily distracted by a cawing bird in the tree above them. "Totally get it," Grace said in a low voice. "Sick days are the worst."

"So, Ethan, did you and Noah have fun today?"

Ethan nodded enthusiastically. "We threw *water balloons* and they exploded *everywhere!*"

"Wow, that *does* sound fun."

"Noah dropped his and it exploded on his feet, and he cried, but then Miss Donna gave him another one, so he was okay."

"Aw, that's good. Though I have to say—I think you just told me more about your camp day than Noah has the entire summer. Maybe you're the one I need to be asking about how Noah's day went."

Grace tousled Ethan's hair. "To be honest, that was the most I've heard either. Maybe we need to swap kids."

"No!" Ethan protested.

"I'm kidding, sweetie." She looked at Amy and subtly rolled her eyes. "Although some days . . ."

"Some days what?" He looked at her suspiciously.

"Nothing. Anyway, Ethan and I have to get to the haircut place before it gets too crowded, but I've been meaning to call you today—are you and Rob free this weekend?"

"I think so." Amy quickly went through her mental calendar. The truth was, since moving, they rarely had elaborate weekend plans. Their date night on Tuesday was the first they'd had since moving, and they hadn't set up anything else. "Yeah, we're around."

"I was thinking . . . maybe the four of us could go out to dinner? Nothing fancy—just a neighborhood place. But I thought it might be nice for us to get together. I had a lot of fun on our girls' night, and I think Rob and Julian would get along."

"Oh—sure. That sounds great. I mean, I'd need to find a sitter. Which, frankly, right now means my in-laws."

"Why don't you drop Noah at our place? Or I guess my parents' place. They'll be out, but we have a sitter we use all the time— Kara. She's fabulous. The boys can play, and Noah can conk out in Ethan's room until we get back."

Ethan gasped. "Noah is coming for a *sleepover?*"

"Not exactly. Just for part of the night. If his mommy and daddy are okay with it."

He started jumping up and down. "Please, please, please, please!"

"I'd need to talk to Rob, but . . . I'm sure it's fine. Let me just make sure he doesn't have any plans that I didn't know about. Which day were you thinking?"

"Saturday? We're flexible, but usually Saturdays work better for us."

"I'll check with Rob and will let you know tonight."

"Great. We can take care of the reservation. Anything I should know before I do? Allergies, food aversions, that kind of thing?"

"Rob is allergic to shellfish, but otherwise he pretty much eats anything. And I really do eat everything, shellfish included."

Grace tapped her fingers against her bottom lip. "Hmm. Okay. We'll come up with something. There's a Mediterranean place in Elkins Park that's pretty good. It's BYO, though I guess Julian isn't really drinking these days, so we might not 'B' anything."

"You can always have some of ours. Unless us bringing a bottle would be . . . unhelpful."

"No, I think it's probably fine." She paused in a moment of thought. "Actually, let me ask him. He doesn't like to make a big deal about it, especially in front of other men. He may just say he's the designated driver and leave it at that."

"It's fine with us either way. I haven't said anything to Rob about . . . the situation." She chose her words carefully, knowing that although Ethan was distracted by an oddly shaped rock he'd found on the ground, he could still hear them.

"I'd say you can tell him, but then Julian doesn't really know I've said anything to you, so . . . I'd rather not make a fuss. I can tell you from experience, it definitely isn't something he'll want to discuss at dinner."

"Oh, I'd never bring it up."

"I'm not saying you would—I'm just flagging it. We were out with his brother a few weeks ago, and his brother started asking a thousand questions, and . . . yeah. It didn't go well. I don't think he's ready to talk about it with anyone other than his group, or me. And frankly he doesn't even like talking about it to me."

"Understood."

"*Mommy*, can we just *go*?"

"Yes, we're going." Grace threw her eyes to the sky. "Like I'm some kind of chauffeur or something."

"Sounds familiar. Time for me to pick up my charge."

"Let me know what Rob says about Saturday, and we can go from there."

"Will do. Have a good haircut, Ethan! Hopefully Noah will come play on Saturday."

"Yaaaaay!" he squealed, and chased his mother up the gravel path to the parking lot.

That Saturday, Amy and Rob dropped Noah off at Grace's parents' house, a grand stone estate set on three acres of property with a gated driveway, lush gardens, and a tennis court. Grace had told Amy to pull up in front of the carriage house where she, Julian, and Ethan were staying.

"This is the guesthouse?" Rob asked in amazement.

"Apparently." Amy's eyes ran up the front of the carriage house, which looked less like the detached garage she'd imagined and more like . . . well, an actual house. It was smaller than their house, but then shouldn't it be? Who needed that much space?

"Jeez," Rob said. "I think it's bigger than you're mom's place."

"I think you're right."

"What do her parents do again?"

"I can't remember. I'm not sure she ever told me. Whatever it is, it's something that has made them very rich."

They got out of the car and knocked on the front door of the guesthouse. Amy could hear small footsteps clambering toward them.

"They're here, they're here!" Ethan's muffled voice rang out behind the door.

Grace opened it and smiled. "Hey, guys. Come on in."

She led them into the living area, which had an open floor plan, with the main family room area leading into an open kitchen outfitted with a sink, a gas range, a dishwasher, and a round, wooden table surrounded by four chairs.

"This is lovely," Amy said. "The whole property is. Did you grow up here?"

Grace nodded. "My parents have done a lot of renovations over the years, though. It doesn't look exactly the way it did twenty years ago."

"Well, it looks pretty amazing now."

"You guys are RICH!" Noah shouted.

Amy's face started burning up. She wanted to dissolve into the floorboards. "Noah," she said, her jaw tight.

"What?"

"That isn't polite."

"But you said that in the car."

Her mortification deepened. "No, sweetie. Daddy and I were talking about something else."

"You *did*. You *did* say that." He stomped his foot on the floor.

*Shut up, shut up, shut up!* Amy wanted to scream.

"Her parents are rich. It's true." Julian appeared at the bottom of a small staircase, which led upstairs.

"Julian . . ." Grace gave him a look.

"What? They are. No reason to make the kid feel bad about it. It doesn't take a rocket scientist to realize the person who owns this property has money. And from what I understand"—he came over and nudged Noah in the side—"this kid might *be* a rocket scientist someday."

Noah smiled sheepishly. Julian knew just how to stroke Noah's ego.

"Anyway," Grace said, clearly wanting to move the conversation along, "I ordered a pizza, which should be here any minute. Kara, I left you money, right?"

Amy looked over Julian's shoulder and noticed the babysitter for the first time. She was sitting on the couch, trying to find a movie for the kids on the TV.

"Yep," she said. "Ah! There it is! Guess what I found, boys?"

"What, what, what?" Ethan cried.

"I'll give you a hint. It starts with an 'M' and rhymes with 'zinions.'"

"*MINIONS!!!!*" they shouted in unison. They started jumping up and down and speaking in high-pitched gibberish.

Grace shook her head. "Have fun, boys. And good luck, Kara. Call if you need us. We shouldn't be late."

"Take your time. We'll be fine!"

"Yeah, I'm not sure who'll be having more fun—them or us," Julian joked.

Amy had to admit, she wasn't sure either.

The restaurant was a comfortable Mediterranean BYOB only ten minutes from Grace's parents' house. Julian drove, which made sense from an environmental and logistical standpoint, but Amy also knew it was his self-created out from drinking that evening. *Whatever it takes*, she thought to herself.

The hostess seated them at a table in the back and offered them an ice bucket for the bottle of white Amy and Rob had brought. Grace had told Amy that *not* bringing wine would be more uncomfortable for Julian because he'd have to explain things he didn't want to talk about. "It's not like his problem was with booze," she had said. "It'll be fine."

Amy sat next to Rob and across from Grace, and the four of them started making small talk: the kids, summer camp, the latest tweets from the president. Once the waitress had recited the specials, she got out a corkscrew and opened the bottle of wine.

"None for me," Julian said, reaching his hand over the top of his wineglass before she could pour. "I'm driving."

"Just three then?"

They nodded, and she filled up their glasses while they all scanned the menu.

"So how are you guys liking the house?" Julian asked once the waitress had taken their order.

"It's great," Rob said. "You guys took really good care of it."

"Thanks," Grace said. "We loved that place. Especially the neighborhood. But . . ." She shrugged. "Life, right?"

An awkward silence lingered. Amy knew the dinner could take an uncomfortable turn at some point, for myriad reasons, but she hadn't expected it so early in the evening. Maybe coming out with them was a mistake. Rob, in particular, was loath to accept the Durants' invitation, but Amy had convinced him it was the polite thing to do. He was still convinced they might be running some sort of credit card scam, but she did her best to disabuse him of his prejudice without betraying Grace's trust.

"Have you run into the crazy cat lady?" Julian asked, puncturing the silence.

"I don't think so . . . ? Does she live on Sycamore?"

"No, around the corner on Juniper. She has, like, eighteen cats or something, and she dresses them all up in different sweaters that she knits herself."

"Just in the winter," Grace added.

"Well, I mean, of course," Julian said in a jocular voice. "Why would you dress your cat in a sweater in the *summer*?"

They all laughed. The mood of the table lifted—thanks to Julian, Amy noted. He did have a way about him. Magnetic wasn't quite the right word, but it was close. He knew how to work a room.

"She sounds special," Rob said. "I look forward to meeting her."

"Oh, you will. If not before, then definitely on Halloween. She does up her house with a zillion tacky decorations and dresses her cats up in costumes. It's really her moment to shine."

"Ethan will really miss it this year," Grace said. "He loved trick-or-treating at her house."

Again, the tenor of the conversation darkened. What was up with Grace tonight? Amy knew the subject of the house could be sensitive, but they'd discussed it before, and it had been nearly two months now. Grace was also usually so positive, easygoing. Why the sudden change in mood?

"He's welcome to come trick-or-treating with us," Amy volunteered.

"That would be fun," Julian said. "And anyway, it's not like it's a gated community. Parents from all over drive their kids into the neighborhood and take them around because it's such a great place to visit on Halloween. I don't know why Grace is being Debbie Downer over here."

"Sorry. I'm just—it's been a long week. My parents are driving me crazy. I'm really ready to be out of there, which is probably why I'm all nostalgic for the old place."

"Remind me what happened with the other house you guys were supposed to buy?" Rob asked.

Amy felt her shoulders stiffen. It was a reasonable question. As far as he knew, the story the Durants had originally given was the truth. And she wasn't even supposed to know the real reason they needed to sell the house. If anything, Rob's question underscored his ignorance, which extended to her by default. But Grace was obviously in a funk, and Amy wondered how she would handle it in front of their husbands.

"It fell through," Grace replied quickly. "Long story. Too many problems after the inspection—mold in the basement, stuff like that."

"Got it," Rob said. "And no other prospects?"

"Not yet. We've talked to a builder about building a new place, but most of the land is so far outside the city. I like being a quick train ride from downtown."

"It's not that quick," Julian said.

"Twenty-five minutes."

"On a good day."

"I've had pretty good luck with SEPTA," Rob offered, obviously trying to cut the tension. *You have no idea the can of worms you've opened*, Amy thought.

"Where's your office?" Julian asked.

"Sixteenth and JFK. I just hop on at Jenkintown and get off at Suburban Station. I can catch multiple lines, so for me, it's usually about twenty-five to thirty minutes."

"See?" Grace said, her eyebrow raised.

Julian groaned. "Sorry, I forgot: The wife is always right."

"How could you forget?" Rob joked.

The wives elbowed their husbands simultaneously.

"Anyway," Julian said, as the waitress placed their appetizers in front of them, "tell me more about your job. You work in telecom, right?"

"For MediaCom, yeah. I'm in their digital marketing department."

"That's awesome. I had a friend who worked over there. Grant Abrams?"

Rob shook his head. "Doesn't ring a bell."

"He might not be there anymore. We sort of lost touch."

"It's a huge company, so there's a good chance he's still there and I just haven't met him."

"So, hey, does your department ever deal with sponsorships and cross-promotion?"

"Not directly. I mean, we support all departments when it comes to promotion, whether it's an internal launch or something else. But I don't deal with sponsorships at all."

"I only ask because my nonprofit, Food Fight, is looking for sponsors for our fall benefit. I realize when you hear food access you don't necessarily think telecom, but MediaCom is one of the biggest companies in Philly, so I figured it was worth a shot."

"Well, I know the company is big on corporate social responsibility, and food access is a major issue in Philly. I'm sure I can put you in touch with the right person."

"Really? That would be awesome. We've partnered with a bunch of local community groups, so the money we raise will go toward increased programming and support for them. If you want, I can shoot you some materials about who we are and what we do. Not that I expect you to pitch someone at the company—that's my job. It just might grease the wheels for when I actually give a call."

"Sure, that would be great. I'd love to learn more about what you do anyway."

There was a touch of suspicion in Rob's voice, though Amy knew she was the only one who heard it. But she knew her husband. He thought Food Fight was a money-laundering front or some other shady venture. Amy was actually curious how far Rob had let his imagination run. Human trafficking? Arms deals? Rob was a very practical guy who tended not to get ahead of himself—as their conversations about her career had demonstrated. But he also loved a good psychological thriller, and she wondered if he'd used his latest read as a model for the Durants' behavior. She knew she'd been sworn to secrecy, but now she was going to have to tell him the truth about Julian, if only so that he'd stop suspecting him of something far worse.

"So that was a little awkward, huh?" Rob said on the car ride home. Noah was out cold in his car seat.

"A little. But mostly fine. Even fun at times."

"I guess. But the tension between the two of them . . . yikes."

"You think? I mean, I know it got awkward about the house, but otherwise?"

"I don't know. I got a weird vibe. She seemed kind of pissed off with him all night."

"Well, maybe he did something to piss her off. Husbands do that sometimes, you know."

"Wives, too, from what I've heard." He grinned. "I don't know. Maybe I'm reading too much into it. But then all that stuff about Food Fight. Like, 'Oh, sure, recipient of much sketchy mail that I have accidentally received. Why don't I help my company sponsor your big event?'"

"You're not going to put him in touch with the people at MediaCom?"

"I probably will. It's just . . . all those letters. Something isn't right."

"It isn't what you think."

"What isn't what I think?"

"The 'not right' thing. It isn't money laundering or a credit card scam or something."

"And you know this because . . . ?"

"Because Grace told me."

Rob gave her a sideways glance. "Told you what, exactly?"

"Why they've had . . . money troubles."

"And what did she say?"

"Well, she sort of told me in confidence."

Rob huffed. "Okay . . . So, is this supposed to make me feel more comfortable about asking my company to sponsor his?"

"You aren't asking. He's asking."

"Whatever. You know what I mean."

Amy thought for a long while, then sighed. "Okay. I'll tell you. But you can't say anything to anyone, do you understand?"

"Shouldn't I have a say in whether or not it's relevant when my employer is involved?"

"Of course. But it's a personal issue that I think the Durants would like to keep that way."

"Does he have gambling problem or something?"

"No, but funny you should say that. Grace says that's what her parents think."

Rob thought for a second. "Is he an alcoholic? I noticed he didn't drink at dinner."

"No, but you're getting closer."

Rob furrowed his brow and looked over at her. "Drugs? Seriously?"

"You can't tell anyone," Amy said. "I promised Grace I wouldn't say anything."

"Jesus. What kind?"

"Pills. I don't know how bad it got, but . . . obviously you and I know it led to some financial troubles. But he's clean now. Grace said he's in therapy and is throwing himself into work to keep busy. I'm sure that's part of the reason he's planning a benefit dinner. Those things create a lot of busy work, which it sounds like he needs right now."

"They also generate a fair amount of money. . . ."

"Yeah, but not for him. It sounds like most of the money will go to the community groups. Listen, if you'd feel better about it, you could always vet some of those recipients yourself. He said he'd send you some materials. Call around to some of the places he supports and see what they think."

"Oh, sure, with all that free time I have."

"I'm happy to help. I just . . . I guess I've watched my brother go through so much, and I wonder if things would have been different if someone had helped him start fresh the first time he got clean. Doesn't everyone deserve a second chance?"

"Of course they do. But your brother is on, what, chance number five?"

"That's my point. Maybe if he'd had something meaningful to occupy his time, he wouldn't be on chance number five. But he didn't. And look where he is."

"Mommy?" Noah croaked from the back seat. Amy had woken him up. She didn't realize how loudly she had been speaking.

"Almost home, sweetie," she whispered. "Go back to sleep."

"Okay." He yawned and closed his eyes.

Rob sighed. "I'll take a look when he sends me the materials and will let you know what I think. Okay?"

"Thank you," Amy said, as if he were doing her a favor, even though none of this had anything to do with her.

# Chapter 10

As promised, the next week Julian sent Rob an e-mail with information about the fall Food Fight benefit. Rob passed the information along to Amy, who took it upon herself to do a little sleuthing about the organization. She knew her time would be better spent writing up marketing materials for her new client, or even drumming up new work, but ever since dinner the previous weekend, she felt obliged to vet Julian's nonprofit. She barely knew him, but at this point she knew his wife and son fairly well, and she wanted stability for them.

From what little investigation she was able to do, Food Fight seemed not only legitimate, but also quite respectable. They'd worked for many years to improve access to fresh food in several North and West Philadelphia neighborhoods and had the accolades to prove it—stories in the *Philadelphia Inquirer* and *Philadelphia Magazine*, reviews on Yelp, and even mentions online in discussion forums, where other nonprofits and community groups heaped praise on the organization for the good work it was doing. It was only a cursory review, and Amy knew that, but there was nothing to suggest untoward behavior of any kind.

Amy wrote a quick reply to Rob's e-mail:

> Looks legit. I can call around to a few of these places later, but even just a quick skim online shows they are a known quantity

doing good work. Check out the profile in *Philly Mag* that I
linked to below—lots of quotes from community orgs that
have worked with Food Fight. Pretty open and honest about
the relationship and what they've done. Doesn't seem shady
to me.

Amy shot off the e-mail just as her phone started ringing. She
didn't recognize the number. She considered ignoring it, but it was
a 215 number. What if it was Noah's camp and something had happened?

She grabbed her phone. "Hello?"

"Hi, Amy?"

"Yes?"

"This is Emily. Jake's mom? We met the other day at Be Well
Café?"

"Oh, right—sorry, I didn't recognize the number."

"Did I not text you after you gave me yours?"

"I don't think so? I don't remember seeing one."

"I could have sworn I did, but I am so ridiculously sleep de-
prived at the moment. Anything is possible. Anyway, I was calling
to see if Noah wanted to come play this weekend."

"Oh. Sure. That would be fun." Amy tried not to sound too surprised. After their run-in at the café, she knew Jake and Noah got
along at camp, but she was still getting used to her son having a
bustling social life. "What day were you thinking?" she asked.

"Either would work. Want to say Sunday? Around lunchtime?"

"Sure, that works. What can we bring?"

"We have a pool, so he should bring a bathing suit. Assuming he
likes swimming."

"Well . . . he . . . um . . ."

The truth was, Noah was still terrified of the water. They'd tried
numerous techniques, including private swim lessons last winter at
a swim club in DC and then enrollment at his current day camp,
which provided swim instruction, but by all accounts Noah had
spent the entire session in both experiences sitting at the edge of
the pool, refusing to get in. Surely Jake must already know about
Noah's water fears if they went to camp together. Maybe he hadn't

told his mom. Or maybe Noah had suddenly made progress in the pool and just hadn't mentioned it? Amy somehow doubted this was the case. Noah was notoriously bad at providing details about his daily activities, but he probably would have mentioned something as monumental as getting in the pool.

"He doesn't . . . love the water," Amy finally said.

"Oh. Well, that's okay. We have plenty of other stuff. Would he do a sprinkler? Or a Slip'N Slide?"

"Probably. He can be a little unpredictable lately."

"Uh, I think that's true for pretty much all four-year-olds. As for lunch, any dietary restrictions I should know about?"

"Nope, no allergies. Noah pretty much eats anything."

"God I'm jealous. Jake eats like five things, and they're pretty much all beige. I hope Noah is okay with PB&J."

"Definitely. Crusts and all."

"He eats crusts? Jeez. So let me get this straight: He can read and spell, he eats pretty much anything, he's polite to all the camp counselors. How are you raising the perfect kid?"

"He's far from perfect. I mean, he's the light of my life, but like any kid, he has his issues. Like I said, he doesn't really love the water . . ." Amy decided to leave it at that and not mention the instances in DC where he spent playdates playing by himself. He'd clearly moved beyond that with Ethan. She hoped that would be the case with Jake.

"Please—my sister still doesn't love the water, and she's thirty-three. I'd hardly consider that a failing. Sounds to me like you have the perfect child."

"No one is perfect," Amy said, and although she tried not to sound defensive or condescending, she realized she probably did.

On the way to pick up Noah from camp later that week, Amy's mom called. The two had spoken a few weeks prior, after Amy and Rob had agreed to send half the money her mom had asked for. Ellen had been audibly disappointed that Amy hadn't convinced Rob to send the full two thousand dollars, but in the end she didn't argue, mostly, Amy assumed, because she was grateful for any bit of help she could get.

"Hey, Mom, what's up?"

"Just checking in to say hi," she said, though Amy suspected there was more to it than that. They didn't speak infrequently, but they also didn't have the sort of mother-daughter relationship where they talked every day over any old thing. Most of that was down to Ellen, who wasn't much of a phone talker. She never had been.

"What's the *point*?" she'd always say. "Fancy having all that time to waste talking about nothing. Some people have work to do."

Amy knew her mom had been overworked and overtired, but she'd also always held her emotions close to her chest. She'd lost her husband a few weeks before their eighth anniversary, and yet as far as Amy knew, she hadn't really talked about that loss with anyone. The memories from that time were fuzzy at this point, but Amy remembered friends stopping by a lot right after her father's death—usually bringing meals and gifts for her and Tim—but the visits gradually dried up, and Amy couldn't remember seeing any of those people at her house after that. At the time, Amy didn't understand why, and then when she was older she assumed people forgot about them once the shock wore off. But in recent years, she'd begun to wonder if her mother had actually pushed those friends away because she didn't want to talk about her husband's death with anyone, not even people she considered close friends. The few times Amy had brought up the subject, Ellen shut her down before the conversation could even begin.

"It's always good to hear your voice," Amy said. "How are things?"

"It's been wicked hot. I don't know if the heat wave has made it down to Philly, but we're dying up here."

"I've seen a few stories online. It's been hot here, but ironically not as bad as farther north."

"Noah looked pretty sweaty in those photos you sent of him at the park."

"Those were from a few weeks ago. It got really hot for a few days there."

"That photo of him drinking from the bubbler cracked me up. I haven't seen one of those in years—looks like something out of the fifties."

"It's an old park, but they keep it up really well. I also haven't heard someone say 'bubblah' in almost twenty years, so thanks for that."

"Never forget your roots!"

Amy laughed. Her mom lacked sentimentality about nearly every aspect of life, but she was a diehard New Englander, through and through. That Amy had settled down in the Mid-Atlantic was no doubt viewed as a huge insult.

"So I assume the money came through?" Amy asked, though as soon as the words came out of her mouth, she regretted it. She wished she'd let the conversation go on longer before turning to financial matters, which always cast a pall over the conversation. She didn't expect her mother to start talking suddenly about her life and feelings, but the sooner she began talking about money and, by association, Tim, the sooner the conversation would spiral downward and then abruptly end.

"It did," her mother said. "Thank you."

"You're welcome. I hope it helps."

"It will. It already has."

"How is Tim doing?"

"Good. Really good. I mean, you know, he has his days. But this time feels different to me. I think he's turned a corner."

"That's great. I'm really glad to hear that."

"He'd love to hear from you."

"I'm not sure *that's* true . . ."

"It most certainly is."

"How can you be so sure?"

"Because you're his big sister. You need more of a reason than that?"

"No, I just meant . . . it's not as if we talk all the time. It's been a while. Years, actually."

"And whose fault is that?"

"I . . . hope you're not suggesting it's mine."

"Well, you're the one who moved away."

Amy pulled to the side of the road and put the car in park. "You're kidding me."

"What? You left. That's a fact."

"I've been back numerous times to help him detox and get back on track."

"All I'm saying is, how hard is it to pick up the phone?"

"This coming from the woman who says talking on the phone is a waste of time."

"It is most of the time. But this is different. Tim needs you. You're his *sister*."

Amy closed her eyes and took a deep breath. "I know that. And I tried to help him—for *years* I tried. But every single time, no matter what hoops I jumped through, no matter what sacrifices I made, he ended up right back where he started. And at a certain point, for my own sanity, I needed to step away. I'm happy to provide financial support to help him get better, but I'm just not sure I can travel down that emotional avenue again until he proves he is serious this time. It hurts too much. There are only so many times I can volunteer to have my heart broken."

"Yeah, well, a mother doesn't have that luxury," her mother snapped back; then she hung up.

Amy didn't want to start something with her mom. She never did. But discussing Tim was always like tiptoeing across a field studded with land mines. Now that she was a mother herself, Amy appreciated even more the struggles Ellen had gone through with Tim, and she understood why it was such a sensitive topic. But that didn't change the fact that Amy had pretty much reached her emotional limit when it came to her brother. To throw so much of yourself into helping someone . . . to have it not make any difference . . . she just couldn't bring herself to get caught up in it all again. She still loved Tim deeply, but she wasn't ready for a call. Not yet.

So that Friday, instead of carving out time to call her brother, she busied herself with chores and eventually took Noah with her to Target, where they ran into Grace and Ethan.

"Hey, Noah, look who it is," Amy said.

"Ethan!" He ran over to Grace's cart.

Amy smiled at Grace. "What a nice surprise."

"It was bound to happen at some point. I practically live here."

"I can relate."

"So how are you guys? I keep meaning to tell you how much fun we had Saturday."

"We had a great time, too. I was really impressed with the food. Do you guys go there often?"

"Not really. We kind of forget about it, to be honest. Every time we go back, I'm like, 'Why don't we come here more?' And then I forget about it for a while and the same thing happens again. I hear they're getting a liquor license, which will probably help me remember." She laughed.

"I think I saw your mom the other day at drop-off."

"Oh, yeah, she's been doing drop-off and pickup this week because Julian and I had conflicts. She didn't mention that you guys met."

"We didn't really. We just sort of said hello to each other, but she was with Ethan and looks a lot like you, so I figured she had to be your mom."

"You think we look alike?"

Grace sounded a little surprised, but Amy couldn't understand why. Her mother was Southeast Asian, and although Grace's ethnicity was more muted, she had the same eyes and smile. They weren't twins, but they definitely resembled one another.

"You don't think you do?"

Grace shrugged. "I guess. I've always thought I looked more like my dad. I mean, he's Mr. WASP, but we have the same face shape and nose."

"I'll have to reserve judgment until I see him at pickup."

Grace choked on a laugh. "My dad? At pickup? Please. He never even picked *me* up from school. Neither did my mom most of the time, now that I think of it. It was mostly the nanny."

"Did they both work?"

"Oh, no. My dad did—still does—but not my mom. You might ask why she needed a full-time nanny if she didn't work, and to that I say . . . you got me. I don't think she liked being a mom very much. I mean, hello—if we could afford help, I would definitely take it. But I don't think I'd need someone all day, seven days a week. At that point, it's sort of like . . . why did you have kids?"

"It sounds like you guys are closer now, though . . ." Amy hesitated lingering on what was likely a sore subject, but she wasn't sure how to pivot the conversation without entirely changing the topic. She couldn't relate at all to Grace's upbringing. Her mom wasn't always around when she and Tim were young, but that was because she was working several jobs and raising them alone. Amy tried to picture Ellen's response to hearing that Grace's mother didn't work and had a full-time nanny. She would probably first ask whether the woman was disabled, and in discovering the answer was no, she would say something like, "Real rough life." Or, more likely, her usual, "Fucking rich people."

"I wouldn't say we're super close, but she's definitely stepped it up since finding out about Julian's financial issues."

Her eyes drifted to Ethan and Noah, who were ogling the boxes of Tim Tams on the shelf. "Oh my God, have you ever tried those things?" Grace said, swiftly changing the subject, much to Amy's relief.

"Tim Tams? I don't think so. They're like chocolate cookies, right?"

"Chocolate cookies with a chocolate cream filling, and the whole thing is covered in fudge icing. They're originally Australian, though I think Pepperidge Farm owns the company now. One of my best friends from college had family in Australia, and last time I saw her she taught me about the 'Tim Tam Slam.'"

"Which is . . . ?"

"You bite off opposite corners of the cookie, and then you use it like a straw to drink some sort of hot drink—coffee, hot chocolate, tea, whatever. The Tim Tam starts collapsing, and you shove the whole thing in your mouth at once."

"That sounds . . ."

"Magical?"

"Pretty much."

"It is. We should do it sometime. In fact, if you're free this weekend, we could arrange a Tim Tam Slam session. Ethan can't have them because they might contain traces of nuts, but I have some nut-free cookies for him that are similar."

"I'll never say no to chocolate."

"Want to say Sunday?"

"Sure!" Amy paused. Sunday. The playdate with Emily and

Jake. Crap. "Actually . . . I take that back. We're supposed to go to Jake's house that day."

Grace's mood deflated, and Amy suddenly felt very awkward, as if she were back in middle school and was deliberately leaving Grace out of a social engagement. The reality was, in middle school Amy was the one regularly being left out, whereas Grace had probably never experienced such exclusion.

"Oh. Never mind then. Maybe another time."

"We're around Saturday," Amy offered.

"We're actually supposed to have brunch with my parents Saturday for my mom's birthday."

Amy didn't know why she felt so guilty for arranging a child-oriented social engagement that didn't involve Grace and Ethan, but she did. It's not as if she owed Grace and Ethan anything. Except . . . well, she sort of felt as if she did. They were the first people other than Rob's family to welcome her and Noah to Philadelphia, and Ethan was Noah's best friend. And from what Emily had said, the three boys were like the Three Musketeers at camp, which meant they'd be down a musketeer on Sunday. That gave Amy an idea.

"Why don't you guys join us at Emily's on Sunday? I'm sure she wouldn't mind."

"That's okay—I don't want to impose."

"I really don't think it would be a big deal. The kids are just going to play outside, and she's making peanut butter sandwiches—though I guess Ethan couldn't have that."

"He can have peanut butter. He's only allergic to tree nuts."

"Oh, well . . . see? What's another peanut butter sandwich? It's not as if she's making lobster."

"I guess. If you're sure? I really don't want to screw things up."

"I'll give her a call this afternoon. I'm sure it's fine. The more the merrier, right?"

"Sure," Grace said, though she didn't sound convinced, and if Amy were being honest, she wasn't either.

On the way home, Amy called Emily from the car. "Hey, Emily?"

"Amy, hi, what's up?" She sounded out of breath.

"Sorry, am I catching you at a bad time?"

"No, no, I'm just cooling down from my run. It's fine."

"Oh. Okay. So the reason I'm calling is because I just ran into Grace Durant at Target—"

"Grace shops at Target? Wow, didn't expect that."

Amy furrowed her brow. "Doesn't everyone shop at Target?"

"Well, *I* do, and I'm sure *you* do, but Grace . . . I don't know. Target seems so basic for her. Like anything she'd buy there she would buy on Amazon so no one would know she needed toilet paper and laundry detergent like the rest of us."

Amy wasn't exactly sure what Emily meant. Sure, Grace's clothes tended to be pieces that Amy hadn't seen anywhere else, but she wasn't a snob. Considering her background, Grace struck Amy as pretty down to earth.

"I get the impression she shops there a lot, actually."

"Huh. Times have changed. Anyway, you were saying?"

"So I ran into her and Ethan, and we got talking about these cookies—Tim Tams?—and she—"

"Tim what?"

"Tim Tams. They're these Australian cookies . . . I can tell you about them on Sunday. But to make a long story short, she asked if Noah could play with Ethan Sunday. I told her we already had plans with Jake, but I was wondering . . . would it be okay if they joined us? I know the three boys love playing together."

There was a brief pause on the other end of the line. "Um . . . yeah. I guess that would be okay."

"It's totally fine if it isn't. They sounded pretty busy, so I'm sure they have other things to do."

"No, no . . . I mean, I'll have to get a few more snacks. . . ."

"Grace will bring Tim Tams. And I can bring something, too."

"Okay. That's . . . yeah. I'm sure Jake will be thrilled."

But by the sound of Emily's voice, she didn't sound thrilled at all.

# Chapter 11

Sunday arrived, and Amy headed off for Emily's house. She glanced down at the bowl of fruit salad sitting on the floor of the passenger seat. She'd gone a little crazy with it. There was easily enough to feed twenty-five children. Maybe thirty. Why had she gone overboard? She knew why: Because she'd invited a friend to someone else's house, and she felt guilty about it. *Oh, sure, a fruit salad will make everything better.* She hoped Emily would just think she was being generous.

"What time is Ethan coming?" Noah asked as Amy stopped at a red light.

"Same time as us."

"What if we get there first?"

"Then we'll play with Jake until he arrives."

"I want us all to get there at the *same time*."

Amy took a deep breath. "Hopefully we will."

"But what if we don't?"

"Then we don't. But we will all be there eventually, and everything will be fine. It doesn't matter exactly when we get there."

"Yes, it does."

"Noah . . ." Amy couldn't muster the energy to argue with him, and really there wasn't any point. Even if it didn't matter exactly when they arrived—and it didn't!—it mattered to him, and so no line of reasoning would make any difference.

"What?" Noah said, prompting her to finish her thought.

"Nothing. Never mind. It's just—ah! Would you look at that? Ethan's mommy is pulling up at the same time." *Thank God*, she added to herself.

Noah clapped his hands together excitedly as she parked in the driveway. "Yaaaaay!"

They piled out of the car and met up with Grace and Ethan as they all walked to the front door. Emily's house was a split-level, nestled in a community with other split-levels, with sidewalks and big trees and well-maintained front lawns. The neighborhood wasn't quite as quaint as Glenside Park, but given the number of driveways filled with tricycles and Fisher-Price toys, it seemed like a perfect place to raise kids.

"Look what I have," Grace said as she held open her tote bag.

Amy peered inside. "The legendary Tim Tams. Oh, boy."

"It's a little warm for hot chocolate, but coffee should do the trick. It's *never* too hot for coffee."

"Never."

"Ever."

Amy rang the doorbell while the boys spoke in Minion to one another. Emily opened the door, and a scruffy gray dog poked out his head before she could even say hello.

"Bastian, sit! No, sit! I said *sit*. Good boy." She shook her head. "I'm sorry. He is . . . well, suffice it to say he was Brent's idea."

"He's cute," Amy said. "What kind of dog is he?"

"No idea. Brent got him from a rescue league. He's some kind of mutt." Bastian started to push through the door again, but she gave him a fierce look, and he stopped. "Anyway, come in, come in! I'm so glad you're here!"

She smiled and opened the door wider, and only then did she notice that Grace was on the front stoop, too. "Oh. Everyone's here."

"Hi, Emily," Grace said.

Emily's smile dimmed. "Grace," she said after a beat.

Amy already felt guilty for her potential social engineering, but now she realized there was more to it than that. There was a palpable tension between Grace and Emily, a frostiness that instantly chilled the air around them. Did it have to do with the children? Or was it something else?

"I brought fruit salad!" Amy chimed in, trying to lighten the mood.

Emily tore her eyes from Grace and glanced at the bowl. "Yes, you did! Wow, that's a lot of fruit. But then I remember you at the coffee shop the other day—you have quite the appetite!"

Amy flushed. That stupid muffin. "I just figured the kids might want some with lunch. Or as a snack."

"Please—I would probably eat that whole bowl myself, left to my own devices. It's perfect." She ushered them inside.

"I brought Tim Tams," Grace said, lifting the package from her tote.

"Tim . . . oh, right, those were the cookies Amy mentioned on the phone, right? I'm sure they'll be huge hit with the kids. Speaking of which . . ." She peered over their shoulders. "*Hi*, Noah and Ethan. Jake is so excited to play with you! Hey, Jake?" She waited for a reply but didn't hear anything. "I think he's in the kitchen."

The group moved into the kitchen, where Jake was half-naked, apparently in the process of changing into his bathing suit.

"Jake! What did I tell you about getting dressed in the kitchen? I don't need your naked tush on the floor."

The boys all started laughing. "She said *tush*," Ethan giggled.

"Tush!" Jake called back.

"Butt!" Ethan said.

"Farts!"

"Boogies!"

The mothers all eyed each other. "Boys—enough," Emily called out. "No potty talk outside of the bathroom."

"But you said tush!" Jake protested.

"I said that because you are half naked in our kitchen, which I've told you a million times is not okay. Can you *please* put on your bathing suit—in the powder room, preferably?"

"Ohh-kay," he said, and stomped off.

"Does either of your boys need to change?"

Amy had brought a bathing suit for Noah, but she noticed Ethan was already dressed for the pool.

"Noah needs to get his suit on," Amy said.

His eyes shot up at her, and his smile disappeared. "But, Mommy . . ." he said in a loud whisper. "I don't *want* to get in the pool."

"We have a Slip'N Slide," Emily offered, before Amy could reply.

He furrowed his brow, looking highly skeptical. "What's that?"

"It's like a long plastic carpet with sprinklers attached. You put it on the lawn and run, run, run and slide across it on your belly."

His eyebrows pressed closer together. Amy knew her son, and this description did nothing to make the activity more appealing. "Maybe you watch the other guys try it a few times and then see what you think," Amy said. "But first you need to get your suit on."

"Mommy . . ."

Amy crouched down next to him. "Please? We came all the way here, and Ethan and Jake are both in their suits. You don't even need to get wet. Just put it on."

"Why do I need to put it on if I'm not going to get wet?"

"Just . . . because." Amy was trying not to sound tense, especially in front of the other mothers, but she was struggling. Why was he suddenly being difficult again? Why couldn't he just go with the flow?

Noah stomped his foot on the floor. "Fine," he said. He grabbed the bag with the bathing suit out of her hands and stormed off to the room where he'd seen Jake go.

Emily smiled as she pulled some juice boxes from the refrigerator. "Are we having fun yet?"

For the next thirty minutes, Noah sat on a pool chair watching the other boys play on the Slip'N Slide. Amy thought she'd gotten in a time machine and traveled back to their life in DC: other kids playing while Noah stood on the periphery, observing and showing no interest in joining in. What happened? He'd made such progress. Emily called them the Three Musketeers! This looked more like the two musketeers and their mute, simple cousin.

"Noah, sweetie, don't you want to join the other kids?" Amy whispered, once the half hour mark had passed.

He shook his head.

"You don't have to get wet. You could just . . . kick a ball around or . . . I don't know. Suggest another game."

He shrugged. "In five minutes."

Amy knew he still didn't have a very good grasp of time, but she was too tired and frustrated to argue. "Okay," she said, and made her way back inside with Emily and Grace, whom she'd left alone.

When she returned, Grace and Emily were talking, and watching the kids through the window. The two barely made eye contact, even as they chatted about such inoffensive topics as summer vacation and paint colors.

"It's been this color for a while," Emily was saying as Grace ran her hand up and down the kitchen wall.

"It can't have been that long . . ."

"About a year."

"Oh. Has it been . . . I guess it has."

The silence lingered as Grace let her hand slip down the wall, her eyes wandering around the kitchen and into the living room. Amy cleared her throat.

"It's a really pretty color," she said, trying to ease the tension. It was a pretty color—a faint celadon that highlighted the veining in the granite countertops. "Did you guys redo this kitchen, or was it like this when you bought the house?"

"We redid it. You should have seen the original—it was a mess."

"I remember," Grace said. "That stove with the electric coil burners? The whole thing was rusted."

"Ugh, it was terrible." She flashed Grace a subdued smile. "Anyway, we fixed it up shortly after we moved in. I couldn't deal."

Before they could say anything further on the matter, the boys came tearing into the house. "MINIONS!!!" they shouted as they started speaking in gibberish and chasing each other around the family room. Amy was relieved to see Noah had joined in.

"Freaking Minions," Emily said as she watched them run around her sectional. "I mean, they're little and yellow and cute, but honestly, I don't get the appeal."

"The fact that adults don't get it probably *is* the appeal," Amy offered.

"Probably. But I swear, if I have to spend one more meal listening to Jake go, 'Bakayarou! Bee-doh, bee-doh!' I'm going to shoot someone."

Amy laughed. "Sing it, sister."

Grace laughed, too, though a little uncomfortably, which made Amy feel as if she were elbowing her way into someone else's friendship. Except she wasn't. In all of their conversations about camp and school, Grace had never once mentioned Emily, and she obviously hadn't visited her house in more than a year. What did any of that have to do with Amy? Nothing.

"Mommy, I'm hungry," Jake whined as he came back into the kitchen.

"Then let's eat! PB&J okay with everyone?"

Noah hurried into the room. "Peanut butter is nuts, right?"

"Technically it's a legume," Grace said. "Don't worry: Ethan can have peanut butter."

"Oh, right, of course." Emily flushed. "I didn't even . . . I forgot."

"It's fine. Let me just double-check the peanut butter jar." She skimmed the ingredients and nodded. "All good."

Emily threw together the sandwiches, and the boys changed into dry clothes and sat around the table. Noah didn't actually need to change, considering he didn't get within ten feet of the Slip'N Slide, but he changed anyway. He seemed to have gotten back into the groove and was playing nicely with the other boys, though Amy did notice Ethan and Jake seemed more connected. Or was that just her imagination? She hated the impulse to jump in and make every social situation perfect for her kid, and she fought it with every ounce of her being, but gosh it was hard. Would she have wanted Ellen to jump in and fix her own social problems growing up? Definitely not. There was nothing she could have done, and if anything, her mother's meddling would only have made things worse. Still, the urge was there, and she had to make a concerted effort to control it.

"So, Emily . . . you wouldn't happen to have any coffee lying around, would you?" Grace asked.

"I think there's some left over from breakfast . . ." She glanced over her shoulder. "Maybe a mug or two?"

"That should be enough. You ladies up for a Tim Tam Slam?"

"A what?"

"I'll show you."

Emily poured the remains in the coffeepot into two mugs and heated them up in the microwave. She added a splash of milk to both and pushed them across the counter toward Grace, who had retrieved the package of Tim Tams from her tote bag.

"Okay. Here's how it goes. Bite off pieces from opposite corners like this. Then you dunk it into the coffee like a straw and suck, suck, suck as hard as you can. . . ."

"That sounds a little dirty," Emily said in a lowered voice. "You sure this is PG with the kids around?"

"It's fine. Watch." Grace stuck the cookie into the coffee, then sucked through it for a few seconds before shoving the whole thing in her mouth.

"Wait, did you just eat the whole thing?"

She nodded as she raised an eyebrow and smirked. There was a little bit of fudge along the corners of her mouth, and she looked a little like a squirrel with her mouth completely stuffed. The whole exercise seemed totally out of character for Grace, or at least what Amy thought she knew of her. The woman Amy knew was chic and subdued and fairly private. She wasn't the kind of person who shoveled chocolate cookies into her mouth. But there was a girlish mischief in her eyes as she swallowed the Tim Tam and washed it down with a little more coffee.

"Either of you want to try?"

Emily and Amy looked at each other and shrugged. "Why not?" Amy said.

They followed Grace's lead, and after many seconds of sucking, Amy felt the interior of the cookie begin to soften and collapse. Panicked, she looked to Grace for guidance, but Grace just said, "Shove it in! Shove it in!"

Amy did, but as she pushed it into her mouth, she managed to smear a huge glob of fudge all over her lower lip and chin. Emily started laughing hysterically as she did the same, and the three of them were giggling like old friends. Amy had to admit, it felt nice.

"See, what did I tell you? Amazing, right?"

"Pretty good," Amy admitted.

Emily burst out laughing again. "I'm sorry. Your teeth—you look like you're missing at least three."

Amy licked her teeth. The fudge was stuck on like mortar. "Oh, jeez."

Grace and Emily laughed as she downed some of the coffee.

"Yours aren't much better," she said, pointing to the two of them.

"Still?" Grace said. "Oh, boy. Okay, I have to go to the bathroom anyway. Back in a second."

She excused herself to the powder room.

"Mommy, what are you eating?" Noah asked.

"Nothing. Just . . . eat your peanut butter. And your fruit. You can have a cookie when you're finished."

The boys' eyes lit up. "COOKIES!!!" they shouted.

"Sandwich and fruit first," Emily said.

The boys agreed begrudgingly and returned to their lunch. Amy took another sip of coffee and blotted the corners of her mouth with a paper towel.

"Wow, I haven't laughed like that in a while," she said.

"Me either."

"I'm glad we did this. Not the slam—that was fun, too. But I mean all of us hanging out. It makes me feel more settled. Like I'm finally meeting nice people here."

"Aw, good, I'm glad." Her eyes quickly flitted to the hallway. She lowered her voice. "Just . . . be careful with that one. Everything isn't what it seems."

Amy opened her mouth to respond—was she talking about Julian's problems, or something else?—but Grace returned before she could say a word.

That night while Amy and Rob were making dinner, her friend Jess called. Amy and Jess had met at Georgetown during their freshman year and ended up living together for the next three. Amy had always seen college as an opportunity to reboot her social life, and Georgetown proved her right. All of her bookishness and precociousness had caught up with her sometime around middle school, and she soon became persona non grata among the cliquish girls in her class. In middle school, she was actively left out of birthday parties and sleepovers, and by high school no one even thought to invite her in the first place. She pretended not to care ("I'm too busy studying and trying to get into college anyway."), but she did, and she couldn't wait to flee Rhode Island and leave her social reputation behind.

When she arrived in Washington, she couldn't believe her luck. Everyone she met was smart and interesting and engaged. These were her people. She supposed some of them may have struggled socially like she did, and others almost certainly didn't, but it didn't matter. They were all in the same boat—young, intelligent people looking to learn new things and make new friends. Her past didn't matter, at least not to anyone there. This was before the advent of social media, which allowed your youth to haunt you like a ghost. Amy could wipe the slate clean simply by being herself with a new set of people. It was empowering.

She and Jess hit it off immediately. They were in the same section for their political science lecture, and Amy had barely introduced herself when Jess invited her to a party that night in her dorm. Amy couldn't remember the last time she'd been actively invited to something. She went and had the most fun she'd had in years, and from then on she and Jess were nearly inseparable.

Jess was exactly the sort of friend Amy could have used in Woonsocket. She was pretty and bubbly, and a good time seemed to follow her wherever she went. But she was smart, too—smarter than Amy—and loved a good debate. Around her, Amy didn't have to worry that her interest or knowledge of a subject would make her seem like a know-it-all. Jess would either be genuinely delighted to learn something new, or would counter her with a more nuanced view. She introduced Amy to all of the people on her debate team, roped her into numerous social clubs, and generally broadened Amy's social circle beyond anything she could have imagined. By the time they graduated, Amy's social confidence had exploded, and she knew a lot of that was down to Jess.

Amy had stayed on in Washington after graduation, but Jess had moved to Durham, North Carolina, for law school and after a bunch of moves had settled with her husband and two kids in Seattle. They kept in touch, but the physical distance combined with the kids meant they didn't do so as often as either of them would like.

"Helloooooo, my long-lost friend," Jess crowed into the phone when Amy picked up. "I hope this isn't a bad time."

"Anytime I get to talk to you is a good time. We're making dinner, but Rob hasn't even put the pork chops on yet, so I have a few minutes."

"Oh, duh, it's dinnertime on the east coast. You'd think I'd have gotten used to the time change after living out here for five years, but no. Can you imagine how much more we'd talk if we lived in the same time zone?"

"Probably not *that* much more. The kids are the real problem."

"I know. My sister's kids are, like, eight and ten, and she promises me it gets easier, but I'm not so sure. Like, at least when they're really little they still nap. That's why I can call you now. Penny is sleeping, and Dave is out with Zander—allegedly on a hike, but I heard something about ice cream, so who knows."

"How is everyone? I feel like we haven't caught up in ages."

"We're good. Zander starts kindergarten in a few weeks, and Penny is off to preschool. I kind of can't believe it. I swear I just brought Zander home from the hospital two days ago."

"Right? That's how I feel. It doesn't help that I haven't seen him in person since he was like a year old."

"Another problem of living on opposite sides of the country. So what about you guys? How's the new house? Are you finally feeling settled?"

"Pretty much. Rob's job is going well. The house is coming together. In a total shock, Noah is making friends left and right."

"That's great! You always sounded down about his social life in DC."

"This is definitely an improvement. I'm really happy for him."

"What about your social life? Have you connected with anyone in your neighborhood?"

"Yeah, sort of. Believe it or not, I actually befriended the woman who sold us our house."

"Interesting. How's that going?"

"Pretty well. Noah is, like, best friends with her son, so we see a fair amount of them. I mean, she and I aren't close like you and I are, but we're friendly."

"Well, no one could be as close as you and I are."

"Obviously."

They both laughed, and Amy wondered how it was possible to be closer with a person she hadn't seen face-to-face in several years than with a person who was relevant to her everyday life right now. The truth was, at certain specific moments, she *did* feel closer to Grace than Jess—when they were talking about something that had happened at camp, or were caught up in the moment of a play-date. But there was a difference between her friendship with Grace—and even her budding friendship with Emily—and the years-long friendship she'd had with Jess. When she spoke to Jess, she was completely relaxed. It was like talking to a sister, someone who had seen her at her best and worst, who had stumbled home with her after a night of too much drinking on M Street or had comforted her after a boyfriend broke up with her. Sometimes Amy wondered if it was possible to make adult friends who would ever know her as completely as her college friends did, especially Jess. There was just so much history with those people, which meant you didn't always need to explain yourself. Then again, sometimes that history got in the way. Amy knew she'd changed since college, and she knew Jess had, too, and yet on some level she knew they both still thought of each other the way they were more than a decade ago.

"What about work? Are you still freelancing?"

"Yeah, I'm not loving it, though. I'm ready to get back into something more substantial."

"I still can't believe you quit your job back in DC. I mean, I totally get it, but you were always such a gunner! I thought you'd be running your own nonprofit by now."

That was the other thing about old friends: They didn't mince words. Amy tried not to feel insulted, but it was hard, especially when she knew Jess was right. "Yeah, well . . . kids," she finally said.

"Trust me, I understand. I wish I could step back and spend more time with ours. But we need the extra income."

She was careful not to add what Amy assumed was the reason, which was that they had two kids and not just one. Jess had always been sensitive to the fact that Noah wasn't an only child by choice.

"So when are you going to visit us?" Amy asked.

"When my kids are old enough to fend for themselves for the weekend?"

Amy laughed. "Seriously—I miss you. I'd love for you to visit."

"We'd love it, too. It's just hard for us right now with the two monsters. But maybe if we could get my parents to visit and then stay on to watch them . . ."

"The kids are welcome to visit, too."

"You say that, but you haven't witnessed one of our dinnertimes. The kids—they're animals. I love them, but honestly, I don't know what we're doing wrong. Penny usually spends most of the meal on the floor, screaming because her blood sugar is low and she is refusing to eat. And Zander . . . whatever. He has his own issues. All I'm saying is, it would be a lot more peaceful and fun without them."

"I think Rob's company might be sponsoring a benefit for a friend of ours in the fall—actually the husband of the woman I mentioned earlier."

"The one who sold you the house?"

"Yeah, I don't know the details, but it could be a fun night out.

Plus, with MediaCom as the sponsor, there might be people Dave wants to talk to for business. Last we talked he was working on some telecom deals."

"Actually . . . yeah. That isn't a bad idea. If I can sell it to Dave as both a social and a business trip, he would probably be on board." She paused. "Oh my God, are we doing this? Are we *actually* going to see each other?"

"I need to get the details on the fall benefit, but assuming that all works out—"

"Don't say any more. I don't want to jinx it."

"Okay, I won't. Let's just think positive."

"Yes, positive. I'll send good vibes into the universe, and you do the same, and hopefully all of those vibes will come back to us."

Amy knew that wasn't how things worked, or at least she didn't think it was, but at this point she was so anxious to see an old friend—a real friend without secrets or boundaries or agendas—that she was willing to give anything a try.

# Chapter 12

Amy didn't actually know much about the Food Fight sponsorship. She didn't even know if Rob's superiors had signed off on it. But he'd run the idea up the chain and seemed to feel positive about the response he'd received, so she felt fairly confident MediaCom would back the event.

Before, she'd hoped the idea would move forward because she wanted to give Julian the second chance her brother never had. But now that the event might entice her best friend to visit, Amy was even more enthusiastic. She hadn't seen Jess in almost three years, and that last encounter was only a brief drink at a bar in DC as Jess passed through on a business trip. Jess was extremely pregnant with Penny at the time—possibly even too pregnant to have been flying, though Jess was the type who wouldn't let pregnancy get in the way of a free trip to her old stomping grounds. The two laughed and commiserated like old times, but before Amy knew it, they were hugging goodbye so that Jess could make her red-eye back to Seattle. Amy remembered feeling like the evening was such a tease. "We need more *time*," they both kept saying. And now, if Jess could fly in for a weekend, they'd get it. Amy tried not to get her hopes up, but she was already getting excited.

For Amy, getting excited about something meant planning, and when she started planning, she ended up chattering at Rob and peppering him with dozens of questions.

"Would we pick them up at the airport? What do we need to do to fix up the guest room? Do you think your parents would babysit both nights so that we could take them out to dinner the night before the event? Or maybe we could use the Durants' sitter. What was her name? Kara?"

And on and on. To most of these questions, Rob would merely shrug, which didn't really bother Amy because most of the questions were just her way of processing her anticipation. But she did want a little more reassurance that the event would actually go forward, and unfortunately, Rob didn't have much useful information.

"I told you," he said, when Amy asked for a status update for what was probably the eleventh time. "I'm not in charge. I sent the information to the team in charge of corporate sponsorships, and they sounded intrigued, but that's the last I heard about it."

"The event is only, like, two and a half months away. I feel like if MediaCom were in, we'd know by now. Don't you think?"

"Maybe? Why don't you ask Grace? I was just the messenger. She probably has more up-to-date information."

Amy conceded this was probably true and rang up Grace that Wednesday while the kids were at camp.

"Your ears must have been burning," Grace said when she picked up the phone.

"Oh, yeah? Why is that?"

"Because I was just telling my mom about the Tim Tam Slam and how I made you and Emily do one on Sunday."

"Aha. Well, in case you couldn't tell, I was a fan."

"Pretty sure the chocolate all over your face was a giveaway. I mean, come on, what's not to like?"

"What's dangerous is how easily they go down once they're all soft and gooey like that. I could easily have eaten five or six that way."

"I think that's kind of the point." She covered the phone and told someone she'd be off in a second. "Sorry, my mom just stopped in." She lowered her voice. "Between you and me, I think she wants us out of here ASAP, so she keeps checking on whether we are still comfortable, mostly by commenting on how cramped we must feel in such a small space."

"Subtle."

Grace laughed. "Trust me, I want us out of here, too, but we need all our ducks in a row before we can do that. We actually found a place in Elkins Park that we like, but there's always a lot of red tape with buying a house. You know how it is. Anyway—sorry, I've totally dominated the conversation, and you're the one who called me. What's up? Everything okay?"

"Oh, yeah, everything's fine. I was just wondering if Julian had heard anything from MediaCom about his fund-raiser."

"Yeah, I thought . . . didn't he call Rob?"

"Not that I know of. Rob said he hadn't heard anything, but he was just the messenger anyway."

"Seriously? I'm going to kill him. Yes, he heard back from the guys at MediaCom, and they liked his proposal. I think they still have to work out the contract, but they're going to sponsor the event."

"That's great!"

"I know." Grace didn't sound as overjoyed as Amy expected.

"Is it . . . I mean, this is a good thing, right?"

"Oh, yeah, of course. No, it's great. Sorry." She paused. Was she still annoyed that Julian hadn't thanked Rob? Amy supposed that was understandable. Rob had stuck his neck out when he didn't have to, and doing so meant the profile of Julian's event would now be raised exponentially. At the very least, Rob deserved to know.

Or had Julian lied to Grace?

"So when do the invitations go out?" Amy asked, trying to chase that last thought from her mind. Because Julian wouldn't *lie* about something like that, would he? Not when it would be so obvious by the time the event rolled around. When there weren't black-and-red MediaCom logos all over the event, it would be pretty obvious they weren't a part of it. And what would be the point of lying, anyway? Grace already knew about his problems and his recovery. It's not as if he had anything to hide.

"In a few weeks. I think part of the sponsorship deal involves the MediaCom logo being on the invitation and response card."

"Ah, got it. Well, I was talking to one of my college friends last night, and she was thinking of coming out to visit this fall. I thought she and her husband might have fun at Julian's event, so I invited them. I hope you don't mind."

"Mind? Why would I mind? The more, the merrier. Every ticket sold means more money for Food Fight's programming."

*Every ticket sold.* A sudden panic swelled in Amy's chest. She knew the event would cost money—obviously. It was a fund-raiser. But in all of the excitement over Jess's visit, she forgot that sometimes tickets to fund-raising events cost a lot of money. Hundreds of dollars—sometimes thousands if the events are targeting a particularly moneyed crowd. Jess and Dave were both lawyers and made good money, but Amy had invited them as her guests, and they'd be spending hundreds of dollars on plane tickets. What if the tickets were $500 each? Could she and Rob really afford to spend $2,000 on a night out? The answer was an unqualified no.

"Great," Amy said. "If you don't mind my asking . . . how much are the tickets . . . ?"

"I'm not sure. Nothing crazy. Maybe seventy-five bucks a head or something like that."

Amy's shoulders relaxed. Seventy-five was doable. It would still mean $300, which was still a very (very) expensive evening out, but this would be for a good cause. Community centers would get money to increase their programming, Julian would get a fresh start, and Dave might even make some professional contacts.

"Definitely put us on the list," Amy said. "Rob and I would love to support you and Julian."

"Thanks," Grace said, and though Amy tried to ignore it, should couldn't help but note the continued lack of enthusiasm in Grace's voice.

"So Julian finally called me today," Rob said as he rested his briefcase on the counter. He loosened his tie and gave Amy a kiss. He always looked thoroughly drained after work these days, but even at his most exhausted, Amy found him utterly adorable. The tie certainly helped. Amy had always had a thing for men in ties, and Rob looked particularly good in one, like her very own James Bond.

"I thought that might happen," she said.

"Why?" He gave Amy a suspicious look. "What did you do?"

"Nothing! I talked to Grace and asked if they'd heard anymore from MediaCom. Apparently they had, and Grace was pissed that Julian hadn't said anything to you about it."

Rob shrugged. "I was only the messenger."

"That's what I said. But come on, it's a little weird that he didn't thank you."

"What's to thank? All I did was get his proposal in front of the right person. It was a seriously low lift on my part." He poured two glasses of water and handed one to Amy.

"Yeah, but for a period of time, you weren't even sure you wanted to do that much, given his history."

"He doesn't know that."

"True. Still, I think a one-sentence e-mail letting you know everything worked out would have been nice. It just seems like common courtesy."

"I don't disagree. But for all I know, he has all sorts of other shit going on, and this fell through the cracks."

Amy took a long sip of water and stared at her husband. "I can't believe I'm more peeved about this than you are. And the fact that you don't seem bothered is making me even *more* peeved, on your behalf."

Rob heaved a sigh. "Do you want me to make some snide, sexist comment about women and emotions and grudges? Is that where you're trying to take this conversation?"

Amy's eyes widened. "No, but since such a comment seems to be right at the tip of your tongue, have at it! By all means."

"Mommy?"

Amy jumped as Noah crept up behind her. He had been playing in the family room, and she didn't know how long he'd been within earshot of their conversation.

"Yes, sweetie?"

"What are you and Daddy talking about?"

"Nothing important. Have you washed your hands? We'll be eating dinner soon."

"You were yelling," he said.

"We weren't . . . we were just having a conversation."

"A . . . what do you call it? A dis . . . a . . . ?"

"Disagreement."

"Yeah."

Amy's and Rob's eyes met. "We weren't really disagreeing," Rob said. "Someone just didn't say thank you to Daddy, and Mommy thinks they should have."

"Saying please and thank you is the nice thing to do," Noah said.

Amy smiled smugly. "That's right."

Rob grinned in spite of himself. "The two of you. Like peas in a pod."

Noah frowned. "Like *peas?* Whaaaaat?"

"It's an expression." Amy tousled his hair. "It means we're alike."

"I'm like Daddy, too. Why can't we be three peas in the pod?"

Rob wrapped his arms around both of them and squeezed them tight. "How's this for a pod?" He kissed the top of Amy's head.

"Oh, I like this pod," Amy said. "I've got my best guys right here with me. Couldn't be better."

"It could maybe be a *tiny* bit better with a puppy," Noah said. Amy's and Rob's eyes caught and rolled in tandem. "And maybe a baby brother."

Amy's smile faded as she looked at Rob again. Noah hadn't brought up a sibling in months, much to her relief. For period of time, from about age three to three and a half, he brought it up almost every day. She knew that was because several kids at his school had become big brothers and sisters, but the constant nagging only added to her stress and frustration. How was she supposed to explain to a three-year-old that acquiring a sibling was not like acquiring a train set? Eventually he started asking only once or twice a week, then once or twice a month. But since the move, he hadn't said a word about it, and Amy assumed he'd given up on the idea, like she and Rob had.

"Sweetie, we've talked about this . . ." Amy said delicately.

"About the pea pod?"

"No, about . . . a baby brother."

"Oh. Yeah, I know." His shoulders slumped.

"Hey, listen—it's cool being the only child. You get all the love from me and Daddy, you never have to worry about anyone taking your toys, you learn to be really independent. And Ethan is an only child, too. How cool is that?"

Noah's eyes brightened. "Maybe Ethan and I could be brothers!"

Amy smiled. "Sometimes when you find a really good friend like that, it feels like having a brother, which is the next best thing."

"Could he come live with us?"

"No, silly—he lives with his parents."

"But I mean if something happens to them."

Amy and Rob gave each other a worried look. "That's not a very nice thing to talk about," Rob said.

"No, no—I just mean if they get in trouble or something and need to go away and can't take Ethan with them, could he stay with us?"

A chill ran through Amy. What was Noah talking about?

"Who said anything about Ethan's parents going anywhere?" Rob asked.

"No, I'm just *saying*. If they *did*."

Amy and Rob were both momentarily at a loss for words. Amy knew this was probably just another instance of Noah's imagination gone wild. He frequently asked what-if questions that strayed into somewhat morbid or inappropriate terrain. "What if you and Daddy die before I'm a grown-up?" "What if I eat a mushroom and it turns out it's poison?" "What if a bee stings me in my eye?" Those were just a few of the questions that had rendered Amy speechless. The *What to Expect* books didn't really prepare you for those sorts of queries, and although Amy eventually came up with suitable answers, they weren't the sort of responses that leapt from the tongue.

"If something did . . . well, he'd probably live with his grandma and grandpa."

And although she knew this isn't the response he was looking for, she kissed him on the head, grabbed the box of spaghetti off the counter, and decided to leave it at that.

Amy and Rob were reading in bed, when Rob put his copy of the latest Harlan Coben novel facedown in his lap.

"Do you think we should get a puppy? Or maybe a kitten?"

Amy's eyes remained glued to *The Hate U Give*. "Absolutely not."

"I don't mean right now . . . although I guess we *could* . . ."

"No."

"I mean in a few years. If the kid can't have a sibling, don't you think we at least owe him that?"

"We don't *owe* him anything, other than the best parenting we can provide, which will enable him to be a fully functioning adult in the real world."

Rob let out a long gust of air. "Well, okay then."

Amy's retort had come out snippier than she'd intended, but any discussion of her inability to provide her son with a brother or sister put her in a foul mood. Even though they'd given up on the idea, talking and thinking about it still stung. The subject made her feel . . . well, like a failure. She'd gotten pregnant with Noah. Why couldn't she do it again? As she'd learned, with "secondary infertility," it didn't matter that she'd conceived once before. In fact that was the point; that's what made it "secondary infertility." She knew that intellectually, and she knew it wasn't anyone's "fault," but emotionally she couldn't help but feel that her body had let her, Rob, and Noah down. About a year ago, they'd discussed the possibility of adoption, but Rob was never entirely on board with the idea. Rob's lack of enthusiasm, combined with the cost and red tape, meant that they'd eventually given up on the possibility of adoption, and of a sibling for Noah. She had nothing against puppies—she'd always loved dogs—but part of her resented feeling like they needed to overcompensate for her fertility woes by buying their toddler a pet.

"I just think," Rob said, after a long pause, "that Noah might really benefit from the companionship, not to mention the responsibility."

"He's four. How much responsibility do you actually expect him to take on?"

"You can build it up over time. And like I said, I don't mean right now. I mean when he's like eight or ten or something."

Amy sighed and put down her book, which she didn't want to do because she had gotten to a really good part. "Okay. I'll think about it. But do not, under any circumstances, say anything to Noah. I haven't said yes, and even if I do, I'd mean in four or five years, and Noah cannot abstract like that."

"Fair enough. Thank you." He leaned over and kissed her temple.

"So now that I'm out of the flow of my story . . . I wanted to ask at dinner, but then with Noah there and his fixation on the Durants' demise . . . what exactly did you and Julian talk about on the phone?"

"Just that he'd heard back from the guy in charge of sponsorships for MediaCom, and the deal was a go. I think they still need to work out some of the contract language, but everything is moving forward. They're giving like ten grand or something."

"Ten grand? Wow."

"Meh. I mean it sounds like a lot, but for a company like Media-Com it's nothing, and to put on a big event like Julian is doing, it's probably a drop in the bucket. He mentioned he has other sponsors and funders lined up, too, although MediaCom will be the only named one."

"I wonder if they'll comp us tickets for helping out. . . ."

Rob gave her major side eye. "Amy. This is a benefit to help poor people. I think we can manage a couple hundred dollars in tickets."

"You're right, you're right. Sorry." She immediately felt awful. She hadn't meant . . . well, she supposed she had meant what she said, but for a minute she'd forgotten what the entire event was about. It was hard for her to see Julian in any context other than "Ethan's dad" or "recovering addict." She had to remind herself that he was a smart, successful director of a nonprofit that tried to get healthy food into poor neighborhoods. He was those other things, too, but they were secondary, at least when it came to this event.

"Anyway, if everything is moving forward, I can start getting serious with Jess about making plans. Gosh it would be great to see her."

Rob reached out and squeezed Amy's hand. "You really miss her, huh?"

"It's just hard to make friends like that as you get older, you know?"

Rob nodded. "But it happens. You're feeling more settled here, right? You've got Grace, and Emily . . ."

"I do. And they're great. But with Emily, it's still that early superficial sort of friendship where you can talk for thirty minutes and still not reveal anything about yourself. And Grace . . . I don't know. She's complicated. Every time I think I get her, I find out something else that alters the picture."

"Isn't that the case with most people? I guess some are open books, but most human beings are complex. The interesting ones, anyway. We only get more so as we get older."

"I know, but I feel guarded around Grace—like I'm afraid to ask too many questions because of what I might find out. I mean, what was that with Noah before dinner?"

"Asking what would happen if Ethan's parents went away?"

"Yeah. That was weird, right? Suddenly I'm thinking, 'Are Grace and Julian planning to make a run for it? Have they done something bad? Is Grace on drugs, too?'"

"Amy, that's crazy."

"I know. But how can I get close to someone when I'm constantly questioning her motives?"

"You can't blame her for your overactive imagination—one you seemed to have passed on to our son, by the way."

She knew he was right. Grace had actually been fairly open with her—about Julian, about her relationship with her mom, about motherhood. But she'd always had the strong sense that beneath the surface, Grace's story was even more complicated, and what she couldn't tell was how much of that was imagined and how much was real.

# Chapter 13

The rest of the summer flew by, and before Amy knew it, she was packing Noah's lunch for his first day at Beth Israel. He started the day after Labor Day, and for the first time, the two of them were equally excited for the school year to begin.

In past years, the start of school ushered in a wave of anxiety on everyone's part. Noah would start complaining about tummy aches, and Amy would fret about him fitting in, and for a good month or so, getting to Bright Futures Academy on time was a painful struggle. The angst didn't only happen at the beginning of the school year either. Anytime there was an extended vacation—winter break, spring break, a week of illness—the process started all over again. Amy was never sure who hated it more: her or Noah.

But this year was completely different. Noah already had two close friends in his class, and he probably knew more, since there was apparently a big overlap between Beth Israel and Green Hills Day Camp. And more than that, Noah was *happy*. He'd bounded into the meet-and-greet the week before and introduced himself to his teacher, Miss Karen, with a smile that took up his entire face.

"Ethan and Jake are coming, *too*!" he'd informed her, so giddy he nearly knocked over the can of paintbrushes.

Ever since, he had been talking about his new school to anyone who would listen: her, Rob, random people at the grocery store.

Amy adored his enthusiasm and only hoped the preschool could live up to his expectations. She'd only signed him up for three days a week, with the understanding that she could always bump him up to four or five days later, if the budget allowed for it.

"Noah!" Amy called up the stairs. "You ready?"

She had lain out his clothes the night before, and he had insisted that he wanted to get dressed and brush his teeth without assistance. As excited as he was, she knew he was also a little nervous, and the ritual of getting dressed probably calmed him down.

He appeared at the top of the stairs, his arms lifted to the sky. "Ready," he said.

She knew she was heavily biased, but she thought he was the cutest four-year-old she'd ever seen. He was wearing the green plaid shorts and gray polo shirt they'd picked out together, and his strawberry-blond tresses were combed neatly to the side. He'd obviously wet and brushed them and seemed pretty pleased with himself.

"You are *the* handsomest boy I've ever seen," she said as he marched down the stairs.

"Handsomer than Daddy?"

"Hmm, I'd say you're tied. Frankly, with your hair like that, you look an awful lot like Daddy. Only about thirty years younger."

"Thirty-*two*," Noah corrected her.

"Right. Thirty-two." Sometimes she forgot what a stickler her son was when it came to numbers.

Amy ushered Noah into the kitchen, where a piece of buttered toast and a glass of milk were waiting for him. He scarfed down the toast before Amy even finished packing his backpack, and the next thing she knew, they were in the car, heading to school.

The drive was short, and they didn't talk much. Amy had to bite her tongue to keep from making conversation, but she knew her son, and he needed this time to process. She could almost see the wheels turning as she glanced in the rearview mirror. He stared out of the window, watching the houses and trees go by.

When they got to school, Amy held Noah's hand as they walked from the parking lot to the entrance. His soft hand held hers tight, and she took a deep breath and tried to savor the moment. She knew someday he wouldn't want to hold her hand in public, and sometime after that, he wouldn't need to anymore. She tried not to be overly sentimental about moments like this, but she couldn't help herself.

"Good morning, Noah!" Miss Ruth crowed as they entered the school. Miss Ruth was the director of Beth Israel's preschool and so far had lived up to all the kind things Grace had said about her. She was enthusiastic, warm, and, most of all, present. From what Amy had heard, she greeted the kids at the door every morning, checked on each class all day, and stayed until the last child went home. She also regularly wandered the hall with her guitar, which was strapped to her at this very moment.

"Good morning," Noah said, a little shyly.

"Are you ready for your *big* first day?"

He nodded without saying anything. Amy suddenly felt a little anxious. Was this day not going to go as smoothly as she'd hoped?

"Miss Karen is very excited to see you. She's waiting in room four with your friends."

Noah brightened. "Ethan and Jake are here?"

"I haven't seen Jake yet, but Ethan just arrived a minute ago."

Before Amy or Ruth could say anything else, Noah took off for room four. Amy put his backpack in his cubby, and by the time she entered the classroom, Noah had already found Ethan, and the two were building some sort of tower.

"Well, that didn't take long."

Amy whirled around and saw Grace standing behind her, smiling.

"So much for a transition period, right?"

Amy laughed. "I didn't even get to walk him into the class. As soon as he heard Ethan was here, he raced in without me."

"Good for him. Look at him. Fits right in."

Amy could hardly believe it, but Grace was right. Noah was acting like he'd gone to Beth Israel for years. She'd definitely made the right choice in sending him here. She was also very glad she'd savored the feeling of his hand in hers because at this rate, he'd be dissing her by next week.

"Have you ladies signed your boys in?"

Miss Karen appeared next to them and extended a clipboard. Both Grace and Amy initialed the appropriate boxes.

"Here is the information about pizza day, which begins tomorrow. It's every Wednesday, $160 for the year. If you're interested, you can send this form in with them tomorrow with a check."

Amy took the form. "Noah loves pizza. . . ."

"It's the most popular day of the week. Everyone loves pizza day."

Amy slid the paper in her purse and crept toward Noah. "Bye, sweetie. Have a good day."

He came and gave her a quick hug and then scampered back to Ethan. Amy took the opportunity to slide out of the classroom without too much of a scene.

"That was easy," Grace said, as she came up beside her. "Usually the first day is a little tearful, even for the stalwarts. But our boys barely noticed we were there."

"That's a good thing, right?"

"That's what I'm telling myself, anyway."

"So do you guys sign up for pizza day? What's the deal with that?"

"We usually do. We did last year. Ethan loves it. But I don't know about this year . . . We're trying to cut some corners, given everything that's going on. I mean, a hundred and sixty bucks isn't going to keep us from buying a house, but Julian has been pretty adamant about keeping costs down. I could ask my parents, but I'm sick of going to them for things and don't want to do it anymore. Ethan won't like it, but he'll survive."

"Do most people sign up?"

"Pretty much everybody, yeah."

"Well, I could just pack lunch for Noah so that Ethan isn't the odd man out."

"Are you kidding? I mean, that's incredibly sweet, but don't make your kid suffer on our account. It's fine—give the kid some pizza! Ethan will just have to deal."

Amy thought about it. A hundred and sixty bucks wasn't that much. Three hundred and twenty was more, but if she could spread it over the year, like every month or so. . . . Rob might not go for it, but then Rob wouldn't understand. Amy knew what it was like to be left out of the fun because she couldn't afford it. She hadn't had the experience at Ethan's age—in Woonsocket, all of her classmates were generally in the same working class boat—but she had in college. At Georgetown, it seemed as if money really did grow on trees, and Amy had somehow missed out on the harvest. More than once, Amy had to turn down a social invitation—which killed her, given her history—because she didn't have the money to spend at an M Street tapas joint or cocktail lounge. Ethan was too young to understand about income and expenses, but he wasn't too young to feel left out. Why not do something about that if she could? He was Noah's best friend. Noah would buy him the pizza himself if he could.

"You know what—I forgot, I have to talk to Ruth about something," Amy said as they were halfway to the parking lot.

"Oh—okay. No prob. I'll see you at pickup, I guess. Is Noah staying until three?"

"Yep. See you then!"

Then she turned around and headed for Ruth's office so that she could figure out a way to pay for Ethan's pizza.

Amy worked out a deal with Ruth where instead of paying $160 for Ethan up front, she would pay in eight installments of $20, which meant Rob would be less likely to ask about it. She didn't *want* to keep it a secret from Rob, but she could already see the eye roll and hear his objections. He wouldn't care about the money per se; he would care that they were further entangling their lives with the Durants. But Amy had taken a shine to Ethan, and it just seemed so unfair for him to be the only kid in the class who couldn't have pizza.

The question now was how to break the news to Grace. She could keep it a secret and just have Ruth say there'd been an oversubscription, so there was plenty for Ethan. But Grace could always say no thank you and send a packed lunch in with Ethan anyway. Or she could tell Grace some vague version of the truth ("I worked out a deal with Ruth so that Ethan could have pizza, too."), but Grace might be annoyed with Amy for meddling. There was no right answer.

In the end, Amy decided to go with some variation of the latter option. Flat-out lying to Grace would only end in disaster, and there was really no upside for either of them. So when she arrived at pickup at three, she called out to Grace as soon as she spotted her walking into the building.

"Oh, hey," Grace said. She sounded a little harried. "Sorry, I didn't even see you."

They walked toward the entrance together, and Amy tried to find a good opportunity to pipe up about the pizza. She didn't want to say anything once they were inside, and she certainly didn't want to say anything in front of the kids.

"So . . . funny story." Was it funny? Not really. Not remotely, actually. But it was the sort of stock phrase people led with before getting into uncomfortable territory. "I was in Ruth's office today, getting more details about the pizza program, and I asked if I threw in a few extra bucks if that would cover pizza for the whole class. She said it probably would, so I went ahead and wrote her a check. So Ethan can have pizza after all!"

Grace slowed her step. "You're paying for Ethan's pizza?"

"No. I mean, sort of. Just . . . you know, extra pizza for the class so that no one feels left out." It wasn't the real story, but Amy was quickly realizing the real story would not go over well.

Grace furrowed her brow. "If all they needed was a few extra bucks, then why are they charging all of us $160?"

"I . . . think that's probably for overhead and stuff. I'm sure it's a scale issue."

"Huh. Well, thanks, I guess. Ethan will be thrilled."

"Don't mention it. I know what it's like to be on a tight budget. That pretty much describes every year we lived in DC."

"It's sort of a first for me, to be honest. We've always had a budget, like most people, but we never really had to worry about the occasional hundred bucks. This is definitely . . . different."

"Well, if you ever need anything else—money for a class trip or a class dinner or something—just let me know."

She stopped in front of the school entrance. "We're not *poor*," she said.

"I never said . . . I didn't mean it like that. All I was saying was that if you need help from a friend—"

"Got it," she said, then opened the door and walked inside.

"And THEN, after lunch we found a ladybug, and Miss Karen put her in a special house, and we all got to look at her with a special glass."

"A magnifying glass?"

"Uh-huh. We could see EVERYTHING."

Noah had been talking nonstop ever since Amy had picked him up. At first she had welcomed the runaway chatter because it distracted from the palpable frostiness emanating from Grace in waves. But now her ears were going numb. She could barely keep up.

"And Miss Karen has so many math games—like seven thousand of them."

"Seven thousand sounds like an awful lot."

"Maybe just fourteen. I can't remember. But it's a LOT."

"Sounds right up your alley."

Had covering Ethan's pizza bill been a huge mistake? It had seemed like such a good idea at the time—a gesture born out of kindness, not pity. But now she wished she'd just minded her own business. She barely had any friends here. The last thing she needed was to alienate her closest one.

Amy pulled in their driveway and got Noah out of his car seat. On the way inside, she checked the mail. There were three bills for Julian, all with the words "PAST DUE" in bold red lettering. The notices had started slowing to one or two a week, but in the last week or so, the volume had picked up again, and now Amy was finding letters for him nearly every day.

"Mommy, are you listening?"

"Uh-huh," she lied. She was too distracted by the assortment of threatening mail meant for the Durants. She shuffled them to the back of the pile. She'd give them to Grace at drop-off or pickup tomorrow.

"Mo-MMEEE." Noah stamped his foot as Amy opened the front door.

"Don't raise your voice at me."

"But you're not *listening*."

"Yes, I am."

"Tell me what did I say?"

"You said . . ." Amy was at a loss. He was right: She hadn't been listening. "Sorry, I forget."

He let out an exasperated sigh. "I *said*, can I have a yogurt tube for a snack?"

"Oh, sure. Let me just put all this stuff down. Go wash your hands."

Noah rushed toward the bathroom, and Amy made for the kitchen, where she laid the mail on the counter. On top was a big envelope addressed to her and Rob. She flipped it over. The return address was printed on the upper flap: It was from Food Fight.

Amy tore open the envelope to find a simple, tastefully designed invitation: Food Fight's Fall Fund-raiser ("sponsored by MediaCom").

"Say that four times fast," Amy muttered to herself.

"Say what?" Noah snuck up behind her.

"Food Fight's Fall Fund-raiser."

"Food's Fall Fightraiser." He laughed. "Say it again?"

She tousled his hair. "Food Fight's Fall Fund-raiser. It's an event for Ethan's daddy's company."

"What does it do?"

"The event? Or his company?"

"Both."

"Well, his company helps poor people get healthier food, and the event raises money so that he can help more people."

"How?"

"How do they raise money?"

"Yeah."

"Well, for Daddy and I to go, we have to pay for tickets, so some of that money will help. And a lot of times at events like these, they have auctions, where people offer to pay money for certain prizes."

"PRIZES?" Noah's eyes lit up. "What kind of prizes?"

"It depends on the event. But a lot of times it's something like dinner at a nice restaurant or a gift certificate to a spa or something like that."

"Oh." Noah looked thoroughly unimpressed.

"Yeah, it's mostly adult stuff. Sorry. But I promise if I see anything you'd like, Daddy and I will bid on it."

"Is it tonight?"

Amy laughed. Only in a four-year-old's mind could an invitation received today be for an event tonight. "No, it's not until November."

"Can I come?"

"No, it's for adults only."

"Awwww!" He crossed his arms over his chest. "I want to come, *too*."

"Trust me, it wouldn't be your thing."

"Then what am I going to do?"

"We have two months to figure that out. But I'm guessing either Bubbe and Zayde will babysit, or maybe Kara."

"From Ethan's?"

"Yep."

His mood brightened. "Can I sleep at Ethan's again?"

Amy was tempted to clarify that last time he hadn't actually spent the night at Ethan's; they'd brought him home after he'd fallen asleep. But she didn't want to argue over details that didn't really matter.

"We'll see. I have to discuss all of this with his mommy." *Assuming she's still talking to me.*

"Okay." His eyes drifted toward the refrigerator. "Can I have my yogurt tube now?"

"Of course."

She settled him in with his snack and sorted through the rest of the mail—bills, junk, a few catalogs. She put the Food Fight invitation to the side and snapped a quick photo of it, which she proceeded to send to Jess.

The event is a go! You guys in?

Last she heard, Jess's parents were able and willing to fly out at some point in the fall to see the kids and watch them for a weekend. Amy only hoped the offer stood.

She put the invitation on top of her pile next to the refrigerator. Rob always called it her GDS (for "Get Shit Done") pile, but lately shit didn't seem to be getting done. The pile was now several pieces of paper thick—fund-raising requests from the Georgetown and Yale alumni societies, appeals from local charities, coupons from stores that (hopefully) hadn't expired. She always paid medical bills and other important invoices right away. But somehow all the requests for donations had piled up this month. Maybe it was because she knew she'd be donating $300 to Julian's charity—and probably more the night of the event. Or maybe it was because she felt like she'd be throwing money at the house and her family (and even the Durants) lately, and she needed to put a few things aside for now to keep her financial anxiety in check.

"Sometimes mommies and daddies fight, and that's okay," Noah said.

Amy turned around and looked at him. Where had *that* come from? "Did you talk about that in school today . . . ?"

He shook his head as he slurped the last of his yogurt tube. "No."

Amy racked her brain. Had she and Rob said something in front of him recently? She couldn't think of anything. They rarely fought, and they certainly never did in front of him. The last time they'd had a disagreement was about a month ago, about Julian's delayed call to Rob, and frankly that wasn't even really a fight. More like a difference of opinion.

"Then where did you . . . why are you worried about mommies and daddies fighting?"

"I'm not. I'm just saying. It's okay if they do sometimes."

"That's true. Mommy and Daddy don't really fight, though. We occasionally disagree, but we still love each other very much."

"I know."

"Because you can be upset with someone and still love them. Just like when I sometimes get upset with you. I still love you—I always love you."

He rolled his eyes like a cranky teenager. "I know."

"Hey, you're the one who brought it up."

"I didn't. *Ethan* did."

"Ethan isn't here."

"No, at *school.*"

Amy's antennae went up. "He did? What did he say?"

His expression brimmed with exasperation. "That sometimes mommies and daddies fight, and that's okay!" By his tone, he might as well have said, *Haven't you been paying attention, you idiot?*

"Did he say anything else?"

"No, just that."

"You're sure?"

He pressed his hands to his temples. He looked entirely fed up with her. "Mommy, seriously. Yes."

"Okay, sorry. I was just checking." Because it now seemed that Grace's sour mood at pickup may have had nothing to do with Amy at all.

# Chapter 14

She didn't see Grace at drop-off the next day. Ethan wasn't in the class when Noah arrived, and after lingering for a few minutes after she signed him in, Amy decided she was better off running into Grace another time. What would she say, anyway? *Are you and Julian having problems?* In front of Miss Karen and all the kids? Please. If she weren't already on Grace's shit list, she would be after that.

As she returned to her car, she saw she had three alerts on her phone. The first was a text from Jess.

WE ARE SO IN! OMG THIS IS HAPPENING! I'll look at flights today. Will let you know. Xo

Amy looked at the time stamp: 9:01 a.m. That meant Jess must have texted at 6:01 her time—a reasonable time for a lawyer with two kids to be up, but earlier than Amy had arisen in months. She had to admit, as much as she missed aspects of working in an office—the camaraderie, the regular paycheck, the title—she did not miss having to wake up extra early so that she could get to work on time. Noah was also a great sleeper and regularly slept until 7:30 or 8:00. Part of her couldn't imagine going back to waking several times in the night with an infant, or taking a gamble on a kid who regularly chose 5:45 as a wake-up time. She knew this was partly a self-preservation mechanism on her part (she had no idea what time Penny woke and whether she had anything to do with Jess's early morning text), but it worked, and she wasn't going to fight it.

The second alert was a reminder that she had a call at 10:30 with the organization for whom she was drafting fall conference materials. They wanted to go over format and content, and Amy had a few questions of her own that she wanted to bring up. Even though the pay was abysmal, she'd taken the gig mostly because she believed in the organization's mission. Well, that and the fact that she didn't want a huge hole in her résumé. Part of her felt that as long as she was working on *something*, she was more likely to find another project or job she liked better. It hadn't worked out that way so far, but she was eternally optimistic.

The final alert was another reminder, only this one made her stomach sour:

### Call Timmy

She'd plugged a reminder into her phone last night when she was feeling a twinge of guilt for not having spoken to him in so long. But seeing the note in front of her now, she couldn't think of anything she'd rather do less. It wasn't that she didn't want to talk to him. It was more that she was . . . well, scared. It had been so long. Almost three years, when she thought about it. She missed Tim and wanted him to get better, but she really wasn't sure she could travel down that treacherous emotional path again.

The last time they talked was shortly after Tim met Noah for the first time. She and Rob had taken a summer road trip to Woonsocket with Noah, so that he could spend time with his Mimi and meet Uncle Timmy. Amy's mom had already met Noah on several occasions, but that was because the Kravitzes had paid for her to fly to Washington. Tim never made his way down, though, and both he and Ellen gave various excuses as to why not. They were all legitimate—the most salient being his probation-related travel restrictions due to a drug charge earlier that year—but it meant that her brother still hadn't met his nephew after more than a year.

She knew something was off when they finally met. He seemed distracted and aloof, like he hadn't gotten enough sleep or was stressed about work. But for Amy, the telltale sign was his eyes. It was always the eyes. When Tim was a kid, and even through high school, his eyes could tell stories. They danced and sparkled, the magnetism of their green-flecked irises drawing people in and refusing to let go. There was a bit of mischief in those eyes, too, a twinkle that used to make Ellen say, "That boy's got a bit of the devil in him." She'd say it with a smile because she didn't mean it, not really. His eyes told you he was up for a good time, but also that he'd never hurt a soul. As it turned out, the only person he'd hurt was himself.

But when Amy saw Tim on that visit, his eyes were dead. There was no life behind them—no joy, but no mischief either. Just . . . nothing. It was hard to explain to someone who didn't know him. By then, he'd gotten very good at hiding his addiction. He wasn't lying strung-out on the couch, a trickle of drool running from the corner of his mouth. Until things got bad, he could fake it pretty well. But he couldn't fake the eyes. The second she saw him, she knew he'd started using again.

She spent the trip building up courage to say something. She'd been through this enough times to know that attacking him or coming out aggressively would only work against both of them. She also knew that unless he truly wanted to get better, nothing she said would make a bit of difference.

Then one morning Rob had taken Noah for a walk in the stroller while Amy showered and dried her hair. Her mom was at work (she wasn't able to take the whole week off and needed to put in two days while they were there), and Tim was sleeping in the basement. According to Ellen, he'd been staying with her for two months, while he looked for another apartment. His former landlord sold the building and the new owner jacked up the rent, so he couldn't afford it anymore. At least that was the story.

When Amy went to dry her hair, the circuit breaker tripped, and all the lights in her bedroom went out. The outlets didn't work either. This had happened to her before—the wiring in her mom's house was in desperate need of an upgrade—and it usually required a quick visit to the electrical panel in the basement, where she could flick the breaker back into place.

She scurried downstairs, not thinking to knock before she entered the basement, and when she got to the bottom of the steps, she found Tim sitting on the basement couch, sticking a needle in his arm.

"Are you KIDDING me?" she shouted before she could stop herself. She'd wanted to approach him with love and kindness, without judgment or aggression, but the shock of the situation took a match to whatever plans she'd had. She wasn't surprised, in the sense that she already suspected he was using again. But catching him in the act—that had never happened before. And for it to happen under the roof where her one-year-old was living and sleeping . . . she was furious. What if Noah found some bits of paraphernalia when he was toddling around? They never took him into the basement, but still. If Tim was willing to be so brazen to shoot up in his mother's house—the mother who'd paid for his rehab stints and sacrificed so much to help him get better—then anything was possible.

"Ame, I'm sorry—I just . . . I need help again."

At that moment, she was so furious with him that she wanted to tell him to fuck off, that he was on his own. Instead, she flipped the breaker and took a few deep breaths before turning around to face him. "You want help? You're going to get it."

As soon as Rob and Noah got back to the house, she sent them back to DC. She stayed on for the next two weeks while Tim detoxed and got back into a program. She visited him every day, saw him through every grueling step, and watched the life return back into his eyes. Sherrie had come to DC to watch Noah, so Amy knew her son was in good hands, but she missed him terribly. She'd never been away from him for more than a few hours. But as she watched her brother get sober, she knew the sacrifice had been worth it. He told her every day how thankful he was for her, how important it was to him that she was there for him. In some ways, she felt closer to him at the end of those two weeks than she ever had. On her last day, he hugged her and said, "I'll make you proud this time. I promise."

Three months later, she got a call from her mom. Tim hadn't

come home the night before, and she was worried. He showed up the next day, strung out and filthy. He was using again.

He called Amy shortly after that to apologize, to tell her it was just a brief relapse, but that he was going to get back on track. At the time, Amy couldn't pinpoint what she was feeling. It wasn't anger. It wasn't pity. It was a deep, crushing sadness she hadn't quite experienced before.

She didn't say much, just wished him well and hung up the phone. Later, she realized what she was feeling. It was heartbreak.

Now, she looked down at the reminder on her phone. "Call Timmy." Her thumb hovered over the reminder.

"Not today," she said to herself, then slid the phone into her purse and unlocked the car door.

At pickup that afternoon, Amy ran for the door as another mother opened it. The building had self-locking doors and required a key fob for entry, and Amy realized she'd left the fob at home. She'd been meaning to attach it to her keychain, but in an uncharacteristic bout of laziness still hadn't done it yet.

"Could you hold that?" she called out. She was far enough away that she wasn't sure she'd make it.

The mother turned around, and Amy realized it was Emily. She was wearing a denim shift dress, and her honey-blond hair spilled over her shoulders in long waves.

"Hey," Emily said, smiling. "How's it going?"

"Good. Sorry—I didn't even realize it was you. I've never seen you with your hair down. It looks great."

"Yeah, occasionally I manage to pull myself together. Don't get used to it—I'll probably be back in gym clothes and ponytails tomorrow."

Amy laughed. "Please. If I manage to brush my hair, it's a good day."

She followed Emily inside and made for Noah's classroom. The hallways were decorated with cheerful "back-to-school" pictures and crafty projects: trees with apples featuring the children's names, colorful books with children's names on the cover, a wall full of bedazzled kites. The school was such a welcoming place.

"So I was thinking—we should get the boys together again," Emily said before they stepped foot in the classroom.

"Definitely. Noah would love that. Ethan, too, I'm sure."

"Oh, I meant . . . well, I guess Ethan could come, too, depending. I was thinking more just Noah. But whatever works."

"We're fine with anything. I just noticed that Jake and Ethan seem to get along really well."

"They do—of course. I mean, my God, they were inseparable in the two-year-old class and most of last year. But then, well—"

"Mommy!"

Jake came running out of the classroom. Amy figured he must have heard them talking. She found it amazing how in tune kids could be to their own parents' voices.

"Hi, sweetie. I was just talking to Noah's mommy about scheduling another playdate. Would you like that?"

"Could Ethan come, too?"

"We'd have to ask Ethan's mommy about that. But Noah would love to get together!"

"See if Ethan can come, too."

Amy tried not to take it personally that Jake seemed to prefer a diluted version of her kid. It made sense, given how long he'd known Ethan. There was probably some territorial stuff going on, too. She'd seen it countless times over the years—as a kid herself and as an adult. Three was almost always a crowd, and there was usually a favorite, in this case Ethan. The two other people both wanted to be the "best" friend of the favorite, and the favorite was either completely unaware of his or her role, or aware but uninterested in doing anything to change the dynamic. She foresaw some tears on the horizon.

"I'll check, but in the meantime, let's plan on something this weekend. Maybe Saturday?"

"That works for us," Amy said.

"Ask Ethan's mommy—she's right there!" Jake cried.

They turned around and saw Grace walking through the glass doors to the school. She'd changed since that morning and was now dressed in wide-legged linen pants and a loose tank top. Her long, almost black hair was tied into a low side ponytail.

"Hey . . ." Grace said cautiously. Amy realized they were all staring at her.

"We were just talking about you," Amy said, by way of explanation. As soon as the words came out, though, she realized they only made the situation more awkward.

"Uh-oh," Grace said. "That doesn't sound good."

"No—nothing bad. It's just . . . we were talking—"

"Can Ethan play Saturday with me and Noah?" Jake cut in. Amy was relieved to have him do the explaining for her.

"This Saturday?"

"It's totally fine if you guys are busy," said Emily. "I know it's short notice. I'm sure you have a zillion things going on."

The way Emily said it made it sound as if she almost hoped they wouldn't come.

"We can't do Saturday. Sorry. But thanks for the invitation."

"Speaking of invitations, we got ours for the fund-raiser," Amy said. "They look great."

Amy assumed both Emily and Grace would appreciate the topic change, but their expressions indicated otherwise.

"Are you and Julian throwing a party?" Emily asked. She tried to sound friendly and curious, but a hint of resentment bubbled below the surface.

"It's Food Fight's Fall Fund-raiser."

"Well, *that's* a mouthful."

"That's what I keep telling Julian. Anyway, Amy's husband, Rob, helped Julian bring on MediaCom as a sponsor, so we added them to the guest list. If you and Brent are interested, I can add you, too."

"I don't want to cause any trouble."

"It isn't trouble." The tone in Grace's voice made it sound like it actually was. "It's a fund-raiser. The more people the better."

"Okay, well, go ahead and add us to the mailing list. I can't make any promises—you know how weird Brent can be about making plans—but it's always nice to be invited."

Amy wasn't sure why the conversation had gotten so uncomfortable and confrontational, and she also wasn't sure why Grace and Julian hadn't invited everyone in the whole school, or at least the parents they vaguely knew. If it was a situation where more people meant more money, then why hadn't they invited everyone they'd ever met? And who *had* they invited, other than Rob and Amy?

"My friends are actually flying in from Seattle to come. They're super excited."

"Wow, even people from across the country got an invitation?" The unspoken postscript being, *And I didn't?*

"They're my 'plus twos'—my best friend from college and her husband. I haven't seen her in years, and we figured this would be a fun thing to do together when they come out to visit."

"The more the merrier, right, Grace?"

Amy hated being in the middle of whatever was going on between the two of them, so instead of digging herself deeper in a hole, she decided to leave.

"Ah, Noah, there you are!" she said, grabbing his lunchbox and backpack. "Come on, time to go home."

"Can I play on the playground for a little bit?"

"Not today, sweetie."

"Why *not?*" he whined.

*Because I've walked into an awkward situation and want to eject myself from it as soon as possible?*

"Because we have stuff to do," she said.

"Stuff? What stuff?"

It was times like this when Amy wished her curious, inquisitive son would mind his own business. What did it matter what stuff? She was the mom. She was in charge! Why couldn't he just go along for the ride?

"Well, first of all, I still have to pick up stuff for dinner."

"Let's get pizza."

Amy wanted to explode. *Can you not see the ferocity in my eyes, child? Are you blind? Do you not see that I need you to SHUT YOUR MOUTH?*

"Mommy is trying to be a little healthier lately," she lied. She'd had Nutella on toast as a snack an hour earlier. "I'd rather not do pizza tonight."

"Please?"

"We're actually going straight home today, too," Grace said.

Amy wasn't sure if this was true, or if Grace had just decided that on the spot, but either way, Amy was relieved and grateful.

"Awwww." Noah crossed his arms and sighed. "Fine. Let's go."

She walked with him down the hallway, and as she looked over her shoulder, she caught Grace's eye and mouthed, "Thank you."

"No problem," Grace mouthed back, and as they gave each other a quick smile, Amy noticed the only one who wasn't smiling was Emily, who'd been watching them the entire time.

That Saturday, the doorbell rang while Amy was in the powder room.

"Coming!" she shouted. It had to be Emily, and if it was, she was early.

She dried her hands quickly and hurried down the hallway to the front door. Through the panes of glass lining the sides, she could see Jake, his eyes cast at the ground. He didn't look particularly eager to meet up with Noah. The word "sullen" came to mind.

"I hope it's okay that we're a few minutes early," Emily said as Amy opened the door.

"It's fine! We're just hanging out. Hey, Noah?" She called toward the family room, where she'd left Noah before popping into the bathroom. "I think he's watching TV. Come on in."

She ushered them into the house and down the hallway, the audio from the TV becoming louder as they approached the family room.

"Hey, Noah—Jake is here."

Noah tore his eyes from the screen and waved shyly. "Hi."

"What are you watching?" Emily asked, in an overly friendly tone that worried Amy. Something told her Jake had done little to encourage this playdate.

"*Ready Jet Go!*"

"Oooh, that's a new one for us."

"I don't like that show," Jake said.

"What? Don't be ridiculous—you've never even seen it!"

"Yes, I have, and I don't like it."

Emily's cheeks flushed. "Jake, you're being silly. Just—"

"The kids don't need to watch TV. Frankly they probably shouldn't. Noah, sweetie, why don't you turn that off and show Jake some of the toys in your room."

"But it isn't over yet," he whined.

"I know, but Jake doesn't really like it. We can always record it so you can finish watching it later."

"But I want to watch it *now*."

"Noah."

"I'm really sorry," Emily said, wringing her hands. She looked at her watch. "Jake, there are only about five minutes left anyway. Just watch it until it's over and then you can play something else."

"I don't *want* to."

"Jake."

He sighed loudly and stomped over to the opposite side of the couch from where Noah was sitting. "Fine."

He collapsed onto the cushion, his arms folded across his chest. Amy wasn't sure who was being a bigger pain, but they were both acting like little jerks.

"Oh, thank God," Emily said as she and Amy left the boys and made for the kitchen. "I have no idea what's gotten into him, but ever since he woke up this morning, it's like something crawled up his ass and died."

"Been there."

"It makes you want to sell them on the street, right? I mean, seriously." She pulled a box from her bag. "Mind if I stick these in your freezer? I bought some yogurt pops for the boys."

"Sure—that sounds great."

Emily nestled the pops between a bag of frozen peas and a box of chicken nuggets. "The house looks great," she said as she looked around. "A lot more traditional than the Durants had done it up, but then it's a traditional house. You've done a really nice job."

It hadn't even occurred to Amy that Emily would have already spent time at 120 Sycamore—on numerous occasions, most likely. She knew she shouldn't feel self-conscious about how her style compared (or didn't) to Grace's, but she did, as was always the case when it came to Grace. Why did she care? And why couldn't she just accept that Grace was more stylish and design-savvy than she was without allowing it to translate into her own character flaw? Different people were good at different things. She didn't look at Stephen Hawking and feel like a failure because she hadn't contributed to the theory of relativity. Why couldn't she just acknowledge that Grace was better at decorating and leave it at that?

She knew why: Because as progressive as she was, there was still some unspoken understanding that styling one's home was something that middle-class women were supposed to be good at. This wasn't some idea spun by conservative bloggers in a particular corner of the Internet. It was something promoted—wordlessly, but consistently—by women she knew from all different phases of her life, from all different backgrounds. Having a messy or unfashionable home still reflected on the woman of the house, even if she was just as overworked and uninterested in the domestic arts as her husband. No one expected Rob to know how to decorate a living room, but somehow she was supposed to know, and more than know, she was supposed to be interested. Well, she wasn't. Not really. She wanted things to look nice, and she hated clutter, but she didn't really care, not the way Grace obviously did. But then when faced with a direct comparison—120 Sycamore under Grace vs. 120 Sycamore under Amy, Grace's outfit vs. Amy's outfit—she suddenly did care, not so much about the style itself, but more about the gaping character flaw that put her in last place. It was bullshit, and she knew it, but somehow she couldn't overcome her feelings of domestic inadequacy.

"Thanks," Amy said, suppressing the insecurities of her interior monologue. "We haven't changed all that much, structure-wise. They did a great job of keeping up the house."

"Yeah, well, that's Grace and Julian for you. Anything house-related? Grace loves it. Pinterest was invented for her, I swear."

Amy laughed. "So it sounds like you two spent a lot of time together . . . ?"

She didn't want to pry—okay, she did. Frankly the tension between them was killing her. It had become obvious that something had gone down between Grace and Emily, and Amy was dying to know what it was.

"We did," Emily said. "Like I said, two years ago the kids were inseparable, so we hung out a lot."

"Did the kids fall out or something?"

"The kids? Oh my God, not at all. Jake adored Ethan. It was more . . . well, I don't really know how to explain it. The Durants just stopped . . . being available. Like, I'd ask if Ethan could come play, and he never could. And Brent and I used to go out with Grace and Julian all the time, but all of a sudden they were never free. After hearing 'no' a dozen or so times, I stopped asking. And that was sort of that—until the other weekend when you guys came over."

"Did she ever explain why?"

"Nope, that's what kills me. I keep thinking . . . did I do something? Say something? I racked my brain for weeks. I even e-mailed her to see what was going on because I missed her. Nothing. So in end I said, fuck her." She craned her neck to make sure the boys hadn't heard, but they were still in the family room, out of earshot. "Sorry. Potty mouth. Anyway, that's as much as I know. So you can see why I was a little hesitant to throw her and Ethan into the mix again. There's something up with her. I mean, who just ghosts a friend like that?"

Amy knew why, and she desperately wanted to say something to Emily. *It wasn't you! It was Julian's addiction! She was embarrassed!* She'd seen her mother and brother do the same thing over the years. Embarrassment and shame were the ugly stepsisters of addiction, and they had pushed away dozens of friends over the years, too humiliated and blinkered to realize they needed those people most of all.

"Mommy?" Jake tugged on Emily's shirt.

"Hey, sweetie, what's up? Is the show over?"

"Yeah. Can we go home now?"

"Home? We just got here!"

"I know, but I want to go."

"Jake, you're being silly."

"I liked this house better when it was Ethan's," he snapped back.

Amy felt as if she'd been smacked in the face. Emily's eyes went wild.

"*Jacob Benjamin.*"

Jake scowled. "Sorry. Can we just go?"

"We haven't even had our yogurt pops yet."

"Can we go after yogurt pops then?"

Emily's cheeks were pink. She tightened her jaw. "Let's just have the yogurt pops, okay? We can talk about going later."

She went for the freezer, and though part of Amy felt deeply wounded that Jake so obviously didn't want to play with her son today, she was also a little relieved that Emily might leave sooner rather than later. It wasn't her place to say anything about the Durants and the reason behind their aloofness, but the longer Emily lingered, the harder it would be not to tell her the truth, and Amy didn't trust herself to keep her mouth shut.

# Chapter 15

To Amy's surprise, Noah didn't show any hesitation when he awoke for school the following Monday. It was his first day back following the Emily and Jake debacle, which had ended with Jake stomping off with arms crossed after they had been playing T-ball outside. Emily had cajoled him into staying after the boys finished their yogurt pops, but the rest of the afternoon was an emotional roller coaster. One minute the boys were playing nicely; the next, Jake was crying or demanding to go home. Amy was much older than Noah when her social life went pear shaped, but if it were her, she'd be uneasy about going to school the Monday after such a rocky get-together. But Noah bounced out of bed that morning as enthusiastic and cheerful as ever.

"Someone's in a good mood," Amy said as he hummed his way through his Cheerios.

"Today is bounce day."

"Oh. Right." She'd forgotten. The school had rented a bounce house for the day, and each class would have a chance to use it at recess. "Do you need to wear something special?"

"No, I need socks, but that's it." He scarfed down the rest of his cereal and ran for his shoes, which were by the door. He had so much more resilience than she ever had. She felt proud and also grateful.

They arrived at Beth Israel ten minutes early, but Noah assured her it was fine. She suspected he thought he'd be able to use the bounce house early if he was the first to get there, and she also suspected this was a false assumption. But given that she had work to do, she was just as happy to go with it.

When they reached the front door, they heard a squeal behind them. "Noah!"

Ethan charged at Noah, as Grace tried to keep up. "Ethan, slow down!"

"It's bounce day!" he cried.

They jumped up and down. Grace rolled her eyes. "Looks like someone was as eager to be first as we were."

Amy swiped her key fob and let them all in. "Do we tell them they haven't even blown up the bounce house yet?"

"Nah, let them figure it out. Life lessons and all of that." She shoved Ethan's backpack in his cubby. "So how'd it go with Emily and Jake?"

"Honestly? It was kind of a disaster."

"Really? What happened?"

"I don't think Jake wanted to be there. After about fifteen minutes he said he wanted to go home. He stayed longer, but he must have asked to leave at least ten times before he actually did."

"Typical. Jake pulls that all the time."

"Really?"

"Oh yeah. Well, I mean, it's been a long time since we've had a one-on-one playdate with him, but he was famous for wanting to go home as soon as something didn't go his way."

"Even with Ethan? I thought they were best buds."

"They were. But even best friends have disagreements."

"That's such a relief. I thought we'd done something wrong. He obviously doesn't like that we're the ones living in that house."

"As opposed to . . . us?"

"Yeah."

The faint tension that arose anytime they discussed 120 Sycamore reared its head. "Well, that's no reason to act like a little asshole. Which, between you and me, is exactly what Jake is."

Amy stifled a laugh. "Kids are kids. Noah has his moments, too."

"Noah seems like an angel pretty much anytime I see him."

"False advertising, I assure you."

There was a slight lull in the conversation, and Amy was tempted to bring up what she'd learned about Emily Saturday—that she was hurt at having been cut out of Grace's life and didn't know why it had happened. Amy knew it wasn't her place, but now that she'd heard both sides of the story, she wanted to encourage Grace to reach out again. But before she could even pave the way to such a suggestion, Emily appeared beside them.

"You too?"

They all laughed. Amy continually marveled at the way being a mother of kids the same age in the same class could smooth over any potential friction or awkwardness.

"Should we tell Miss Ruth and Miss Karen that next time they decide to do something special for the kids, they should surprise them? Honest to God, I've been up since six o'clock. I nearly had to tie Jake to a chair to keep him from trying to walk to school."

"I don't think they've even inflated anything yet."

"Oh, great. Meltdown coming in five . . . four . . . three . . ."

Just then, Jake burst out of the classroom. "Mommy! *Where* is the bouncy house?"

"I don't know. Ask Miss Karen."

He disappeared back into the classroom.

"That kid. I'm telling you. Did Amy tell you what he did on Saturday?"

"She mentioned it," Grace said.

Emily shook her head, as if she were reliving the episode all over again. "I was furious. Furious. I'm so sorry, Amy—we must have ruined your weekend."

"Hardly. Noah was happy to have someone to play with."

"I told her not to take it personally—remember when Jake pulled that kind of stuff with Ethan back in the day?"

Emily nodded, then a look of realization washed over her face, as if she suddenly realized, *Wait, you two were talking about me? What else did you discuss?*

"He's gotten better about it, at least most of the time," she said. "I think it freaked him out seeing 120 Sycamore under new ownership. Has Ethan been back?"

"No," Grace and Amy said in unison.

"Though you're obviously welcome," Amy added quickly. "I just figured . . . given his age . . . it might be too soon."

"Probably. To be honest, the only one of us who's seen it since the move is Julian."

Emily looked surprised. "Was there a problem or something?"

"No, he just forgot to forward our mail, so he picked it up a few times."

"How could he forget to forward the mail?" Emily looked incredulous.

"I know. Don't get me started. Thankfully that chapter seems to be coming to a close."

Amy decided not to mention that she actually had three letters for Julian in her purse that very moment. She'd get them to Grace soon, maybe even at pickup, but handing them over now, in front of a curious but wounded Emily, would serve no purpose other than to pique Emily's interest in a subject Grace obviously didn't want her knowing anything about.

That afternoon, while Amy worked in a nearby coffee shop, she got a text from Jess.

Flights booked. Childcare sorted. IT'S ON.

She squealed and clapped her hands, only remembering she was in a public place when the middle-aged man to her right looked at her as if she'd just thrown confetti in his face. Whatever, she didn't care. Her college roommate was coming to visit, and they were going to get dressed up and go to a party, and it would be fabulous. She opened up the calendar on her phone. Only seven and a half weeks to go. She could barely contain her excitement.

She texted Jess back with a series of celebratory emojis and then texted Grace to let her know Jess and Dave's RSVP was confirmed; they'd definitely be a party of four. Shortly after she sent the text,

Grace called. Amy stared at the number. Why was Grace calling? Was there a problem? She tried not to let her overly active imagination get the best of her and answered the phone.

"Hello?"

"Hey—sorry, is this a bad time?"

"No, it's fine. I'm wrapping up work on a project, but I have a few minutes," she said.

"Are you sure? I can call back."

"No, it's fine."

"Okay. I'll make it quick. I just saw your text, and it reminded me that I've been meaning to talk to you about the fund-raiser."

"What about it? Is there a problem?"

"Sort of. Nothing major. It's just . . ." She took a breath. Amy braced herself. Had she changed her mind about Jess and Dave being allowed to come?

"If there isn't room for my friends, it's okay. Just let me know."

"What? Oh my gosh, no—of course they can come. That isn't the problem."

Amy's shoulders relaxed. "Oh. Then what's wrong?"

"Julian doesn't have the support staff to do all the grunt work necessary to make this event happen. His assistant and a few others resigned when things got bad with him, so he's really scrambling. I'm trying to pick up the slack until he hires some new people, but I can't do it all myself. I know you have your own work going on, but I was wondering . . . is there any way you'd be able to lend a hand?"

"Oh. I . . . sure. I guess."

"You don't have to—no pressure. I know you're busy."

"No, it isn't that. I mean, I'm working on a few projects, but I'm about to wrap one up, and the rest are small. It's more that . . . well, my background is in education policy. I am clueless when it comes to the kind of stuff Food Fight works on. I'm not sure how much help I'd be, unless it's really menial stuff like stuffing envelopes or picking up stuff from the printer."

"Okay, first of all, some of it is menial stuff like that. I mean really, we need as much help as we can get. But also, don't you write up and edit proposals all day?"

"Mostly. My latest is actually promotional materials."

"Even better! Julian has written up a bunch of stuff that I'm happy to format into brochures and booklets. My background is in graphic design, so that's a low lift for me. But the wording . . . let's just say Julian is an ideas man. There is a lot of good stuff in there, but I'm sure it could be organized in a better way. We're trying to get people interested in Food Fight's work, not put them to sleep."

Amy thought about it. She wasn't necessarily the best person for the job. Or non-job, really, since she was just helping a friend and wouldn't be getting paid. Food access wasn't her area of expertise, and she should probably be spending her free time trying to drum up new business in the area she knew something about—a position that would pay and would possibly lead to something full time. But she also wanted the fund-raiser to be a success. On some level it had to be if Julian was to get the fresh start he and Grace needed. And Jess was flying all the way from Seattle. Amy didn't want the event to be a dud.

"So?" Grace said, after Amy had been quiet for what was probably a bit too long. "What do you think?"

"Happy to help," she said, even though she wasn't entirely sure that she was.

Over dinner that night, Rob picked at his chicken while Noah went on and on about the bounce house at school.

"And THEN, Ethan jumped up to the roof, and Jake jumped at the same time, and they CRASHED into each other."

"That sounds painful," Amy said. She glanced at Rob, who seemed distracted.

"It WAS. Ethan cried a lot, and Jake did, too, and Miss Karen had to get ice and Band-Aids. Jake wanted Spider-Man ones, but she only had plain, and he got really mad and wanted to go home."

"Sounds about right." She raised an eyebrow at Rob, but he was busy pushing some rice to the side of his plate. "Is dinner okay?" she asked.

Rob looked up. "What? Yeah, it's great. Sorry. I'm just not super hungry. They had some event at work today, and whoever was in charge ordered too much food, so I ate an Italian hoagie at, like, four-thirty."

"Ah."

"What's a hoagie?" Noah asked.

Rob shook his head. "What kind of Philadelphian am I that my kid doesn't know what a hoagie is? It's basically a big sandwich on a long roll, with lots of meat and cheese and seasonings, and it's very filling."

"Apparently," Amy said. "Had I known, I wouldn't have bothered cooking dinner."

"Sorry—I should have said something before I got on the train. My fault."

"It's okay. I'm not annoyed." Rob gave her a look, and she smiled. "Uranium?"

Rob always joked that he'd never met someone who could express her irritation in as few words and gestures as Amy. She radiated annoyance like a hunk of uranium, he said. It was such a nerdy analogy that every time she thought about it, no matter how annoyed she was, she couldn't help but smile. She wondered if that was his objective.

"You can't help yourself," he said.

"*Anyway*," she said, still smiling, "I heard from Jess today. She and Dave booked their tickets for November. It's full steam ahead."

"That's great."

"I know. I'm super excited."

"So what's the deal with the fund-raiser? What exactly will it entail?"

"Funny you should ask. I'm not a hundred percent sure, but I will know more soon because I volunteered to help with some of the final details and planning."

"Doing . . . what?"

"I'm not exactly sure. It sounds like some menial stuff like picking up pamphlets from the printer and writing place cards, but she mentioned some writing and editing, too."

"Writing and editing what?"

"Promotional materials, that kind of thing. Grace's background is in graphic design, so she can mock all this stuff up, but she needs help with the words."

"And you said yes."

"Of course."

"What do you mean, 'of course'? Are they paying you?"

"No, I'm not working for them. I'm just . . . lending a hand."

Rob frowned. "Isn't this stuff Julian's employees should be doing?"

"Yeah, but apparently his assistant and a few others quit back when . . ." Her eyes flitted toward Noah, who was chomping on a green bean. "Before," she said.

Rob's eyebrows rose in unison. "And now you are going to jump in to bail him out."

"I'm doing a favor for a friend. It benefits no one if this event is a disaster—not the people who need better food access, and frankly not us either, considering you greased the wheels for MediaCom to sponsor the event."

"I was only the messenger."

"Still."

He sighed. "Man, these people really have a grip on us, don't they?"

"Who?" Noah asked.

Amy looked at Rob. They shouldn't be discussing this in front of Noah, and they knew it. The time had long since passed that they could talk about anything and everything in his presence, and they needed to be more careful, especially when discussing his best friend's parents. Who knew what he might hear or misinterpret or relay to Ethan in a moment of misunderstanding? The fact that they'd mentioned any of this in front of him was a mistake, and Amy only hoped he had been too preoccupied with his memories of "bounce day" to have heard anything.

"No one, sweetie," Amy said. She kissed him on the head. "Now finish your green beans."

# Chapter 16

The virus that took down the Kravitz family arrived the last week of September, and it was a doozy. First, Noah came home early from school with a fever, which developed into a fever and upper respiratory infection and, eventually, an ear infection as well. Rob caught it next and was out of work for three days. And then Amy caught it, by which point the virus had morphed into a heinous beast the likes of which she'd never experienced, at least not in recent history.

She couldn't get out of bed. That was the problem. She tried, but when she got to the bottom of the stairs, she was sweaty and delirious and had to lie down for a minute to catch her breath, by which point she forgot why she came downstairs in the first place. Was it for food? Unlikely. She had no appetite at all. Did she want to watch TV in the family room? Maybe. What she really wanted to do was sleep, but that's all she'd been doing for six days—*six days*, and she still had a fever and felt like death.

"You should go to the doctor," Rob said when he called to check in on her.

"I don't have a doctor here yet." Her throat was so sore it hurt to speak.

"Then go to the ER."

"I'm not going to the ER. This isn't an emergency. Anyway, that'll cost a fortune."

"Okay, so go to urgent care."

She pressed her cheek against her pillow. Thank God she couldn't smell. She hadn't washed her hair in days. It probably smelled horrible. "Which one?"

"I don't know. There are, like, seven of them within a ten-minute drive. If you want, I can text you a recommendation."

"No, that's fine. I'll Google it."

"Do you want me to come home and take you?"

"I can drive. It's fine." She wasn't entirely sure this was true, but she didn't want to make her husband come home all the way from Center City just to take her to urgent care. As it was, his mother was shuttling Noah to and from school. She'd imposed on people enough already.

"I'm worried about you. I've never seen you like this."

It was true. Throughout their marriage, she had always been the "tough one." A virus would take her down for a day or two, but she rarely complained and was back on her feet as soon as she sensed she was on the mend. Rob, on the other hand . . . well, he didn't exactly suffer in silence. Every cold was the worst cold anyone had ever had. Every pulled muscle was tantamount to being crippled. He would cough and hack and limp his way around the house, like an invalid nearing the end of his days. Amy had once said something along the lines of, "Oh, cut me a break." To which Rob replied, "How can you have so little sympathy for the *infirm*?" She burst out laughing, assuming he was joking, but he wasn't, and she quickly apologized. For such a self-aware, intelligent person, he clearly had no idea how ridiculous he seemed, acting like a runny nose was tantamount to the Black Plague. So now Amy just bit her tongue and bought plenty of Tylenol and NyQuil.

"It's just a cold," she said, then burst into a coughing fit that seemed to have no end.

"Ame . . ."

"Sorry."

"Don't apologize. You're sick. You should probably be on antibiotics or something."

"Maybe then I can get back to helping Grace. I've really dropped the ball."

"Don't worry about Grace. She'll be fine."

"There's just so much to do . . ."

"You've done way too much already."

She wasn't sure she'd done "way too much," but she had certainly done a lot. It all sort of snuck up on her. At first, she only had to proofread the dinner menu. Then she needed to pick up the menu from the local printer and follow up with the caterer. Before she knew it, she was the caterer's primary contact, and she was copyediting the pamphlets, confirming silent auction participants, and ordering balloons. Some days it felt like a second job. Or, really, like her primary job, and the grant proposals were just a side gig she occasionally dipped into.

Rob kept saying, "I can't believe you're doing all of this for free," which at first made Amy roll her eyes, but after a while, she couldn't believe it either. She didn't mind helping, especially when it was for such a good cause, but at some point between the table arrangements and the balloons, it became a bit much. Did Julian really not have *anyone* else who could help? She knew budgets were tight and staff members had left, but now she was wondering . . . had *everyone* left? Couldn't he hire an intern? Surely there were hundreds of ambitious college students looking for experience who'd be willing to work for free. Amy tried to tell herself she was making useful connections for when she was ready to reenter the workforce, but at this point, the only real contacts she'd made were with the catering staff and a local printing company.

"I'm trying to be a good friend," she said.

"You're an *amazing* friend. Frankly, I'm not sure Grace deserves you."

Amy coughed into the phone, then sniffled loudly. "Yeah, it isn't just anybody who's worthy of a gal like this."

"Stop. You are super sick, and the Durants will just have to deal. You've gone above and beyond already, and you know it."

She rolled over and stared at the ceiling. "I really do feel like a shit sandwich."

Rob paused. "A shit sandwich? Is that like . . . two pieces of bread with shit in the middle? Or is everything made of shit, like a shit patty inside a shit bun?"

"I don't know. I don't even know what I'm saying at this point. Earlier I almost put my phone in the toaster. It's bad."

"Which is why you need to go to the doctor. Okay?"

She sighed. "Okay. I'm going. I just . . . need to summon the energy to actually get out of bed. But I'll do it."

"Good. Call me after you see someone and let me know what they say. I'll call my mom and tell her to take Noah back to her place after school. That'll buy you a little time."

"Thank you. You're the best."

"Nah, you are. Haven't you noticed how crazy everything has been since you got sick? You're the glue that keeps this house together. We need you back."

"I'll get there, don't worry," she said, even though at the moment, she couldn't imagine feeling anything other than awful ever again.

Amy somehow managed to clothe herself. She wasn't sure how. One moment she was in bed clutching her phone, and the next she was in her bathroom wearing clothes, and she wasn't entirely sure how any of it had happened. The mirror reflected an image back at her that was . . . well, there was no way to be gentle about it. She looked horrible. Her greasy hair slithered down her neck, and her skin was so pale it was nearly translucent. Under normal circumstances she would either hop in the shower or throw on enough makeup to make herself look human, but today she couldn't be bothered. She needed to conserve all her energy to drive to urgent care.

Her purse and jacket were still situated on a kitchen chair, where she'd left them nearly a week ago when she'd told Rob and Noah she didn't feel so great and needed to lie down. Did she need a jacket? She had no idea what it was like outside. She hadn't actually been outside since this ordeal began. She checked the weather: sixty-two degrees. Screw the jacket. It was just one more thing to do.

Clutching her keys and purse, she dragged herself to the car.

The air felt chillier than she'd expected, but she wasn't going back for the jacket. The only direction was forward.

When she went to start the car, though, nothing happened. Had she forgotten the key? Their Jeep was the kind that used an automatic fob that didn't require an actual key. All she needed was to have it on her person, and the car would start when she pressed the ignition. She rifled through her purse, and sure enough, there it was. But if she had it on her, why wasn't the car starting?

She called Rob.

"Hey, where are you? Have you seen the doctor?"

"No, I'm in the driveway. The car won't start."

"Shit. I just drove it last night to pick up dinner. Is it the battery?"

"I don't know. Maybe?"

"Stay on the phone with me and try it again."

She stepped on the brake and pressed the ignition button, and that's when she noticed something illuminate on the dashboard: REPLACE KEY BATTERY.

"Shit. It's the battery—not the car's, the key's."

Rob let out a sigh of relief. "We can deal with that."

"Can we?"

"Definitely. We have an extra fob."

"Where?"

"I think . . ." He made a rustling noise. "Oh. Crap. I have it."

"Great."

"Sorry. Oh! But I think I have extra batteries somewhere in the house. Try the junk drawer in the kitchen. Just replace the battery and you should be good to go."

She closed her eyes and took a calming breath. On most days this wouldn't even be an issue, but feeling like she did, she could barely dress herself, much less perform a mechanical task she'd never done before.

"Okay. I'm on it."

She hung up and plodded back to the house, where she searched through the junk drawer and several others for the batteries. She couldn't find them. They weren't in the basement either, nor were they in the buffet in the dining room, nor the media console in the family room. Just when she was about the dissolve into a heap on the floor, she remembered: Hadn't she seen a strip of small lithium batteries in Rob's sock drawer? She raced upstairs—well, "raced." More like lumbered. She yanked open his sock drawer, and there they were, all ten of them.

"Hallelujah!" she cried. Then she needed to lie down for a minute. All the moving and shouting had taken it out of her.

She finally made it downstairs and laid the key fob and battery in front of her. The problem was, it was entirely unclear how to get the battery out. Obviously it was inside somewhere, but how were you supposed to open the damn thing without breaking it?

Found batteries. How do you open fob?

Rob texted back:

No idea. Check manual?

"God, fucking help me," she said to herself. She managed to walk back to the car, open the glove compartment, and find the manual; when she got back inside she opened it. She'd started seeing floaters a few minutes earlier, which meant reading the minuscule instructions was next to impossible. There were illustrations, but they made it look so easy. It wasn't easy! How was she supposed to get the top off, like the picture showed? She jabbed at it with a pen, then a butter knife, then a paring knife, but nothing worked. She slammed it on the counter once but decided not to repeat that maneuver, both because she worried she would break the fob and because she didn't actually have the energy. By this point, she was sweating but also shivering, her back and chest beaded with sweat. Another fever was coming on, she could feel it. She started bawling.

"I . . . just . . . want . . . to . . . see . . . a . . . doctor!" she cried into the air. No one was there to hear her, of course, but she felt better just letting it all out.

She rubbed her eyes and nose on her sleeve and stared down

the key fob. It was just a *key fob*. It wasn't a bank safe. She could do this. She had to do this.

She grabbed the paring knife again and wedged it between a ridge in the side of the fob, and at last she felt something give. The plastic top popped off.

"Yes! YES! Oh, thank you. THANK YOU!"

She popped out the battery and pressed in the new one, and moments later she was hoisting herself into the driver's seat of their Jeep. The car turned on, and she threw it in reverse down the driveway. In her delirium and excitement, she hadn't checked the urgent care address, so she didn't know where she was going. Actually, she hadn't even picked an urgent care. Like Rob said, there were at least seven close by, but her brain was too foggy to remember where any of them were.

She grabbed her phone, pulled up the map app, and plugged in "urgent care." A smattering of red dots appeared across the map of their area. She picked one at random—the one that seemed closest to her house—and got directions: a five-minute drive. She could do that. She would make it.

If anyone she knew had seen her driving, they would have stopped her and offered to drive her instead. She looked terrible. She *felt* terrible—cold and clammy and feverish. But it didn't matter. She was going to get herself to urgent care, and some doctor was going to make her better. She believed that now. All she needed was a prescription for something from a medical professional who knew what he or she was doing. Help was moments away. She was counting down the seconds.

From the moment she pulled into the parking lot, something seemed off. The lot was packed. At first she figured the cars were overflow from another lot, but when she walked through the front door, the waiting room teemed with people as well.

*This virus is even worse than I imagined*, she thought. By the looks of it, at least thirty people were also waiting to see the doctor. Could she really wait for that many people to go ahead of her? Not really. But at the moment, she couldn't fathom getting back in the car and attempting to find another office. This one would have to do.

She signed in at the front desk. It was one o'clock in the afternoon, and already the place was on its eighth page of sign-ins. This virus was a beast. It was going to take out all of Montgomery County.

The receptionist looked her up and down. "Insurance and ID."

Amy handed over her cards. The woman threw a clipboard at her, catching Amy off guard.

"Fill this out," she said.

"Here? Or do you want me to have a seat?"

"Do I look like I care?"

Amy looked around to see if she was the only one who thought this woman rude beyond all reason, but no one seemed to be paying attention. She decided to fill out the forms at the counter, mostly because she didn't want to lose sight of her cards. She didn't know this woman at all, but she didn't trust her.

Once she'd finished filling in the information, she handed the clipboard back to the receptionist, who tossed Amy's insurance card and driver's license back on the counter.

"Have a seat," she barked, as if Amy were trying her patience. Maybe she'd had a long day, with all of these sick people. Amy was willing to give her the benefit of the doubt. Still, she couldn't see why the woman needed to be so rude about it. It's not as if Amy wanted to be here. Given the choice, she'd rather be pretty much anywhere else in the world.

There weren't any available seats, so Amy found a place to stand in the back corner of the waiting room. She could barely keep herself upright, so it would be a miracle if she didn't pass out before the nurse called her back. She leaned against the wall and closed her eyes. Whoever was called back next, she would take their seat. That was the only thought that kept her from crying.

The room was noisy. Not with people talking—no one really was—but with lots of ambient sound. Sniffling. Creaking. Scratching. A lot of scratching. Amy opened her eyes and looked around. Something was off, but she couldn't put her finger on what. The people all seemed so . . . fidgety. Granted, she wasn't exactly in top form and wasn't acting herself either, but most of the people in the room didn't seem very . . . well, *sick*. She knew there were lots of reasons someone might go to urgent care—sprains, shallow cuts, fever, sore throat. But the people around her seemed more anxious than anything else.

"Katrina, you're up."

A nurse held open the door to the back part of the office, and a rail-thin woman arose from a chair and went to meet her. The woman's ash-blond hair hung in straggly waves, and she wasn't wearing any makeup.

*Okay, so maybe some of these people do look sick*, Amy thought. She made for the woman's empty seat and snagged it before a middle-aged black man could beat her to it. She sunk into the vinyl seat, her sweatpants squeaking against the sticky black surface.

"Katrina, baby, hurry up. We don't have all day."

Amy tried to mask her surprise, but she was sure her face broadcast her disapproval. What kind of nurse talked to a patient that way? Frankly, what kind of nurse said "you're up"? It sounded so unprofessional.

"There you go. Good girl. Back we go."

Maybe the nurse already knew her. That would make sense at a primary care office or some other doctor's office that had regular patients. But who would be a regular at urgent care? If you had that many "urgent" situations, you probably should be seeing a specialist because there was probably something wrong.

Amy folded her hands in her lap and waited.

Ten minutes.

Fifteen.

Thirty-five.

At forty-five minutes, she started having an internal debate. Did she get up and speak with the receptionist to ask how much longer it would be, thus risking her seat being taken by another patient? Or did she hold on to her seat, but risk sitting for another two hours, in which time she could go to another, less crowded urgent care facility? She looked at the clock on her phone. It was getting close to two o'clock. Sherrie would pick Noah up at three, and though she'd bring him back to her own house for a while, she'd eventually bring him to 120 Sycamore. Amy wanted to get in another nap before having to be "mom" again. She decided to take her chances on the seat. If someone took it, another one would open up eventually.

The receptionist raised an eyebrow as soon as she clapped eyes on Amy. "Yeah?"

"I just wanted to check on how things are moving along. I've been waiting for about forty-five minutes and—"

"Some people been waiting longer than that."

"I'm sure, but I was just wondering if you had an idea of how much longer it will be."

"Let me look into my crystal ball." She picked up a pencil holder on her desk and shook it. "It says the doctor will see you when he sees you. So there you go."

Amy was speechless. How had the office not fired this woman already? As she tried to find the right words, she overheard someone in the hallway beyond the receptionist's desk say, "Shit. Should we just tell them to go to the ER?"

She got a sinking feeling in her stomach. Had she chosen the wrong urgent care? As Amy looked around, she noticed how dirty the office was. The floor was littered with gum wrappers and plastic bottle tops and random pieces of paper. How had she not noticed that before? Probably because she was so sick. She desperately wanted to see a doctor, but she was becoming worried that no one here would be able to help her.

The door to the exam rooms opened beside her. "Amy Kravitz?"

"That's me."

The receptionist huffed. "Looks like it's your lucky day."

She followed the nurse down the hallway to an exam room. "Kravitz, huh? You related to Lenny?"

"No relation."

"That would be pretty cool, huh? I guess you'd have to be black, though."

"I guess . . ." Amy had hoped the nurse would make her feel better about the quality of care here, but she was quickly realizing her hopes would probably not bear fruit.

She followed the nurse into an exam room. "Have a seat on the table."

She went to sit on the table but stopped when she realized they hadn't replaced the protective paper. The table itself was ripped and dirty, and she swore she saw mucus in the far corner. "I . . . think it needs paper."

"What? Oh." The nurse went for the roll of paper but jumped back when she saw the mucus. "Aw, come on. Gross."

She wet a paper towel and wiped it off. She stretched a clean sheet of paper over the table. "Right. Up you go."

Amy was about to ask if the table should be sanitized first, but before she could the nurse started in with questions.

"So what brings you in today?"

Amy described her symptoms.

"And what's your pain level?"

"I wouldn't say I'm in pain, per se. More achy and uncomfortable and generally miserable."

"But if you had to give it a number. Like a five? A two?"

"I don't know. Maybe a three."

"Okay. And have you had any lacerations prior to these symptoms beginning?"

"Sorry?"

"Have you had any lacerations prior to these symptoms beginning?"

"Lacerations? Like . . . cuts?"

"I guess so."

Amy was baffled. What did cuts have to do with a virus and possible sinus infection?

"Um . . . no."

"Any gunshot wounds?"

"*What?*"

"Gunshot wounds. You have any?"

"No."

The nurse typed a few things into the computer. Then she grabbed a blood pressure cuff and attached it to Amy's arm. She stared at it for a long while. "Hmmm. I think this one is broke."

"I . . . think you need to squeeze the pump," Amy offered. She didn't care if she sounded snarky. This woman was supposedly a medical professional. What kind of nurse didn't know how to take someone's blood pressure? Was *anyone* in this office competent? Also, she wanted to correct the woman and tell her the word is "broken" not "broke," but right now grammar was the least of her worries.

The nurse glared at Amy. "Uh, yeah, thanks."

She squeezed and squeezed, until the cuff was so tight around Amy's bicep that she thought she might cry. "Ouch," she winced. "That hurts."

The nurse sighed. "Like I said. It's broke. Let me get another one."

She left and slammed the door behind her, and Amy heard a stream of obscenities as she chatted to another employee. "Watch out for the bitch in room three. Telling me how to do my job. I mean really."

Amy started panicking. She shouldn't be here. Whatever this place was, it wasn't a competent urgent care center, and she no longer had faith they could correctly diagnose her, much less make her better. She grabbed her purse and snuck out of the room, heading down the hallway.

"Hey, where are you going?" the nurse called after her.

"I changed my mind," Amy said.

"Yeah, well, good riddance. We still get paid anyway."

Amy wasn't sure if that was true or not, but she figured she'd deal with the financial fallout later. She burst into the waiting room and headed for the door, but as she opened it, she bumped straight into Julian.

"Julian—hi." Amy self-consciously tucked her hair behind her ears. She knew there was no way she looked anything other than terrible.

"Hey," Julian said. He sounded as uncomfortable as she felt. "How did you . . . what are you doing here?"

"I have the cold of the century. I've been out of commission for six days. Rob and I agreed it was time for me to see someone."

"Ah, got it. Yeah, I think I'm fighting something similar myself."

"Yeah, well, a word of advice: Don't waste your time here. I just left in the middle of the appointment because the nurse couldn't figure out how to take my blood pressure."

"Yikes."

"That's putting it mildly. I'll probably have to wait another hour at another urgent care, but I'd rather do that than risk my health at the hands of one of these clowns."

Julian glanced over Amy's shoulder. He hesitated. "Eh. I'm already here. Might as well take my chances."

Amy shrugged. "Maybe you'll have better luck than I did." She doubted that was possible.

"Julian, baby, come sign in," the receptionist called across the room.

"Sorry, gotta run. But good luck to you. And hey, thanks for all of your help with the fund-raiser. I really appreciate it."

"No problem. Once I'm back on my feet I can dive back in."

"Sounds great. Take care."

He walked past her into the waiting area and as the door shut behind her, she thought how odd it was that the receptionist already knew his name.

# Chapter 17

Amy eventually got better. She found a competent urgent care, where the nurses knew how to use blood pressure cuffs and the doctor diagnosed her with sinusitis and prescribed a course of antibiotics. Rob was furious when he heard about her experience at the first urgent care and had already filed a report with the Better Business Bureau. She wouldn't repeat that experience for all the money in the world, but she did get a lift out of seeing Rob all riled up on her behalf.

For her part, Amy had gone onto Yelp to write a scathing review and was astonished at how many people had identical experiences to hers. One woman, who went with her eight-month-old, was told that babies don't have sinuses. Another found feces on the exam table. Another was prescribed penicillin even though she had an allergy. The complaints went on and on. Why hadn't Amy checked here first? If only she hadn't been so deliriously sick and impatient, she could have saved herself hours of frustration.

But now she was better, which meant she could get back to helping with the Food Fight gala. She didn't mind helping—some of the tasks, like helping with the menu, were actually pretty fun—but it was starting to feel more like a job than like helping a friend. She didn't want to feel stressed the entire evening of the event because she somehow felt responsible for it. Part of her worried, as

Rob suggested again and again, that she was diverting time away from potentially more productive and lucrative work to help Julian get a fresh start.

Nevertheless, she was in too deep now to abdicate responsibility. The fund-raiser was in a month, and she had already taken charge for many aspects of the evening. One issue she was determined to resolve was figuring out what all of these community centers and other recipients of Food Fight's help actually *did*. Amy knew the money raised at the event would be distributed to these places to bolster their programming, but Julian had merely given her a list of groups to include in the reading materials, rather than explain what each group did to improve access to healthy food. He didn't have to provide details, but Amy knew people would be more likely to pony up if they knew exactly what their money was going to support.

One morning while Noah was at school, she pulled up the list of groups and decided to start calling them one by one. First up: St. Luke's Community Center. She plugged the number into her phone and called. A receptionist picked up after the third ring.

"Hi, could I please speak to Leroy Harris?"

"I don't think he's . . . oh, wait, let me check, hold on." The woman covered the phone and after about a minute returned to the conversation. "He's here. Let me transfer you."

A few moments later, a man with a deep and slightly hoarse voice picked up the line. "Leroy Harris, how can I help you?"

Amy explained who she was and how she was helping Julian with his upcoming fund-raiser.

"Oh, sure, sure. Food Fight. They've helped us put on some great programming."

"That's why I'm calling. I figured if he includes more specifics in some of the reading materials—what kinds of programs you've been able to offer, what kind of difference it's made—people might be more inclined to donate."

"Makes sense."

"Tell me a little more about what you do."

"Well, we do a lot of things. Obviously we have a religious affiliation, so we provide spiritual counseling to those in our community. But we also offer activities. We have a basketball court where kids come to play. We bring in speakers to talk about issues relevant to our neighborhood. We have celebrations and gatherings. Our main purpose is to enrich our community, in any way we can."

"Where does Food Fight fit in?"

"Julian and his group have provided us with funding and resources to offer cooking classes a few times a month. A lot of people in our community eat a lot of fast food, mostly because it's quick and cheap, but also because a lot of them don't really know how to cook for themselves. So our classes have shown people how to take cheap, fresh food and turn it into a meal quickly. A lot of our people are on food stamps, but thanks to work by Julian's group and some others, most of the farmers' markets in the city accept SNAP benefits."

"And you've seen a change in the way people are eating?"

"Yes and no. It's definitely empowered people to cook for themselves, but the truth is, a lot of the healthy food is still far from home. After a busy day, it's still easier to do Burger King. One thing I'm trying to work on with Julian is to bring a farmers' market into our own community. We've even laid the groundwork for St. Luke's be the site. But of course implementing that kind of stuff takes resources and money."

"Which I'm guessing is where this fund-raiser comes in."

"Exactly. For a lot of these things, we have the space and the interest. We just need the money and know-how to make it happen."

Amy typed furiously on her laptop as she tried to get down everything he was saying.

"So Julian's got you working like crazy on this event, huh?" he asked as Amy typed.

"It's not too bad. I volunteered. It's nice to be actively involved with a nonprofit again. I used to work in education policy in DC before I moved here."

"Ah, so you were messing around with those clowns down in Washington, is that right?"

Amy smiled. She didn't want to get into a political discussion, but it seemed inevitable these days. "Something like that."

"Well, welcome to Philadelphia. It's a little different up here."

"So I'm learning," she said. "Anything else you want to tell me about Food Fight or what you have planned?"

"Not really. We just really could use the help. The cooking classes have been popular, but we can't continue them without some extra funds, and the farmers' market won't get off the ground without some additional resources. I'm not taking millions of dollars here—any small amount would help."

Amy typed away. "Well, if all goes according to plan, Julian should raise more than a small amount to pass on to you."

"That would be much appreciated. So let me ask you—you working for one of them education nonprofits up here now?"

"No, I'm sort of . . . freelancing at the moment."

"I see, I see. I guess that's where Food Fight fits in."

"Sort of. Like I said, I'm just volunteering."

"We know all about that over here. Couldn't survive if it weren't for some good volunteers. I'll make sure I tell Julian you're doing a great job. You're a kind soul, I can tell."

"I must have said something right."

He laughed. "I've been around a long time."

"Hey, listen, I'll take it."

"You take care, all right? Hopefully we'll speak again after the fund-raiser."

Amy hoped so too and said, "Thanks, Mr. Harris. I truly look forward to it."

Amy made her way through the rest of the list, and minutes after she finished her last call, Grace phoned. Amy stared at the screen with some amount of trepidation. She hadn't mentioned to Grace that she'd run into Julian at urgent care—she wasn't entirely sure what to make of the encounter herself—but now every time they talked she felt as if she were hiding something. Grace hadn't once mentioned Julian being sick, but then why else would he have been there?

"What's up?" Amy said as she answered the phone.

"We've run into a babysitting issue. For the night of the fund-raiser no less."

"Uh-oh." Grace had offered to let Noah come over that night, while Kara babysat the two of them, so if her babysitter plans fell through, that meant Amy's had as well. "What happened?"

"Turns out Kara is out of town that weekend. I swear I asked her and she said she was free, but apparently there was some sort of miscommunication."

"Oh boy. What about your parents?"

"They'll be at the event."

"Oh. Right. Duh."

"I tried a few other people I know, but for some reason everyone on the planet already has plans that night. Do you happen to know of anyone?"

"Honestly? The only people we've used since the move, other than Kara that one time, are Rob's parents."

Grace hesitated. "Would *they* sit?"

"Oh—I don't know. They have a pretty busy social calendar. But assuming they're free, I'm sure they would. They love spending time with Noah, and Ethan is so easy."

"I don't know about *that*, but he'd be good for your in-laws. We'd make sure of it."

"Why don't I call Sherrie and see what she says, and I'll let you know ASAP."

"Perfect. Sorry to pile one more thing on your plate. You're doing so much already."

"Not a problem at all."

"No, really. I feel so guilty. You're doing all this stuff that someone else should definitely be doing, and it just seems . . . I don't know. Like, I don't want Julian to take advantage of your generosity, you know?"

"He isn't. Don't worry," she said, even though in her heart, she kind of thought he was.

Amy called Sherrie. Even after all these years, she still didn't love calling Rob's mom. They got along fine—quite well, actually—but no one could get out of a conversation with Sherrie in under fifteen minutes. It wasn't possible. The woman had the gift of gab and sometimes Amy didn't feel like losing a chunk of her day over a minor request. Sherrie was exactly the kind of person texting was made for. But Sherrie didn't text. Or at least not in any sort of timely fashion. By the time she saw the message, days had possibly passed, and by then the matter was moot. If you needed an answer right away, you had to call.

"Hello?" Sherrie always answered the phone in a singsong voice, as if she were serenading you with her greeting.

"Hi, Sherrie, it's Amy."

"Amy, hi. Is everything okay? Are you feeling all right?"

Amy realized now that the last time she called Sherrie, she was feverish and semi-delirious on over-the-counter cold medicine.

"Oh, yeah, I'm fine. Thanks for asking. The antibiotics worked wonders."

"See? I told you that's what you needed."

Amy didn't remember her saying that at all, but then she wasn't exactly in the best state of mind to remember anything that happened over the course of that week.

"Oh, but Rob told me about that urgent care. *Horrible.* They should be put out of business."

"I think Rob is trying. He's filing complaints all over the place."

"That's my boy! Always a go-getter." Amy could hear her smile through the phone. "So what's up?"

"I have a babysitting request. Are you free Saturday, November 5?"

"Hang on. Let me check my calendar." She rustled through some papers. "Okay. What did you say? November 5?"

"Yes."

"It looks like we're free . . . hang on. Bruce? BRUCE! Oy, I'm telling you, his retirement is killing me. BRUCE!"

A faint voice replied in the background. "Yes?"

"I love how you sound so defensive when I've been shouting your name at the top of my lungs. Anyway, Amy wants to know if we can watch Noah on November 5. There's nothing on the calendar, but I want to make sure you haven't concocted one of your plans that you haven't told me about."

"When do I concoct plans?"

"Oh, I don't know. Like two nights ago when apparently we

were having dinner with the Goldsteins? Some little get-together you and Bill came up with at tennis, and I ended up having to talk to *Marsha* all night."

"Come on, you had fun."

"Did I? Because that isn't how I remember it."

Amy cleared her throat to remind Sherrie she was still on the line. There was definitely a chance she'd forgotten, and Amy felt a little uncomfortable listening to her in-laws partake in a marital spat.

"Anyway," Sherrie continued, "we're free on the fifth, right?"

"What, like a month from now? If there isn't anything on the calendar, then we're free. I don't plan that far out."

"Of course you don't . . ." Amy could almost hear the eye roll. "Okay. We're free."

"Great! Thank you so much. Oh, and is it okay if Noah's friend Ethan is there, too?"

"The kid who used to live in your house?"

Amy felt a twinge of guilt. She'd said she wouldn't invite Ethan over until enough time had passed that he wouldn't feel sad about not living at 120 Sycamore anymore. But Grace had suggested the plan in the first place, and at this point, Ethan coming to their house seemed like the only option left.

"Yes," she said. "They can't find a sitter for that night. Ethan is a really good kid, so he won't be any trouble."

"Oh, it's fine. Of course. It'll be fun! I'll have to bake something special."

"You don't have to go through any trouble. Honestly—we're just grateful that you're willing to give up your Saturday night."

"Please. For my grandson? It's a pleasure. I couldn't live with seeing the disappointment on that little face if I came empty-handed."

"If you're sure . . ."

"Of course I am. So where are the four of you going that you're planning this far in advance?"

"Julian's nonprofit is having a big fund-raiser that night."

"Remind me what he does?" Sherrie asked.

"He runs an organization called Food Fight. They promote access to healthy foods in poor neighborhoods."

"That's wonderful. Would Bruce and I be able to contribute, even if we don't attend the event?"

"I could ask. I'm sure he wouldn't turn down your money. They have a bunch of exciting new programs they want to launch this winter and could use the extra funds."

"Find out for me, would you? We'd love to help."

"Will do. I'll mention it to him or Grace next time I see one of them. I've actually been helping a lot with the event, so it's not the kind of thing that would slip my mind."

"That's nice that you've found something to keep you busy."

Amy wasn't sure if Sherrie intended to sound so condescending, or if it just came out that way. She suspected it was a combination of the two. Her career had always perplexed Sherrie, even when she worked in a proper office five days a week. Part of that was because she didn't fully understand what Amy did, and part of that was because once Noah came along she thought Amy should stay at home. When Amy ultimately left her job, Sherrie didn't bother to hide her relief.

"You made the right choice," she'd said at the time. "For your family."

Amy didn't disagree (she wouldn't have done it if she'd believed otherwise), but there was something about the way her mother-in-law said it that rubbed her the wrong way. Sherrie had quit her job to raise Rob and his sister and knew that Amy's mom barely took maternity leave. She didn't know all the details of Tim's problems, but she knew enough. All of that combined, it seemed a little smug when she suggested leaving the workforce was the right decision. It was almost as if she were saying, *Your mom kept working, and see how that turned out?*

"Trust me, I already have plenty to keep me busy," Amy said.

"Well, sure, with a little one running around. Kids are a lot."

"They are. And with this fund-raiser and my work projects—"

"Oh, are you still doing that . . . grant writing stuff or whatever it was?"

"Yep, still at it," she said. Amy had to laugh that even after all these years, Sherrie still didn't understand her work.

"Oh. Well, that's good. As long as it isn't too much. It'll be nice to have something to go back to someday."

"That's the idea."

But the truth was, Amy wasn't sure what, exactly, she'd be going back *to*, and when that someday might be.

The gala-related chores continued. There were seating arrangements to finalize and silent auction vendors to confirm. Did they want a signature cocktail, or just an open bar? How much could they realistically afford to spend on centerpieces? Amy felt as if she were planning her wedding all over again. She knew it was for a good cause, but part of her felt Julian cared a little too much that the event look a certain way. If this was truly for charity, who cared if the centerpieces were balloons and not flowers? What did it matter?

She ultimately convinced Julian to save money on flowers and go with balloons and other décor, but in return she got roped into filling out place cards. She could have said no, of course, but then she could have said no to any of it—to all of it—and she hadn't. What made place cards any more over-the-top than the other chores and requests? *I finalized the menu, called every one of your community partners, drafted a summary of your work with them, and picked up programs from the printer, but this*—this *is where I draw the line.*

That said, Amy wondered if she was even capable of saying no, and not just to the Durants. She'd taken that poorly paying freelance gig because she wanted to keep her résumé current and fresh, but part of her also feared saying no would reflect badly on her. Maybe word would get around that Amy was just the sort of can't-do person you shouldn't even bother calling about potential work. Growing up, she took any work she could get—dishwasher, cashier, stock girl—because her mom had impressed upon her the need for her to develop a strong work ethic and contribute to the family till. Somehow Amy had internalized that so deeply that she was now doing work that didn't even pay. Her mother would be horrified.

A little more than a week before the gala, Amy pulled out the stack of blank place cards and list of table assignments and got to work. She'd found a template online that she could use to do everything on the computer. There was no way she was going to fill out one hundred some place cards by hand. *I guess I can draw the line*, she thought, though she realized the line was so faint and far as to be nearly invisible.

As she cut and pasted the names for Table 1 into their respective spots, the doorbell rang. She wasn't expecting anyone or any packages, so she hesitated. She didn't love answering the door when she was home alone. It could be anyone—a friendly neighbor at best, a violent criminal at worst. If something bad happened, no one could help her. But it was midday on a Thursday, so she decided to take her chances. There were enough retired and nosy people in the neighborhood that if she screamed loudly enough, someone would hear and see her.

She crept toward the front door, but as soon as she spotted the man standing on her front stoop, she knew she'd made a mistake. He was a burly guy in a leather jacket and a pageboy hat, and Amy didn't like the look of him. His jowls were covered in a stubbly beard, and he stood with his hands in his jean pockets. She considered turning around, but he clapped his eyes on her. It was too late.

She put on a polite smile as she opened the door. "Hi. Can I help you?"

The man looked over her shoulder. "Yeah, I'm looking for Julian."

"Oh, sorry—he doesn't live here anymore."

"Says who?"

"We bought the house from him a few months ago."

"Is that so?"

Amy nodded. "I'm really sorry. I think there's been a lot of confusion regarding the change of address."

He stared at her for a beat. She noticed his front tooth was chipped. "So you're not his wife or nothing?"

"Me? No, definitely not."

"Ex-wife?"

"No, like I said—my husband and I bought the house from him. He forgot to change his address. We've been getting a lot of mail for him, too."

"Really." He said it more like a statement than a question. "And what have you been doing with that mail?"

Amy was about to tell him the truth, but she caught herself. If she admitted to knowing the Durants and seeing them on a semi-regular basis, she could put them—and herself—at risk. She didn't know who this guy was, but he seemed like trouble. The fact that he was looking for Julian at his old house and didn't want to take no for an answer only added to this perception.

"I send it back," she lied. "Sorry I can't be of more help. Maybe the post office has an updated address. Good luck."

She started to close the door, but he reached out with his thick hand and stopped her.

"So you haven't seen him since you moved then?"

"No . . . like I said, we bought the house from him. That's it."

He looked over her shoulder and cast his eyes on the console in her hallway. "Looks like you know something about Food Fight."

Amy followed his gaze to the stack of Food Fight brochures sitting on the console in the foyer. *Crap*, she thought. *Why did I leave those there?*

"What about them?"

"So you haven't seen Julian, but you have a big stack of brochures about his company."

"Is that . . . Julian runs Food Fight?"

Amy's mouth was running faster than her brain at this point, but she didn't know how to get herself out of this, and she was desperate for this man to leave.

"Don't bullshit me, lady."

"I'm not . . . like I said, we just happen to have bought his house. And I volunteered to distribute some flyers and stuff for a friend of mine. I didn't realize there was a connection to the former owners of this place."

"What friend?"

"Sorry?"

"What friend asked you to distribute those brochures?"

"Emily . . . ?"

"Emily what?"

Amy's eyes darted nervously around the neighborhood. Was anyone home? Could anyone see her? Would they hear her cries for help?

"I don't . . . listen, I'm getting a little uncomfortable. I've helped you as best as I can, and now if you don't leave, I'm going to have to call the police."

"That would be a mistake."

She swallowed as she pulled out her phone. "Sir, I will ask you one more time. Please leave."

"Hey, listen—put that away. I'm outta here. Have a good day."

"Thank you."

He narrowed his eyes as he cracked his knuckles. "But you tell my friend Julian that Lev is looking for him, and he wants his money."

Then he turned around, walked down the front path, and disappeared down Sycamore Street.

# Chapter 18

When she told Rob about the incident that night, he went ballistic and threatened to call the police.

"Please don't do that. Please?"

"Oh, so it's totally fine to have hitmen coming to our door?"

"He wasn't a hitman."

"How do you know?"

"Because that's ridiculous."

"What, that the former drug addict with serious debts who lived in our house might have interacted with some dodgy people who might now be after him?"

"He just owes the guy some money."

"Okay. But you know what? Legitimate businessmen who lend money don't show up at people's houses and threaten the new owners."

"I just don't see how calling the police is going to do anything. He didn't actually do anything to me. And I don't have any information on him, other than his name, which might not even be his real name."

"Listen, I'm just trying to protect our family. Who are *you* trying to protect?"

The truth was, Amy wasn't exactly sure. Obviously she wanted to shield her own family from harm—obviously! But when she really thought about it, she realized part of her wanted to keep the Durants safe as well. Why? She supposed part of it had to do with Ethan and Noah's friendship. Their connection was clearly something special, and she felt very protective of it. Exposing Julian's past to the police would no doubt make life for Ethan a lot more complicated. And then there was Grace. There was no reason for Amy to feel more drawn to Grace than she did to, say, Emily, but she did. Part of that was due to their children's friendship, and part of that was due to Grace's inherent cool, but whatever the case, Grace had cast a sort of spell over Amy. She didn't want to stir up trouble before she'd even told Grace what was going on.

"Our family comes first," Amy said. "But let me talk to Grace or Julian. This is their problem, and they should handle it. Okay?"

He sighed. "Fine. But tell her Julian's 'friends' need to back off, or I'm going to the cops. I don't care what he got up to in the past, but if it puts me and my family at risk, that's a problem."

"Agreed. I'm on it."

That ended up being only sort of true. She hoped to bring up the subject with Julian the next time he called about a fund-raiser–related task, but in the two weeks that followed, all requests and tasks went through Grace. Amy decided she'd take up the issue of Lev with her instead, though she was still struggling with how, exactly, she would to do that.

In the end, she resolved to bring it up in person, rather than over the phone. Later that week, when she picked up Noah from school, he begged to play football with Ethan on the playground, and she agreed, figuring it would be a good opportunity for her and Grace to chat. She and Grace found a spot next to each other on a bench while the boys chased each other.

"I know nothing about football, but . . . I don't think that's how it's played," Grace said.

Amy laughed. "Doesn't matter to me, since this is the closest he'll ever get to the sport."

"True that." She leaned back against the bench and sighed. "So when do your friends arrive?"

"Next Friday."

"Nice. You excited to see them?"

"Very. I haven't seen Jess since Noah was a baby. We're way overdue."

"You guys will have fun. And hopefully they won't be too bored at the fund-raiser."

"They'll love it. Speaking of the event, how are you guys feeling? Is Julian ready?"

"I think so? I never know with him. He can be very hard to read."

"He's probably a little nervous. I mean, jeez, *I'm* a little nervous, and I only helped with odds and ends."

"You did more than that. Honestly, I'm not sure he could have pulled this off without your help. He owes you big-time. We both do."

"You don't owe me anything. I was just trying to help a friend."

"Well, thanks. We really appreciate it. Julian tends not to be as vociferous with his praise, but he's really grateful, too."

"Speaking of Julian, I've been meaning to mention . . ."

Amy played with the hem of her jacket. Why the sudden hesitation? She supposed it was because Grace would almost certainly not be happy to hear what she had to say, and Amy hated being the bearer of bad news.

"Yes?" Grace said, her eyebrow raised. Amy realized her pause had lasted a beat too long.

"I had a run-in with an acquaintance of his last week."

"Of Julian's? Who?"

"Someone named Lev?"

Grace frowned. "Never heard of him. How did he say he knew Julian?"

"He didn't, exactly. He just said he was a friend." His demeanor indicated he wasn't actually a friend of Julian's at all, but Amy didn't want to alarm her just yet.

"Huh. Are you sure it was Lev? I know he's friends with a Leonard. I thought he went by Lenny, but maybe he's going by Len these days."

"Maybe? What does he look like?"

"Lenny? He's tall, thin, curly brown hair. Kind of geeky looking, but a real sweetheart."

"No, that's not him. I'm pretty sure he said Lev."

"Weird. He's probably someone from work. Where did you meet him?"

Amy swallowed. "At the house, actually."

"One twenty Sycamore? What was he doing there?"

"He stopped by looking for Julian. He didn't seem to know you'd moved."

Grace's expression cooled. "Did he say why he was looking for Julian?"

"He said . . . well, he seemed to suggest that Julian owed him some money." Amy's cheeks flushed. She wasn't sure why. Maybe she was embarrassed for Grace that her husband was in this position.

"Money? How much?"

"He didn't say. It must be a fair amount."

"No, that isn't possible. Julian has paid back all his debts."

Amy raised an eyebrow. "This guy was pretty pushy. I feel like he wouldn't have been so pushy if it wasn't a lot."

"So you think Julian is lying to me?"

"No, I didn't—I'm not saying that."

"What other explanation could there be?"

"I don't know . . . Maybe there is some kind of misunderstanding."

Grace looked across the playground, her knee bouncing furiously up and down as she tapped her heel on the ground. "Yeah. Maybe."

She didn't sound convinced, though, and despite her attempts at reassurance, Amy wasn't either.

The following Friday, billboards flew by as Amy cruised down the highway. Jess's flight landed around 4:30, and she couldn't wait. She'd managed to pick up Noah and escape without a request to play on the playground, which seemed like a small miracle. The weather was unseasonably warm, and on any other day, he would have wanted to hang out for hours. But Grace had already picked up Ethan before she arrived, so he was less inclined to stay without his BFF.

"Mommyyyyy, when are we going to be there?"

"Soon, sweetie. Only a few more miles."

She hadn't spoken to Grace in the week since the conversation about Lev. They'd e-mailed and texted, but only about event-related issues, and Amy never felt right bringing it up. She'd told Grace about it, and there wasn't much more she could do, at least for now. But she couldn't help but wonder what Grace had said to Julian about it. It seemed like such a jarring secret to learn your spouse was keeping.

It's not that she and Rob didn't have secrets. Every couple did. But they were minor secrets, like when she bought and hid a jar of Nutella so that Rob wouldn't finish it all, or when Rob claimed he was going upstairs to do work but she discovered he had fallen asleep watching ESPN. They didn't keep major secrets from each other, ones involving money and loan sharks and drug addiction. She was actually impressed that Grace and Julian had lasted through his addiction and recovery. Many couples didn't.

Eventually she came to the exit for the airport. She glanced down at her phone. She had a text from Jess:

At arrivals. Standing near "yield to pedestrians" sign.

Amy followed the exit toward Arrivals, and as she came around the bend, she spotted Jess. She was wearing a bright red wool coat, her wavy brown hair tucked beneath a cream knit cap. Amy flashed her headlights, and Jess beamed and waved. She elbowed Dave and pointed. He smiled and waved as well, though he looked exhausted.

"Who are you waving at?" Noah asked.

"See the woman in the red coat? That's Mommy's friend Jess."

"*Auntie* Jess," he corrected her. He was at that awkward stage where it wasn't really appropriate for him to call adults by their first names, so she and Rob were regularly correcting him to call people "Mr." and "Mrs." or, in the case of a close friend like Jess, "Aunt" or "Auntie." He somehow hadn't yet grasped that the rules did not always apply to her and Rob. She had tried to explain that some rules only applied to kids, but either he willfully refused to grasp that concept or it was developmentally beyond his reach.

She pulled the car next to the curb and popped the trunk. Dave piled their suitcases inside as Jess hopped into the front seat. She and Amy let out happy squeals and hugged each other tight.

"It is so good to see you!" Jess cried. She pulled away and looked Amy in the eyes. "You haven't changed a bit."

"I'm pretty sure I have a few more crow's-feet and gray hairs than the last time you saw me."

"Where? I see nothing but glowing youth. Me, on the other hand . . ."

"Please. You haven't changed either. You look great."

She did. She had the same bright, smiling face Amy had encountered their freshman year at Georgetown. She had a few wrinkles now, but didn't they all? In Jess's case, she had two little kids at home. Amy was impressed that she didn't look like a ghost of her former self. That's how Amy felt sometimes, and she only had Noah.

Dave closed the trunk and got in the back seat next to Noah. "Hey, Noah—nice to meet you." He reached out his hand. Noah smiled and shook it. Amy could tell he felt very grown-up. "Cool shoes."

Noah looked down at his sneakers—metallic and neon ones that Amy thought were a *little* too bright, but that Noah had insisted on buying. "Thank you. Mommy says they're a little flashy."

They all laughed. "Hey, I like flashy," Dave said.

Noah smiled again. "Did you know that tomorrow my friend Ethan is coming over for six *hours*?"

Dave raised his eyebrows. "No way!"

"Uh-huh. And my Bubbe and Zayde are coming, and they always bring me treats. Bubbe is a very talented baker."

Dave chuckled. "Is she? You, my friend, have an excellent vocabulary."

Noah flashed a self-satisfied look. "Thank you."

Amy put the car in gear and carefully navigated her way out of the airport. Soon, she was on 95 again, though the traffic was noticeably worse than on the way there. She looked at the clock: It was approaching rush hour. Hopefully they'd beat the worst of it.

"So tell me more about this party tomorrow," Jess said.

"It's a fund-raiser for a nonprofit run by the guy who used to own our house."

"What kind of nonprofit?"

"He tries to improve access to healthy food in poor neighborhoods. The group is called Food Fight."

"Cute name. So Rob's company is sponsoring it?"

"Yeah, although Rob hasn't really had much involvement. It's not his department. Frankly, I've had more involvement than he has. I offered to help with a few odds and ends, and the work sort of . . . snowballed."

"No, really?" Jess feigned shock. She knew Amy too well.

Amy smacked her playfully in the arm. "Hey now."

"What can I say? The old ones are the old ones." Jess grinned. "So there will be MediaCom people there other than Rob, right?"

"Yeah, I think there's an entire table." Amy shot her a sideways glance. "Why, you thinking of ditching us for a better group?"

"Psh, are you kidding? Like I'd fly across the country to dine with a bunch of corporate nincompoops. I can do that in Seattle, thanks."

"I'll be interested to hear what you think of Julian and Grace."

"They're the couple who sold the house?"

"Yeah, sorry—Julian and Grace Durant."

"Wait, Julian Durant?" Dave chimed in from the back seat. "Do you know where he went to college?"

"I'm not sure. Why?"

"I went to UNC with a guy named Julian Durant. We weren't tight, but I know the name."

"Maybe? I guess you'll find out tomorrow."

"For sure. If it's the same guy, he was pretty well-liked around school. Social butterfly type."

"That fits. He's definitely very charismatic."

"Athletic, too. I think he played on the soccer team for a while."

"I don't know how active Julian is these days—assuming it's the same guy. I think he had an injury."

"Oh, yeah? That's a shame. What happened?"

Amy glanced in the rearview mirror. Noah didn't seem to be paying attention and was watching the cars pass, but Amy knew it wasn't appropriate to bring up Julian's issue with painkillers, regardless of whether Noah was there or not.

"I'm not sure," she finally said. "You'll have to ask him tomorrow."

By the time they got home, Noah had fallen asleep in the back seat, and Dave looked like he was about to as well. Since Sherrie and Bruce were babysitting the following evening, Amy didn't feel right sticking Noah with a babysitter two nights in a row, so she'd planned on a low-key dinner at home after Noah went to sleep. It wouldn't be the wild night on the town she'd envisioned when she first invited Jess, but these days, a quiet, home-cooked meal was more her speed anyway.

She prodded Noah awake and led the group inside, showing Jess and Dave to the guest room upstairs.

"The house is *great*," Jess said. "I can see why you fell in love with it. It's so cozy. I mean that in a good way—not like it's too small or something."

"It does have a warm feeling, right?"

"The whole neighborhood does. Two thumbs up."

Amy didn't need a friend's approval to feel confident in her choice of domicile, but she had to admit, getting Jess's endorsement felt good. Jess had always had excellent taste in art and design, and in college Amy often looked to her for style advice. Given Grace's artistic flair and the traces of it she'd left behind, it made sense that Jess would feel a connection with 120 Sycamore. Frankly, some days Grace reminded her a little of Jess. Maybe that was another reason she felt so drawn to her.

Jess and Dave unpacked while Amy cooked Noah's nuggets and green beans; then they met in the kitchen for wine and cheese while Noah ate. Rob came in just as they'd poured the second glass of Pinot Noir.

"You made it," he said, smiling as he shook Dave's hand and gave Jess a hug. Amy had always loved how seamlessly Rob blended in with her friends, as if they'd been his friends for as long as they'd been hers.

"Noah was just telling us all about poisonous frogs," Jess said.

"Ah, yes, a favorite pastime."

Jess and Dave laughed. "He knows way more than I ever did about them, I'll tell you that," Dave said.

"He knows more than I do about a lot of things," said Rob. "That may be more a reflection on my memory and education than anything else, but nevertheless."

"Hey, Noah, sweetie? Finish up your nuggets and then Daddy will take you up for bath."

"But I want dessert."

Amy sighed. "Fine. One piece of chocolate and then it's bath time."

"Can Dave come, too?"

"In the tub? Uh . . . no thanks, dude." Dave winked at them jokingly.

"*No*," Noah said. "Not in the *tub*. In my *room* for story."

Amy and Rob looked at each other and shrugged. "Fine," Amy said. "But only if you promise to go straight to bed after."

Noah wiggled excitedly and scarfed down the rest of his nuggets before practically inhaling a Hershey's Kiss. Rob and Dave accompanied him upstairs, and Amy got on with cooking dinner, a simple sausage and kale pasta with a side salad.

"So, Ame, how's your family? I've been meaning to ask."

Amy crumbled the sausage into a skillet and pushed it around with a wooden spoon. "Oh, you know . . . the usual . . ." She sighed. "My brother is in rehab again. Or recovery I guess at this point."

"I'm so sorry to hear that."

"Better in recovery than the alternative, right?"

"For sure. Have you spoken to him?"

A wave of guilt washed over Amy. She still hadn't called him, even though she'd been thinking about doing so for weeks.

"No, I've been meaning to, but . . . you know how it is. Life with kids is busy, and this time of year is even worse than normal."

"Well, sure, and I'm guessing it doesn't help that you've been through this a dozen times before with him."

That's what Amy loved about Jess. Not only did she speak freely and honestly, but they'd also known each other long enough that she completely understood where Amy's head would be with all of this.

With new friends—well, with most new friends she didn't even mention her brother. But with those she did, like Grace, she wouldn't dare admit that part of her didn't want to talk to her brother, even though she knew she should. She didn't have to pretend with Jess, though. Jess knew she loved Tim, but as an old friend, she had also lived through nearly every iteration of his addiction and rehab saga. She'd watched Amy throw herself into emotional turmoil as she tried to help Tim time after time. Amy had vented to poor Jess on dozens of occasions, unleashing her frustrations and sorrow over the course of a phone call because there was no one else she could talk to about it. So Jess knew why Amy hadn't called Tim. They didn't need to pretend it was Amy's busy schedule.

Amy shrugged. "It's just too much, you know? After last time."

"I hear you. You've done a lot for him. After a while, you need to step away, for your own sanity."

"Which, let's be honest, has always been questionable."

Jess laughed. "Please, you're the sanest person I know."

"Uh, that's troubling." Amy added the blanched kale to the sauté pan. "What kind of people have you been hanging out with in Seattle? I'm concerned."

Jess sipped her wine. "Oh, you know . . . nice people. Friends from work. Other people with kids. All perfectly friendly folks, just not . . . you know. *This*." She gestured back and forth between her and Amy.

"Do you think we'd have done anything differently if someone had told us that making close friends as an adult is so hard? Like, would we have made more of an effort to live in the same city?"

"Probably not."

"You don't think?"

"Young people think they're invincible. We wouldn't have listened."

"Hey, we're still young."

Jess looked unconvinced. "Maybe young*ish*. But we're old enough to know how stupid we were at twenty."

"True." She poured some chicken stock into the pan and looked over her shoulder. "We were pretty stupid, weren't we?"

"So stupid. But you know, sometimes I kind of miss that version of me. She was gutsy. She had big dreams. These days the biggest dream I have is being able to sleep for nine consecutive hours."

"I don't know, that sounds pretty ambitious to me."

They both laughed. "You're right," Jess said, "that's probably even less realistic than my dreams of becoming attorney general."

"All in good time, my friend."

"What, becoming attorney general or getting a good night's sleep?"

"Why not both?"

"You're right. Why not?" She raised her glass. "To good friends and crazy dreams. May neither of them fade."

"Hear, hear."

Amy clinked her glass against Jess's and thought how her friend's visit was already better and more perfect than she ever could have imagined.

# Chapter 19

The next day did not go nearly as smoothly. All of the adults woke up with hangovers after staying up too late talking and drinking wine. Then Amy's plans for everyone to spend the morning and lunch downtown were held up when Grace called with a last-minute event request. Amy had told Grace she had friends visiting and wouldn't be able to help that weekend, but somehow Grace hadn't internalized the message.

"I'm sorry—I know you're busy—but Julian is having second thoughts about certain parts of his speech, and I was wondering if you could take a look."

"We were actually just heading out the door. . . ."

"This won't take long. I promise. He could just use a second pair of eyes that aren't mine."

Amy sighed. "Okay. Send it to me."

Once again, Amy's inability to say no reared its head. The truth was, she'd spent so much of her own time on this event that she didn't want Julian to ruin it by making a fool of himself. The rational part of her brain knew that if she'd said no earlier on, she wouldn't feel so invested and could more easily say no now, but it was too late to do anything about it.

Grace took an age sending the e-mail, and by the time Amy had finished reading it and writing comments, it was too late to make it downtown for lunch and an activity and still make it home to get dressed for the gala. So instead, they headed to Morris Arboretum to grab a bite and check out some of the sculptures and installations. The weather had turned, though, and it was a little too cold to spend more than an hour or two outside, so once they'd seen the Bird's Nest and the Garden Railway, they piled in the car and headed back to Jenkintown.

The rest of the afternoon involved napping, snacking, and getting dolled up for the fund-raiser, and before Amy knew it, the doorbell was ringing. She quickly fastened her earrings and hurried down the stairs.

"Bubbe's here! Bubbe's here!" Noah shouted as he ran down the hall. He nearly crashed into her at the bottom of the stairs.

"*Somebody* sounds excited to see me," Sherrie said as Amy opened the front door.

"Me, me, me!" Noah jumped up and down as he fixed his eyes on the foil-covered tray in her hands. "What's *that?*"

"Oh, I don't know . . . just a little something for some boys who've been well behaved."

"I have, I have!"

"Then I guess you will get to have some . . . peanut butter swirl brownies."

"Yay! Yay! Yay!" Amy thought his head might actually spin off his body.

"You have to eat your dinner first," Amy said, patting him on the shoulder. "Okay?"

He sighed. "Of *course.* Why do you even say that?"

"Noah . . ."

"Oh, he's fine. He is perfect, in fact." Sherrie leaned over and kissed his head. "Doesn't Mommy look beautiful?"

Noah nodded, his eyes wide. "Like a princess."

"Or a movie star," Rob said as he came down the stairs behind her. "Very Audrey Hepburn in *Breakfast at Tiffany's*, don't you think?"

"Maybe if Audrey had reddish hair and less desirable bone structure," Amy joked.

"Stop," said Sherrie. "You look gorgeous. And Rob—so handsome!"

"Thanks, Mom." He gave her a kiss and reached out to hug Bruce, who had been lurking behind his wife as she fussed over Noah. "Let's head back to the kitchen. We're still waiting on Ethan, and Jess and Dave are still upstairs getting ready."

They crowded into the kitchen, where Sherrie put her brownies on the counter and piled her coat with Bruce's on one of the kitchen chairs. Ethan climbed up on a stool and peeked beneath the foil.

"Ah, ah, ah—not until after dinner, remember?" Amy said.

"I'm just *looking*."

"You should keep the foil on—they might dry out."

"Fine." He gave them one last probing look and then replaced the foil. "Ethan can have those, right? Even though they have peanut butter?"

Sherrie blanched. "Ethan is allergic to peanuts?"

"No, just tree nuts. Peanuts are fine."

"Oh, thank God. You scared me for a second."

"You're fine. Not to worry."

"That's odd, isn't it? Tree nuts but not peanuts?"

"Peanuts are technically a legume, so I guess it's a completely different allergy. There are definitely kids who are allergic to both, but not Ethan."

"Lucky for him. It seems like peanuts are in everything, especially for kids."

The sound of footsteps echoed down the hallway, and Dave and Jess appeared in the kitchen with the rest of them. Jess looked stunning in a raspberry crêpe de chine gown with long sleeves and a plunging neckline. She extended her hand as she approached Rob's parents.

"So good to see you again," she said. "The last time—well, I think the last time was their wedding nine years ago."

"I think you're right," Sherrie said. "Gosh, it's hard to believe it's been that long. Isn't it, Bruce?"

Bruce nodded but seemed a little dazed by Jess's beauty.

Jess clapped her hands together. "So! Are we off then?"

"We're still waiting for Ethan."

"Oh. Right." Her eyes drifted to the clock. "Aren't his parents the ones running the event? Is someone else dropping him off?"

"I think Grace is dropping him off. Julian went ahead to Old Pine Community Center. I offered to give her a ride. It seemed silly for them to have two cars downtown."

"That makes sense." She looked at the clock again. "Remind me what time the event starts?"

"Six," Amy said.

"Ah. Okay."

Amy knew what she was thinking because Amy was thinking it herself: *It's time to leave, and the wife of the guy spearheading the event isn't here yet? Seriously?* Given how much effort Grace put into the event, Amy was surprised she hadn't wanted to leave earlier so that she could get there well before the guests arrived. Even Amy wanted to be there at least a few minutes early, just to see how everything looked. It wasn't her event, and she didn't want to take public credit for the work she'd put in, but she had done enough that she was more than a little curious to witness the fruits of her labor.

"Let's get our stuff together," Amy said. "I'm sure she'll be here any second."

It was many seconds before Grace finally arrived—1,800, in fact (not that Amy had counted, though Noah would have been ecstatic if she had). When she hadn't answered any of their calls, they debated leaving without her. Maybe she'd made alternate plans and forgot to tell them.

But then at 5:30, the doorbell finally rang. Amy hustled down the hallway as fast as she could in her long black satin dress and heels. She tried to calm herself so that she didn't come off as annoyed as she felt. What kind of spouse showed up late to her partner's event—and worse, made her friends late as a result?

Amy threw open the door, but as soon as she set eyes on Grace, she felt guilty for being pissed off. Grace didn't look herself. Her hand, which rested on Ethan's shoulder, was trembling, and her eyes were red and a little puffy. She looked as if she'd been crying.

"I'm so sorry we're late," she said as she pushed Ethan through the front door.

"It's fine—we were just . . . are you okay?"

Grace smiled tightly as she escorted Ethan down the hall. "Fine. Thanks."

"You just look . . . we were trying to get ahold of you, but no one answered."

Amy was floundering, but she didn't know exactly what to say. If it were Jess who had shown up late and looked as if she'd been crying, Amy would know exactly what to say and how to say it. But her friendship with Grace was so new. She wasn't sure how to approach the subject of her puffy eyes without being pushy or rude.

"Things just didn't go as planned this afternoon, that's all. Julian took a nap but forgot to set his alarm, so he overslept, and the day has been chaos ever since."

"Wow, I can only imagine. I assume he is already on his way downtown?"

"Oh, yeah, he's already there. Thank God."

They entered the kitchen, and immediately Noah pounced on Ethan. "Wanna see my space puzzle? It glows in the dark!"

The boys hurried off to the family room, and Amy quickly introduced everyone.

"The house looks great," Grace said, a little morosely. Her eyes wandered around the kitchen.

"Thanks," Amy said. She felt herself flush. "You guys took such great care of it."

"I love your dress," Sherrie said to Grace. "It's so interesting."

The dress *was* interesting—and, Amy thought, fabulous—but more than anything Amy was grateful to Sherrie for changing the topic. Grace already seemed upset about something, and dwelling on the fact that this was no longer her home wouldn't improve anyone's mood.

Her dress consisted of two pieces: a short-sleeved cream chiffon top, the front of which was studded with gold sequins and a band of coral beads around the neck and waist, and then a long cream chiffon skirt with bands of gold and coral beads. The sleeves and waist were pleated and flared out delicately, as did the bottom hem of the skirt. She looked like a Greek goddess. The dangly gold earrings and gold bangle around her bicep only added to the impression.

"Thanks. I thought it was a little different."

It was more than a little different—it was truly unique. Amy had never seen anything like it. Her own dress may have been classic *Breakfast at Tiffany's*, but that also meant something similar had been worn by hundreds of women—thousands of women—for decades upon decades. Jess looked stunning in her raspberry gown, but Grace, as always, was a class above.

"Anyway, we should go," Grace said. "I'm really sorry for holding everyone up."

"It's fine, it's fine," everyone said, even though mere minutes ago they'd all been complaining about how late they were going to be.

"Thank you so much, Mr. and Mrs. Kravitz, for watching Ethan. You have no idea how much we appreciate it."

"It's our pleasure," Sherrie said.

"I promise he'll be good. He likes a lot of the same things Noah does, and if you run into any trouble—"

"We won't. You're fine. Go, go—before you're really late."

Grace flushed. "Right. Sorry. See you when we get back."

"Have fun," Sherrie and Bruce called after them.

The group hurried together toward the car and headed for the city.

The event looked even better than Amy had expected. The hall in the Old Pine Community Center had been transformed into a festive wonderland. A sea of tables spread out before her covered with balloons and confetti, the programs she had so carefully edited distributed at each place setting. Julian had apparently found an intern willing to help transport the décor, which was lucky for him, considering the day's turn of events.

The community center was located in Society Hill, a historic Philadelphia neighborhood that reminded Amy a little of Georgetown. Primarily a residential neighborhood, the streets—many of them cobblestone—were lined with Federalist and Georgian brick townhouses, old-fashioned streetlamps, and ruddy brick sidewalks. It was the kind of neighborhood where Amy could imagine the Founding Fathers living while they drafted the Constitution. It wasn't the sort of neighborhood that needed Food Fight's services (it was one of the wealthiest neighborhoods in Philadelphia and was home to one of the best farmers' markets in the city), but the Old Pine Community Center was much like many of the ones Julian's nonprofit would benefit, so the location worked both in terms of aesthetics and mission.

"Wow, this looks *great*," Jess said as they peered in the banquet hall. "You had something to do with this?"

"A little."

"She did more than a little," Grace said. "She was a lifesaver."

"I wouldn't go that far."

"I would." She peered over Amy's shoulder toward the small lobby area, where people were having cocktails and hors d'oeuvres. "I guess the bar is over there. Shall we?"

She led the group to the bar area, and they each ordered a drink. Amy knew Julian had bought his own wine, beer, and liquor to keep costs down, but with a hired bartender pouring the drinks, no one could tell the difference. Amy thought it was admirable the extent to which Julian had stayed on or below budget. Aside from the question of flowers versus balloons, he had been remarkably frugal, considering he'd gotten ten thousand dollars from MediaCom. *Good for him*, Amy thought. *Better to put that money toward local programs than filet mignon for dinner.*

Thinking of MediaCom, Amy noticed the logo appeared all over the cocktail area—on the napkins, above the doorway to the banquet hall, on the pens situated along the tables where the silent auction was taking place. They'd done a good job. The logo was noticeable but not intrusive. The company seemed to be doing a nice thing but weren't being over the top about it.

"Should I bid on that Prada bag?" Jess whispered in Amy's ear.

"Go for it. Someone has to win it. Might as well be you!"

"Or you."

"Jess, dear, the amount I can afford to bid on that bag probably wouldn't even pay for the zipper."

She laughed. "How about this: If I win, we can share it, since you were kind enough to pay for my ticket here tonight."

"Share a purse? With you in Seattle and me in Philadelphia?"

"Sure. We can have joint custody. Half the year it will live with me, and half the year it will live with you. And either of us has visitation rights when the other is in possession."

"Spoken like a lawyer."

"A lawyer who misses and loves her friend."

"Okay. You have a deal."

Jess scurried over to the bidding table and made an offer on the purse, and Amy surveyed the room. She didn't recognize many people here, but then that wasn't surprising since she was still relatively new to the city and didn't actually work for Julian. Everyone seemed to be having fun, and Rob had even managed to introduce Dave to a few MediaCom employees who would make useful contacts. In Amy's fantasies, one of them would eventually offer Dave a job, and he and Jess would move to Philadelphia with their kids. She knew the likelihood of such a thing happening was infinitesimal (Dave seemed to love his job, and they both seemed to enjoy Seattle), but she held out hope that maybe, someday, it would happen.

The one person in the crowd Amy didn't see was Julian. She figured he was probably pressing the flesh with as many of the 148 attendees as he could, but as hard as she tried, she couldn't locate him. Grace was standing behind her making small talk with an older couple she seemed to know, and when the couple moved on, Amy came up beside her.

"This seems to be going really well. Julian must be thrilled." Amy waited for Grace to reply, but she just nodded. "Where is he, by the way? I haven't seen him."

"Don't know, don't care." She took a sip of her wine and stared out over the crowd.

"Oh. I didn't . . . did you guys . . ." Amy tripped over her words. "Sorry. I'm not trying to . . . you just looked upset when you arrived, and I wanted to make sure—"

"I'm fine," Grace said, a little coolly.

"Good. I'm glad. But if you ever want to talk about anything—"

"Now doesn't seem like a great time for that, does it?"

"No, definitely not. I just meant—"

"You guys, I just went *crazy* at the bidding table," Jess said, coming up behind them. "I hope Dave likes soft pretzels. . . ."

Amy forced a grin, but Jess could tell by her expression that she'd walked into an awkward situation.

"Sorry—did I just interrupt something? Ignore me. Carry on."

"No, I was just telling Amy I needed to check on the caterer," Grace said. "I'll see you ladies inside."

Then she walked away, sipping her wine, looking like the loneliest woman in the room.

They all took their seats around 7:30. Amy knew (or at least knew of) most of the people at her table: Emily and Brent, Jess and Dave, another couple from Beth Israel, and then another mid-thirties couple she didn't recognize. Her table wasn't far from the head table, where she saw Grace chatting to an older couple. As she looked at them more closely, she realized they must be Grace's parents. The man looked to be in his early seventies and was tall and thin, with a head of gray hair that was thinning at the top. His wife looked a bit younger—maybe early sixties—and was the woman Amy had seen at camp dropoff.

She still didn't see Julian, but she figured he was probably milling around somewhere in the crowd. Grace's frostiness had definitely piqued her interest about what had happened earlier this afternoon. Whatever problems had occurred in the past, Grace seemed very adept at putting on a happy face and pretending like nothing was wrong. If she hadn't let it slip at the brewhouse that Julian was in recovery, Amy probably never would have guessed. But tonight was different. Grace wasn't happy, and she wasn't doing a very good job at disguising it. Even talking to her parents, she looked irritated, though Amy figured she might often look that way when in their presence, given what she had said about their relationship. Were they asking where Julian was? Were they as curious as Amy was about the sudden change in Grace's demeanor?

"I should introduce myself—I'm Emily. My son Jake is in school with Noah and Ethan."

Amy snapped out of her trance and saw Emily leaning in to chat with Jess.

"I'm Jess. Amy and I went to college together."

"Sorry," Amy said. "I should have introduced everyone. Jess, Emily. Emily, Jess."

"No worries," Emily said. "We were on top of it. You know me—incapable of minding my own business."

Amy laughed. "I probably wouldn't have put it *that* way, but since you're the one who said it . . ."

"Seriously, I'm terrible. Did Amy tell you I basically stalked her at a local coffee shop? Oh, yeah. Came right up to her and interrupted her work so that I could introduce myself and set up a play-date."

"That sounds like being friendly," Jess said.

"Does it? I mean that's how I meant it, but people are always telling me to tone it down a little. Aren't they, Brent?"

Brent lifted his shoulders. "There's really no good way for me to answer that, is there?"

She pursed her lips. "Agreeing with me is the good way."

"Okay, then yes. People tell you to tone it down. Including me. Right now."

Jess nearly spit out her wine as Emily glared at her husband.

"Anyway," Emily said, "it's great to meet you. Such a wonderful coincidence that you could visit the same night as this event."

"When the stars align, the stars align."

"Sounds like Amy had a hand in some of the planning . . . ?" Emily raised an eyebrow as her eyes landed on Amy.

"I guess so," Jess said, "though I still haven't had a chance to meet the mysterious Julian."

"Ha! Mysterious." Emily rolled her eyes. "That's one way of putting it. Have you met Grace?"

"We gave her a ride tonight. She seems really nice, though definitely a little . . . stressed."

"Stressed? That doesn't sound like Grace. Grace is full of . . . well, *grace*. I always called her unflappable. When we were still close."

Jess caught Amy's eye. She knew there was a story there but was studying Amy to see if now was the time to talk about it. It wasn't.

"It's a major event for Julian," Amy said, moving swiftly along. "I'd probably be stressed if Rob were putting on something like this—especially if I'd had a part in some of the planning."

"Yeah, but you did have a part in some of the planning for *this*, and you don't seem flustered at all. Anyway, it's just interesting to hear you say—ah! There's Julian! Well, *he* looks dapper, doesn't he?"

They all turned and looked as Julian approached the podium. He did look decidedly handsome. His dark brown hair was parted to the side and held in place with some sort of pomade or gel that made his tresses glisten. He wore a slim-cut navy suit with a lavender shirt and dark magenta tie, and though she was seated a bit far to see exactly what kind of shoes he was wearing, she could tell they were brown leather lace-ups that looked as sleek as the rest of the ensemble.

"*That's* Julian?" Jess whispered in her ear. "Meow."

Amy elbowed her before she could say anything inappropriate.

Dave reached across Jess and tapped Amy on the shoulder. "Hey—I think that *is* the guy I went to school with."

"No way," Amy and Jess said in unison.

"Yeah, looks just like him. Like I said, we weren't close, but we knew some of the same people. Remember Henry? He was tight with Julian."

"You mean Henry could have set me up with that?" Jess said. She feigned a sigh. "What could have been . . ."

*If only you knew*, Amy thought.

The crowd quieted as Julian adjusted the microphone at the lectern and cleared his throat.

"Welcome," he said, "and thank you all for coming. Before I dive in to my remarks, I want to thank the Old Pine Community Center for providing a venue for tonight's festivities. Community centers like yours all around the Philadelphia area enrich our city and make it the vibrant, diverse, and dynamic place it is today. Without community centers, the work we do at Food Fight wouldn't have nearly the reach and impact it currently does. And with the funds raised at tonight's event, we think we can stretch that reach even farther, and touch corners of the city that have long been ignored, belittled, and abandoned."

The audience applauded, and a few people raised glasses while cheering, "Hear, hear."

Julian continued with his remarks, outlining the successes the organization had over the previous years and the challenges that lay ahead. At the beginning of the speech, Amy had noticed that he was swaying almost imperceptibly from side to side as he spoke, which she attributed to a nervous public speaking tic. Her former boss Debbie used to do it all the time—they called it the Debbie dance. But as the speech went on, even as his voice became more relaxed, the lilting became more exaggerated. Then, somewhere in the middle of the speech, he started stumbling over words, slurring other words together, and skipping lines so that he needed to apologize and go back. After a stumbling over the phrase "fresh food suppliers" three times in a row, he chuckled and tried to make a joke of it.

"Sorry, I shouldn't have let Bill buy me that whiskey."

The crowd laughed, a little uncomfortably Amy thought. She also wondered if someone named Bill really *had* bought him a whiskey. Aside from the fact that Julian supposedly didn't drink anymore, the event had an open bar. There was no need for anyone to "buy" him anything. Maybe it was just a turn of phrase? Or maybe he was covering for being nervous. Or maybe it was something else.

The speech went on and became increasingly awkward, at which point Amy's phone started buzzing on the table. She looked down. Sherrie was calling.

She couldn't answer right there in the middle of Julian's speech, so she grabbed the phone and slipped out the door to the cocktail area. By the time she was in a quiet place, she had just missed the call, but before she could call back, the phone rang again. Sherrie.

"Sherrie, hi—sorry, Julian was in the middle of his speech, and I—"

"Amy!" Sherrie shouted. "Stop. We have an emergency."

Amy nearly stopped breathing. Noah. Oh God. "What happened?"

"We ate dinner, and then I gave the boys some of those brownies for dessert and Ethan . . . you said he wasn't allergic to peanuts!"

"He isn't."

"Well, his face is blowing up like a balloon and he's wheezing, and I can't find his EpiPen anywhere. He pointed to his bag, but it isn't in there."

"Are you sure?"

"YES, I'm sure." Amy had never heard Sherrie like this. She sounded utterly panicked.

"I don't . . . I mean . . . shit. Can you take him to the ER?"

"Of course, but I'm worried he'll stop breathing before we get there. It's bad, Amy. BAD."

Amy thought she might throw up. If Ethan died on her in-laws' watch . . . the bile crept up the back of her throat.

"Wait," she said. "Rob has an extra EpiPen in his medicine cabinet."

"Oh, thank God. Is it in date?"

"I think so? Go—it's upstairs."

"I'm going."

Amy could hear her thumping up the stairs as she made her way into their bathroom. Amy's palms were so sweaty she could barely hold on to the phone.

"I found it. It's here. But it's the adult one. Not the one for kids."

"Fuck." Amy took a deep breath. "Hang on. Two seconds."

She raced back into the banquet hall and snuck over to her table. She grabbed Rob's arm and pulled him out of the room with her.

"What the—"

"Can your mom use your Epi on Ethan?"

"What do you mean?"

"He's having a reaction and doesn't have one with him."

"Oh. Shit. I don't know. Mine is for people over sixty-five pounds. He needs the junior dose."

"Yeah, but he doesn't have the junior dose. My question is: Will the adult dose give him a heart attack, or will he just feel shitty? Because the latter is better than him dying of anaphylaxis."

Rob looked completely freaked out. He obviously didn't feel comfortable having another kid's life in his hands.

"From what I remember learning when I was a kid . . . I think any epinephrine is better than no epinephrine."

"Sherrie?"

"Yeah?"

"Give it to him. And then go straight to the ER. We'll meet you there with Ethan's parents."

"If you're sure."

"I am. We'll be there in, like, forty minutes. Okay?"

"Okay."

Amy hung up and ran back in the banquet hall, trying to find the words to break the news to Grace.

# Chapter 20

Forty minutes later, they arrived at the Abington Hospital ER. All five of them came—Amy, Rob, Jess, Dave, and Grace. Given that they'd carpooled, there was no other way to split up the group. Julian couldn't leave in the middle of his speech, and they couldn't abandon out-of-town friends at an event where they knew no one. So they stormed into the ER as a posse, one outfitted in satin, chiffon, and worsted wool.

Grace was immediately taken back to see Ethan, the pleated hem of her chiffon skirt fluttering as she hurried beside the nurse. The rest of them sat in the waiting area, still dumbstruck at the unexpected turn the evening had taken.

"Do you think Julian is okay?" Jess asked. It was the first any of them had really said since leaving the fund-raiser. "I mean, we all just took off before he'd finished his speech without any explanation."

"I'm sure Grace's parents filled him in."

"Why didn't *they* drive her here?"

"They didn't have a car nearby. Apparently they have a pied-à-terre on Rittenhouse Square, and the car was parked somewhere around there. We were two blocks away."

"The whole thing is just so crazy. Why didn't he have his EpiPen?"

"I don't know. Grace seemed really flustered and upset when she showed up late. Maybe she just forgot."

"I guess . . . But an EpiPen seems like something you wouldn't forget."

"You say that, but have you ever switched to a different purse and forgotten something you always carry around? I've done that at least a dozen times. Just last week, I accidentally left my wallet in my gym bag and got all the way through the grocery checkout before I realized I couldn't actually pay for anything."

Jess chuckled. "Nice."

"What, you've never done anything like that?"

"Oh, no, I totally have. I once forgot to refill the diapers in the diaper bag, and Dave took Penny while he did some errands and she did an epic poop. He ended up having to wrap her in a bunch of paper towels—which, in case you're wondering, are in no way a diaper substitute."

"See? Shit happens."

"Literally."

They both laughed, but caught themselves when they saw Sherrie heading toward them. Rob rushed to meet her and gave her a hug.

"How are you? How's Ethan?"

"He's okay. Very nauseous, but okay."

"So what happened?"

"We gave him the adult Epi. They say it saved his life, but he won't feel well for a few days."

"No, I mean, how did he have a reaction in the first place?"

"The doctor says it must have been something in the brownies. I told him I didn't use any tree nuts, but he said sometimes there are traces in chocolate or peanut butter. I didn't even think to check the label. It's been so long since I've had to think about anything like that." Her voice caught. "I feel awful. Just awful."

"Mom, it isn't your fault. You didn't even know he had an allergy when you baked them."

"But if I hadn't fed him those brownies, I'd be sitting in your family room with Bruce while the boys slept upstairs. Poor Noah. I've never seen him so scared. He'll probably be having nightmares for months." She buried her face in her hands. "Oh God, I can't believe it."

Rob hugged her close and rubbed her back. "It isn't your fault. He's going to be fine. You did everything right—you saved his life."

She sniffled. "Thanks to your EpiPen. You'll need a new one by the way. Which I'm sure will cost you a pretty penny."

"Mom, stop. It's fine. I'm glad you were able to use it—especially since he didn't have his own."

She wiped her eyes and pulled away. "I couldn't believe it. With an allergy like that, to not have an EpiPen . . ."

"I'm guessing Grace forgot it," Amy chimed in. "She was in such a rush after Julian overslept that she probably just threw a bunch of stuff into a bag without really thinking about it."

She didn't know why she kept defending Grace. She didn't *know* that Grace had forgotten it. But Grace was a good mother. Amy knew that. She'd never done anything brazenly irresponsible in all the time they'd known each other. Amy couldn't imagine her knowingly doing anything reckless when it came to her son, and as a fellow mother, Amy wanted to give her the benefit of the doubt.

"Maybe." Sherrie glanced over her shoulder, then lowered her voice. "Is she usually that . . . scattered?"

"No, but tonight wasn't a typical night. This event was a big deal for Julian. He's had some issues in the past, and this fundraiser was meant to be sort of a comeback for him."

Sherrie's antennae went up. Even Jess seemed to lean in a little closer.

"Issues?" Sherrie said.

"Just . . . you know. Business stuff. Funding issues."

"Mmm." Sherrie looked suspicious. Amy could see the wheels turning, as if she were trying to figure out how Ethan's incident could be tied to some sort of nefarious behavior by Julian.

A nurse appeared in the waiting area and made for their group as soon as her eyes landed on Sherrie.

"Mrs. Kravitz?"

Both Amy and Sherrie turned around, but within seconds it was clear she was referring to Rob's mother.

"Yes?"

"Mrs. Durant is going to stay with Ethan until we release him from observation, so you are free to go."

"Oh. Okay. He's going to be okay?"

"We think so. We have to wait four hours to make sure he doesn't have a secondary reaction, but right now his biggest complaint is the nausea from the epinephrine."

"I'm so sorry—it was the only dose we had."

"It's fine. You did the right thing."

"Okay, well, I—oh! I just realized. I'm the one who drove Ethan here. How is he going to get home? Grace's car is still at my son's house."

"She said her parents are coming to get them."

"What about her husband?"

Sherrie was pumping the nurse for information, but everyone in the group was just as curious.

"She . . . didn't mention her husband. Sorry."

Amy knew he was probably still tied up at the event—he'd been giving a speech when they left and had other responsibilities there—but she couldn't help but wonder if Grace's omission had been due to some other reason as well.

Sherrie took a deep breath. "Well, I guess that's that. Would it be okay . . . could I say goodbye to Ethan?"

"Mrs. Durant asked for privacy until her parents arrive. I'm sorry. I'm sure she'd be happy to speak to you tomorrow, though. She sounded very grateful for everything you'd done."

"Oh. Okay." She cleared her throat. "Well, thank you for all of your help. I'm glad he is going to be okay."

She slipped on her coat and zipped it up, and the five of them filed out of the emergency room, hoping they'd left the evening's drama behind them.

They got home just after 9:30. Bruce had fallen asleep in the family room arm chair and was snoring so loudly they could hear him as soon as they walked in the house.

"Do you see what I have to put up with?" Sherrie said. "Every night is like this. Every. Night."

Dave laughed. "You need to invest in a good set of earplugs."

"The plug that will block out that sound doesn't exist. Trust me. I've tried. Eight pairs and counting."

Rob squeezed Amy's shoulder. "See what you have to look forward to?"

"If I were you, I'd pray for early deafness," Sherrie said. She stopped at the threshold to the family room. "I mean, look at him. *Look* at him."

Amy tried not to laugh but couldn't help herself. Bruce's arms dangled over the side of the chair, and his legs sprawled out before him, his nose pointed to the ceiling as his mouth hung wide open.

"God forbid Noah would need him for something. I mean, really." Sherrie shook her head in disgust. She walked over to the chair and nudged him. "Bruce. *Bruce!*"

He shook awake with a snort. "What's happening? Oh, you're back. Is everything okay? Where is Ethan?"

"He's still at the hospital under observation, but his mother is there with him now."

"Oh, good."

"Did everything go all right with Noah?" Amy asked.

"Sure did. He's upstairs asleep. He was a little shaken up by all of the commotion, but he calmed down once they'd gone to the hospital. He'll have a lot of questions for you tomorrow, though."

"I'm sure."

"Anyway." He smacked his hands on his knees. "I think we've all had enough excitement for one evening. Sherrie? Shall we?"

He got up and grabbed his coat off one of the kitchen chairs. Sherrie went over and inspected the leftover brownies.

"Do you want these? I can't even look at them without feeling queasy."

"We actually didn't eat dinner, so . . ." Amy surveyed her friends' faces. They nodded. "Yeah, we'll take them."

They showed Bruce and Sherrie out, and Amy called in a pizza order while the other three dug into the brownies.

"Dessert before dinner," Jess said as she inhaled an entire brownie. "We're really living on the edge."

"The pizza should be here in twenty minutes or so. Anyone want some wine?"

All three raised their hands. Amy got out four glasses and poured some Malbec into each. She brought the glasses to the kitchen table, where everyone was sitting, and leaned back in her chair.

"Well, I'm guessing this wasn't what you expected when you bought your plane tickets, eh?"

Jess laughed. "No, but it'll make for a great story."

"I'm so sorry. This is not how I saw this evening going. We didn't even find out if you won the Prada purse!"

Dave frowned. "You bid on a Prada purse?"

"And a case of soft pretzels. And maybe a mixology gift basket and a signed Eagles jersey . . ." Jess winced.

"I don't even like the Eagles!" Dave protested.

"Hey—watch it," said Rob.

"It was for charity." Jess put on her cutest smile. Amy knew Dave wouldn't be able to resist it.

"It's fine, it's fine." Dave took a sip of wine and shook his head. "Hopefully someone outbid you on at least one of those things."

"I'm guessing Julian will let me know if you won anything," Amy said. "I'll call him and Grace tomorrow to check on Ethan."

Jess reached for another brownie. "You said something at the hospital about Julian having some issues? What was all that about?"

Amy looked at Rob. On the one hand, Julian's past wasn't any of her friends' business, but on the other, what did it matter if she told them? They'd probably never see him again. Jess and Dave also weren't the types to spread gossip. Even if Dave talked to someone who'd known Julian in college, he was too polite to bring up Julian's problems. That wasn't his style.

"Promise not to say anything?"

"Of course."

"Okay, so a year or so ago, Julian got into some trouble with pills."

"Painkillers?"

Amy nodded. "I don't know all of the details, but it got bad enough that his nonprofit started suffering. Grace found out, and he went into rehab, but they cut a lot of ties with friends in the process. Like Emily at our table tonight? They used to be really close, but now they barely talk to each other."

"I thought something seemed off when she mentioned Grace," Jess said.

"Exactly," Amy said. "And apparently when things were bad, most of his staff either quit or were let go. That's part of the reason I ended up doing so much to help with tonight's event."

"That and the fact that you are almost incapable of saying no."

"True. But I think he was really hoping tonight would put Food Fight back on strong footing."

"Speaking of footing . . . did you notice how he was swaying back and forth tonight during his speech? That was weird, right?"

Amy had wondered if anyone else had noticed besides her. She nodded.

"His speech was kind of all over the place, too," Rob said. "Like, that whole thing about the whiskey? I thought he didn't drink."

"He doesn't. Or at least that's what Grace said. Maybe he was just really nervous, and that was a line to play it off."

"Except it got even worse after that. When you went out to take my mom's call? It was painful. Part of me was relieved when you pulled me out of the room."

Amy looked at Jess and Dave. "That bad?"

Dave nodded. "Pretty bad. I mean, there was some really interesting information in there—possibly stuff you finessed this morning, I don't know. But the delivery . . . it needed work."

Amy wondered if everyone else was thinking what she was thinking. She was too afraid to say the words out loud. But from the looks on everyone's faces, she realized she didn't need to say anything. They were all on the same page.

"It's just crazy to think that someone like that would have a problem," Dave said.

Jess furrowed her brow. "Someone like what?"

"I guess . . . well, like in college, he was Mr. All American—athletic, smart, popular, engaged in campus issues. He wasn't one of the guys getting obliterated at frat parties every weekend. I can't even remember if he was in a frat. He just seemed so . . . I don't know. Decent."

Amy tried not to glare at him because she knew he didn't know better. He held the same prejudices a lot of people did about drug addicts—that they were usually degenerate or sleazy in some way, that they looked like the characters in *Trainspotting* or the bums walking the streets. As a teenager, Amy had held those preconceptions, too. But if her experience with Tim had taught her anything, it was that addiction was indiscriminate, and people from all different backgrounds—rich, poor, shy, outgoing, tough, weak—could become its next victim. Her reasons for distancing herself from Tim had nothing to do with a lack of decency on his part; it had more to do with emotional preservation on hers. Her brother wasn't a bad person. Most days, she felt like the bad person for not contacting him.

"A lot of decent people have addictions," she said. The doorbell rang. "I'll tell you more about it over some pizza."

The next morning, Grace called while Amy was driving her guests and family to Chestnut Hill. She'd arranged brunch at a cute café on Germantown Avenue so that Jess and Dave could see the quaint, cobblestoned section of northwest Philadelphia that was only about fifteen minutes from her house.

Amy debated whether or not to answer, but everyone in the car—including Noah—was desperate to know how Ethan was doing. As long as she was open about the fact that Grace would be on Bluetooth, for everyone to hear, she figured she had nothing to worry about.

"Grace?"

"Hi—am I catching you at a bad time? You sound like you're in the car."

"I am. You're on Bluetooth."

Jess, Dave, and Rob said, "Hi!" in unison.

"Oh. Hi."

"Sorry," Amy said. "We can talk later. I just wanted to answer to see how Ethan was doing."

"Is he okay?" Noah called from the back seat. He'd been up a few times in the night with bad dreams about Ethan being sick. Amy hoped Grace could put his mind at ease.

"He's much better today, thanks. The doctors said he wouldn't be a hundred percent for a few days, but he's so much better than he was last night."

"We're so glad to hear that. We've been worried about him."

Amy had a dozen more questions she wanted to ask, but she figured she'd wait until Noah wasn't within earshot.

"Will Ethan be allowed to play at my house again?" Noah asked. "I promise I won't make him sick next time."

Amy cast a sideways glance at Rob, whose eyes locked on hers. *Oh, boy*, they said.

"Oh, sweetie, of course," Grace said. "It wasn't your fault *at all*. We've had this happen at our own house. It's no one's fault. He has an allergy."

"Okay," Noah said. Amy couldn't decide whether he sounded convinced or not.

"Anyway, I'll let you guys go. Amy, we can talk another time. Oh, but before you go—in all of the commotion last night, your friends never found out they won some prizes." ·

Amy caught Jess's eyes in the rearview mirror. "You're kidding."

"Yeah, hang on." She riffled through some papers. "Jessica Parrish won the case of soft pretzels, and . . ."

"The purse, the purse, the purse," Jess whispered in the back seat.

"Oh, wow. The Prada purse."

"YES!" Jess shrieked.

"That hurt my ears," Noah said, placing his hands over them.

"Sorry. It's just—yippee! I really wanted that purse."

"Of which I have joint custody," Amy added.

"Of course."

"Joint custody of a *purse*?" Dave muttered.

"I think what you mean is 'thank you.' I won you enough carbs to satisfy every craving you've ever had."

"Anyway," Amy said, barely able to contain her smile, "we're on our way to brunch now, but why don't we swing by after to pick up the goods?"

"Oh. That would be . . . you don't have to. I'll just drop them off."

"Don't be silly. We're out anyway. It's a low lift for us to stop by on our way home."

There was a long pause on the other end of the phone. "Things are just a little . . . we aren't really up for having guests. Ethan is still recovering."

"We don't have to come in. I could just pull in the driveway and you could hand the stuff through the window."

"I guess that would work." She paused. "Okay. Sure. Just make sure you call when you're on your way so that I'm ready for you."

"Will do. See you in a few hours."

Amy hung up and wondered if it were her imagination, or if Grace sounded even more aloof than she had the night before.

"This is their *house?*" Dave's eyes widened as they drove down the Sterling's driveway. "Wow. Major upgrade from 120 Sycamore— not that there's anything wrong with your place. It's great. But it's not . . . this."

The paved drive curved past some sort of modern sculpture. "This isn't the Durants' place," Amy said. "It's Grace's parents'. The Durants are living in the guesthouse."

"Oh." He peered out the window. "Sweet deal."

"I don't think it's an ideal situation for any of them, but they had to sell the house, and this was pretty much the only option."

Amy met Jess's eyes in the rearview mirror. Jess nodded. Without knowing all of the details, she got the gist of the Durants' circumstances, partially due to the conversation they'd had last night and partially due to the near-telepathic relationship she and Amy had after only a few days back together. Amy missed having a connection like that in her life.

She slowed the car as they approached the front of the house. Grace's mother happened to be out front, surveying an arrangement of pumpkins and cornstalks on the portico. She squinted as she tried to peer through the passenger window from afar. Amy rolled down the window.

"Hi, I'm Grace's friend, Amy."

"Of course." She had a slight, almost undetectable accent. "We've been expecting you."

Amy tried not to look too surprised, but she wasn't exactly sure why Grace's mother knew anything about it. Grace hadn't even picked up when Amy called en route to let her know they were on their way.

"Your friends' prizes are inside. Let me get them."

She hurried up the front steps. Moments later, she appeared with a small bag bearing the Philly Pretzel Factory logo, along with a shopping bag that presumably contained the purse. Amy popped the trunk.

"The pretzels are just a sample," Grace's mother said as she loaded everything in. "They will overnight a case of fresh ones to your house. You just have to contact the company and arrange it. The number is in the bag."

She closed the trunk and came around to the passenger window.

"Grace sends her apologies. None of them is feeling one hundred percent today."

"I'm sorry to hear that," Amy said. "Send them our best. Tell Ethan we hope to see him at school next week."

"Grace thinks he'll be fine by tomorrow, but I keep telling her he should take it easy. The whole evening was quite an ordeal." She turned to Rob. "Thank your mother again, will you? We are so grateful. I can't *believe* Grace forgot the EpiPen."

"It was a busy and stressful day," Amy said. "I could see myself doing the same thing."

"Anyway, thanks for coming by." She craned her neck to get a view of Jess and Dave. "Congratulations on your prizes. I hope you enjoyed your visit."

"We did," Jess said. "I'm glad we could help Julian's organization. They seem to do great work."

"Yes, well. We think so. Are you staying the week?"

"No, we fly back to Seattle this afternoon. Amy is taking us to the airport in about an hour."

"Ah. Safe travels, then."

"Tell Ethan I say hi!" Noah shouted from the back seat.

Grace's mother smiled as her eyes landed on him. "I will. He's been talking about you, you know."

"What did he say?"

"Just that he's sorry he never got to finish building that Lego rocket ship with you."

"He can come play another time and finish it."

She smiled and looked at Amy. "He's a very sweet boy. I'm not surprised they're friends."

"Ethan is very sweet, too," Amy said.

"Yes, he is. It's just such a shame about . . ." She caught herself. "Anyway, enjoy the remaining time with your friends. I'll send Grace, Julian, and Ethan your regards."

She walked up her front steps and turned around to wave good-bye, the expression on her face inscrutable.

# Chapter 21

Jess and Dave left, and life for Amy and Rob returned to normal. By now, Rob had settled into his job, and Amy had gotten into a routine that revolved around her fluctuating freelance work and Noah's schedule. She hated to admit it, but she actually missed the busy work that came with helping Julian plan his event. At least then she was regularly in touch with someone—either him or Grace or one of the community centers—and felt as if she were a part of something. With her freelance work, she felt disconnected from the organizations for which she was drafting grant proposals and editing program materials. The truth was, she was no more a part of Food Fight than she was a part of the Association of American Educators, but the face-to-face contact with Julian and Grace augmented her sense of belonging.

More than the professional engagement, though, Amy realized how much she missed Jess. It wasn't only Jess (though she was the college friend with whom Amy had stayed the closest), but really any friend with whom she had a deep bond. Emily and Grace were great. But they weren't the kind of friends she would cry in front of or discuss her deepest secrets—at least not yet. She'd thought maybe Grace could become that kind of friend, but ever since the fund-raiser, she had become increasingly withdrawn. She would be polite when they ran into each other, but at pickup she'd hurry

Ethan out the door, even when the weather was nice and the other kids wanted to hang around to play. Combined with Jess's departure, Amy felt lonelier than she had in a long time.

Nevertheless, it wasn't Amy's style to mope or wallow. The weeks went by, she kept her chin up, and life generally kept to its everyday rhythm. Noah still loved school and stood front and center in the Thanksgiving show Miss Ruth put together. From there, his attention turned to the Hanukkah show the school would be putting on for the parents before winter break. For Amy's part, she couldn't believe it was already December. It seemed like just yesterday it had been summer and they were moving into their new house. The year was flying by.

Amy had just come in the house with some art supplies for Noah's latke crown when her phone rang. She looked at the screen and didn't recognize the number. It was a 215 area code, meaning the caller was based in Philadelphia, but she couldn't think who it could be. She hesitated but decided to pick up in case it was someone from Beth Israel calling about Noah.

"Miss Kravitz?"

"Yes?"

"It's Leroy Harris. We spoke about two months ago, when you were planning that fund-raiser for Food Fight."

"Of course—how are you?"

"I'm good, I'm good. Getting ready for Christmas. Always a busy time around here. Lots of programs in the mix."

"I'm sure. So how can I help you?"

"I don't mean to trouble you, but I can't seem to get ahold of Julian."

"Oh. Is there a problem?"

"Well, as a matter of fact, there is."

Amy braced herself. Something in his voice told her she was not going to like what he was about to tell her.

"Shortly after you and I spoke," he continued, "Julian reached out to discuss the projects we were working on together. At that point we obviously didn't know exactly how much money we'd have to work with from the fund-raiser, but we knew we'd have a few thousand. So the Monday after the event, a bunch of us community centers got an e-mail about how much money was raised that night—$50,000. We were ecstatic. Divided among us, that would allow us to do a lot of the stuff we'd discussed with him. The problem is, that's the last I've heard about it. I waited a week or two before following up with Julian, but I couldn't get ahold of him, and it's been about a month now since the event. He doesn't answer his phone, and he won't return my e-mails."

Amy got a sinking feeling in her stomach. "Have you tried anyone else at the organization?"

"Yeah, I've called the main number dozens of times. No one picks up. That's why I'm calling you. You're the only other number I have for someone affiliated with Food Fight."

"I'm not really affiliated with them. I just helped a little with the event."

"That may be, but I'm asking for your help. If you're friends with him and his wife, you know how to get in touch with them. I need you to find out what's going on."

"Okay. I . . . I'll try. I'm sure it's just a misunderstanding."

"That may be, but it doesn't change the fact that we have all sorts of programs lined up and a bunch of people very excited about them, without the means to pay for everything. Julian made the funding sound like a sure thing—I wouldn't have green-lighted all these projects if he hadn't. We were counting on that fund-raiser to help us out."

"I understand. I'll see what I can do."

But a part of Amy dreaded what she might find because she was already beginning to suspect the worst.

Before Amy could look into anything, the calls started coming. It wasn't just Leroy Harris. It was Shonda White from the Hunting Park Community Center. Yvonne Lewis from the North Philly Rec Center. Adam Rivera. Isaiah Wilkins. Martha Ramos. By the time the weekend was through, pretty much everyone she had called from the list of community centers had contacted her with the same question: "Where is the money?"

Amy didn't have any more luck than the rest of them in getting ahold of Julian, or Grace for that matter. She called a few times and left voice mails for both, but neither of them called her back.

When the weekend passed without her hearing from the Durants, she decided she needed another strategy. She saw Grace nearly every day at Beth Israel. Grace no longer lingered to chat with the other parents, but Amy knew if she caught her at the right time, she could get an answer out of her or at least try.

So on Monday morning, Amy dropped Noah off at school a few minutes earlier than normal and lingered by Noah's cubby until she saw Grace come in with Ethan. Grace was so preoccupied with Ethan's various accessories (backpack, lunchbox, hat, mittens, *Star Wars* mask) that she didn't seem to notice Amy standing there until she was halfway through helping Ethan out of his coat.

"Oh—hi," she said, looking surprised. "Sorry—I didn't even see you there."

"Is Noah here?" Ethan asked.

"He is. I think he's working on some sort of latke number tree. He could probably use your help."

Ethan bolted inside while Grace hung his coat in his cubby. "The day Noah needs Ethan's help with anything number related is the day we all spontaneously take flight. . . ."

Amy laughed. "Noah will be glad he's here, whatever the case."

Grace slid into the classroom and signed Ethan in before saying goodbye to him and joining Amy in heading to the parking lot. They made small talk (how Ethan was doing, holiday plans, gift lists) until they approached Grace's car, at which point Amy began to panic. Time was running out. *Say something!* a voice in her head shouted.

"By the way," she said, "did you get my voice mail?"

"I did. Sorry—things have been really crazy."

"That's okay. I just wanted to talk because . . . the other day I got a call from Leroy Harris."

"Who?"

"The guy from St. Luke's Community Center?"

Grace shrugged. "Don't think I've met him."

"No. Right. I guess you wouldn't have. St. Luke's is one of the community centers working with Food Fight. They were supposed to get money from the fund-raiser."

"Oh, okay. Sure." She smiled. "Figures that you'd get close with all of those people. You certainly did enough work on the fundraiser to warrant it."

"We aren't really close. We're just—I mean, we have a good rapport, and he seems like a lovely person, but it's not like we talk all the time or anything." *Get to the point!* the voice said. *Stop prevaricating!*

"So he was just calling to—"

"He wants to know where his money is."

The words echoed off the car windows and pavement. A chilly silence hung between them.

"What do you mean?" Grace finally said.

"He hasn't received any of the money from the fund-raiser. None of the community centers have."

"I'm sure it's just a processing issue."

"That may be, but Julian isn't returning any of their calls or e-mails."

She looked down as she hunched up her shoulders and tucked her hands in her coat pockets. "He hasn't been feeling well lately."

"It's been a month."

"Yeah, but there are a lot of details to sort out when this much money is involved."

Amy stared at her for a beat. The wind whipped at her face. "I don't want to cause any trouble, but we were both there the night of the fund-raiser. Julian didn't seem himself. Frankly, you haven't seemed yourself lately, either, and I'm guessing the two things are related. The fact that Food Fight raised $50,000 that night, and none of the people the money was supposed to benefit has seen a penny, is . . . well, it isn't good, Grace. It's concerning."

Amy wasn't sure if it was their conversation or the cold, but Grace's eyes were wet. She sniffled and wiped her nose with the back of her hand. "Okay. I'll talk to Julian."

"Thank you. Honestly, I'm telling you this as much for your own benefit as for theirs. I don't want you and Ethan caught up in something. Fifty grand is a lot of money, and it's missing."

"I know, okay? I know." She pulled out her keys and unlocked her car. "I'll look into it. I promise."

Then she got into her car and drove off.

Amy waited until Grace had pulled away; then she returned to her car. She started the engine, but as she glanced at her phone, she noticed she had a voice mail from her mother, who must have called while she was talking to Grace. She pulled the car into gear and played the voice mail on Bluetooth.

The first few seconds, all she could hear was her mother sobbing. Then: "Amy . . . give me a call as soon as you get this. Something's happened and . . . *ohhhh!*" The sobbing resumed.

Amy could barely breathe. She played the message again. A car behind her honked, and she realized she had stopped smack in the middle of the parking lot. But she couldn't move. She couldn't take her foot off the brake. Even without her mother saying much of anything, Amy knew why she had called.

Tim was dead.

# Chapter 22

The funeral was set for Friday. Ellen didn't want a fuss. It was to be a small, private affair: just her, Amy, and three or four other family members. There wouldn't be a viewing, as had been traditional in Amy's Catholic family, since Ellen had decided on a closed casket. Amy had tried to persuade her to open the funeral to more people—friends of the family, other relatives—but Ellen refused. She didn't want to be around so many people. All Amy could think was, *It's like losing Dad all over again.* When confronted with grief, Ellen's natural reaction was to push people away. The circumstances of Tim's death only made it worse.

On Tuesday, Rob dropped Amy at the train. She was taking Amtrak to Providence, where her mother would pick her up and drive her back to Woonsocket. She would stay through the week and return to Philadelphia Sunday morning. Part of her wanted Rob to come. He hadn't known Tim very well, but he'd supported Amy through much of the roller coaster of Tim's addiction. But Ellen had made it clear Rob wasn't invited, so he would stay home and watch Noah.

Amy looked out the train window and watched the trees and buildings whiz by. She replayed the conversation with her mother in her mind. She had dreaded such a call for more than a decade. She'd had nightmares about it. On dozens of occasions, she'd awoken to Rob rocking her in his arms, saying, "Shhh, shhh, everything is okay, it was just a dream." The nightmares took various forms. In some of them, she found the body. Sometimes she'd have done so mere moments after he'd overdosed; other times his body had been rotting for weeks. In other dreams, though, she'd get a call from her mother, much like the one she received on Monday. Part of her had hoped—prayed!—yesterday's call was just another dream, another nocturnal manifestation of her anxiety and guilt. But even in her shock, she knew it was real.

When she called her mom back, Ellen had confirmed what Amy had suspected: Tim had died of a heroin overdose. She had seen him Sunday during the day, but then he'd left for one of his NA meetings. He was supposed to come back for dinner afterward, but he never showed. She'd called his phone again and again, but he didn't pick up. Then she called his NA sponsor, who said Tim hadn't come to the meeting that day; he'd tried calling him as well, to no avail. Late that night, Ellen got a call from the police. Tim had been found in a McDonald's bathroom on Diamond Hill Road with a needle sticking out of his arm.

"My Timmy. Oh, my Timmy's *gone*!"

Amy had never heard her mother cry so much. Amy assumed she must have when her dad died, but she never witnessed it. Ellen had been adamant about protecting her children in the throes of such a traumatic event. But Tim's death cracked her wide open. She could barely get through the call.

"I'm coming tomorrow," Amy had said. "We will get through this together."

She'd meant it, but somehow the words sounded hollow. How would she help her mom get through this? What could she possibly say to dull the sharp edges of a mother's grief?

Amy leaned her head against the train window and watched the factories and industrial buildings pass. Scenes from her childhood played through her mind, a montage of her relationship with Tim. The first time they rode the Ferris wheel together at Rocky Point. The time they snuck downstairs at 3 a.m. on Christmas Eve and opened a present each before Ellen caught them and sent them back to bed. The time Tim short-sheeted Amy's bed. Amy didn't want to think about the later memories, the ones where she caught him trying to steal Ellen's jewelry or found him passed out in his car. She wanted to think of the good times because there *were* good times, before it was all drugs and rehab and relapse.

But most of all, she didn't want to think about the fact that she never called him, that she never got to hear his voice one last time, that she didn't do what she had promised to do, which was to talk to him about his recovery and encourage him to keep going.

So she closed her eyes and let those early scenes play, like a carefully edited movie that didn't make her think too hard.

"West Kingston! Next stop, Providence. This stop West Kingston. All aboard!"

Amy awoke with a start. She'd fallen asleep for . . . well, she wasn't sure. A long time, she suspected. She glanced at her phone. Two hours. She couldn't remember the last time she'd taken a two-hour nap.

Her stop was next, so she gathered her things. As she waited for the train to reach Providence, she checked her e-mail and Facebook, where she saw a post by Emily about a local news story.

"I KNEW this place was shady," she wrote. "Good riddance."

Amy clicked on the story, which had the headline: "DEA RAIDS LOCAL URGENT CARE; 3 ARRESTED."

Her eyes widened as she scrolled through the story. This wasn't just any urgent care—it was *the* urgent care, the one she'd visited when she was sick back in September. Apparently, she wasn't merely feverish or delirious when she thought something was wrong with the place. The head doctor and owner of the franchise had been arrested on the suspicion of prescribing opioid painkillers for non-medical purposes. No wonder the waiting room had been so crowded with a strange assortment of characters. And the nurse she'd seen—was she even really a nurse? The pieces were all coming together. Reading the story in front of her, she couldn't believe she hadn't connected the dots sooner.

But there was one dot she didn't want to connect, even after the Food Fight event, even after the call from Leroy Harris. She didn't want to, but she couldn't ignore it any longer.

The receptionist who'd known his name . . . his insistence on waiting even though Amy told him not to . . . his discomfort at seeing her there . . .

"Oh, *Julian*," she said to herself.

"Providence! Providence, this stop!"

Amy looked up to see the train slowing to a stop. She slid the phone back into her purse and hurried down the aisle, her mind awash with explanations, none of them any good.

When Amy emerged from the train station, she spotted her mom's white Ford Focus about twenty yards away, parked behind a black pickup truck. Her mind was still reeling from what she'd read on the train, but she tried to push the story aside as she prepared to see her mother. Whatever trouble Julian was in—whatever he'd done—it could wait until Amy was back in Philadelphia. For now, she had to focus on comforting her mother.

Amy waved as she approached the car, and moments later, the trunk popped open. She tossed her belongings inside and slid into the passenger seat, reaching across the center console to give Ellen a hug.

"Hi, Mom," she said, squeezing her tight. Ellen squeezed back.

"Okay trip?" Her voice was tight.

Amy rubbed her back, then pulled away. "Not too bad. I slept for a chunk of it."

Ellen swept at her eyes with the back of her hand. Amy suddenly realized how much older her mother looked. She hadn't seen her in almost a year, but she suspected the past twenty-four hours were responsible for the rapid deterioration in her appearance. Her mousy hair somehow looked mousier; the bags under her eyes were more pronounced. Her entire face seemed to sag. It was as if every aspect of her biology was projecting sadness.

Her mom started up the car, and soon they were on 146 North, headed toward Woonsocket. Ellen was quiet for most of the drive—not uncharacteristically so, given that she'd never enjoyed deep, emotional conversations, but the silence made Amy uncomfortable. There were so many things she wanted to say ("I'm sorry

I never called Tim," "I'm sorry you had to go through this alone," "I'm sorry I can't make any of this better for you"), but she knew her mother well enough to know that if she wasn't talking, it was because she didn't want to.

Thirty minutes later, they were pulling up the driveway to the house where Amy grew up. The home was a ranch, with butter-yellow siding, black shutters, and a glossy black door. Some of the houses on the street had seen better days (damaged shutters, mossy roofs, mildew-ridden siding), but Ellen had kept hers up well. It actually looked better than Amy remembered it.

"The house looks great," she said.

"What's that?" Ellen's mind was somewhere else.

"The house. It looks great. Did you repaint the door? I don't remember it being that shiny."

"Tim did it." Her voice was strained. She could barely get the words out.

She parked the car and helped Amy unload. The two of them settled into the kitchen, were Amy poured herself a glass of water. In the kitchen door, she noticed a bottle of Autocrat Coffee Syrup.

"Oh, wow, I haven't had this stuff in years. Do you mind?"

"Have whatever you want. I'll never finish the whole bottle myself."

Amy poured some milk into a glass and then squeezed a healthy squirt of coffee syrup over the top. Coffee milk was one of those Rhode Island traditions that somehow hadn't migrated to other parts of the country, other than New England. It was like chocolate milk, but with coffee syrup instead of chocolate. She mixed the milk and syrup together with a spoon and took a long sip. It tasted like her childhood.

Her eyes welled up with tears as she thought about all the times she and Tim drank a tall glass of coffee milk after school. It was Tim's favorite. Nowadays, most of the yuppie parents she knew wouldn't let their kids near the stuff ("All that high-fructose corn syrup! And why should kids acquire a taste for coffee anyway?"), but Amy was tempted to bring a bottle back for Noah. He would never know Tim, but at least he could know a little about him and the things he enjoyed.

Amy caught her mother staring at her. She blinked back the tears.

"He still loved that stuff, you know. Even at thirty-three. He'd go through a bottle a week, I swear."

"That doesn't sound like a particularly healthy habit. Then again, I guess Tim wasn't all that concerned with whether habits were healthy or not."

"Hey—watch it." Ellen's voice was sharp and bitter.

"Sorry, I didn't mean . . . I was only joking."

"Do I look like someone in the mood for jokes?"

"No, sorry."

Her mom looked at her for a long while. "You never called him, did you?"

The guilt that had enveloped Amy since Tim's death tightened around her like a straightjacket. "No," she said. "I didn't."

She shook her head slowly, her lips tightly drawn. "I am so disappointed in you."

"In me?"

"Yes, in *you*. All I asked—all I asked!—was that you call him. That's it. I never asked much of you, but this was important. He needed you, and you weren't there for him. You let him down. You let all of us down."

Amy's lip quivered. The tears were coming fast now. She lay the glass on the counter as she wiped her eyes. "Don't you think I feel guilty? I hadn't heard his voice in years, and now I'll never hear it again. Sometimes I can't breathe when I think about it."

"Maybe if you'd called him, he'd still be alive."

The blood rushed to Amy's head. "That isn't true."

"You were never there when he needed you."

Amy's face felt as if it were burning. "How can you even say that? Maybe you don't remember the hours and weeks I spent here helping Tim detox when Noah was a baby. I spent time away from my own kid—my own kid, who was only a baby and needed me—so that I could get Tim back on track. Or what about the time when I was in college, when I missed a major exam so that I could help Tim get into a different rehab program? Or the countless other times I put my own life on hold so that I could resuscitate his? Don't tell me I wasn't there when he needed me."

"You weren't there this last time, and that's what counts."

"Do you honestly believe that a phone call from me would have prevented Tim from relapsing? Because I've got news for you: it wouldn't have."

"You don't know that."

"Okay, then why did he relapse every other time I reached out and tried to help him? What makes this time so different?"

Ellen started trembling. Her face went red. "Because this time he's DEAD!"

"That isn't my fault!"

"Then whose is it, huh? Is it *mine*? Is that what you're trying to say?"

"Of course I'm not!"

They were shouting at each other now. Ellen was shaking. Amy tried to bring herself under control.

"How can you not see that this was Tim's fault? These were his choices."

"It's a disease, Amy. He didn't choose to have a disease."

"I know he didn't. And it breaks my heart to think of all the suffering he went through. But I wasn't the cure, and neither were you. He was the only one with the power to turn his life around."

"He wanted to. He told me that. He really wanted to this time."

"I know he did. But sometimes wanting something isn't enough. There's so much more to it than that."

"It's just . . . he was . . . he was . . . he was my *baby*. Do you understand? He was my *baby boy*, and now he's gone." The sob that came of her was so expansive it seemed to swallow up the entire room. The sadness crashed over Amy like a wave and pulled her out to her mother's grief-stricken island. If something ever happened to Noah . . . if she were powerless to save him . . . if she lost him . . .

She went over to her mother, and Ellen collapsed in her arms. Amy held her tight, lifting her up and keeping her close.

"It wasn't your fault, and it wasn't mine," she said, tears streaming down her face. "We did everything we could."

She knew that was true, but she also knew it would take the rest of her life to believe it.

The funeral was the solemn, private service Ellen had wanted, and Amy held her hand throughout. Afterward, they went back to the house along with Amy's two aunts and one uncle. Her aunt Cindy had made some chowder and bought some rolls from Stop & Shop, so they warmed up from the frosty December temperatures while sitting around the dining room table slurping soup. No one said much.

Once everyone had left, Ellen retired to her room, where she stayed until the next morning. Amy would occasionally knock on the door and ask, "Mom, you okay?" The answer was either silence or a muffled answer like, "Fine, just resting." Amy had lived through her mother grieving over her father, but this felt different. She almost seemed to have given up, as if nothing mattered anymore, as if she had nothing to live for. Part of Amy understood, but another part wanted to shout, "Live for me! Better yet, live for *Noah!*"

Finally, on Saturday evening, she knocked on Ellen's door with a plate of eggs and toast. As far as she knew, her mother hadn't eaten all day.

"I have dinner," she called through the door.

"Thanks, but I'm not hungry."

"Mom, you have to eat something."

"I told you, I'm not hungry."

Amy took a deep breath and stared at the plate of food. "Do you want me to throw it out, then?"

A pause, then the rustling of sheets. Ellen hated wasting food. She couldn't resist that threat.

The door opened. Ellen looked terrible—puffy eyes, dark circles, gnarled hair. She glanced at the food. "I guess I could pick at it. I won't finish it, though."

She took the plate and shuffled back to her bed. Amy followed behind.

"I was going to FaceTime with Rob and Noah in a minute. Want to say hello? Noah would love to see you."

"I'm not really up for it."

"I know, but I think it would be good for you to talk to him."

"I don't want him to see me like this."

"Okay, but . . ." Amy trailed off. She wasn't sure how hard to push her. On the one hand, she had just lost a child. She was entitled to wallow. But on the other, Amy wanted her mother to see that there were people out there who still needed her. For more than a decade, Tim had consumed an outsized proportion of her bandwidth, and now he was gone. Who was going to fill that space? Realistically, no one would. No one could. But Amy wanted to show her mother that other people could fill at least some of it.

"I know you think I'm being pathetic," Ellen said.

"Mom, look at me. I do not think that. Not even for a second. You lost your son. I cannot even imagine the pain you are feeling. But Noah is your grandson, and he misses you. He asks about you every time I call to check in."

"He does?"

"Yes."

She sniffled. "I just . . . I don't want to scare him, you know? I mean, look at me. *Look* at me!" She patted her tangled head of hair.

"So run a brush through your hair and splash a little water on your face. The video quality isn't that good. And anyway, Noah doesn't care what you look like. He's a four-year-old boy."

"I guess."

"I know Tim has left behind a big hole. But I'm still here. Noah is still here. Aunt Cindy, Aunt Diane, and Uncle Mike are still here. And we love you and need you, too."

Ellen's lip quivered. "I know. But his addiction . . . it was all I thought about for so long. Worrying about him, helping him, working with him. And now it's over. All that worrying, all that help—what good did it do?"

Amy brushed a tear away from her mother's cheek. "You couldn't save Tim, but maybe you could save someone else. Have you ever thought about that?"

"Someone else like who?"

"Other people with addictions. Other families going through what you went through."

"I don't think I'm ready for that."

"I'm not saying you should do it right now. But once the fog has lifted a little, you may want to think about it. Helping other people might really help you, too."

She took a deep breath and let it out slowly. "I'll think about it."

"Take your time. But if that's something you might be interested in, let me know. I'd like to help, too."

"Okay. We'll just . . . we'll see."

Amy kissed her on the forehead. "Now, should we give Noah a call?"

She nodded. "Let me just have a bite of this toast first, and then I'll freshen up."

She took a bite of the toast, and before Amy knew it she'd eaten the entire slice, along with the scrambled eggs, which were probably cold and rubbery by this point, but Ellen didn't seem to notice or mind. She excused herself to the bathroom and ran a brush through her hair, and when she returned, she looked like a modestly improved version of the mess Amy had encountered a few minutes prior. It was a step in a positive direction.

Amy pulled up Rob's number and called him via FaceTime. When he picked up, the first face she saw was Noah's, not Rob's.

"Mommy, Mommy, guess what?"

"Hi, sweetie. What?"

"Daddy downloaded Candy Crush Soda, and I'm already on level TWENTY!"

Amy smiled. "Ah, so Daddy is doing some very hands-on parenting down there, eh?"

"Hey!" Rob called out in the background. "You're lucky the house is still standing."

She laughed. "I'm not judging. I'm sure it's been a long five days. Hey, Noah—want to say hi to Mimi?"

He gasped. "Yes, yes, yes!! Mimi, Mimi, Mimi!"

She handed the phone to her mother. "Hi, sweetheart. How are you?"

"I'm great! Can you come visit soon?"

Her mother was suddenly beaming, though her eyes were wet. "Yes, sweetie," she said. "I would really, really love that."

# Chapter 23

Amy returned to Philadelphia Sunday afternoon. She was glad she'd gone and worried how Ellen would cope in her absence, but she missed Rob and Noah and was ready to return to real life.

"Spending time with your mom doesn't feel like real life?" Rob had asked when she told him how she felt.

The truth was, it had felt surreal. She'd expected the funeral to give her closure in the ongoing heartbreaking saga of her brother's addiction. But really, it had opened up old wounds and made her realize how much of her relationship with her mother had in some way been tied to Tim. They were starting over now, and Amy wasn't sure what their future relationship would look like.

She had barely settled back into the familiar rhythm of her daily routine when Monday morning she received another call from Leroy Harris.

"I still haven't heard from Julian," he said, skipping the pleasantries. He voice didn't carry the same warmth it had in other conversations either. It was all business.

"Really?"

"Not a word. Have you?"

"No, but then I've been out of town for almost a week. My brother died."

"Oh. I'm very sorry to hear that. I'll pray for your family."

"Thank you." Some days she wished more people had prayed for her family while Tim was still alive, but she knew saving Tim would have taken a lot more than prayers.

"Anyway, I did manage to talk to Grace before I left," she continued. "She promised she'd look into it and help to resolve the issue."

"Well, she hasn't. I've tried to contact both her and her husband multiple times, and I have it on good authority that I'm not the only one. We community organizers talk. Something funny is going on."

"Now you don't know for sure—"

"Ma'am? Don't. You know as well as I do that this smells rotten. If I don't hear anything in the next day or two, I'm going to the police."

"The police?"

"And maybe the press."

Amy's throat tightened. If Leroy spoke to the authorities, the Durants' life could unravel very quickly. And if he talked to the press, their life wouldn't so much unravel as it would implode. At this point she didn't really care if that happened to Julian—maybe it would even encourage him to seek treatment—but she didn't want it to happen to Ethan. He wasn't her four-year-old boy, but he was *a* four-year-old boy, and she couldn't bear the thought of someone Noah's age having his world completely ripped apart. The fact that he was also Noah's best friend made her feel even more protective of him.

"It's not even about my programs at this point," Leroy said. "It's about all of us. A lot of people gave money they thought was for one thing, but if he's using it for something else, that ain't right."

Amy agreed, but she wasn't sure what to do. She'd already spoken to Grace once. She'd hoped that would be the last time she needed to talk about it. But it was becoming increasingly clear that a casual run-in outside her kid's preschool wasn't going to be enough. Maybe if Grace knew the police and press might get involved, she'd be more likely to fix things. Or had she already tried, and it was too much for her to do on her own?

"I'll talk to Grace again," Amy said.

"Doesn't seem to me like talking is doing any good."

"I'll get through to her this time. I promise."

"You know what they say about promises?"

"No, what?"

"They're like piecrust: meant to be broken."

"You can trust me, Mr. Harris. I won't let you down."

"That would be wonderful. But I'll believe it when I see it."

"You'll see it. I'll make sure they set things right," she said, even though at the moment she had no idea how she would possibly do that.

As soon as Amy hung up with Leroy Harris, she called Grace. The call went to voice mail. She didn't leave a message and instead vowed to call back in an hour.

She did, and the call rang and went to voice mail again. She tried one last time, thirty minutes later, and although it went to voice mail again, this time she decided to leave a message.

"Hey, Grace. Sorry I've been out of touch. I don't know if Rob saw you or mentioned, but my brother died, so I was in Rhode Island last week for the funeral. Anyway, could you give a call when you get a sec? I need to talk to you about something."

She didn't leave specifics, mostly because she didn't want to spook Grace by saying, LEROY HARRIS IS GOING TO THE POLICE, CALL ME RIGHT NOW. But when Grace still hadn't called back by the time Amy left to pick up Noah at school, she worried she hadn't been forceful enough. There was no chance of running into her at Beth Israel either because Ethan hadn't been at school that day.

"Was he sick?" Amy asked.

"Uh . . . I think so. Yeah, actually. He was SUPER sick, like barfing and coughing and everything."

"Is that what Miss Karen said?"

"Uh . . . maybe? I can't remember. I think so."

Amy was highly suspicious of this story. Noah was a horribly unreliable narrator. He had a tendency to take small snippets of reality and weave them into a fanciful, and often very dramatic, tapestry. Ethan may have had a stomach bug. He also may have had a doctor's appointment or been on vacation.

"Huh," she said. "I'll have to ask his mommy when I talk to her." *Which at this rate will be never*, she thought.

They piled into the car and headed to a nearby pharmacy in Rydal to pick up some wrapping paper and holiday cards, along with a few small gifts. Unlike the chain pharmacies, the independently owned ones in the area sold all sorts of unique mementos, from scented candles and diffusers to cheese boards and fancy chocolates. Amy wanted to pick up a holiday gift for Miss Karen, as well as a hostess gift for Rob's coworker, who had invited them to a holiday party that weekend.

"Mommyyyyy, where are we going?" Noah whined in the back seat. She hadn't mentioned the planned detour because Noah hated running errands, but by now he knew the route to and from school well enough that he could tell something was amiss.

"Meadowbrook Pharmacy. It'll only take a few minutes."

He groaned. "I want to go home."

"We will. After we stop at the pharmacy."

"But I don't *want* to."

"I'd be a little more enthusiastic if I were you. Meadowbrook Pharmacy is the one with the fancy chocolate-covered pretzels. Remember . . . ?"

He suddenly perked up. "Oh! Okay! I like that place! Can I get a pretzel? Pleeeeeease?"

"If you behave."

"I will, I will! I promise."

Amy smiled to herself. She knew bribing her four-year-old with chocolate probably wasn't good parenting, but if it meant she could accomplish an errand quickly and without whining and hysterics, she didn't care.

She found a parking spot right in front of the store and held hands with Noah as they made their way through the front door. As soon as they stepped inside, they were surrounded by charming gifts: shiny picture frames, milled soaps on ceramic soap trays, hand-painted mugs, and artisanal tea sets. In the center of the store, a circular candy bin reached from floor to ceiling, filled with everything from jellybeans to gummy peaches, like something out of Willy Wonka. Noah's jaw dropped as he clapped eyes on it.

"Candy," he whispered. He'd clearly forgotten that the chocolate-covered pretzel store was the same as the magical candy store. "Can I have some? Please, please, please?"

"It's either candy or chocolate-covered pretzels. You can't have both."

He scrunched up his lips. A tough decision.

"Let me think about it," he said.

"You do that. In the meantime, I'm going to find something for Miss Karen and Daddy's coworker."

She scanned the aisles and shelves and decided on a sparkly mug filled with Jordan almonds for Miss Karen and a box of chocolate truffles for the holiday party host. Noah was still deep in thought when she was ready to head to the register.

"Okay, kiddo, what's it going to be?"

He stroked his chin. Amy tried not to laugh. Sometimes his gestures were so adult-like.

"I think . . . I want some pretzels. But I want to choose which ones."

She walked with him to the chocolate counter, where dozens of truffles and chocolate-covered pretzels lined the inside of the glass case. The pretzels came in all different flavors: milk chocolate with M&M's, white chocolate with crushed Oreos, dark chocolate with toasted coconut, milk chocolate with peanut butter chips. Amy couldn't blame Noah for wanting some. She wanted some herself.

"Can I help you?" asked a young woman behind the counter.

"Yes," Noah answered before Amy could. The woman smiled at Amy, who simply shrugged. "I want . . . that one. And that one. And that one. And . . ."

He kept pointing until the woman had filled up a half-pound box. Amy let him because she knew she and Rob would have some for dessert that night.

"Do you need this wrapped?" the saleswoman asked.

"No, thank you. Oh, but I do have these things as well." She placed the gifts on top of the counter.

"No problem. I'll ring you up."

Noah jumped up and down excitedly as the woman keyed the information into the register. Amy smiled, but her expression hardened when she glanced over her shoulder toward the pharmacist's counter. The pharmacist was in a heated discussion with a customer whose back was to her, a man with dark hair and a slim build. As she stared at the man, she realized how familiar he looked, even from behind. Her shoulders tightened.

"I'm sorry, Mr. Durant, but we don't fill prescriptions from that facility."

"You said that last time, which is why I went somewhere else."

"That may be, but wherever you went is another place whose prescriptions we can't honor."

"Bullshit. I have chronic back pain. The doctor prescribed medication for it. You're telling me he doesn't know how to do his job?"

"What I'm telling you is that I am legally barred from filling this for you." He handed over the paper script.

"That's fucking ludicrous!"

"Take it up with the DEA."

He snatched the prescription from the pharmacist's hand and turned to leave.

"It comes to $48.28," the cashier said.

Amy watched as Julian headed for the door, her stomach in knots. She had been trying to contact Grace all day, but here was the man responsible for the fund-raiser—and for getting the money to the supposed recipients. If she let him leave . . . if she didn't stop him . . .

"Hang on one second," she said. She glanced down at Noah. "Stay right here, sweetie. I'll be two seconds. The nice lady at the counter will watch you."

She ran toward the door, knowing she was breaking about five different parenting rules, but Julian was already outside by the time she reached it. She followed him.

"Julian!" she called out as she burst through the front door.

He stopped and turned around. "Amy. Hi."

He was already in the parking lot. Amy looked over her shoulder into the store and made eye contact with the cashier. One minute, she mouthed, holding up a finger. Noah was probably having a conniption, but she couldn't let this opportunity go. She hurried to meet Julian.

"Hi. Sorry. I didn't meant to—I've been trying to get in touch, and when I saw you here . . ." She trailed off as she registered his face. His eyes looked sunken and his skin was pale, paler than she'd ever seen it. He did not look well. "Are you okay?"

"Me? Yeah, sure. I've just . . . I hurt my back the other week and have been in bad shape ever since."

Amy stared at him for a long while. "Julian," she finally said. She said it gently but firmly, like she would if she'd caught Noah doing something he shouldn't.

"What?"

"Julian," she said again, this time more forcefully.

"*What?*"

"We both know 'what.' Don't play dumb."

"I literally have no fucking idea what you're talking about."

"Really? Then explain to me what you were just doing in there." She nodded toward the pharmacy.

"Picking up a prescription from my doctor. You have a problem with that?"

"I don't know, should I?"

"Jesus, what is your deal?"

"What's *my* deal? I'm not the one who's been avoiding people's calls for weeks. *I'm* not the one who ran a fund-raiser that has failed to distribute any of the money it raised."

He stared at her coolly. "You have no idea what you're talking about."

"Is that so? Then why would Leroy Harris and Shonda White and Yvonne Lewis and a bunch of other people call me complaining they haven't received their money? Why would they do that, Julian?"

"Beats me."

"Really. You have no idea? I find that hard to believe."

"I don't know what you're trying to suggest, but—"

"You know exactly what I'm trying to suggest. And more than that, you know I'm right. Do you know where I was last week?"

"I don't—"

"At my brother's funeral, Julian. That's where I was. He was thirty-three. And do you know how he died? A heroin overdose." She looked at him pointedly.

"Listen, I'm sorry for your loss, but that has nothing to do with me."

"Doesn't it? Did you know his addiction started with pain-killers? A bunch of Oxy his doctor prescribed when he tore his ACL in college. And when that got too expensive and he couldn't find anyone to write him prescriptions anymore, he moved on to heroin. And last week, it killed him."

He sniffed the air. He'd started tapping his foot nervously on the ground. "That's a shame. But that's your brother's story. It isn't mine."

Amy took a deep breath. She wasn't getting anywhere, and she knew she wouldn't, at least not standing in a parking lot on a cold winter's day while a cashier kept an eye on her four-year-old.

"Fine. Whatever. Do what you want—it's your life. But get the money to the people you promised to help. Because if you don't? They've threatened to go to the police, and I can guarantee that won't end well for you."

Then she turned around and marched back into the store, her blood boiling.

"And THEN, Mommy LEFT ME in the store with the lady be-hind the chocolate case, and she didn't come back for almost TWO HOURS."

Noah was recounting the afternoon's outing to Rob over dinner. Rob glanced at Amy, his brow furrowed.

"That isn't exactly how it went," Amy said.

Rob looked thoroughly bemused. "How did it go, then?"

She sighed. "I saw J-u-l-i-a-n at the pharmacist's counter—"

"Julian? Like Ethan's daddy?" Noah asked. Rob and Amy's eyes met. Sometimes they hated that their son could spell already.

"Yes. And I wanted to grab him before he left, since I've been trying to get in touch with him and Grace for more than a week.

But he was already outside, so I needed the cashier to watch Noah for a second."

"Not a second. TWO HOURS."

"It was more like five minutes, max."

"My name isn't Max," Noah whined.

"I said 'max.' As in maximum."

"Oh. Okay."

"Anyway, I got his attention and talked to him, though I don't think it made any difference."

"You say you saw him at the pharmacist's counter?" Rob raised an eyebrow.

Amy nodded, her lips drawn. She didn't need to go into detail. He understood.

"BUT, the good news is . . . we have chocolate-covered pretzels!" Amy smiled brightly as she cleared the dinner plates and went to retrieve the box of pretzels. Noah had already eaten one as a snack, but considering she'd left him with a stranger this afternoon, she was happy to let him eat as many as he wanted today.

He got first pick—a milk chocolate one covered in crushed Kit Kats—and Rob and Amy chose one each. Chocolate-covered pretzels were very much a Philadelphia convention, but they were one Amy could get behind. Sweet, salty, chocolaty—in many ways, they were the perfect treat. Amy was glad they'd bought enough for the family, but was also glad they'd gone with a half pound and not a pound. She had visions of her stuffing her face with the remains while Noah was at school.

Noah made quick work of his pretzel and then started babbling about everything and nothing, his chatter supercharged by sugar and chocolate.

"He kind of never stops, does he?" Rob said as the two of them loaded the dishwasher. They had thought they'd occupied him with a space activity book she'd bought for him in Rhode Island, but he continued jabbering, currently about something to do with Saturn's rings.

"Nope. It's exhausting, huh?"

Rob let out a gust of air. "Let's just say I'm glad you're back to carry some of the load."

Amy smirked and rolled her eyes, but Rob wrapped his arms around her and leaned down to kiss her.

"I know you do most of the heavy lifting on a daily basis, and I want you to know how grateful I am. I've always been grateful, but the six days you were away really rammed home how hard it is to do what you do."

"Well . . . thanks."

"No, thank you. Seriously. He's such an amazing kid, but he's fucking exhausting."

Amy laughed and gave him another kiss. As she pulled away, the doorbell rang.

"Want me to get that?" she asked, still smiling.

"Nah, I've got it."

He headed down the hall while Amy put a few more dishes in the dishwasher, but after a few seconds she heard elevated voices coming from the foyer.

"You have a lot of nerve coming back here," Rob said.

Amy's shoulders tensed. Whom was Rob talking to?

She snuck down the hall behind him, and as she peered over his shoulder, the blood drained from her face. The leather jacket, the pageboy hat, the stubbly jowls . . .

Lev.

Amy tried to duck out of sight, but before she could, Lev spotted her.

"Hey—you. I know you lied to me."

She could barely swallow. "About what?"

"Our friend Julian. You know where he lives. Don't bullshit me."

Amy didn't understand why Lev couldn't just find Julian himself. How hard was it to track down the Food Fight office?

"Why don't you just find him at his work address?"

"Oh, hey, look, we have a fucking Sherlock Holmes."

"Don't talk to my wife like that," Rob said.

"Listen, I already tried his work office, and there's nothing there."

"What do you mean there's nothing there?"

"The place is for rent. Empty."

"Empty?"

Amy tried to contain her shock. Had Julian moved offices? And if not . . . where was he working?

"That's what I said. So why don't you tell me where I can find him?" He stood with his shoulders back. Amy couldn't be certain, but she thought she spotted a gun tucked into his pants.

"I told you—"

"Do not bullshit me, lady. I can make this very unpleasant for both of you."

"This has nothing to do with us. And anyway—"

"Mommy?"

She and Rob turned around to see Noah treading warily down the hallway.

"Hi, sweetie. Mommy and Daddy are just talking to this nice man. Why don't you go back to the kitchen and finish your activity book?"

He looked at her skeptically. *He doesn't* look *like a nice man*, his expression said. That was one of the downsides of having a bright kid. He saw right through their lies.

"I have a question about black holes," he said.

"Mommy will come help you really soon."

He hesitated. "How soon?"

"Just another minute or two."

"Okay," he finally said. He padded back to the kitchen.

"Nice kid," Lev said. "Smart."

Amy and Rob stared at him coolly. She didn't like the menacing expression on his face.

"Be a shame if anything happened to a kid like that—someone with so much potential."

"Listen, you piece of shit." Rob spat out the words like bullets. "Don't you dare threaten my family. I'm calling the fucking police."

"Whoa, whoa, whoa, we're just talking here."

"No, we aren't," Amy said. "I asked you to leave me alone, and now I'm asking you again."

"If you'd just tell me where your friend Julian is—"

"He isn't our friend," Rob said.

"Oh, okay. Sure. Well, if you'd tell me where your 'non-friend' is—"

"You want to know?"

"Rob . . ."

"No, listen, I'm sick of this. We have nothing to do with any of it, and I want to get back to living my life."

"I'd love to make that happen for you," Lev said.

Amy's stomach was in knots. She didn't care about Julian at this point—he'd created this mess, and her anger from this afternoon's interaction was still palpable—but if Rob told them where the Sterlings lived, he was putting Ethan and Grace at risk. Whatever Julian had done, whatever mistakes he'd made, none of it was poor Ethan's fault.

"Last I heard, he was staying with his in-laws," Rob said. Amy felt a little sick. What if Lev did something to Ethan? Or what if Ethan saw him do something to Julian?

"Is that so? And where might they live?"

"Meadowbrook. I don't know the exact address."

This was actually true. Rob knew the area better than Amy did, but she was the one who'd plugged the address into their GPS anytime they'd gone there.

"Street?"

"Honestly, I'm not a hundred percent sure. I'm pretty sure it's Stocton."

Lev stared at them for a beat. Amy feared he'd realize she knew the exact address, even if Rob didn't. It was Stocton Road, and she knew the number, but she wasn't volunteering the information. He would figure it out. Frankly, with the information Rob had given him, any idiot would be able to.

"Good," he said. "You've been very helpful—finally."

He started to walk away, but Rob called after him. "If I ever see you anywhere near my house or my family again, I'm calling the police."

Lev turned around. "If the information you just gave me is true, you'll never have a reason to see me again."

Then he disappeared into a black pickup truck and headed down the street.

* * *

When Amy finally shut the door, she could barely breathe. Her eyes welled up with tears.

"Ethan," she managed to say.

Rob went on the defensive. "What was I supposed to do? Let him come in the house and harass my family?"

"No, and this is all Julian's fault, but . . . if Lev threatened Noah, imagine what he could do to Ethan. He could kidnap him, Rob. Hold him hostage until he gets his money."

"I had to put our family first. The fact that Julian potentially put his child in harm's way isn't my fault. He's the one who got himself into this mess, not me."

Amy knew he was right, but she couldn't stop thinking of worst-case scenarios that involved something happening to Ethan—a botched kidnapping, a stray bullet during a shoot-out. She knew many of these scenarios were not only worst case but also highly unlikely, but nevertheless, she couldn't keep herself from worrying.

"At the very least I can warn Grace, so that Ethan doesn't get caught up in this," she said.

"Fine. If you think that'll help."

Amy hurried toward the kitchen to find her phone.

"Mommy, what would happen if your spaceship went past a black hole? Would it suck you inside?"

She riffled through her purse. "Maybe, I don't know."

"Where would you go? What would happen to you?"

She grabbed the phone and looked up at her son, who was staring at her expectantly. "What?"

"Where would you go if you got swallowed up by a black hole?"

"I have no idea."

"Would you die?"

"I don't know."

"What would happen to your body?"

"I DON'T KNOW!"

Noah's eyes welled up with tears. Normally Amy would feel guilty for having made him cry, but tonight she was emotionally tapped out.

"Noah, I'm sorry, but Mommy has to do something very important right now, okay? We can talk about black holes later. Or maybe Daddy can talk about them with you."

She looked over her shoulder at Rob, who couldn't look less enthusiastic about the prospect if he tried. He'd just spent six days as a single dad and moments ago was fearing for the safety of his family. The physics of black holes wasn't a topic he was eager to discuss at any time with anyone, much less tonight with a four-year-old.

"No, I want to talk about them with *you*." His eyes were still wet.

"Then you're going to have to wait a few minutes."

"But I already waited a few minutes!"

Amy tried not to lose her cool. Nothing would be improved or accomplished by exploding at her four-year-old, but at the moment, all she wanted to do was shout at him to SHUT UP SHUT UP SHUT UP.

"I told you: I have to do something very important right now. When I'm finished, I will help you. Okay?" She said the words slowly and deliberately. By Noah's expression, he seemed to have understood.

She hurried upstairs, pulling up Grace's number as she did. She called. Grace didn't pick up, just as she hadn't all day. Amy decided to try her one more time, and this time she picked up.

"Amy?"

"Hi—sorry to bother you."

"It's fine. I got your message earlier, but today has been . . . well, anyway, I was going to call you later tonight." Amy wasn't sure she believed that, but at this point, it didn't matter. "What's up?"

"Listen, that guy Lev—the one who came by the house looking for Julian?—he dropped by again tonight. He was pretty agitated, and he threatened Noah, which scared the crap out of us and sent Rob through the roof. I wanted to warn you because he knows where you guys are staying, and I'm a little worried for your safety."

"Whoa, whoa, whoa—how does he know where we're living?"

"Well, he doesn't know the exact address, but he knows you're on Stocton in Meadowbrook."

"Right, but how does he know even that?"

"Because things got really heated, and he was threatening us—"

"So you *told* him?"

"He threatened Noah. Okay? Do you understand? He threatened our child. And anyway, let's back up for a second. If it weren't for Julian's involvement with this guy, he never would have stopped by our house in the first place. If you want to direct your rage at someone, direct it at your husband."

She was quiet for a beat. "So what am I supposed to do?"

"For starters, you should tell Julian that Lev is looking for him."

"Julian isn't here."

"Where is he?"

"Does it matter?"

*It did and it didn't,* Amy thought. Was he out with friends? At a meeting? Out buying pills? Given their earlier interaction, Amy was suspicious of his whereabouts.

"Then call him. Because if Lev finds your parents' property, he doesn't seem like the kind of guy who's going to make it very pleasant for either you or your parents. Frankly, if I were you, I'd get out of there."

"Fuck," she muttered under her breath.

"Do you have anywhere else you can stay?"

"I don't know. I'd . . . I'd have to think about it."

"Do your parents have a security system? Maybe you could stay in the main house until this blows over."

She hesitated. "I guess that's possible. They're in New York until tomorrow anyway. They have pretty good security—cameras, an alarm. Maybe that's what we'll do. Although . . ."

"What?"

"I just don't want to have to explain any of this to them when they get back. With all the cameras and everything, they'll know we slept in their house. I'm just really sick of lying to them."

"So don't."

"Easy for you to say."

Amy wished Grace could see how much harder she was making everything for herself. If she'd been truthful with her parents about Julian's addiction and recovery, maybe she wouldn't be in the position she was in now.

"You can come here, if you want," Amy offered. She knew she

was enabling Grace's secrecy, but in the near term, her biggest concern was Ethan's safety.

"Why would we do that? Wasn't that guy just at your house?"

"Looking for Julian, not you. Why don't you and Ethan hang here for the night?"

"Are you sure Rob would be okay with that?"

The answer was almost certainly not. He wouldn't want to give Lev a single reason to revisit 120 Sycamore, and she didn't blame him. But she wasn't inviting Julian. Whenever he came back from wherever he was, he would return to the Sterlings' guesthouse and deal with the consequences himself.

"I'll work on Rob," she said. "Just pack your things and get over here."

# Chapter 24

As expected, Rob was not on board with Amy's plan.

"No, no way. Have you already forgotten how fucking terrifying that guy was? I don't want the Durants anywhere near this place."

"It's just Grace and Ethan. Lev will find Julian where you told him Julian was."

"I hope he gives him a good punch to the gut."

"Rob!"

"Seriously—who puts his family in danger like this? I can't believe someone would fuck up an otherwise amazing life for, what? Some pills?"

"He isn't intentionally fucking up his life."

"Well, intentionally or unintentionally, he's doing a spectacular job at it."

Amy didn't have the energy to give the "addiction is a disease" speech she'd given dozens of times before. Every time she did, Rob nodded his head and seemed to understand, but then when her brother would do something reckless, like break into a neighbor's house or shoplift from Walmart, Rob would seem to forget everything they'd discussed. She realized part of this was because he was observing Tim's behavior from a distance—closer than most, but not as close as her or her mother. The natural instinct of someone relatively unfamiliar with addiction was to say, "Jesus, why can't he get his life together?" Frankly, she felt that way herself sometimes, even though she knew better. If she had to remind herself, she supposed it was only natural that Rob and others would forget, too.

The doorbell rang. Rob's eyes met hers. "Amy . . ."

"It's just for tonight. Please."

She hurried down the stairs and opened the door. Grace was there with Ethan, whose ebullience seemed incongruous, given the circumstances.

"We're having a sleepover!" he said.

Noah came running down the hall from the kitchen.

"What? We are?"

She hadn't had time to brief Noah on their plans, which meant Ethan's arrival was even more of a delightful surprise.

"Just for tonight," Grace said. "Special treat."

The boys jumped up and down, and Grace ushered Ethan into the house with his backpack and sleeping bag.

"Where should I set this up?" she asked.

"In Noah's room. I'll help you. Rob, why don't you take the boys into the family room and put something on the TV."

"*Minions!*" they cried in unison.

"We don't have time for a whole movie."

"Just part of it? Pleeeeease?" Noah begged.

"Fine, whatever. Rob?"

Rob took a long, deep breath. "Okay. Boys, come with me."

The boys clapped and giggled as they scurried down the hallway. Amy showed Grace upstairs.

"I like what you've done with his room," she said, after Amy had flicked on the light. "It's really cute."

"Oh. Thanks."

For a brief moment, Amy had forgotten that this room used to be Ethan's. Of course it had. How else would she know the Durants? Why else would Grace be here?

Amy stood by and watched as Grace unrolled the sleeping bag and fixed it up with a few of Ethan's favorite stuffed animals.

"I ran into Julian earlier today," she said as Grace fluffed a small pillow.

Grace looked up. "You did? Where?"

"Meadowbrook Pharmacy."

Her cheeks reddened. "Oh."

"He's using again, isn't he?"

Grace stared at her for a long while. "I'm not sure. We don't . . . he hasn't been around a lot lately."

"Grace . . ."

"Listen, I'm trying my best. Okay? I'm just . . . everything is really fucked up and crazy right now."

"I'm sure it is. But nothing is going to improve if you keep burying your head in the sand."

"I'm not!"

"Then *do* something."

"About what?"

"Julian's addiction, the missing benefit money—take your pick. Leroy Harris called again. He still hasn't seen his money from the benefit. No one has."

"I'm still looking into it, okay? It's . . . complicated."

"What is?"

"Everything."

"Grace, look at me. No, *look at me.*"

Grace looked up from the sleeping bag. Her eyes were wet.

"The money's gone, isn't it?"

Her lip started trembling. She wiped at her eyes. "I don't know. I mean, yeah. I think it might be."

"Julian needs to fix this."

"Like I said, it's complicated."

"Stop *saying* that!" Amy was nearly shouting, but she didn't care. She could hear *Minions* playing downstairs, so the boys wouldn't be able to hear. "It isn't complicated. It's pretty fucking simple. Julian has taken a lot of money from a lot of people, and he's using it to either buy drugs or pay off debts or both. Forget all those people at the benefit for a moment, the ones who thought they were giving money to a good cause. Think about yourself, your parents, *Ethan.* I mean, Christ! Julian drained Ethan's trust fund, for crying out loud!"

Grace looked stricken. "What?"

"Ethan's trust. The one in your dad's name. There's almost nothing left in it."

"What are you talking about? How do you know that?"

Amy opened her mouth, then paused. How did she know that? Then she remembered: the letter. The one she never should have opened.

"Because one day I accidentally opened a letter for Julian, thinking it was for us. But it wasn't. It was a letter informing him that the trust's holdings were valued at $500 or something."

"And you never told me?"

"I figured you already knew."

"Well, I didn't. I didn't know about any of it. Fuck." Her lip started trembling. "You should have said something."

"Hey, don't turn this around on me! Your husband is the one who took the money."

"Okay, and what am I supposed to do about it now, huh? The money is long gone, and God knows where he spent it."

"You know what you can do about it? You can get Julian into a serious rehab program."

"He's already been to rehab."

"And it clearly didn't work. He needs something more intensive."

"He doesn't need something intensive. It's just *pills*."

"It isn't just pills!" She stomped her foot. "Don't you understand that by now? Haven't you been watching the news? It started as 'just pills' with my brother, Tim, and then it progressed to heroin, and now he's dead. Is that what you want for Julian? For *Ethan*?"

"Of course that isn't what I want!" Tears were streaming down Grace's cheeks. "But I don't know what else I can fucking do. I can't *make* him want to stop."

Amy couldn't argue with that. If Julian didn't want to go back to rehab, it wouldn't work in the long run. The times Tim had gone under someone else's direction, he hadn't stayed clean for more than the length of the program, often less.

"At the very least, you can fix this Food Fight mess. Leroy

Harris is threatening to go to the police, and I don't think he's bluffing."

Grace suddenly looked scared. "The police?"

"The police and the press. Once he does that, you won't be able to control any of this anymore."

Grace rubbed her cheeks and nose on her sleeve, leaving a trail of tears and snot. It was strange to see her unhinged like this when normally she was so refined. The Grace she had met all those months ago would have politely blown her nose in a tissue, probably out of earshot. Grace's carefully constructed façade was falling away. Maybe now that Grace felt free to be emotionally naked in front of her, they could establish a true friendship.

"I just . . . I'm not sure how I can fix this. All that money . . . all those people . . ." The tears came faster now, and Grace covered her mouth to keep the sobs from reaching Ethan on the floor below. Amy knelt next to her and wrapped her arm around Grace's shoulder.

"You do whatever it takes. If that means telling your parents the truth and getting their help, then that's what you do. Or you find another way—friends, family, a Kickstarter. But you can't keep closing your eyes and hoping all of this will just go away. It won't unless you do something."

Grace leaned her head on Amy's shoulder, her body shaking as she choked on the tears. "This isn't how I wanted my life to turn out," she said.

Amy held her tight and rubbed her shoulder. "I know," she said. "But the good news is, you still have plenty of time to start over."

When Amy woke up the next morning, Grace and Ethan were gone. She wasn't sure when they had left. She hadn't heard anyone making noise in the night, although she was so exhausted from the day's events that she probably would have slept through it. But Rob usually armed the security system, which would have gone off if Grace had tried to slip out the front door. The only explanation she could come up with was that they'd snuck out just after Rob left for work. He'd left at 6:30 for an early meeting, at which point

Amy and Noah were still fast asleep. If Grace had gone then, Amy wouldn't have heard it.

She tried not to worry too much as she ate breakfast and packed Noah's lunch, but given what had happened the day before, it seemed only natural that she'd be a little concerned. Had Grace gone home? Or had she taken Ethan somewhere else? Was Lev still looking for Julian?

"Mommy . . . where's Ethan?"

Noah rubbed his eyes as he toddled into the kitchen. His face was still puffy with sleep, and he had a big crease across his cheek from his pillowcase.

"I'm not sure, sweetie. He left with his mommy before I got up."

"But I wanted to have breakfast together." He frowned.

"I know. But I'm sure there are plenty of sleepovers with Ethan in your future, and you will definitely have breakfast together at one of those."

He sighed. "Okay."

"What do you want to eat? Cereal? Toast?"

"Toast with peanut butter and honey."

"Done.

"But, Mommy?"

"Yes, sweetie?" Amy grabbed the loaf of bread and stuck a slice in the toaster.

"I'm sad because I wanted to have breakfast with Ethan *today*."

"I know you did. But you'll see him in about an hour at school, so that's like the next best thing."

Except he didn't see Ethan at school because Ethan wasn't at school that day. Nor was he at school the next day, or the one after that. When he hadn't appeared by Friday, Amy began to worry. Had something happened to him? She'd tried to call Grace to check in the day after Lev's visit, but Grace hadn't picked up, nor had she picked up the other two times Amy had called. Where were they? Was everything okay?

When she went to pick Noah up from school Friday afternoon, she noticed through the glass in the door that he was sitting sullenly on a small couch in the corner of the room. His arms were crossed, and his head was tilted down. She could barely see his face, but she could tell his bottom lip was sticking out. She didn't know why, but she was almost certain his pouting had to do with Ethan's absence.

Amy made eye contact with Miss Karen, who nodded to the assistant teacher to take charge while she stepped outside. She met Amy in the hall.

"What's up with Noah? He looks miserable."

"He's been like that all day," Miss Karen said. "Ever since I announced that Ethan wouldn't be in our class anymore."

"What do you mean? What happened?"

"I'm not exactly sure. As you know, he hasn't been here all week. I think they're moving."

"Moving? Where?"

"I don't know. I don't have any details. All I know is that Grace called Ruth this morning and said Ethan would no longer be attending Beth Israel."

Amy couldn't believe it. No wonder Noah was devastated.

"They didn't even say goodbye," she said. She was talking to herself as much as she was talking to Miss Karen.

"I know. A number of the kids took it very hard. But none as hard as Noah."

"He was Noah's best friend—his first best friend. This is going to destroy him." Amy's eyes were wet. She tried to hold back the intense heartache she felt for Noah, but she was doing a very bad job.

"He's a tough little boy. He'll be okay."

Amy opened the door to the classroom and went inside. When Noah saw her, he ran over and threw his arms around her, burying his head in her belly as he began to cry.

"Shhh, shhh, shhh," Amy said, rubbing his head. "It's okay."

"N-n-n-no it's n-n-n-not. I m-m-miss E-e-ethan."

She leaned down and kissed the top of his head. "I know, sweetie. I know."

She escorted him out of the classroom and gathered his things. She could barely get him to put his coat on. He was inconsolable.

In the past when he'd had meltdowns, as any preschooler did, they'd blown over fairly quickly. But she wasn't so sure this one would.

When she finally got him into the car, she brushed the tears off his cheeks. "What if I called Ethan's mommy to see what's going on?"

He sniffled. "Could I talk to Ethan?"

"Sure. Let's do it at home, though, okay?"

They made it home without another explosion of tears, and when they got inside, Amy pulled out her phone and called Grace. Given recent experiences of trying to get in touch with her, Amy worried she wouldn't pick up, but to her relief, she picked up after three rings.

"I guess you've heard the news," she said.

"Sort of. All Karen said was that Ethan wouldn't be coming to school anymore. She seemed to think maybe you were moving?"

Grace took a deep breath and released it slowly into the receiver. "I just need to get away for a while."

"Away? Where?"

"Texas. A friend of mine lives in Austin. Ethan and I are going to stay with her for a few months."

"What about Julian?"

There was a pause on the other end. "We've separated."

"Oh. I wasn't . . . I didn't know."

"That's okay. We haven't told anyone."

"Are you all right?"

"Not really? But it had been building for a while. That's why things were so frosty between us. I just felt as if I couldn't trust him anymore. There were too many lies, too many excuses that didn't add up. I realized I couldn't live my life questioning his every move. The story about Ethan's trust fund only confirmed that."

"I'm sorry."

"Me too. I thought he was the love of my life." She sniffled, and Amy heard her blow her nose. "Remember when we had drinks all those months ago and you told me about your mom raising you and your brother by herself, and I was like, 'I could never do all of this alone'? Well, here we are." She laughed bitterly.

"You'll be okay. People will help—I will."

"You'll be almost two thousand miles away."

"When you get back, then. You are coming back, right?"

"That's the plan."

Amy glanced at Noah, who was nibbling on a graham cracker and hanging on her every word, and gave him a thumbs-up. She had to be careful about what she said, but luckily Grace was doing most of the talking. She was grateful to Noah for being so patient. The snack helped, but she also suspected he was so distraught about Ethan's departure that he was counting on her to figure out what was going on.

"How is Ethan doing?"

"I haven't fully explained everything to him yet. For now, I've just told him that we're taking a big vacation where it's warm. I'll get to the rest later. It's kind of a lot for a four-year-old to understand."

"Too much."

"Exactly. It was bad enough when we were on the run from some sort of loan shark. At least he never picked up on what all that was about."

"Whatever happened with that? Did Lev find Julian?"

"He must have. He hasn't bothered me and Ethan, anyway. We've been staying in the main house with my parents, so maybe that's why."

"Do your parents know what's going on?"

Grace sighed. "Mostly. They're both furious, but my dad is off the charts. They're kicking Julian out of the guesthouse."

"Where will he go?"

"They've offered to pay for his rehab. At first he said he didn't need their money, but then I think he realized he's broke and the only way he'll see Ethan again was if he goes, so I think he'll accept the offer."

"What about all the money from the fund-raiser?" Amy had been scouring the Internet lately for news stories about Food Fight and Julian. She hadn't seen anything, but she hadn't heard from Leroy Harris either. Part of her thought it was only a matter of days before Julian's scandalous story was plastered across the web.

"Honestly? I don't know. I mean, the money raised that night is gone—God only knows what he spent it on—but whether or not he can replace the money he stole? I'm not sure."

"Could your parents help?"

"Maybe. It's a big ask. I think they're torn between wanting to hush up a scandal and wanting Julian to get slaughtered in the press. The news about Ethan's trust fund really put my dad over the edge."

"*Mommyyyyyy.* You've been talking for HOURS. Can I PLEASE talk to Ethan?"

Grace laughed. "I guess we've been talking too long, huh?"

"I guess." The truth was, it hadn't felt too long to Amy. It felt as if she was finally getting somewhere with Grace, who after all these months seemed to be opening up. She wished they could keep talking, but she knew Noah wouldn't stand for it, and she couldn't blame him. He'd been so patient.

"Want me to get Ethan?"

"Could you? Noah is dying to talk to him."

"Sure. Hang on. Hey, Ethan?"

Amy could hear footsteps as Grace walked down some stairs.

"Ethan?"

"Yeah?"

"Want to talk to Noah?" There was a loud squeal in the background. "Should we FaceTime?" Grace suggested.

Amy switched over to the video function and handed the phone to Noah. "Say hi to Ethan," she prompted.

Noah grabbed the phone. His face lit up as Ethan appeared on the screen. "Uh . . . bello! Boo-chee boo-chee ya ya."

Ethan replied saying something in Minion-ese. Under normal circumstances she might roll her eyes, but right now she was glad to see Noah happy again.

"Do you guys even speak to each other in English anymore?" Grace said in the background.

"Uh . . . si, si! Korabeedoo!"

The continued on like that, interjecting with the occasional "butt" or "poop" or "fart."

"No potty talk, please," Amy said.

"Sorry," they said in unison.

Ethan made a silly face, and Noah laughed.

"Ethan, sweetie, we need to pack. Say goodbye to Noah."

Noah's smile faded, and his lower lip started trembling. "I don't want you to go," he whispered.

Ethan looked over his shoulder at Grace. "My mommy says we'll come back soon."

"In the spring," she added.

Noah gazed up at Amy. She'd never seen him look so sad. "When is spring?"

"Like late April until June."

"No, but how long from now."

She mulled over the best way to answer. At four—even an advanced four—he didn't have a sense of how long a month was.

"About three months. So like remember when you started school? From about then until now. That's how long until Ethan will be back."

The edges of his lips curved downward. "But that's so *long*."

"Not really. It's shorter than the amount of time we've lived here. Shorter than the amount of time you've known him."

"I guess." He looked back at the screen. "Make sure you come back, okay? In the spring."

Ethan nodded fervently. "I will. I'll probably be as tall as my daddy by then."

"Me too," Noah said.

"And then we can reach the top of the trees with our HANDS, and we can jump up and climb up and FLY!"

"Yeah!" Noah yelled enthusiastically. "And we can do it again and again and AGAIN, and when we get tired we can just have some chocolate and then we can do it AGAIN!"

Amy and Grace threw their eyes upward and smiled.

"Ethan, sweetie, we really need to go," Grace said.

He sighed. "Okay."

"Bye, guys," she said, waving. "Keep in touch."

"We will," Amy said. "Safe travels."

She hung up, and immediately Noah burst into tears and buried his head in her chest. "It's okay," she said again and again. "It's okay. He'll be back."

She thought about everything Grace must be going through—the upheaval of her life, the emotional turmoil. Did she have people she could talk to? Amy assumed she did. She had a friend in Austin she knew well enough that she could live with her for a few months. But Amy couldn't stop thinking about Tim, about everything he was going through in the months before he died. She still believed calling him wouldn't have changed the course of his life, but it might have made a difference, however small, in how he felt about himself, if only for a few minutes. Sometimes people just needed a reminder that you were there.

She pulled Noah close, breathing in the sweet smell of him. He was so fragile, more fragile than she'd ever realized, but also more emotionally intelligent and complex, in the most wonderful way. She used to think he would be such a good friend to someone someday, and here he was, at the tender age of four, already proving her right. How wonderful to be young, to be so openly vulnerable and innocent. In most instances, she and Rob were teaching him how to be more like a grown-up, to say please and thank you and hold his knife and fork properly. But today, today she wished she could be more like him. She wished she could be even half the friend to Grace that Noah was to Ethan.

She pulled out her phone again with one hand as she stroked Noah's hair with the other. She wrote Grace a quick text:

I know I'm not an old friend and we don't go back a long way, but I'm here if you ever need to talk.

She squeezed Noah tight and glanced down at the screen on her phone. The timestamp showed that Grace had read the message. She hadn't replied, and Amy didn't really expect her to. But that was okay. She knew. She knew Amy would be there, whenever she was ready, and for now, for right now, that was all that mattered.

# Chapter 25

The week after Grace and Ethan left, Noah went into what Amy could only describe as a toddler depression. He didn't want to go to school, didn't want to eat, didn't want to do much of anything. Amy hated seeing her newly sociable and gregarious son retreat, but Rob kept telling her it would pass, and she knew he was probably right.

In the meantime, she tried to keep the rest of Noah's life as steady and predictable as possible. They visited Sherrie and Bruce for Sunday night dinners, made Noah's favorite foods even if he didn't eat them, and forced him to go to school, even when he resisted. After a few weeks, he began to perk up, and after a month he seemed like his normal self again. He still asked about Ethan, but the questions were less frequent. It reminded Amy of the way he used to ask for a sibling. The questions eventually just . . . petered out. She supposed that's how he thought of Ethan—like a brother—only she suspected he'd never give up asking about Ethan entirely, and that was fine.

For now, she was just glad to see him happy playing with other kids in his class. All those worries she'd had about him making friends, all that anxiety about his intelligence—she realized now she was merely projecting her own lived experience onto him. But Noah wasn't her. In a lot of ways, he was more self-aware than she'd ever been. He was a great kid, and he'd be just fine. He didn't need her getting in the way.

One day at pickup, she peered through the door and saw him playing a board game with Jake. Amy had noticed how much closer the two of them had gotten without Ethan in the mix. Now that no one was competing for Ethan's affections, they could develop a friendship on their own terms.

"Are they cute or what?"

Amy turned around and saw Emily peering over her shoulder. She smiled. "The cutest."

"We'd love to have another playdate. I promise no hissy fits this time. What am I saying? I can't promise that. Jake is . . . well, they're all capricious little dictators, aren't they? But I've noticed a change in him lately. He seems a little more reasonable—I'm talking fractions here, but nevertheless. It's a positive development."

"Kids change. Thank God."

"Thank *God*." Emily laughed, then turned more serious. "I wonder if any of it has to do with the Durants moving. Don't you think it was sort of odd how they just . . . disappeared?"

"I think Grace needed a change." She wasn't sure how much Emily knew about the Durants' situation, including the separation, so she didn't want to disclose too much.

"Maybe. I guess I shouldn't be surprised. 'Disappearing' is sort of Grace's MO."

Amy studied Emily's face. She knew it wasn't her place to share Grace's business, but at the same time, she didn't think it was fair to either Emily or Grace for Emily to go around thinking that she'd done something wrong or telling people Grace simply "disappeared" on people as a matter of course.

"You know . . . when you and Grace fell out . . . it wasn't because of anything you'd done," Amy said.

Emily stared at her. "You guys talked about me?"

"No, no—sorry, not at all. I just meant . . . I know Grace was going through some tough times back then, and I think she sort of cut herself off from everyone."

"You mean like she's doing now?"

"When you put it that way . . . yeah, I guess."

"What's so tough about being Grace? She's gorgeous and popular, her husband is smoking hot, her parents are loaded. If that's tough . . . I'll take it."

"Things aren't always what they seem."

Emily raised an eyebrow and opened her mouth, as if she were about to say something, but before she could, Noah and Jake burst out of the classroom and threw their arms around their respective mothers' legs.

"I'm *starving*," Noah whined. "Can we go home for a snack?"

"Sure." She looked back at Emily. "Let's be in touch about that playdate. We'd love to get together."

Then she zipped Noah's coat, gathered his things, and led him out of the building.

The first thing Amy saw when she got online the next day was a big and bold headline on Philly.com:

## LOCAL FOOD NONPROFIT SHUTS DOWN AFTER BENEFIT FUNDS GO MISSING

She clicked on the link, and sure enough, it was an article about Food Fight. Leroy Harris had made good on his threats to go to the press, who proceeded to investigate Julian and his organization. The reporter not only uncovered the story of the embezzled fundraiser money, she also found that Julian had stolen from the general Food Fight coffers as well, which is why he'd needed to fire most of his staff. He'd managed to fill the gap with a mixture of donor and "personal" funds (Amy wondered if some of this was from the house sale or Ethan's trust fund), but in the end it wasn't enough to save the organization, especially when the dishonest behavior continued. The reporter also laid out Julian's problems with addiction, citing several anonymous sources. Had Grace been one?

Further down in the article, Grace's parents were quoted:

> "We are shocked and saddened to hear about Julian's deceitful behavior. What he has done is inexcusable, and the beneficiaries of Food Fight's

services deserved better. We are glad to hear that
he is currently in a rehabilitation program getting
the help he needs and will pray for him in his recovery."

The article went on to say that the Sterlings would make good
on the money raised at the benefit and would compensate the community groups directly. Amy had to admit, it was a shrewd move. Julian got shamed publicly, which is what they wanted, but they also
came off as the heroes. Amy wondered how Grace would feel about
the situation. She was probably glad she was far away from it all in
Texas.

When she'd reached the bottom of the article, her phone rang. It
was Rob.

"Did you see the news about Food Fight?"

"I'm reading it right now."

"Nothing we didn't already know, but yikes. What a mess."

"At least the community groups will get their money," Amy
said. "That's a silver lining."

"True. Although it still makes me mad when I think about the
fact that the money we spent on tickets and everything was ultimately used to buy drugs or pay off drug debts."

"I know. But nothing we can do about that now. At least he's in
a program."

"Do you think it'll actually work?"

Amy thought about it. If she were to draw from her experience
with Tim, she would say probably not. This was Julian's second
time in rehab, and he was essentially being forced by his in-laws.
But Julian had a son—he had someone to live for. Maybe that
would make a difference. She knew there would be all sorts of
forces working against him, but in her heart she wanted to believe
that Julian would do whatever it took to get better. Even if when it
got hard, even when he wanted nothing more than to take another
pill, he wouldn't because he had a boy, a gorgeous little boy who
loved and missed and needed him. Maybe that wouldn't be
enough—maybe nothing would—but Amy held on to the thought

that Julian's story didn't have to end like Tim's. There was still time for him to write his own ending. He just needed to keep his pen on the paper.

"Yes," she said, because even if she wasn't certain, even if she had her doubts, she realized if Tim's death had taught her anything, it was that she'd rather hold on to hope than fear.

# Epilogue

***Six Months Later***

"Noah—slow down!"

Amy chased Noah down the walking path as he bolted for the playground. It was early June, and Ethan and Grace had just come back from Texas, two months later than expected. The delay had caused some consternation in the Kravitz household, mostly on Amy's part as she worried that maybe Grace and Ethan would stay in Texas for good. But they'd stayed only so that Ethan could finish the preschool he'd enrolled in there before they moved back. They'd just arrived two days ago, and as soon as they did, Grace had called to set up a playdate.

"You guys up for the park?" she'd asked.

"Like you even need to ask."

"See you there at noon?"

"It's a date."

She and Grace had kept in touch over the past six months, mostly over e-mail. Initially, they hadn't delved into the thorny subjects of rehab and marital separation, but gradually Grace started to open up about her sense of betrayal (Julian had lied about things other than money and drugs, including an affair with a coworker). Amy imagined this was easier to do in writing, rather than over the phone, and she knew how therapeutic it could be to simply write things down. Sometimes she felt as if she were reading pages from Grace's diary, but she always made sure to respond, so that Grace would know she was listening. They didn't e-mail every day or even every week, but they were in touch enough that they generally knew what was going on in each other's lives.

"It's like you're long-distance dating," Rob had joked.

Amy had to admit, it felt that way sometimes. The problem with long-distance relationships, of course, was that when people were finally in the same city, the relationship often fell apart. She hoped that when they met in person, they'd be able to pick up where they'd left off in cyberspace.

Noah arrived at the playground and looked around. "Where is he? I don't see him."

"He'll be here. We're a minute or two early."

They were actually more like ten minutes early, mostly because she'd run out of ways to tell Noah it wasn't time to leave yet. He was beside himself with happiness when she'd said they were seeing Ethan today. He woke up an hour earlier than normal and had been asking to leave since 7:30 a.m.

Noah climbed to the top of one of the climbing frames, and as he stared out over the park, he let out a yelp.

"ETHAN!!!!!!" He waved his arms animatedly.

"Noah, be careful, you're going to fall."

"No, I'm not!" He climbed down and bounded across the playground toward the parking lot.

"Noah—*freeze*! Do not go near that parking lot!"

He stopped and sighed, but then he started jumping up and down as Grace and Ethan approached. Once they were within about twenty feet, Noah started up again and nearly tackled Ethan to the ground.

"Whoa, I guess someone is excited to see you, Ethan."

Ethan giggled. "Guess what I have?"

"What?" said Noah.

He pulled some sort of foam contraption from Grace's bag. "A stomp rocket."

Noah's eyes widened. "What's that?"

"It's a rocket you can send all the way to the sky."

Noah beamed. "Can I try?"

"Yeah, come on, I'll show you."

The boys scampered off, and Amy reached in and hugged Grace. "It's good to see you. How are you settling in?"

"Getting there. *Lots* of boxes."

"I know what that's like. Let me know if you need any help. A year ago, we were in the same position."

When she thought about it, she got déjà vu. Almost exactly a year ago, she was sitting in this very park next to Grace, talking about how much unpacking she had to do. So much had changed since then.

"Do you like your place?"

She shrugged. "It's fine. It'll do for now. I mean, it's an apartment. That's definitely an adjustment. But it's better than staying at my parents. We needed a fresh start."

"You did the right thing. Plus, if you're still there in the fall, isn't your building in the same catchment as our elementary school?"

Grace smiled. "Yep, that was part of the reason I chose it."

They walked toward a park bench and took a seat next to one another, breathing in the warm June air. It was a beautiful day— seventy-eight degrees and sunny, with almost no humidity, a perfect day for the park.

"How is Julian?" Amy asked.

Grace sighed. "Better, from what I hear. He's been drug free for about six months now. Whatever program my parents paid for seems to be working."

"That's great."

"It is. I'm really happy for him. I just hope he can stay the course. He seems committed."

"Have you seen him yet?"

She nodded. "Yesterday. Ethan was over the moon. It made me realize how much he needs a dad. I think Julian saw that, too."

"That's good. It'll keep him motivated."

"Exactly. So what about you?" Grace said, changing the topic. She'd become more open about things, but she still didn't like to linger for too long on the subject of Julian. "How are things?"

"Same old same, for the most part. Noah is excited to start camp next week. We're planning a trip to Stone Harbor later in the summer."

"Fun. Are you still doing stuff for Leroy Harris?"

"I'm officially working for him now, actually."

"You're kidding."

"Nope."

"You like it?"

"Love it."

"That's great! I'm so happy for you."

Shortly after the Food Fight story broke, Leroy had called to apologize—not for going to the press (because on that front, he didn't have anything to apologize for), but for putting Amy in the awkward position of being the go-between. Amy told him there was no need to apologize; she probably would have done the same thing in his position. He mentioned he'd been impressed with the work she'd done translating St. Luke's mission for Food Fight's fund-raiser and asked if she'd ever be interested in doing a little copywriting and editing work for him. She said sure, and what started as a few tasks evolved into a steady stream of work, and now she was in charge of their after-school education programs. The pay was average but consistent, and the work was meaningful. She finally felt as if she were a part of something again.

She and Grace leaned back against the bench and looked out toward the grassy field beside the playground, where the boys were stomping on an air bladder and sending the foam rocket soaring into the sky. They howled in delight.

"Look at them," Grace said. "You'd never know they hadn't seen each other in six months."

It was true. Noah had developed a better relationship with Jake and many of the other kids in the class, much to Amy's relief. But watching him and Ethan play together, it was clear their bond was something special. It was the kind that doesn't come around all the time, the kind you hope you develop at least once in your life. She and Jess had a friendship like that. They could go months— years!—without seeing each other, and when they did, they picked up right where they'd left off.

"What they have is special," Amy said.

"It really is."

She looked at Amy and smiled, and something in her face—in her eyes, maybe, or in the curl of her lips—told Amy that maybe, just maybe, they would have a friendship like that someday, too.

# Acknowledgments

Many thanks to Esi Sogah, Carly Sommerstein, Lulu Martinez, and the entire Kensington team. Thanks also to Scott Miller and the hardworking staff at Trident Media Group.

A big thank-you to my mom for being an early sounding board, and to Rog for the unfailing support. The publishing journey has been a long, crazy road, and you've been there every step of the way. I couldn't have done any of this without you.

And to Alex and Charlie: thank you for inspiring me to be the best version of myself and for filling my life with such joy. I love you up to God's roof and back.

# THE LAST HOUSE ON SYCAMORE STREET

## Paige Roberts

### ABOUT THIS GUIDE

The suggested questions are included
to enhance your group's reading of
Paige Roberts's *The Last House on Sycamore Street*.

# DISCUSSION QUESTIONS

1. Why do you think Amy feels so drawn to Grace?

2. How much of Amy's perception of Noah is accurate, and how much is colored by her own experience?

3. Should Amy have told Grace about Ethan's trust fund?

4. Why does Amy keep trying to help the Durants? Do you think she goes too far?

5. Do you think Amy should have called Tim? Do you think a call from her could have made a difference?

6. Amy tells her mother that Tim's death wasn't their fault; it was his. Do you agree? If addiction is a disease, how and when does blame come into play?

7. Early in the book, Ellen says Amy is judging Tim, but Amy says she isn't. What do you think? How does she perceive Tim?

8. What role does 120 Sycamore play in the relationship between the Kravitzes and Durants?

9. How does Amy's relationship with Ellen compare with her relationship with Noah?

# Connect with Us

Visit us online at
**KensingtonBooks.com**
to read more from your favorite authors, see books
by series, view reading group guides, and more.

## *Tell us what you think!*

To share your thoughts, submit a review,
or sign up for our eNewsletters, please visit:
**KensingtonBooks.com/TellUs.**